D1601723

THE RIGHTEOUS, THE VAIN, THE FALLEN

Robert Denton

Dedicated to Cindi, my wife and best friend.

All characters appearing in this work are fictitious. Any resemblance to real persons, living or dead, is purely coincidental.

Published 2017 by Robert Denton
All rights reserved

Contact author at:
RobertRDenton@gmail.com
Subject: RVF

PROLOGUE

Five Years Ago

Wall Street blinked.

Virtual Reality Corporation, the high-tech, intellectually-superior southern California based bastion of computer wizardry had burst upon the country, seemingly from nowhere, to become the undisputed darling of professional stock pickers. The product was fun and educational, but most important; it was light years ahead of the competition.

The hype was explosive . . . overpowering. Imagine being able to put on a pair of modified ski goggles and click on a home-computer program, immediately to be whisked into a make-believe, three-dimensional surround-sound environment where you could move about freely and perform spectacular tasks. What parent wouldn't want such a product for their kids . . . for themselves? Think of the endless possibilities. Ski down black-diamond slopes at Breckenridge, stroll through the Louvre, play poker with the likes of Jack Benny, W.C. Fields and Richard Nixon, enter a blazing gun fight at the OK Corral, visit a topless lounge (lockout programming available for the children), witness the signing of the Declaration of Independence or command the bridge of a starship against a Romulan attack.

Such is the stuff that dreams are made of. Such, also, was the environment in which the Initial Public Offering of Virtual Reality Corporation stock rocketed from the pre-offering over-subscribed price of sixteen dollars per share to forty-eight in the first week of trading. Article after article, interview after interview, and speech after speech, the investment community couldn't get enough. During the next twelve months the stock continued to fuel imaginations and investment portfolios while the price soared . . . touching two hundred dollars. Naturally, quite a few VRC employees became instant paper millionaires, not to mention those savvy investors who jumped aboard early enough to ride the stock up.

The first virtual-reality headsets, called 'the VR' by a mesmerized public, hit store shelves with a lofty high-tech price tag: Nine-hundred dollars. They were gobbled up in an unparalleled buying frenzy which left disappointed customers standing in absurdly long lines, waiting to add their names to already-lengthy waiting lists. Offhand remarks in the workplace such as, "I just couldn't take off my VR last night," created a chasm between the haves and have-nots.

Rumors circulated that over two hundred thousand units were on back order, allowing illicit Internet black-market scams to blossom and flourish. One report had scalpers selling VR's to rich oil sheiks for *fifteen thousand dollars* apiece. It was hardly surprising that first-round purchasers were reticent about admitting that available software disks were few, of limited scope, and poor quality. All claimed that it was merely an inconvenience, or the price one must pay to get in on the cutting edge of innovation. Besides, it went without saying that technology soon would catch up and cure all.

High-tech pundits were swept up as well, and with unbridled optimism that both captivated and fascinated throngs of computer devotees and technology-hungry consumers, they literally buried the "insignificant" investment concerns of nonbelievers. The viewing screen was small and rectangular, reminiscent of the pint-sized 1950's-style TV screens . . . so what? The optical-array chip produced low-resolution images that were blurred, faded and indistinct, leaving viewers' eyes to contend with the inherent pixel problem . . . so what? The headset weighed around five pounds . . . so what? The return rate from dissatisfied customers was ever increasing . . . so what? VR was the wave of the future, and anyone who missed the wave was doomed to be swallowed by it!

Management was every bit as optimistic as the investing public, and presumably because of the euphoria gripping them all, corporate spokespersons issued appropriately reassuring public statements like: "We can't fill orders fast enough." Or: "Our latest enhancement is not to be believed." Or: "Next year's profits are gonna go ballistic." The eagerly awaiting world embraced VRC's culture, party line, and revenue growth projections.

But technology couldn't keep pace with the dream. Solutions to brighten the picture, enhance it to film-quality sharpness, and extend the viewing surface to surround the user's field of vision were exorbitantly costly pursuits, and by no means a sure thing. Reality can be cruel.

Wall Street expressed indignant amazement when the stock price quite suddenly started falling. Not by much at first, just a few points (dollars). Simply an opportunity to buy the stock at a more attractive price recited brokers who also babbled advice of, "Don't cash out. Now's the time to build your portfolio!" Meanwhile, production problems continued and back orders got filled with whatever was readily available, which too often included returned units. Customer satisfaction nose-dived. Finally, a smattering of industry articles began painting a far less glowing picture of both the VR and the VRC management team, seemingly incapable of handling unfettered growth or public scrutiny.

To everyone's surprise VRC's stock didn't bounce back as prophesied. In fact, what began as a minor "correction" soon erupted into a meltdown of such magnitude that three different times trading was halted by the stock exchange. The VR's inherent problems could no longer be contained or addressed, and investors were understandably furious. Journalists' calls to previously publicity-seeking corporate officers went unanswered, management was never available for comment, and panicked emails crisscrossed between concerned parties.

While VRC stock continued its downfall, commission driven stockbrokers hastened to remind clients that other companies had experienced start-up problems, nevertheless they weathered the inferno and became lasting and successful investments. All was to no avail. Frenzied selling pushed the price down further and faster, dragging other technology-related stocks right along with it. When the price finally bottomed out it was at an unbelievably low one dollar and twenty-five cents.

Three short weeks later, Virtual Reality Corporation filed voluntarily for bankruptcy protection under Chapter 11 of the United States Bankruptcy Code. Trading was halted once again, this time never to resume.

Those investors too paralyzed to move quickly or whose brokers convinced them to 'hang in' were obliterated. Life savings were lost, loans collateralized by VRC holdings ended in default, grand plans for college funding or early retirement were shattered, and dozens of small software vendors closed their doors. In essence, the lives of tens of thousands of investors and employees were devastated.

* * *

Not everyone ended up remembering the VRC episode with equal parts bitterness and horror. In colossal Wall Street debacles, a few seem always to emerge unscathed, possibly even enriched. One unique maven viewed the spectacle as a singular opportunity to ameliorate her career. Months before the general citizenry became aware of VRC's lethal internal chaos she had stumbled upon (and then taken advantage of) an inside source, who in a moment of understandable weakness had entrusted her with the disturbing truth. Thus armed with reliable insight the clever broker had utilized a simple yet under-appreciated trading technique in order to make a twenty million dollar profit during VRC's collapse.

On the night of VRC's bankruptcy announcement, The Fallen Angel (as she was mockingly nicknamed by "The Street") stood alone on the terrace of her Upper East-Side Manhattan apartment, and raised a glass of chilled 1897 Dom Pérignon in a private victory toast. Her living room television speakers were broadcasting Larry King's voice as he feigned interest in a pudgy young stock analyst hyping his latest publication, *The Bad Investment Protection Handbook*. She shook her head at the naiveté of the public-at-large, wondering if they'd ever comprehend the difference between opinion and knowledge.

On the terrace the late evening air felt clean and crisp, while a nearly full moon cast a pale silver sheen upon the city below. Gusts of warm wind rustled her shimmering, oversized satin pajamas as Ashley Taylor-Bishop grasped the wrought iron railing. She leaned out into the night sky, squeezing her eyes shut and tensing her slender body. Everything had come together today, a true moment to savor. Indeed, she hadn't felt so alive since just before . . . no! Don't ruin the moment. Don't think about Willard Prescott tonight, she chastised herself.

Arching her back, Ashley took in an enormous breath of fresh air and held it as long as possible, finally exhaling in a long audible sigh. Then in one fluid movement she defiantly flung the exquisite elixir into the vast sky as if to challenge the night. At that moment the young woman was wholly sensuous . . . bewitching. She wore an expression memorialized by that fabled spider who had just seduced the hapless fly.

Ashley Taylor-Bishop was in the throes of a new intensity, flush with the realization that there was more to be had and she wanted it, if only to show them all. That's when the thought struck her . . . if twenty million could be gained from the inadvertent burnout of a witless little company which had climbed to undeserved heights, think of the fortune she could amass during the downfall of a corporation twenty times its size . . . why not *a hundred times* its size?

Running her tongue along the edge of the crystal goblet, Ashley gave free reign to her fantasy, also thinking how sweet it would be to accomplish this at the expense of those contemptuous Wall Street hypocrites, those bastards who had driven her out for doing exactly what they themselves did; only, she did it better . . . that was her unpardonable sin.

Refilling her glass and sipping the vintage champagne, she looked out over her adopted city again wondering if there was such a place. Was there a sizable company ready to ignite into a huge fireball? If so, could she discover it before anyone else?

Ashley brushed the cool crystal against her cheek, admitting that it was a remarkable idea, a deliciously wonderful idea. She'd do it. She'd find her Holy Grail . . . and whatever time or resources were necessary would be considered inconsequential.

Peering down twenty-two floors at the street below, Ashley knew in her heart that for the name of but one company she'd gladly jump straight into the deepest depths of Hell . . . even hold hands with the devil himself. Why shouldn't she? What could 'He' possibly do to her that others hadn't already?

PART 1
THE FALLEN

CHAPTER 1

Five Years Later
Saturday, March 2, 6:00 A.M.
Interstate 57, just outside Chicago

The freedom . . . the power! Absolutely incredible!

Kevin Hobart "Hobby" Glassman blasted through all four of the manual gears, thrilling to the car's response. Oh, he was enjoying this. Half a minute back the speedometer glided past eighty and before him lay nothing but straight road and vivid morning sunlight.

As he both expected and demanded, the reconditioned 1971 black-and-silver Ford Mustang Mach 1 hardtop with four-speed transmission and three-hundred-fifty-one cubic-inch Ram Air engine was performing flawlessly. Hobby knew he'd been unbelievably lucky to have found it at that godforsaken estate sale last January. The owners had never known what they had, and after enduring mindless dribble about their only son's car and how after his death in 'Nam they'd felt honor bound to keep it . . . but now needed the money to pay back taxes. Really tragic. So what did he care? He'd made the steal of the century. *That's* what mattered.

Fate. It must have been fate when his good buddy Brett Hollister put him onto the estate sale. Not many knew about it as only a dozen buyers were there when Hobby arrived, and none seemed too keen on an old neglected Detroit muscle car. He'd have to thank Brett at the next board meeting. Just how did that stiff-lipped, square-jawed Texan get wind of an Illinois estate sale? No matter. He'd show his appreciation by keeping quiet about LoneStar's cash flow. Yeah, that would make them about even.

Ahhh, today, right now, life was really worth living. What could be better than flying down a strip of empty road without a care in the world? He loved everything about this car. From the two functional hood scoops designed to gulp massive quantities of air for the four barrel carburetor, to the black leather bucket seats and silver rear-end spoiler. It was one bitching machine. The needle now pointed to ninety-five and hadn't topped out yet. Hobby shot past the odd car sharing the road. As far as he was concerned they deserved to be left in his dust.

The tires hummed, the onrushing wind blended with throbbing engines, and Hobby felt another adrenaline rush. Quick checks of the instrument panel showed all was in order as the speedometer slid past one hundred. He pressed himself further back into the bucket seat to feel the vehicle's vibrations.

Too bad in a couple more minutes he'd have to turn around and head back toward civilization. In truth, Hobby didn't want to push his luck and blow past some donut munching cop lying in ambush up ahead with radar . . .

Inexplicably, the left front wheel locked spinning the black Mustang into a severe right-hand skid, which no amount of driving skill could overcome. The car lost contact with the pavement, flipped and cart wheeled down the concrete highway. Chrome, glass, broken steel fragments flew in all directions. Hobby's upper body was whipped back and forth like a rag doll in a maelstrom, repeatedly smashing his skull against the hard metal, snapping his neck like a pretzel stick. With no way for coherent thought to transmit from Hobby's stunned brain to his consciousness and in the seemingly endless interval just before death, he felt only the floating sensation of complete serenity.

CHICAGO TRIBUNE, SUNDAY
DEATHS LAST WEEK

Kevin Hobart Glassman, 62, passed away March 2, following an automobile accident; the nationally-known businessman and car enthusiast successfully managed his highly-publicized investment-consulting business from Chicago where it started as a one-man operation following his receipt of a master's degree from the Wharton School of Finance thirty-eight years ago; the oft-quoted financier also served on the board of directors of several companies including the National Bank of Illinois and Dallas based LoneStar International Corporation; Interment private.

Sunday, March 10, 1:30 P.M.
A Public School, Manhattan

The sounds of basketballs bouncing while children shouted and shrieked at one another reverberated off the gymnasium walls. "Hey. Watch this!" A boy of about six placed his head on a tumbling mat, throwing his legs high into the air. They wobbled but he managed to hold the headstand for a few seconds before gravity won. The child landed on his back with a thud.

Undaunted, he yelled, "Wait! I'll do it again!" This time his legs stayed up for nearly a full minute. When he finally fell, he rolled to a kneeling position and looked expectantly at the two women regarding him from the lower bleacher section.

Molly McHenry clapped and waved. "That's wonderful, Carlos! Just great!" The boy grinned from one Dumbo-sized ear to the other then dashed off to play with a group of kids on the opposite side of the gym.

The rather plain looking companion sitting next to Molly remarked, "Remember when Carlos wouldn't even say hello?"

It took a second of reflection before Molly replied, "Seems like a hundred years ago." Glancing at her watch Molly noted the time and said, "We'll have to start the lunch break pretty soon. So, what did you bring?"

It was customary for the adult volunteers to provide lunch for the twenty or so youngsters attending these special events every weekend. Today was Ashley's turn. "I did the best I could."

In spite of herself Molly rolled her eyes. "Peanut butter and jelly sandwiches again?"

Ashley shrugged. "It's the only meal I'm good at. Had lots of practice."

"How 'bout next time it's your turn we all chip in and send out for pizza?"

As expected Ashley smiled at the good-natured ribbing, but barely. Anxious to change the subject, Ashley asked, "Shouldn't Ben be here?"

Molly quickly surveyed the blur of youthful bodies careening across the hardwood floor. No one seemed in any mortal danger. "Late as usual," Molly answered then added, "you should be glad you're not married. Men are so irritating. You seeing anyone special?"

"Ah, nope. No one special," Ashley responded in an even tone. To no avail her fellow volunteers kept trying to coerce Ashley into talking about herself, but she'd have none of that.

Fellow adult supervisor, Dave Hanson, wearing blue jeans and a heavy white Northwestern University sweatshirt blew his whistle at mid court. "Hey! Alma! Jodi! Knock it off!" He waited until the two girls freed the unwilling Travis Garber whom they'd managed to hogtie with a pair of jump ropes. Shaking his head he wandered over to join the women on the bleachers. "What's for lunch?"

Molly aimed her thumb in Ashley's direction. "Her turn."

Striving for his own effect, Dave beetled his unruly brows and said, "Oh-nooooooo." The final syllable rolling into a prolonged groan.

"Watch your mouth or I'll bring lunch every week," Ashley threatened. She stood up and trudged off toward the coach's office to collect the Styrofoam cooler containing the infamous sandwiches. The remaining two middle-aged adults chuckled at each other.

Pleased with Ashley's reaction Dave eyed the children and offered, "Everyone seems to be having a good time today."

"Yep. The hospital is thinking about opening up the program if they can get some more volunteers."

"Not likely." Dave pointed toward the door and added, "Here comes the love of your life."

A big burly man walked into the gym, stomping snow off his boots. Ben McHenry walked over and kissed his wife then winked at Dave while dragging a drenched woolen cap off his matted head. "Miserable weather." he said, shaking the cap. "Took me over an hour to get here. Say, is it my imagination or are there more kids than usual?"

"No, you're right," Molly confirmed. "Word's gone out through the children's wing and I was asked if we could handle a few more. I just couldn't say no." She could never say "no."

* * *

Yeah, Molly was truly one in a million. Ben gazed softly at his wife allowing himself a few moments of undisguised sentiment. Numerous lines and wrinkles etched in the otherwise smooth skin of her kindly face were recent tokens of a young life in torment. But her gently curled mousy hair was brushed to a sheen and she had taken pains with her make-up. Molly was slender and diminutive. Today she wore chartreuse sweats, which were noticeably faded and frayed in a few places.

Although Molly was scrupulous in the selection of her wardrobe it had been obvious for months that nothing new was being added. Not that she'd ever complained about the financial havoc Tracy's illness had created. Molly wouldn't . . . whining simply wasn't in her nature. In fact, to her adoring husband it seemed that every waking hour of each day she bubbled with joy, and everyone around her caught that infectious cheerfulness. That's what every kid wanted in a mom.

Turning to scan the area, Ben asked, "Just you two here today? Where's Ashley?"

With heavy heart Dave answered, "She went to get lunch."

Ben sat down rather heavily himself. "Oh. Wish I'd known. I could've stopped and picked something up."

Molly poked her husband in the ribs. "Ashley has a lot of fine qualities."

The men exchanged startled glances, as if to ask if anything could be more important than their proper care and feeding. Molly scrunched her lips together and then added, "You two! I'll bet if a super model dangled a peanut butter sandwich, you'd grab it fast enough."

Ben thought for a long moment before stating the obvious, "Okay. So what's your point?"

"Since you brought it up, Molly," Dave interjected, scooting closer to Molly's other side, "why don't you tell Ashley to try some make-up or something? I mean, she's single, right? You'd be doing her a favor getting her to fix herself up."

Ben's head bobbed enthusiastically. "Yeah. She's got a great smile but she's . . . I don't know . . .

lifeless? Like she doesn't much care. Looks sort of drab . . ."

Molly shook her head at the men and injected, "You two are dipsticks. This is Sunday, her so-called day of rest. She probably looks dynamite during the week and I'll bet she has all the dates she wants. Listen, if you put Halle Berry or Scarlett Johansson in baggy sweats without make-up . . . assuming, of course, that they'd even consider doing this kind of volunteer stuff . . . they'd look pretty lifeless too. I guarantee it."

On the other side of the gym Ashley emerged bearing a cooler so the men took the opportunity to give her a speedy once-over. After a few moments of appraisal Dave shrugged and pronounced, "Uh, sure, Molly, whatever you say." He headed over to help set up lunch, while Ben stood and struggled with his overcoat.

Molly sighed as she witnessed the kids mobbing the cooler. They didn't seem to mind the drab fare. "We need more help," she declared.

Ben considered her statement then replied, "Okay, I'll ask around again. But unless someone has a kid in the hospital they don't much feel like volunteering. I mean, Dave, you, me . . . we'd be the same if our own kids weren't here, right?"

Nodding her head, Molly concurred, "Fraid so. Ashley's the only one without a kid and I don't know why she does it. She's not that comfortable around them."

"Can't figure it out either," Ben agreed, and then opined, "seems to have a chip on her shoulder all the time. Maybe she doesn't like her job. What's she do anyway? For work I mean."

"Oh, something on Wall Street, I think. Some kind of cubical job most likely. She's pretty tight lipped about herself."

"Secretary or something, hmm? How about we ask her boss to help us manage our stock portfolio?"

"Good thinking," Molly replied with a broad smirk. "We need all the help we can get figuring out how to invest our life savings of three hundred and twenty-two dollars."

They chuckled and Ben put an arm around her. "Well, even though it nearly broke us thank heavens we got our Tracy back," he declared. "Look at her jumping and hollering with the rest of them. Sure am glad the hospital got that new equipment. Never would have caught the tumor in time without it."

Molly patted his hand. "Yeah, Tracy's got a guardian angel that's for sure. Now come on, time for lunch."

With very little enthusiasm Ben stretched wearily and said, "Okay, but I'm going under protest."

Same day, 4:00 P.M.
Mid-town, Manhattan

After shepherding the kids safely back to the hospital Ashley decided to walk home rather than flag a cab. The streets were in foul weather gridlock, block after block of vehicles inching along through half a foot of dirty snowy-slush. Besides, she rather enjoyed physical exertion and sidewalks usually provided an excellent opportunity for productive thinking. Today, however, her thoughts ran to shifting fortunes, about how quickly little Tracy's illness had changed the lives of Ben and Molly. They seemed to be good people, hard working. Then out of nowhere . . . the blink of an eye . . . all their savings gone to pay medical bills. Yeah, life wasn't fair, big surprise.

If only she could take back her commitment to supervise all those kids. What on earth had she been thinking? Actually, she knew exactly what she'd been thinking. Somehow she'd expected spending time with ill-fated children would be therapeutic, a way to rationalize her own twisted childhood memories. Subdue them. But it wasn't the case. So now she was obligated to finish out the year. Couldn't very well skip out and leave the McHenry's and Dave Hanson on their own could she? Could she?

Passing a familiar brownstone she began to feel lightheaded and the sidewalk seemed to gently roll under her feet. Reaching out an arm she steadied herself against the closest wall. Pressing her cold, clammy hand on the marble slab she willed herself to block out tormenting images that were beginning to poke into her conscious.

Some time ago she'd discovered that intense concentration to the point of near physical and mental exhaustion would keep her demons at bay. Working eighty plus hours a week became a necessity, basically for mental health reasons. Bygone visions of rage and remorse flashed again. Why wouldn't they leave her alone? Those damned kids must have triggered them. Focus. She needed to drill all thought into something else, anything else. Think about Prescott. Yeah, that's it, Willard Prescott. Focus—

Images came . . . mocking images. Images of years not so long ago. She was a player at a major Wall Street firm. Her analytical prowess coupled with keen intuition, street smarts, and aggressive trading style had reaped huge profits for her and her employer. Investors clamored to have the stunning brunette manage their portfolios and any number of competitors offered to sell their souls to get her to jump ship. Seven-figure compensation packages, unlimited expenses accounts, palatial working conditions, and private chefs were routinely dangled in front of her classic, slightly upturned nose. She loved it.

She had earned it too. Ashley had paid her dues. For over ten years she had dug, scratched, and clawed her way through the snake pit known as Wall Street. In a male dominated world it had never been easy, nor had Ashley been able to overcome her frustration with the fact that a degree from Penn State was less important to managing directors than her 'cute butt.'

How many times had she been stuffed into a limousine with important clients and expected to enjoy watching porno DVD's on the television all the way to a strip club? How many times had she endured roaming hands on her legs and butt? And how many times had errant elbows rubbed her breasts? But she could play that game too.

Male dominated or not Wall Street was the land of opportunity and she wasn't about to leave empty handed. No way! Not even if it cost a husband, which it did. A small price to pay . . . or at least Ashley thought so. She never bothered asking Jim Bishop's opinion.

A blast of cold wind bit at her and she shuddered. No one passing had stopped to inquire about her . . . no one really cared. Okay, so she was alone, big deal. Her choice. She had no intention of being a victim again. She could make it on her own. Anyway, she couldn't afford time-consuming relationships while working eighty plus hours a week. It was sad but telling that her closest friend lived several hundred miles away and they hadn't seen each other since college.

Ironically, the harsh lessons she'd learned during adolescence served her career well . . . Ashley never felt the least bit hesitant about manipulating the weak. She discovered early on that men would do almost anything, spout any secret, betray their best friend, or destroy cherished principles simply to feel her firm breasts rubbing against their arm as they shared a cocktail. It was said she possessed beguiling eyes and a heart-stopping smile, and an indefinable inner fire that melted men's resistance. Understandably, Ashley knew what she could do with men and what they fantasized doing with her. So she manipulated them, all of them . . . come into my parlor said the spider to the fly.

She had planned and executed her rapid ascent on Wall Street with singular determination. Possessing insider information happens to be an obsession on Wall Street providing the holders with a critical, albeit illegal, jump on the competition. Not surprisingly, more than a few admirers who should have known better took their turn confiding to Ashley as they plunged headlong under her spell. Ashley was a good listener. She absorbed information without passing judgment, while the hapless flies talked and prattled on.

So what if her private life was essentially empty . . . a tapestry of meaningless encounters and affairs always with the same sort: Handsome and successful. Like that unusually shy, young, blond programmer she met at a computer software convention five years ago . . . was it five years ago?

Wasn't it odd? She thought as snow swirled around her sweating face. Try as she might Ashley could no longer remember that young blond programmer's name. Even their lovemaking was a faded dream. In fact, Ashley doubted she'd recognize him at the next corner if they happened to bump into one another. Still, the name of his troubled company was indelibly etched inside her memory: Virtual Reality Corporation.

Clear images of other conquests eluded her too. But they all had a hand in sending her portfolios continually soaring. There was that swaggering, conceited executive vice president about to sign a multi-billion dollar federal defense contract, and a corporate lawyer who confessed that he was about to win a major class-action lawsuit. Then there was that bio-tech researcher who scored a brilliant yet undisclosed breakthrough victory in cell mutation. Ah, and the divorced private equity partner whom Ashley entertained for several months . . . who kept her apprised of covert corporate takeovers and spinoffs. Dining at Twenty-One with the social elite or eating Coney dogs in Central Park, the men unburdened themselves to Ashley. To be sure, every scrap of wisdom was immediately fed into her laptop computer later to be digested and acted upon.

A mystique developed around her. The Street could hardly help noticing her curious, indeed amazing ability to predict the price movement of singular stocks. The gift was heralded by her clients of course but it was detested by her peers. Not that they weren't trying to get the same sort of information . . . they were. She was simply better at it.

Not unexpectedly there was a lot of grumbling to which, understandably, Ashley's satisfied superiors turned a deaf ear. To them Ashley's success was proof enough of her integrity. She was promoted to managing director, handed a key to the executive washroom and told to take no prisoners. Her bank account swelled to overflowing with more money than most would earn in a lifetime. But money didn't matter, not really. Her demons couldn't be bribed into going away.

Friday morning . . . it was on a Friday morning. Without preamble Ashley was summoned to the office of her chairman, Willard Prescott. Half expecting to be congratulated on her latest stock-picking coup she waited for the accolades that never came. Prescott was unnaturally solemn. After frowning and stammering he eventually told her that the Securities and Exchange Commission and the Financial Industry Regulatory Authority's forerunner—the National Association of Security Dealers, had been trading suspicions regarding Ms.

Taylor-Bishop's uncanny success. Apparently, insider information was alleged.

While Ashley was his superstar . . . his rainmaker . . . his big dog, the chairman had to concern himself with the "bigger picture," that her success had created powerful enemies. It was only a matter of time until the inevitable launching of a formal investigation commenced. He said that although he regretted it and thought the whole situation a damned travesty, he couldn't possibly tolerate a herd of incompetent regulators thrashing around his trading operations, creating chaos and panicking clients. No, Prescott declared, rather than defend her it would be much better for Ashley to resign effective immediately. "Oh . . . by the way (the pompous ass told her), all your clients have already been divided up among the other managers and a security guard is here to escort you out of the building. Nothing personal, Ashley. Just business."

She was devastated. But the topper came when she demanded to know how he'd learned about this pending investigation. Prescott innocently admitted that one of his married senior partners was sleeping with a highly-situated administrator at the SEC. How else could one get insider information? That did it. Blinding rage sent a thundering right uppercut into the chairman's pious jaw . . . broke it in fact.

Ashley was cured of any desire to work for any pillar of Wall Street again. The hypocrites could go to

Hell before she'd allow herself to be skewered again by a group of overbearing, self-righteous, self-absorbed pigs. Ashley salvaged what she could from her client book, convinced the regulators that the rumors were totally unfounded and began life anew.

Gossip of her sudden fall from grace filled the streets. Everything from incidents of outright fraud to screwing high rollers in limousines was speculated. It made re-establishing herself a thousand times harder. The Fallen Angel found herself once again humiliated, vulnerable, and alone. But this time she answered the challenge by creating a special domain. She threw herself into building her own cocoon, an exclusive sanctuary where the public wasn't allowed—she was bulletproof.

A ray of uncommonly bright sunlight poked its way through the gray clouds, warming her smooth skin and gently bringing her back to the present. The demons were asleep. Taking several deep breaths Ashley exorcized any further thoughts of corporate abuse, self dealing and outright betrayal. Pulling herself together she straightened her shoulders and flicked errant strands of hair away from her jade colored eyes. Move along, she told herself. Find that Holy Grail.

CHAPTER 2

Wednesday, March 13, 4:30 P.M.
I-96, Detroit, Michigan

Richard Blaine's sense of humor was instinctive and infectious, and he often used it to transform fiery situations into harmless skirmishes. A product of the nineteen seventies, Rick's straight brown hair still completely covered his head and his six-foot frame remained reasonably lean since unlike many his age, he didn't overeat and hadn't totally rejected exercise. Rick was also one of those who knew how to hit a happy medium . . . people genuinely liked him. As for being middle aged, it simply seemed to have shown up one day while he wasn't looking.

Technically, Rick Blaine was the president of the First State Bank of Michigan, NA., at least for another hour. Today was his last day with the bank and he evidenced his contempt by wearing his least favorite suit. This was not a joyous occasion. There would be no parties, no well-wishers, no departing speeches, no nothing. After four years as chief executive officer, Rick was odd man out.

A larger bank in Ohio wanting to expand into Michigan had decided that his bank was just what they needed. Their generous buyout offer was readily accepted by his board of directors and approved by the shareholders. The Ohio bank's president made it clear he didn't want Rick hanging around . . . no need for two presidents. Apparently, steady earnings, superior customer surveys, and few, if any, problem loans didn't matter. Rick was thrown under the bus, a casualty of cost cutting.

This whole mess had broken Rick emotionally and spiritually. Especially since banks were being consolidated, acquired and merged at a dizzying pace. The ranks of the unemployed were full of displaced bankers. He was now just one of a growing multitude of senior executives scrounging for a job. Reality check—the banking industry was shrinking. Nothing personal.

Saying goodbye to his secretary, carrying a box of personal effects he left his office for the last time and found himself homeward bound drowning in self-pity. What a disaster. Only a short while ago the certainty of a regular paycheck had never been an issue, now suddenly it was all-consuming. To make matters worse, Stephanie had sacrificed a professional career because they both felt having one parent at home overrode all other concerns. Noble convictions indeed except when the only source of income is abruptly ended. Yeah, nothing personal.

PART 2
THE VAIN

CHAPTER 3

Friday, March 15, 8:00 P.M.
Double Eagle Restaurant
Dallas, Texas

Although he'd often seen it advertised in airline magazines among those boldly-listed Top Ten Steak Houses, it was Gary Nash's first time at the Double Eagle. Gary was the rapidly balding, overweight, mid-fiftyish Treasurer of LoneStar International. Apparently, his two hosts from the Wall Street brokerage firm of Pagent & Associates read the same airline magazines and pulled several strings to secure last-minute prime-seating reservations. Aided with a constant stream of alcohol to limber the brain cells, Pagent's managing director Bob Bell and his young lackey Larry Hendricks, dedicated the evening to educating Gary about something called 'SWAPs.'

Before today, Gary was totally ignorant of SWAPs as were most Earthlings. Undaunted, the men from Pagent took great pains throughout dinner explaining how a SWAP works. "See, Gary. We're gonna swap a fixed rate debt for a variable rate. Just look at these betas and convexities." Then they said something about durations and notional amounts. A highly energized Larry painstakingly went over a vast array of computer generated simulation models containing cash flows and columns of numbers, each proudly displaying 'high' coefficients of confidence.

For Gary, the main idea to grasp was each simulation yielded the same result: A win for LoneStar International of between one and two million dollars a month. It didn't take the native Texan long to figure out these two boys had done this sort of thing before.

As empty drink glasses were swiftly replaced with fresh refills, Messieurs Bell and Hendricks explained how the more sophisticated financial institutions were all using SWAPs and other synthetic securities for additional infusions of income. Gary remembered hearing about synthetic securities from somewhere. Weren't they what got Orange County, California deep into trouble years ago?

Not that it really mattered. LoneStar's Chairman, Brett Hollister was advocating this new endeavor and who was going to overrule Brett? Hell, Gary knew his job tonight was to be a rubber stamp. But once the profit dynamics were conveyed he realized exactly why Brett had hurriedly sent him to 'pin down the details.' Gary knew all too well about his bosses' quest for more earnings.

Reminding himself to ignore his rapidly rising anxieties abetted by the fact that every other word uttered by the Pagent team sounded like a foreign language, Gary played along by grunting intermittently and nodding his understanding. Gary Nash was a CPA, a reputable and good CPA . . . LoneStar's treasurer for Christ sake . . . and he wasn't about to let a couple of Yankees know he was totally lost.

Squeezing his eyes shut and sitting back for a moment as another tray of delectable morsels were served; Gary took a breather from the cavalcade of confusion. Sipping the last of his Old Fashion, he surveyed the Double Eagle. The interior was reminiscent of his idea of an English manor, like the place the wealthy gentry retired after a fox hunt. Their party of three had been charmingly greeted by a pair of exceptionally attractive hostesses attired in body-sculpting low-cut evening gowns, and then, seemingly within seconds, the black-tuxedoed maitre d' appeared, bowing eagerly to show them to this "excellent table," which faced an open-pit fireplace.

Fist-sized lobster appetizers began the gastronomic spectacle, followed by shrimp cocktails, salads, breads, soups, twenty-ounce steaks, perfectly prepared asparagus, new potatoes with a drizzle of clarified butter and just the right amount of fresh parsley, hot apple slices and wine.

Yeah, the wine! Bob Bell and the sommelier, a high-brow name for 'wine steward,' talked and talked while Gary and the youthful Larry sipped and sipped and drank and drank. Nuances of taste among the various bottles being poured escaped Gary entirely but nonetheless he went graciously along with the lavish presentations, as though this were something he did every night.

The waiters smelled high tippers or else they were impeccably trained. Gary had never been so well attended. It was almost as though with every bite of food a straight-backed wait staff would appear with an oversized napkin to dab his mouth. Surely, Gary couldn't be blamed for allowing himself to be taken in by all the pomp and circumstance, the artistic pageantry. Sometime during the third bottle of red wine Gary figured out that being the center of attention afforded the recipient a certain degree of arrogance unavailable to lesser beings. To be sure, feeling important was something to be savored.

It was also extremely self-satisfying having Bell and Hendricks falling all over to please him. My, how the compliments flowed. "I've only met one or two other firms that have treasurers intelligent enough to really grasp what we've been talking about tonight," they told him, and "It won't be long before you'll find yourself being offered jobs by the competition." The Pagent & Associate boys even told Gary he'd probably be asked to speak at industry conferences and co-author a few articles. Talk about an ego boost.

"Hey, Gary," Bob Bell said in noticeably lowered tones, "next time we fly back here, you know . . . once your board approves you hedging with SWAPs, why don't we plan on going to one of those famous Dallas gentlemen's clubs?"

Gary was somewhat taken aback but managed to slur out in a half-drunken stupor, "Damned straight." He had nothing against the clubs. Actually, he'd never set foot inside one of the fancy strip joints but not because he didn't want to; rather, he'd never gotten up the courage to suggest it to a friend or to go alone. While neither he nor Bob Bell would ever be mistaken for Brad Pitt or Matt Damon, how important could looks be at a men's club? Truthfully, the only real question was: Could they live through it?

With fantasies of nimble young lovelies parading in front of him, Gary stole a sideways glance at his host. Bell's pear-shaped body and chubby cheeks hinted at a lifestyle, which by tradition and convention ran rich in both caloric intake and alcohol depletion. Dark-gray, darting eyes encased beneath overgrown brows seemed to see everything but focus on nothing, much like a predator. But it was Bob Bell's ears which drew the most attention, with long bristly hairs sprouted from both lobes like weeds desperately in need of mowing.

Brett Hollister had told Gary that Bob Bell was around forty, although the man could easily pass for someone eyeing membership in AARP. Regarding Bell's substance and personality, a solid gold chain wrapped several times around a Rolex watch and accented by a gaudy diamond pinkie ring spoke volumes. Bob Bell was truly someone Gary wanted to emulate.

Belting back another after dinner glass of brandy the affable and inebriated Larry Hendricks chimed in and said, "Yeah, we certainly will've earned a night of female entertainment, don'tcha think?" He gave a cartoon-caricature wink to the other two men.

A warm feeling filled Gary and it wasn't caused solely by alcohol intake. Outwardly, he seemed literally to glow brighter as the night wore on and inhibitions crumbled. Yep, this was man at his finest, good friends exchanging smirks and making sloppy remarks concerning lap dancers. How much better can it get?

As a grand gesture he decided to really impress Bob Bell and Larry Hendricks. Gary cleared his throat and said in halting speech, "Look, I can fully well . . . ah, appreciate the value of SWAPs. So I'm gonna tell Brett . . . soon as I see him Monday . . . that you boys and your program have my full backing." He smiled and added, "I'm gonna tell him that . . . that we need the best investment advice Wall Street can offer, and that's you boys."

Both men from Pagent gazed momentarily at the large brandy snifters they were clutching, obviously overcome by some shared sentiment. Then Bob Bell looked up, almost choking back the emotion of the moment and told Gary it was a rare pleasure dealing with a man of such integrity and market savvy.

Gary nearly had to choke back tears himself when he replied, "Well, you have my word. I mean, you can count on me *one hundred and fifty percent.*"

Same day, 11: 09 P.M.
LBJ Highway, Dallas

Later, riding in the back seat of a taxi traveling toward the north entrance to D/FW International airport, the sprawling complex serving Dallas and Fort Worth, Bob Bell was lost in thought. This deal was all but wrapped up and with a little bullying he could convince Gary Nash to increase the suggested amount of the SWAPs to realize even greater profits, not to mention substantially higher commissions for himself.

It was amazing what could be accomplished with ultra-sophisticated concepts. Never mind if they were necessary or if they even worked for that matter. These cutting-edge securities were held out to the financial community as necessities. Sporting powerful sounding names like 'Swaps' or 'Derivatives' or 'Reverse Repos,' these synthetic investments garnered instant cult status from the brood of confused treasurers and chief financial officers trying to justify their own careers. Admittedly, if the market turned the wrong way these investments could propel a firm straight into bankruptcy, witness several high-flying technology companies. It often seemed ironic to Bob Bell that the wilder the theory the more salable the product.

His young associate Larry was busting with unabashed glee, which caused Bob to wonder . . . not for the first time . . . what made Hendricks tick? To

Bob and others of his generation, Larry looked more like a world-class sprinter than a financial whiz-kid. But under short-cropped tightly-curled blonde hair (a style and color about which only his hairdresser knew for sure) lurked a crazed carnivore, complete with nose which flared periodically, particularly when Hendricks moved in for the kill.

"Right nice work, Bob," Larry drawled in obvious mimicry of Gary Nash's extravagant Texas accent. "Reeled him in just like a fish. These good ole boys just don't have a clue, do they?" He laughed aloud and it came out as a derisive snort, a quick mean-spirited ha! "But," he continued, "since Nash and Hollister are going to make us fucking rich, who are we to judge? Best thing that's happened to us in months."

At the moment, Bob Bell just couldn't convince himself of that fact. He didn't feel right. Something was wrong and it wasn't just his associate's school boy fun-making. Was *he* getting soft, thinking too much about the other guy? But at the end of the day, Bob admitted to himself, it sure was easy money.

Sunday, March 24, 2:00 P.M.
A Public School, Manhattan

The kids playing in the gymnasium had succeeded in wrapping one of their own up in a tumbling mat. "Hey. Get Janice out of there. Now!" Dave Hanson blew his whistle and pointed to the guilty parties. "I said, *now!*"

Over on the other side of the floor, Ben and Molly McHenry were trying to keep order during a game of dodge ball. Everyone was having a great time except for one little girl sitting with her face to the wall. It was Sara's first trip out of the hospital, the first time the other children had seen her nearly bald head, the first time she realized that she had every reason to be ashamed and the feeling was agonizing. Certain that everyone would make fun of her, Sara had turned her back and hunched her small body into a faraway corner.

Seeing the little girl all alone didn't particularly faze Ashley one way or the other. After all, sometimes being alone was preferable. Thankfully the kid wasn't whining . . . Ashley hated whining. But succumbing to the circumstances Ashley glided over and crouched down next to the girl and said, "Not having much fun, huh?" Sara shrugged and hugged her knees all the more tightly. "Hey, I know!" Ashley offered. "You want to see something? It looks kind of funny. You put it on your head, over your eyes, and then you can see things. It's kind of like going to the movies. Wanna try?"

Sara turned slowly, looked nervously at the lady with pretty green eyes, and finally nodded. In response, Ashley took Sara's hand and together they walked over to the bleachers where Ashley's oversized knapsack stowed a host of personal paraphernalia. Her laptop computer was near the top sheathed within a soft leather case, which she pulled out along with something else buried at the bottom of her carry-all. It was an odd looking mask with a front visor. She tethered it to the laptop using a long electric cord specifically designed to fit a four-pronged plug in the very back of the contraption. Next, Ashley turned on her computer, typed in a few words and clicked the mouse, then turned to Sara. "Okay," she said. "Now this is kind of heavy so I'll hold it for you. You sit in front . . . right there, that's good. Ready?"

The child nodded, clearly skeptical but nevertheless eager to try. Besides, it would help hide her baldness. Ashley lowered the visor and when Sara realized it was almost totally dark inside she started trying to squirm out, but then she saw a picture that caused her to hold her breath. It was like nothing Sara had seen before and the activity enveloped her, as though she were an integral part of the fantasy. She was at a zoo!

Monkeys jumped back and forth, climbing over each other, waving to her and making friendly little noises like they wanted Sara to leap into the tree branches and join the fun. Ashley watched as Sara reached forward to touch the small animals and she heard Sara giggle and then say, "Wow! Awesome!" . . . responses similar to those Ashley had heard before.

The scene changed to tigers and after a few moments Sara noticed that the big cats appeared blurry. Trying to sharpen the focus she squinted, but it didn't help. The viewing screen was sort of small. "Ooooo," she squealed in delight, clapping her tiny hands together. "Zebras!" Sara loved zebras and these were running and kicking out with their hind legs. She giggled and then felt a twinge behind her eyes, some sort of small pain which caused her to place both hands on the visor, pushing it up.

Ashley was quick to react to Sara's discomfort, and when the devise lay between them on the bleachers she asked, "Did it hurt your eyes a little?"

Sara nodded. She looked up at Ashley seemingly unaware that a group of other kids had noticed the weird mask and were skipping towards the bleachers and shouting: "What's that? What's it doing? Can I try? Is it something you play with?"

Suddenly Sara was the center of attention and before she could shy away it dawned on her that the children were talking to her, not making fun. She answered all their questions, but when she came to the part about her eyes hurting only a few of the boys seemed anxious to take a turn. While Ashley helped the curious peek inside a virtual world Sara scampered off to play with a group of girls.

"Whatcha got there?" Molly and Ben had finished their dodge ball game and were allowed a five minute respite by their tiny charges.

"Oh, this is the VR headset . . . VR for virtual reality," Ashley answered.

Ben's eyes lit up. "That thing that created such a commotion a few years back?" he asked, lining up behind three small boys. "So what does it do?"

Ashley spread her arms expansively. "Whatever you want. Put it on your head and it'll whisk you away to wherever the software's been programmed."

"No kidding? What's something like that cost?"

The first little boy pulled his head out of the mask grimacing and another took his place, while Ben moved forward in the line. Ashley's arms were getting tired from holding the dead weight and she shook them out before fitting the headset onto its newest user. "Sorry, Ben. What did you say? Oh, the price! These things started out at nine hundred dollars but I got this one for forty-nine ninety-five at a closeout sale."

"No kidding? Where?"

"Nowhere now. The manufacturer went bankrupt. The images are sort of crude and a lot of people, particularly kids, got headaches from eyestrain."

Ben's turn had arrived and he held the visor overhead then slipped into it. "Kind of heavy."

"Don't I know," Ashley agreed. "The weight didn't particularly help sales, either," she added.

Ben whistled. "How about this?" he said. "Neat picture. Like 3-D movies only better. But it's fuzzy off and on. Not worth nine hundred dollars, that's a fact. Where'd you say you got it?"

"Uh, I sort of stumbled into it."

"Company went belly-up, huh? Well, that's a shame. They were onto something, though. Maybe just ahead of their time. Investors lose everything?"

"Just about. Investors, stockholders, employees . . . almost everyone."

Ben removed the mask. "Say, you work on Wall Street don't you?"

With no emotion what-so-ever Ashley replied evenly, "Yes. That's right."

"The company you work for, did they by any chance get burned by this?"

Involuntarily, Ashley smiled a bit and said, "No." A twinkle in her eyes suggested there was more to the story but they both knew he'd be waiting forever for an explanation.

Ben tried a more direct approach, "So, what do you do for a living?"

"Mostly research. I read a lot," she answered evasively.

"Yeah? Sounds boring but then you probably wouldn't want my job. I work for a meat-packing company."

"So Molly told me. She also said you're up for a promotion."

Ben allowed the corners of his mouth to turn up and he puffed out his chest despite an obvious effort to appear indifferent. "She tell you that? She wasn't supposed to but, yeah, things are looking real good. We can use the extra cash too. Hospital bills and all."

Ashley nodded and said, "I hope it works out for you. You and Molly are nice people."

"Thanks. Bet there's a bunch of nice people in your line of work, right?"

Tilting her head almost imperceptibly, she replied, "Probably."

CHAPTER 4

Tuesday, April 9, 8:30 A.M.
Boardroom, LoneStar International Corporation
Dallas, Texas

The boardroom of LoneStar International was nothing if not opulent. In keeping with the traditional period of mourning, Hobby Glassman's recently vacated chair was draped with a special-ordered black scarf, courtesy of Neiman Marcus. On a day which otherwise promised to be difficult for Chairman Brett Hollister, he was pleased with the scarf's effect. It added just the right touch.

Surveying the room as was his custom prior to board meetings Brett's eyes drifted past the massive French doors inlaid with exquisite hand carved panels, which opened onto a panorama of richly-appointed furnishings, intricate wall moldings and heavy beige drapes. Original oil paintings from the Impressionist period were strategically spaced and hung with special lighting for maximum dramatic impact. The room's focal point . . . a long oval mahogany conference table surrounded by twenty high-back brown leather chairs . . . gleamed under the a three hundred pound tiered crystal chandelier hanging dead center.

He also noted the Edward II wing chairs arrayed along the walls in small groupings for intimate dialogue. On the south side of the room the floor-to-ceiling windows afforded an unobstructed view of downtown Dallas and the surrounding flatlands from ten stories high. Dallas was a Mecca of marble and reflective glass skyscrapers built during the heady days of the 1970s and early 80s when acquiring oil or land had meant guaranteed appreciation of your investment. Rightfully so, LoneStar's monument fit in well. Especially the tenth-floor executive offices, which had been decorated in the same luxurious style as the boardroom.

Expensive antique furnishings had been purchased without budget restraint. Paintings, sculptures, leather bound books, vases and urns, silk screens, lamps and Oriental rugs all contributed to the desired and desirable aura of brazen prosperity. The atmosphere often intimidated clients, as well as adversaries . . . all the better for maximum negotiating leverage.

Also, in further keeping with time-honored traditions, no effort was considered superfluous in preparing for a board meeting. Each piece of sterling silver flatware in addition to the Baccarat drinking goblets, bone china dishes and serving platters, were either washed or polished. A special cleaning crew ensured that every nook and cranny of the room was spotless. Luncheon preparers and servers were brought in from a nearby five-star hotel and given the run of a fully furnished adjoining kitchen designed and utilized exclusively for board meetings. Pomp and circumstance was the order of the day.

Finally, Brett gazed at Hobby's chair. What a terrible waste and what an imposition. Today, the topic of filling this now vacant position would have to be addressed in order for the candidate's name to be included in the soon-to-be-released shareholders' proxy statement. Whoever he proposed to the board would certainly get the nomination and whoever they nominated was virtually assured of receiving overwhelming approval at the upcoming annual shareholders meeting.

Over twenty percent of the stock was held by directors, officers and employees, none of whom would even think of voting against Brett's proffered slate. Besides, never had a board nominee lost, as they'd always run unopposed. No alternative slate of candidates to choose from! But time was short. Hobby's vacancy was giving Brett Hollister problems for which he was sorely unprepared, and being unprepared was unnerving.

Unnerving because Brett had always commended himself for his ability to control board meetings. He spent untold hours of his own time plus hundreds of employee hours orchestrating each and every detail of the monthly events. They were not to start until after lunch . . . a heavy lunch to dull senses just enough to give the chairman a surreptitious edge. As for the agenda, it would contain only those topics which Brett considered "worthy" of such a venerated body. Adjournment would occur promptly at 3:45 p.m., ostensibly to give the out-of-state members ample time to catch return flights, which meant that a mere three hours was devoted to actual deliberations. Three hours was more than sufficient time for board meetings and Brett wasn't about to lengthen it.

Regrettably, Hobby had been one of only two directors from another state. If the new board ended up containing only one foreigner, then Brett's mid-afternoon forced adjournments could be threatened by several local members who would jump at the chance to hang around the lavish surroundings, ask a lot of fool questions, and make pests of themselves. That's how it was before, when he'd first been given the job . . . no discipline. Well, that sure wasn't going to happen again, not while he was still breathing. A non-Texan successor had to be identified and quickly. There were four résumés stacked neatly on his desk compliments of the board's search committee, waiting for his final selection

Brett finished his review of the boardroom and returned to his office to reread each file for the fifth time. The finalists had been whittled from an initial list of fifteen names all supplied by himself, whose altruism belied his true motives. Sitting at his desk Brett wondered who he could trust to give this choice plum.

With so little time to complete the selection process Brett didn't have a chance to develop his typically close working relationship with the prospective candidates. He didn't know which one would follow his lead without question. Damn Hobby for putting him into this predicament.

Not that Brett Hollister believed LoneStar had all that much to hide. The company had been in business for over fifty years with a fairly constant stream of earnings and dividends, at least until recently. During Brett's ten-year tenure at the helm LoneStar had diversified from a local developer of raw land into a national powerhouse with tentacles reaching into all sorts of businesses.

Sure there had been a few bumps along the way, there always were . . . and that's why he wanted an accommodating board. Remember those heady acquisition years and taking on all that debt? That same debt which was now choking them to death. Talk about rude awakenings. Did anyone really know how much they'd actually overpaid? Or to be more precise, how much he'd been 'advised' to overpay? Did he really want to explain all that to the shareholders?

Betrayal, that's what this was all about. The company had spent money to expand like that infamous cliché about drunken sailors . . . no offense to drunken sailors. Brett shook his head in disgust thinking how he'd been screwed by self-serving brokers, attorneys and lenders. And he could add his own management group into the mix. For damned sure he'd been too trusting, at least that's how he saw it.

Anyway, he finally showed them who the hell was running LoneStar. A few years back any executive who brought bad news found himself out on the street. Amazing how the rest of his flock took the hint and stopped screwing up . . . they also stopped showing up. But that was fine with him. If Brett wanted to see someone in person his secretary would issue a summons. If he felt like screaming at them, he would. It was a good system.

Brett wasn't a very complex leader. In fact, even though his singular business philosophy was forged over more years ago than he cared to admit, it was refreshingly simple: Just look around. Every day more and more institutions were finding themselves on the wrong end of a merger or 'strategic alliance,' where hedge funds or private equity groups paid a few extra bucks to the shareholders in return for the right to strip your miserable carcass bare. It was enough to tear your heart out.

Well, it sure wasn't going to happen here, not while he was in charge. Fortunately, the stock was owned by devoted employees, sympatric board members and satisfied shareholders eager to derail any unwanted advances. LoneStar's future was assured as long as earnings held. Earnings was the key. Consistent, dependable, ever increasing earnings.

Closing the cover on the fourth and final résumé Brett cupped large hands behind his thick neck and admitted he'd ridden this damned horse far too long to let some shave-tail, wise-ass director tell him what to do or go poking around where he didn't belong. So without any qualms, but with a ton of fanfare, he'd offer Hobby's empty seat to the candidate who appeared to be the easiest to intimidate. If proven wrong? He'd nail the son of a bitch to a wall.

Same day, 1:45 P.M.
LoneStar Boardroom

"Gentlemen, gentlemen . . . please come to order. Thank you. The next order of business is the selection of a candidate to fill the seat once occupied by our good friend Hobby, whose untimely death is a great loss to us all, I'm sure." Brett let his shoulders droop slightly, lowering his head as if to pay homage to the dearly departed. For a few moments he said nothing but stole glances at the other directors, noting with satisfaction that they were following his lead. For further effect, when the chairman straightened he spoke as though talking to himself. "The most tragic accident, the worst I can think of . . ." Then clearing his throat and speaking with considerable vigor he continued by acknowledging Hobby's "tireless efforts on behalf of LoneStar" and concluded the delicate but necessary transition by saying, "It is with a deep sense of pride that I announce a two hundred fifty thousand dollar memorial fund established at our own Parkland Memorial Hospital in the name of Mr. Kevin Hobart Glassman." As soon as the other eighteen board members had politely applauded their approval, he proceeded.

"Now to the business at hand. In your board book behind tab E you will find the résumé of our selection committee's nominee, Dr. Charles Hilborn. You will note that Dr. Hilborn is a professor, writer, historian, humanitarian, a veteran and founding father of Dream Makers, the well-known and valuable charity for terminally ill children. He still teaches a few courses of philosophy and history at the University of Michigan and currently serves on the board of several community organizations. Dr. Hilborn is fifty-six years old and a periodic guest at various White House functions, an honor apparently not entirely due to his own impressive achievements, but to his wife Jennifer who has been involved with politics for about twenty years.

"Having had the personal pleasure of meeting Dr. Hilborn, I'm able to add that he is a delightfully enlightened individual, and I wholeheartedly concur with our search committee that Dr. Hilborn can infuse this board with new perspectives and insights that might currently be lacking. The floor is now open for questions and comments."

"Mr. Chair-*mon*?"

"Yes, the chair recognizes, Mr. Walker." Brett congratulated himself . . . who would ever know that not twenty-four hours ago, Willis Walker hadn't even heard of Charles Hilborn? Willis was a leather-faced Lyndon B. Johnson clone who'd happily display his appendectomy scar. A retired U.S. Senator turned rancher he possessed enough land, cattle, cash and political favors to do exactly what he wanted, when and for how long. He had served on the board since leaving Washington and never once cast a vote against Brett. With Willis there were no pesky questions or unwarranted intrusions regarding LoneStar's affairs. His canned comment was, "You boys just keep doin' what ya been doin'," and following a private conversation Brett had engineered with Willis only two hours earlier, the rancher promised to give Dr. Hilborn a ringing endorsement.

This was necessary because a vote from Walker was almost as compelling as Brett's. The man was a living legend. It seemed as if Willis alone could get away with verbalizing haphazard statements that left the other directors nodding enthusiastically, while trying to read profound meaning into the benign gibberish. Willis was truly an artful rhetorician.

"Mr. Chair-mon, ah took the liberty of doin' a little checking up on this here good doctor back last week when ah found his name on the committee's short list. Ah don't mind tellin' ya that having a teacher in our ranks didn't sit well with me at first, but hell . . . ah just wanna say he's got ma vote." Willis sat back . . . looking entirely pleased with himself.

That was it? That was the resounding endorsement? Well, with Willis sometimes fewer words were better. Often the eminent senator would just spin yarns out of control and ramble on for hours, and today they had a lot of business to conclude. "Yes, thank you, Mr. Walker."

"Mr. Chairman?"

"Yes, the chair recognizes, Mr. King." Arthur King was the gaunt, thin-necked, bow tie-wearing, forever-grinning, insipid president of a small Fort Worth bank. Almost every prominent board had an Arthur King within its ranks. In this case, he was a pet banker whose daddy once got on the wrong side of Brett and probably still regretted it. Nonetheless, Arthur had his uses.

Business acquaintances called him King Arthur, a nickname he seemed to enjoy. But Arthur's true joy came from being on the board of this national company, a credential of which his friends and family were exceptionally proud. Prestige was a powerful influence in some social circles and Brett knew King Arthur would never compromise his position on the board for any reason, short of treason against the

Republic of Texas. There was no cause for alarm with this man.

"Mr. Chairman, I would like to go on record that I fully and totally support the nomination of Dr. Charles Hilborn to serve on this esteemed board. I look forward to having such a highly-regarded academician working with us as we guide this great ship. A ship I'm not ashamed to state I'm honored to be part of."

What an ass-kisser, Brett thought as he struggled against wincing. As usual, King Arthur had overdone it. Why couldn't the man just stick with the program? Why bore everyone with all that Camelot horseshit? Brett sometimes wondered if a sure vote was worth having to endure King's irritating grandiloquence.

"Mr. Chairman?"

Brett hadn't expected this man to speak. "Yes, the chair recognizes, Mr. Bennett." Chester Bennett was an attorney and LoneStar's general counsel. While this man knew which side to pledge allegiance to, like all lawyers he could be unpredictable. Brett found himself staring at Chester's bald spot, which had widened noticeably during the past year along with his waistline. Brett knew better than most that the past years had been tough, perhaps particularly for the corporate attorney. Those overlapping folds of fat under bloodshot eyes were stark reminders of the toll the job exacted . . . although the generous compensation package made it palatable.

Other than Brett, Chester Bennett was the only LoneStar executive on the board. It was Chester who was charged with fending off hostile suits and closing complex business deals at the eleventh hour, not to mention penning employment contracts for the top executives, the first and best being for Brett Hollister.

Chester was shrewd enough to understand that getting the board to pass his own generous contract would happen only after the precedent had been established with Brett. For that reason, almost two years ago, Chester, with a litigator's typical dramatic style presented to the board a newly created employment contract which clearly aimed to reward and retain Brett. It did both. With all due humility Brett accepted the token of esteem. Quite naturally, the general counsel's own employment contract followed shortly thereafter, along with similar contracts for other key executives.

Normally, Chester Bennet could be counted among Brett's *most* trusted allies and confidantes. Although, the chairman also knew that Bennett's soft and eloquent southern drawl could quickly turn into a torrid rampage of self-righteousness . . . particularly if he thought his veracity or intelligence was being impugned. And as general counsel of a major conglomerate embroiled in litigation throughout the land, it frequently was. Brett could only hold his breath and wait for evidence of Bennett's current mood.

"Mr. Chairman, quite the contrary to most lawyers I shall keep my summation of the matter at hand refreshingly brief." LoneStar's general counsel paused for the obligatory unconvincing chuckles of those couple of board members who could be bothered. As Brett held his breath Chester finally declared, "I support Dr. Hilborn's nomination wholeheartedly."

"Thank you, Mr. Bennett," Brett replied, sucking in air. Anxious to move the proceedings along he asked if there were other comments and received blank stares in return. "No? Well then, in accordance with our by-laws the chair will entertain a motion to nominate Dr. Hilborn along with the nineteen of us at this table to three year terms as directors, thus setting forth our slate of candidates for stockholder approval."

"So moved."

"Thank you. Is there support?"

"Yes, I'll support."

"Thank you, all in favor say aye. The Secretary will note that the motion was passed by unanimous consent. Now on to the next agenda topic, Sale of Commercial Property, which you will find in more detail behind tab F."

Brett was encouraged to see several sets of limp eyelids. Heavy lunches . . . works every time. Now he needed to get through the next two issues without a lot of discussion.

"You will note gentlemen, the forty-million dollar semi-annual interest payment on our eight-hundred million dollars of outstanding debt is due and payable in two weeks. This is a substantial sum of money and inasmuch as our corporate cash is currently employed elsewhere, we have been approached by a group of investors wishing to purchase those properties listed on page F-3."

Brett sighed. This was tricky. It was the same line he'd spouted on three previous occasions when the damned interest payment came due. But this time . . . this time the assets proffered for sale to assemble the much needed cash would *not* turn a tidy profit. LoneStar was looking at a deterioration in earnings for the first time and Brett felt double-crossed. How could real estate values drop like this? To make matters worse, the damned accountants wanted him to start setting aside more reserves for writing down other overstated assets. Son of a bitch, he muttered to himself. I can't do that. Damned stockholders would string me up.

Speaking to the board Brett moved to accept the offer as proposed and asked, "Is there any support?"

"Mr. Chairman, if I might ask a question?"

Dammit, just vote for Christ sake and keep things moving. "Yes, of course, Mr. Whiteside." Brett forced a smile.

"Thank you. It appears that the sales price being offered is substantially below what we think the assets are worth. Now, rather than booking a loss shouldn't we sell our more liquid securities? Like those treasury notes we're holding as investments?"

"Thank you for your question, Mr. Whiteside. While on first blush your suggestion does appear a more thoughtful solution, when we get to the next agenda item you will see that the treasury notes in question are earmarked as security for a highly desirable new opportunity. In brief, we can't sell the notes, so management proposes the sale of property. If there are no further comments, I request a motion for support."

"Support."

"All in favor say aye. Thank you. Mr. Secretary, please note that the motion was passed by unanimous consent. Now for the next topic entitled 'SWAPs.' You'll find the material behind tab G. For this agenda item our treasurer Mr. Gary Nash is waiting outside if we need to bring him in, but I think that everyone here is smart enough to grasp the profit potential without the necessity of copious details. Suffice it to say, a SWAP is a clever but effective Wall Street invention that will help us with these burdensome interest payments. This is accomplished when we replace . . . or swap . . . the fixed interest rate on our debt with a rate which is tied to commercial paper. We all know that as short-term rates continue to fall commercial paper rates will fall too, and these SWAP's will be in the money. So, as long as short-term rates fall we'll end up paying less in interest."

Brett paused, pretending to search for some item in his folder. In reality he wanted to give the SWAP description ample opportunity to sink in and also to survey the room for general reaction. He was expecting them to be too numb to offer insightful discourse or pointed arguments. In fact, tacit approval was the best case scenario. Judging all to be well, he continued. "If interest rates climb we'll be protected by something called a collar. Apparently, a collar sets a maximum ceiling on the amount of risk. The bottom line is we'll receive instant cash from the SWAP. That's about as technical as I can get but you all know Gary Nash . . . well, he's been spending a lot of time with a team of rocket scientists from Wall Street to ensure that we know what we're doing before we do it. Gary told me he's *one hundred and fifty percent* behind this. Are there any comments?"

No one spoke. Some flipped the confusing charts back and forth trying to make sense out of them, while others simply gazed off into the distance. "Mr. Chairman?" It was Arthur King again. Brett recognized him while keeping a wary eye on the others.

"Mr. Chairman, while I must admit that I'm not sure I understand the complexity of this financial instrument, this SWAP, I see by looking at this summary page that we'll get an extra one to two million dollars a month. Do I read that right?"

"Yes sir, you do."

With an expression halfway between amazement and triumph the banker slapped his pen onto his board folder and bellowed, "Then I don't see how we can fail to support the proposal. In fact, I'll be interested in looking at this for my bank."

Not too surprisingly, after the requisite 'thank you's' the motion and carried. The SWAP was passed by a group of tired men growing increasingly weary. The remaining housekeeping formalities continued for another hour with hardly anyone paying the slightest attention. All votes were unanimous. The meeting adjourned on schedule and polished limousines whisked the directors away to individual destinations. Thus concluded another successful LoneStar board meeting.

PART 3
THE RIGHTEOUS

CHAPTER 5

Wednesday, April 10, 5:30 P.M.
Birmingham, Michigan

"Mr. Blaine, I've enjoyed talking with you and perhaps there'll be something in the future, once our new budget is approved. Meanwhile, I'll put your résumé into our active file. Thanks again for taking time to visit us." Rick Blaine managed a half-hearted smile followed by the obligatory handshake, removed himself from the office and walked heavily to his car.

Someone once said that the difference between a recession and a depression was: In a recession your neighbor is unemployed, in a depression *you're* unemployed. Five interviews, scores of résumés emailed, a handful of executive search firms, plus networking, and over thirty calls to business associates and friends all added up to a big, fat, zero. Luckily, his severance package was decent enough to pay off several months of bills, which Rick knew was more than other discharged employees received. But still.

Having little else to do this evening he offered to take over the kids' car-pooling, while his wife Stephanie went shopping. Stephanie's mood improved immeasurably after a shopping spree, and having her happy was of greater import right now than the money she might spend. Anyway, even the blackest cloud held some silver lining, however thin. For Rick the upside was the opportunity to spend more time with his two boys, albeit fleetingly. After dropping the eldest off at his music lesson it was hurry up across town and wave goodbye as their church's weekly Mid-High Youth Group commenced its field-trip to a local skating rink.

With both boys now otherwise occupied Rick realized he had over an hour before the music lesson ended and his presence was required. To kill time and amuse himself he decided to stroll through the church, admittedly an impressive edifice. Built in the 1950's and styled after an ancient Scottish Abbey, which looked more like a castle than anything else, the building was composed mostly of large stone blocks and towering leaded glass windows. Situated on a hill overlooking a two-mile-wide private lake, surrounded by forty acres of church-owned property, lavish with trees, the structure was called The Abbey.

Rick's footsteps echoed as he ascended a winding stone staircase before wending his way through arched walkways leading into the sanctuary. Black wrought iron chandeliers offered dim light which cast eerie shadows on the cut stone walls. In the sanctuary itself Rick passed row after row of dark oak pews with red velvet seat cushions. The altar area was framed within an immense stained glass relief of various biblical characters, and each side of the altar was covered with frescoes depicting Christianity's more historic moments. Approximately sixty feet above Rick's head, massive wooden beams supported a vaulted slate ceiling.

There was virtually no sound save his breathing. More than any other chamber within the church, the sanctuary was humbling and solemn . . . peaceful and conducive to thought. Rick figured it was time for some heavy thought.

He sat in the front pew gazing up at the relief and reflected on his plight. God alone knew that his prospects were discouraging. Assuming he found a job . . . which was a big assumption . . . odds were it would require relocation, something his boys would reject out of hand. For that matter moving wouldn't make Steph too happy, either.

Just shy of his forty-eighth birthday Rick had accepted the fact that he'd have to try his hand at starting over at a much lower position. He also knew that someone offering him such a job was a long shot. More than one potential employer told him they'd be foolish to hire him for any mid-level position because as soon as a better opportunity presented itself he'd be gone . . . and they were right. Adding to that obstacle was the age factor.

Looking around to ensure that he was alone, Rick thought to himself: Might as well try prayer. Rick had never actually embraced worship, although he wasn't put off by it either, at least so long as he didn't have to noticeably participate. Oh, he'd gone willingly enough to Sunday services with his wife and family, but that was more out of convention than need or desire. But, since he was here . . .

"Ah, Father . . . Sir? I'm not too good at this sort of thing. I'm not even sure I'm doing it right, but I, ah, need your help." His own echo made him feel self-conscience and vulnerable. Rick quickly looked around to make sure he was quite alone. Satisfied, he continued, "Ah, Lord? I know it's been a long time, probably because other things always got in the way. Well, I apologize. Sorry if I offended you. But you're a forgiving God, right?"

Rick allowed his eyes to gaze up and he waited. Except for the sounds of his thumping heart the Lord's only response was an ominous silence. Having gone this far he decided to press onward. "I know you can do anything, so if you don't mind doing me a favor, I ah, need a job. I've already done everything I can think of, but no one will hire me and I'm worried sick about my family. They depend on me and I'm failing them."

Rick had a sinking feeling that no miracles were in the offing. The spectacular silence enveloping this magnificent sanctuary made him feel all the more insignificant. Never had he felt so alone or forsaken.

With nothing to lose, Rick raised his voice a notch and added, "See, losing my job wasn't really my fault . . . I guess I should have pushed for a better employment contract last year when I had the chance, but the board wasn't too receptive. Wait till next year they said. Well, Stephanie's terrified that we'll lose our house and all she does is cry. She's completely dependent upon me for income, and feels, oh, I don't know, like she's been cheated. You know, she gave up her career to raise children, so now she can't possibly jump back in the job market and be compensated anywhere close to what she *could* have been making. My fault again. Anyway, I'm out of ideas, so if—"

"*May I help you?*" popped out of nowhere.

God himself never witnessed a more sudden bolt from a pew. Rick flew from his seat, panic-stricken. His racing heartbeat pounded loud enough to overpower all other sounds. With eyes bulging and stabbing chills racking his entire body, Rick blurted in a high-pitched shrieked, "Oh, Lord! Oh, God! Oh, Jesus!"

The ominous voice shot back, "May I help you? May I be of assistance?" That voice again. It was so . . . so God-like. What had he gotten himself into? A sound of soft shoes scuffing the stone floor was followed by Associate Minister Ryan Sladden emerging out from the dark shadows, apparently through a recessed doorway, carrying a stack of papers. "Did I frighten you?"

Sweat driblets trickled from Rick's underarms and his stomach was tighter than an Eagle Scout's double-half-hitch knot. Frightened? He had never been so scared in his life! Gripping the side of the pew to steady himself, Rick laboriously replied, "No. Ah, not at all." Realizing the Almighty hadn't suddenly engaged him in conversation, a curious sense of relief flooded all five senses, weakening his knees and giving Rick a slightly lightheaded feeling. Dropping back into the pew, Rick added, "Um, I'm fine. Just fine."

The minister suppressed a smile and said, "I see. Well, can't I help you anyway?"

Waiting while his head cleared, Rick mumbled, "I'm not sure . . . I mean, I'm just wasting time waiting to pick my son up . . ." Dumb, dumb, dumb, Rick chided himself. He tried again. "I didn't know . . . that is, I thought I was alone."

"In that case we need to establish whether you want to stay alone, or perhaps you'd care for some company, and a cup of coffee? *I'd* like that."

"Oh! Well, I don't know. Yes . . . yes, I would. That would be great," Rick found himself committing before he could stop himself.

"Excellent. My name is Ryan Sladden, and you are?"

"Blaine. Rick Blaine. One of my sons is at the mid-high meeting right now. I dropped him off and was just walking around."

"Try not to feel awkward, Mr. Blaine. As you've just learned, I too walk around from time to time."

"Right. Thank you," Rick said, smiling for the first time. "Ah, you *did* give me quite a start."

"For which I apologize," Sladden said as the two men shook hands. "Now, let's go get that coffee. Nothing like something warm on a brisk night. We can sit in my office and visit."

A few minutes later Rick was ushered into Reverend Sladden's private domain. The office was a mess, impossibly cluttered with all manner of papers and files. Surely there was a desk somewhere, or so Rick reasoned, but, if so, it wasn't visible. On a battered coffee table, perched precariously close to the edge, teetered an outdated IBM Personal Computer covered with dozens of those yellow square pieces of sticky paper each bearing a scribbled message. An overstuffed plaid sofa sandwiched between a pair of tall brass coach lanterns was over laden with books, and across from the sofa were a pair of matching wing chairs with a single ottoman. The motley grouping faced a small hearth, which Sladden tried to light by tossing small matchsticks onto a few twigs laying underneath a mountain of wadded-up magazine paper. A very cozy room all in all, if you could get past the clutter.

"Please. Make yourself comfortable, Mr. Blaine."

"I appreciate it. Call me Rick, and, ah, well, I was wondering if I might help get that fire started?"

"I'd be in your debt," said the Minister, who straightened up with a groan and tossed the tiny matchbox to Rick. "Never was any good with those things," he grumbled, "and me being a camp counselor and all. Oh, and by the way, I respond just as well to Ryan. Now, let me get that coffee, and I'll bring cream and sugar."

By the time the late-thirty-something minister returned bearing a tray with mismatched pieces totaling a full coffee service, Rick had coaxed and blown the hearth's contents into a small inferno. Sladden stopped at the door, genuinely stupefied. "How on earth did you do that?" Without waiting for an answer he moved forward to place the tray on the coffee table, while Rick hurriedly shoved aside notebooks, paperwork and well-used tomes bearing names like *Bible Prophesy*, *To Seek And To Save*, and *Spanish for Beginners*.

Rick was fascinated. In all his almost forty-eight years he never socialized with a minister, not once. Taking in everything around him, he noticed that Ryan Sladden didn't walk so much as he seemed to bounce. That particular trait seemed at odds with the distinctive coarse voice that seemingly mixed equal parts of the Bronx and Ireland. Ryan's blue eyes twinkled . . . literally . . . and that, together with a ready smile and keen wit which he'd displayed during the sanctuary incident, made Rick think of

Cary Grant playing the mischievous angel in the old film, *The Bishop's Wife.*

Sladden poured and talked at the same time. "You'll have to show me how to light a decent fire. Do you take cream and sugar? No? All right then." He finished mixing his own and said, "Well, Rick, what exactly can I do for you?"

Rick sat in one of the wing chairs debating how to proceed. Without a clear outline, but wanting to say something, he stammered, "Well, ah, I'm not sure what to say. Um, things aren't going so good, you see, and I recently found myself unemployed. Prospects don't look very promising and I'm not winning any points at home. I've never been in this situation before. I never even thought about not having a regular paying job." He shrugged and added, "Anyway, tonight it occurred to me to ask God for help."

Ryan took a sip of steaming coffee seemingly lost in reflection. Finally he said, "I'm truly sorry to hear about your misfortune. Unfortunately, I haven't heard of any job openings, although I know of something you'd do well to consider. It's not commonly thought about but there are practically no support groups for men in your situation. You're left to your own coping devices. But there is a group sponsored by The Abbey. I think it might help."

Trying to disguise his disappointment, Rick said, "Thanks, but I can't see telling my wife and friends that I'm attending a support group for failures. No, I don't think so."

Holding up his right arm, palm facing Rick, Ryan continued undaunted. "Hear me out, please. The group isn't an emotional soul searching cult where everyone ends up crying or hugging each other. It evaluates job hunting techniques and career choices. A more accurate description would be that it's designed for men of like circumstances to convene and exchange ideas on what has and hasn't worked for them, in addition to what's available. The group meets here every Thursday evening at seven . . . no reservation required."

"I'll think it over," Rick said without conviction. "Any other advice?"

"Why, yes," the minister said. "Prayer works." Rick raised his eyebrows, an involuntary gesture he regretted immediately.

The minister noted the skepticism and added, "Perhaps you're out of sync, praying on an AM channel while God's receiving on FM. That's usually the situation."

"Or could be there's no channel at all?"

"Rick, let's say you have a lamp but you don't plug it into an electrical outlet. Now, when you turn the lamp on and nothing happens, would you say it's the lamp's fault?"

"You're implying I have to take some responsibility, right? Okay, how do I get onto the FM band wave?"

Sladden smiled and replied, "That, Rick, requires more than the few minutes left before your child finishes mid-high . . ." He looked at his watch and nodded to himself before continuing, "but I'm more than willing to meet with you again. Just call me."

The minister stood and started riffling through a myriad of papers before turning his pockets inside out. At long last he looked helplessly at Rick and said, "Well, I can't seem to find my datebook. Could you call the church office? They'll schedule some time for us."

At least the man was trying to help, Rick thought, which was more than he could say for anyone else. "All right, Ryan. I'll think about it. Now, let me teach you the basics of starting a fire."

A short time later they walked back to the sanctuary. Just before parting Sladden touched Rick gently on the elbow and said, "Consider this: Other than a bit of your time, what would it cost you to come back and talk with me or to attend a meeting? You really have nothing to lose. Even if zero comes of it, are you any worse off?"

The man had a point.

Friday, April 12, 3:45 P.M.
University of Michigan, Ann Arbor

"The year was 1815 and the place was Waterloo, which, as I'm sure you know, is in Belgium. The sound of gunfire could still be heard, but Wellington's victory over Napoleon was assured, and totally unexpected. Now, it seems that a series of couriers had been organized and sped the news to England of Napoleon's defeat. But the message was not delivered to the Prime Minister . . . a Lord Liverpool, I believe . . . instead it was taken to a financier, a wily banker who had reasoned that if by some stroke of luck Napoleon was defeated, English government stocks would soar. It was the banker who had arranged for the couriers and, for his efforts he received battlefield reports a full twenty-four hours before anyone else in London. Naturally, he immediately bought a great deal of stock and added substantially to his personal and family wealth, as prices rose over the next four days.

"And who was the gentleman with such keen business acumen? None other than Nathan Rothschild of the Rothschild dynasty.

"So, would you say Mr. Rothschild was an ethical person? Oh, by the way, that's not a rhetorical question.

"For next week, I want you to read chapters eighteen through twenty-five and write a short paper, a thousand words maximum, on which moral philosophy is at work with Mr. Rothschild. Class dismissed."

With those final two words, books thumped closed and chairs scooted as students made a mad rush for the door. Attending classes on a Friday afternoon was the worst, except that is, for teaching a class on Friday afternoon. Dr. Charles Hilborn's instinct for self preservation kicked in and he shielded himself behind the wood podium. Within thirty seconds he was alone, and before the next two minutes had passed he too had beat a hasty retreat.

Charles loved Ann Arbor and the University of Michigan, with which the city was synonymous. Despite a degree of good-natured griping from academia, the city and U of M were identified with football. Driving past the now empty stadium the professor reminisced on the dozens of times he and Jenny had sat on hard benches surrounded by a hundred plus thousand of their closest friends, watching the maize and blue football team with its distinctive winged helmets play smash mouth with other Neanderthals. Campus life suited Charles to perfection.

The afternoon drive was quick to their three-bedroom Tudor style home, perched slightly off campus along a tree-lined street brandishing similar 1940 and 1950-era houses, the kind with detached garages and the old two-lane cement driveways. Entering the living room under a burden of papers

Charles was greeted with a blast of heat from an old stone fireplace.

Michigan weather is miserable from December through March. But you expect winter to be miserable. April, however, is a totally different matter. Supposedly, April is springtime . . . budding flowers, babbling brooks and clean fragrant air. Not some icy, snowy, mush that refuses to go away. The weather channel was reporting another cold front moving down from Canada into the Midwest . . . one last reminder as to why no one ever retired to Michigan.

"Charles? Is that you, dear?" The question never failed to perplex him. Was a burglar supposed to say "No," or perhaps, "Yes, darling?"

Jenny Hilborn strolled in from the kitchen swiping both hands against her terrycloth apron. She always had a smile for him, although sometimes it didn't last very long, like today. "Hi. How about calling that plumber you said you'd never hire again in a thousand years? Something about him being a merciless, bloodsucking whore. I think that's the way you phrased it."

"I take it our kitchen sink is leaking again?" Not even his high cheekbones, well-proportioned nose, or thick ash-blond hair graying slightly at the temples could charm her today.

"I've stopped it for now, but your stubborn streak is wearing thin. Will you get this thing fixed? Oh, and how was your day? Don't forget to go through the mail, and be ready to leave by six or we'll never get a good table. You also received a call from a Mr. Bennett of LoneStar International, in Dallas. He asked that you call him back tonight if possible. Isn't that where Brett Hollister works?"

Peppered with too many questions to respond to, Charles slipped his paperwork into the V-shaped magazine rack Jenny had purchased years earlier, trying to save the living room from becoming a trash heap. Jenny noted his grieved and befuddled look, took two quick steps forward and wrapped her arms around him. For a few precious moments they stood leaning against each other and rocking back and forth. Finally, he decided to answer her last question first. "I haven't talked to Brett since . . . can't remember."

"Fort Worth," Jennifer offered, loosening her grip enough to look at her husband.

"Oh, right," he exclaimed. "You're absolutely right. The last time was at that political gathering of eagles you dragged me to. Fort Worth, that's it. Seemed Brett was holding court there. We were at the same table."

"Any idea why they're calling?"

"Not a clue. You?"

She shook her head. Jennifer Hilborn loved mysteries, so she asked, "Doesn't it seem odd that all of a sudden, out of the clear blue, you get a summons from Dallas? Makes me think they want something from you."

"Like what? Surely they don't need history lessons."

"Ha ha, funny man," she said. "I'm just saying they've zeroed in on you for something other than your witty remarks."

"Honestly, Jenny!" Charles bristled. "Why must you view everything with a suspicious eye? Probably from those smoke-filled cloak rooms where you politicians and bureaucrats double deal each other, while grinning like Cheshire cats." He always suspected his wife's political involvement had addled her sense of reality. Admittedly, the problem with that theory was the remarkable number of times she turned out to be right.

Same day, 5:10 P.M.
Chairman's Office, LoneStar International

The executive floor . . . 'High-Ten,' it was called by employees who'd never seen it and probably never would . . . was a world unto itself, one which emitted constant waves of nervous energy and excitement. Senses were automatically heightened, particularly for the unwary as they approached the nerve center, which of course was the office of the chairman himself. There were no nicknames for Brett Hollister. The man was too omnipotent to consider using terminology of either endearment or derision, much less affection.

Hollister's eyes! That's what struck people first. They could reach out and grab a person's throat in a death grip, or lull them into a sea of complete serenity, and there were occasions when both reactions occurred within milliseconds of each other. The regal and unarguably domineering presence of the five-foot-nine-inch, barrel-chested former University of Texas defensive lineman intimidated most mortals; thus enhancing his ability to deal with the more rebellious employees, colleagues or adversaries. Hollister was a potent ally or he could be a first-class nemesis, and his attitude seemed to convey the message: You choose.

Brett possessed a gravelly but smooth-flowing Jack Palance oratory style, and it too could cut both ways. Like a sword equally sharp on both sides the chairman's words could without warning make the recipient live the old adage: "A coward dies a thousand times before his death, the valiant die but once."

Standing beside Brett's secretary's desk, Chester listened as she poked a button on her phone and said, "Mr. Hollister? Mr. Bennett is here to see you. He doesn't have an appointment."

The reply was instantaneous. "Thank you, Suzanne. Have him come in and then hold my calls."

Chester Bennett always looked forward to visiting Brett in his office. This was the sanctuary, the corporate inner sanctum, and relatively few individuals were afforded an opportunity to enter. Hell, lesser employees and business associates weren't even allowed on the floor. Chester continually marveled at his bosses paperless atmosphere . . . no stacked files, no memos scattered about, no folders and not a single spreadsheet.

Naturally, being the chairman's office it was also the largest. The occupant had access to a private bath with shower, a small kitchen with a fully stocked refrigerator, a private bar containing every sort of liquor imaginable, and a separate conference room complete with a marble-framed fireplace. The furnishings were lavish, almost garish, bespeaking old money and, most important, power.

Chester enjoyed giving Brett good news and didn't mind dropping by unannounced to deliver it. "I just got off the phone with Hilborn, and it's safe to say he's interested. The word he used to express his initial reaction was 'intrigued.' Obviously, he was surprised that we asked him to serve on the board . . . said that he didn't have a clue what he could offer us. All that aside, he's quite willing to proceed with the next step."

"Excellent. So, what's the next step?"

"Well, I told him we'd be happy to bring him down for a visit, or that I could run up north. He'd like to visit here so we made tentative plans for next Tuesday. That okay with you?"

"Let me think for a second . . . yup, that'll work. Have him meet a couple of the local directors too, set up a luncheon at the club. You can review prior board minutes with him if he wants and have Nash walk him through our financials."

"Sure, but we'll need him to sign a confidentiality agreement."

"Okay, prepare it right away and have it faxed or emailed to him. Just make sure we give Mr. Hilborn and his lawyer a chance to look it over before he gets here."

"Done. Anything else?"

Brett shook his head. "Just put together an itinerary and distribute it to those involved. We want to put on a good show."

"Okay. Now if you have a couple of minutes I'd be interested in your thoughts regarding Hilborn's question. Why *did* you pick him?"

"Well, it might be that I think we need someone with a different perspective. He seems a pretty well versed fellow, you know, and having a respected university professor won't hurt our image. I suspect that his wife's affiliation with the current administration could come in handy too, particularly guiding us to the right people in the Commerce Department. Christ, Chester, we need help to close those international deals—damned New York shyster lawyers have been jerking us around since last year."

"We're interested in Mrs. Hilborn's political contacts?" Chester asked.

"Eventually. But I've met the man at a couple social functions. He carries himself well in groups or one-on-one situations, I was impressed. We won't have to worry about whether he'll project himself properly. Is that enough to satisfy your curiosity?"

Mulling over the details for a moment, Chester replied, "Yes, absolutely. Oh, and apart from everything you've said Hilborn has been out of the corporate loop for so long he'll probably go along with whatever you want. Right?"

Brett grinned at the insightful general counsel. "Watch it, Chester. All that lawyer bullshit is turning you into a cynic."

"Uh-huh, you're probably right. I'll go set things up. Talk to you later." Chester left Brett's office, once again amazed with the man's ability to see around corners.

CHAPTER 6

Sunday, April 14, 2:00 P.M.
A Playground in Manhattan

The shrill whistle kept blowing and blowing. With only half a second to spare a sprinting Dave Hanson caught the little girl falling from the teeter-totter before she hit the hard-packed dirt ground. "Jamal! Don't you ever . . . *ever* . . . pull that stunt again! That goes for the rest of you, too. No one gets off one of these things while your playmate is still in the air, you hear?"

A little distance away Molly and Ashley traded knowing smiles. "Kids are unruly today," Molly concluded, stooping to place a Band-Aid onto a scraped knee. The child leaned over and kissed her on the cheek; she mussed his wavy red hair and sent him back into the fray. "It must be the fresh air," she added. The unseasonably warm weather had indeed refreshed the winter weary little troopers.

Laying on the ground Ashley took a deep breath and leaned back, squinting at the sun as she used elbows to support herself on the soft spring grass in the park. "This is really pleasant. Way better than the gym. Sounds don't carry nearly as much outside."

Molly was busy with lunch . . . it was her turn this week. Ashley had previously snatched several carrot sticks off a vegetable plate and now began nibbling. A few pieces broke loose and fell onto her faded Penn State sweatshirt, which she brushed off before taking a larger bite and repeating the process with another stick. "Where's Ben?" she asked between munches.

Molly paused and put down the knife she was using to spread mayonnaise on slices of bread. "Oh, he's ah, not going to, ah, make it today. Aw, Ashley, I don't know what to say. The truth is, Ben's been laid off."

"*Laid off?* I thought he was in line for a promotion." Ashley raised herself to a sitting position.

"Yeah, so did we," a somber Molly replied. "We were really counting on it, but you know how it is. The plant downsized . . . no one even saw it coming. Ben was older than most so he got cut first. Anyway, he's working two part-time jobs now, and if Tracy wasn't here I'd probably be working too. As it is she'll be released in about three weeks. I hate to leave you and Dave in a spot but I don't think I'll be back after that. I can't . . . I'll have to get a job and who knows who'll take care of Tracy?"

Ashley was totally unprepared and could only offer a: "I'm so sorry."

"Yeah, the hospital is being helpful. They're coming up with a new payment plan." Ashley couldn't tell whether Molly's tone was one of discouragement or sarcasm . . . maybe it was both. She listened while the other woman continued, "I guess I can't blame them, they need money too. But we can't pay it. Doesn't seem fair, does it? Ben's never home anymore and working two jobs is killing him." She looked down and shook her head. "I don't know what we'll do, Ashley. Just manage, I guess."

Moving next to her, Ashley picked up another carrot stick and looked at it for a long while. Finally she said, "Sure you will."

"Ben says we can sell our house, use the money to pay some of the hospital bills." Molly sat down at the picnic table as tears formed.

Ashley sat down beside her giving Molly an awkward hug. "Don't think about the bad," she advised. "You've got a great husband and a little girl who adores you. That's more than . . . a lot of people have. Know anyone who can give you a loan? You know, just to tide you over?"

Molly wiped away a tear. "Maybe my folks but I hate to ask them. They're retired and don't have much either."

In a confidential tone Ashley remarked, "Well, I've heard how sometimes hospitals end up with extra money that they apply against certain hospital bills."

"A medical tooth fairy?"

"Sort of, I guess. I'm just saying that things can happen, Molly. Don't get down . . . don't give 'em the satisfaction."

Molly flashed a sad smile but didn't reply.

Tuesday, April 16, 10:10 A.M.
LoneStar Offices, Dallas

The black limousine deposited Dr. Charles Hilborn at LoneStar's massive entrance. Walking into the lobby Charles decided there must have been some mistake. This can't be the lobby of a business, he thought. It looked like the Ritz, the Grand Hyatt and the Anatole all rolled into one. He stopped, put down his briefcase and stared in wide-eyed bewilderment.

The ceiling vaulted three stories above a Carrara marble floor; a veritable fortune of multi-paneled Chinese silk screens hung at intervals along each wall; handcrafted terra cotta urns overflowed with lavish greenery offsetting a brilliantly colorful display of orchids; a long and complicated geometric fountain spewed a delicate water pattern right in the middle of a foyer that was at least half the size of a football field; chocolate leather sofas were scattered about with beveled-glass coffee tables, and here and there Charles noticed freestanding frames each holding an original oil painting. "Incroyable," he whispered, having deemed that the English word "incredible" didn't make a sufficient statement.

He finally got moving toward a massive circular reception desk where his name apparently carried weight, considering the speed with which he was escorted to a bank of eight plush teak-and-mirror elevators. Ten floors later, in a more intimate but equally magnificent lobby, Chester Bennett was waiting for him. Charles offered his hand while wondering how much all these trappings cost?

The rest of the day was a whirlwind tour of facilities including a high-tech, multi-media center/auditorium where two hundred reclining upholstered seats cradled customers who were barraged with sounds, lights, information, communications, appeals and suggestions. There was also a graphic arts department that created, planned and actually printed an amazing variety of forms and promotional materials headed for customers and potential clients. Other unique areas included a fully accredited preschool and a computer systems complex that made him think of NASA.

Wedged between the tours and a handful of general meetings with key management was the Dallas Country Club luncheon where Brett, Chester and two other board members provided the discourse. Questions and answers bounced back and forth and the smiles were infectious. Also, optimism about LoneStar's' bright future was epidemic . . . not a discouraging word or note of caution was uttered.

Generally speaking, everyone involved behaved with exceeding cordiality and remarkable shallowness. No discussions of any consequence occurred and probing questions were quickly but politely dismissed, or else answered with practiced double-talk. A call to Jenny during an early afternoon break elicited a warning about getting involved with people he knew nothing about. Her advice had definite merit.

After allowing himself to reflect upon LoneStar International he finally deduced that the place couldn't be normal. *They've erected a palace, complete with lords and ladies-in-waiting. There's no telling what's hidden from public view. So, if they wanted him they were going to have to indulge him a bit.*

Same day, 8:30 P.M.
Chairman's Office, LoneStar International

It was far too late to be working. To top it off, Brett's daughter and grandchildren had made a special trip to visit grandma and grandpa . . . except grandpa was stuck at the office, refusing to accept LoneStar's latest quarterly projections. Brett was already in a foul mood when Chester broke the news to him. Throwing his pen down the chairman said, "He said *what?* What the hell do you mean he wants to hire a consultant? Are you fucking crazy? I'm not about to let some stranger poke around here." Brett's face had turned dangerously red.

For his part, Chester would just as soon have avoided this late-night confrontation with Brett, but it couldn't be helped. "Look, I know how you feel, Brett. But Hilborn said his grasp of the inner workings of big corporations is a little lacking and he wants someone else to interview key employees, then give him a thorough briefing. He obviously thinks it's in his best interest and unless we want to call another board meeting to select another candidate, we'll just have to make the situation as painless as possible."

"Dammit, Chester. Dammit to hell and back." Brett was in a hole and he knew it. Time would not allow dawdling at this point and, anyway, he couldn't imagine confessing that he and the search committee had been in error . . . not after all those glowing endorsements. Add to that, wouldn't the board members be more than a little suspicious of his concern regarding an outside audit? No, his only option was to give in to Hilborn's demands. "Okay," he said with jaw clenched. "What exactly does he want?"

"He wants a business consultant to come down here for a couple of days. In addition to interviewing about ten senior managers, he's also asked us to package and ship our 10-K's and 10-Q's to said consultant, plus the last few annual reports and recent press releases. All of which is public information, I might add, so at least there's no confidentiality issue. The consultant will report back to Hilborn within the week and then we'll have his answer. Obviously, the man's not as naive as we thought."

That's not how Brett characterized the man. "He's an ungrateful little prick, that's what he is. Just who does he think he is? This is my company, *my company*! Ah shit, just let me think . . ."

LoneStar's general counsel, hardly a timid man himself, nonetheless felt vulnerable when forced to dispense bad news to Brett. The chairman's reputation as a no-nonsense manager who started as a humble mailroom clerk was true, except Chester had trouble believing the "humble" part. There was always an undercurrent of anger in Brett, a hotheaded tension easily unleashed. Many was the time Brett's patience suddenly snapped resulting in explosive shouting matches . . . witness the ex-director who dared to openly question Brett's obsession with technology.

True, Brett took most of his managers for granted treating them to impromptu tongue lashings, seemingly as the mood struck. Which certainly explained why the senior executives avoided him at all costs. How the guy stayed married for thirty-seven years was a testament to Brett's family values. He simply doted on his wife and grandchildren, for whom he'd do anything. In fact, that's how he dealt with friends and total strangers . . . gracious and charming almost to a fault.

Half expecting Brett to pound the desk and scream "traitor," Chester was relieved when the rising fury passed without incident. "Okay," Brett said. "Wait till sometime next week and then tell the bastard that we'll be more than pleased to honor his request. Tell him that we think it's a great idea and wish we'd thought of it ourselves. Insist on paying all costs associated with the consultant, no arguments. Give every bit of public information he wants. *"Then let's make damn sure we're ready for whoever that son of a bitch is gonna send."*

The chairman took a deep breath and folded his manicured hands teepee-style on his desk. After a few moments in a low and threatening tone, he said, "Chester, I promise you one thing. After Hilborn comes on board I'll personally cut his balls off if he ever pulls something like this again." There was no argument.

Thursday, April 18, 3:55 P.M.
Chairman's Office, LoneStar International

"Mr. Hollister? Mr. Griswold is here for your four o'clock appointment."

"Tell him to wait! We're not finished." Brett disliked meeting with the Controller, Emmet Griswold. The guy never seemed to bring anything but bad news. Just like a squeaky wheel that couldn't be oiled . . . a constant irritation.

"All right, Spence. You're saying that our technology efforts have fallen short and we need to increase our commitment? What about the sales revenue you were supposed to be bringing in?" Brett prized discussing the latest technology initiatives occurring at LoneStar, but today he needed cash.

"Brett, without a state-of-the-art system, which means all the bugs have been worked out and our own business units are totally satisfied, selling the software to major companies would only damage our reputation and prejudice the market against us. When we're really ready to act, we will." Sidney Spence was the chief information officer, a short, ill-tempered, ex-IBM engineer charged with taking LoneStar's internally developed financial software and selling it to the elite of the financial community. Spence had joined LoneStar after IBM's massive reorganization a few years back, hired on the recommendation of Arthur King who knew the engineer because they belonged to the same golf club and both shot in the high 90's.

The systems area was bleeding LoneStar's limited cash resources dry and Brett knew something had to be done. "It's been over eighteen months, Spence. We can't continue tossing tons of money into a project that ain't gonna fly."

"I agree, and if that were the case I'd be the first to suggest we rethink the strategy. But Brett, I know we're just a couple more months away from scoring a touchdown." Spence was a Dallas Cowboys fanatic. To him, life was one long football game. "It's an interface problem, that's all. Let's not punt now, not when we're so close to the goal line. Look at these projected sales figures . . . we'll be pulling in fifteen million by next year. Every Fortune one-hundred firm will be crawling to us, begging us to install our system."

Brett nodded, caught up in the sales hype. He loved technology . . . not that he could program his own name. Hell, just think of the potential he continually reminded the board. "Okay. So what else do you need besides two more months?"

"Make it a handful of months and toss in a couple more systems engineers and five to ten more programmers. And there's a conference in San Diego that we should attend in force."

Brett just couldn't say 'no.' "Alright, but I'll need something to show the board pretty damn soon. They've been behind me up till now, you know. I've always said technology's the future and we can't be left behind."

"I know. You'll get proof, Brett." Spence stood and added, "You know, at IBM everything was always done by committees and it took forever to get a decision. That's why I appreciate working here."

"Good to have you with us, Spence," the chairman said, "and I'm counting on you. Oh, on your way out, tell Emmet to come in. Now go bring me some solid results."

Brett steadied himself and wondered what new crisis Emmet had for him. Damn, he wished his controller would just go away and leave him alone. Seconds later the nemesis poked his skinny head in the doorway. "Oh, hi, Emmet. Come in, sit down. What can I do for you?"

The tall and too thin, military crew cut controller ignored the visitor's chair and perched precariously on the edge of an ottoman. Hardly a confident individual under the best of circumstances, Emmet was noticeably nervous. When the man got nervous he would start talking in a maddeningly slow cadence, then apparently hear himself and speed up, at which point he tended to speak so fast his words ran together into one unintelligible outburst. To make sense of it Brett always had to lean forward and really concentrate, which made Emmet all the more nervous. One day Brett figured out the way to tell when a sentence ended was by watching Emmet's tie . . . when Emmet finished a thought, he'd give the knot a nervous twist.

"I, ah . . . know you're . . . um, busy and don't have much time. But, I, ah, think you should know that, ah . . . wegottrouble." Brett hadn't missed anything consequential, but the next outburst sounded like: "AhthebanksworriedaboutCASHgik--Ó"

Brett held out his hand, palm forward and asked, "Did you say that we're in trouble with cash again?"

Emmet swallowed hard and nodded. Then he started again: "Ah, a fewofthbanks dftmp captialproblemsoxkik--------."

The tie twisted, so Brett interrupted. "The banks are questioning our working capital and how we plan to make the next interest payment?"

Emmet nodded in reply.

"Hell. I don't give a shit what those bankers think or don't think. Screw'em. If they have a problem let their president call me and we'll fix it real fast. One quick phone call and I'll replace them with another damn bank. Got that?"

Another short nod and Emmet said, "Well, we're ah, still spending anawfullotin Spence'sareaioenmkr."

"For heaven's sake, Emmet! I know about Spence's budget and the system conversion problems . . . who do you think just walked out of here? Spence, that's who! For your information he's only a couple of months from turning his division into a damned cash cow."

The next fifteen minutes went by in a deluge of nerve-wracking gobbledygook. Brett picked up enough to know Emmet was worried about increasing expenses and the fact that a group of bondholders had been calling him with uncomfortable frequency. Also, some New York investment firm named Taylor-Bishop was digging around, asking questions.

In a voice brimming with hostility Brett instructed his controller to tell the bond holders they were welcome to ask anything they wanted . . . at the annual meeting. "Until then," he said menacingly, "the policy is that I alone talk to outsiders. Is that clear?"

Emmet nearly fell off the ottoman but managed a hurried nod.

"Good. As for cash flow, we've been offered a deal to sell some of our real estate to the same guys who bought from us last year. The board approved it and it'll happen within the month. That should take care of our cash needs."

The controller started a sentence that bordered on insubordination: "Buuuttt, we're not makeingreturnsweomvokw . . ."

That was the last straw. It was more than Brett could take. "You let me and Gary Nash worry about our damned financial condition! All I want from you is a quarterly report showing we're making more money than the prior quarter!"

Emmet's papers slid to the floor and as he bent over to retrieve them he almost fainted. The chairman stopped, rubbed thumb and forefinger along furrowed brows, and said, "Emmet, if you have nothing else to talk to me about."

The controller hastily shoved the mass of papers together and skulked from the office. Brett told himself to calm down but a few moments later he caught himself twisting his own tie.

CHAPTER 7

Sunday, April 21, Noon
A Playground in Manhattan

As instructed by the hospital administrator, Ben and Molly McHenry handed the pizza delivery man a sealed envelope while Dave Hanson carted the eight greasy cardboard containers over to an empty picnic table, dropped them, and ran for his life while thirty-three kids tore apart the boxes and grabbed handfuls of cheese and pepperoni. They were laughing and squealing and making a mess. They were having fun.

Dave scurried back licking his fingers. "Just like Ashley to skip out on her week to do lunch. But then I sure don't miss the peanut butter sandwiches. Oh, speaking of the cavalry coming to our rescue, I overheard some nurses talking on our floor. They said another big contribution came into the children's wing. Nice to know some people care."

The McHenry's exchanged embarrassed looks. Molly hesitated then asked, "Dave, you have any idea what Ashley does? What kind of job she has? Are her parents rich or anything?"

"Rich? I don't think so, but Ashley keeps pretty much to herself. I can't be sure. Why?"

Lowering her voice a notch, Molly replied, "Probably nothing. A while back we were talking . . . Ashley and me, I mean . . . and, well, something she said might happen came true. Now we're more curious about her than ever."

Dave shrugged. "I thought she was a secretary or something. If she's rich wouldn't she have lunch catered when it's her turn? Why would she keep putting us through the peanut-butter-and-jelly routine? Yuck."

Ben and Molly had to agree with the logic. "Another dead end," Ben murmured and then said, "Where is she, anyway?"

Molly looked at her watch. "Well, the hospital administrator said she might not come today. I'll just bet she had a big date last night and slept in late."

Although Ben and Dave were too gentlemanly to smirk their expressions clearly stated: "I don't think so." Molly shook her head and said, "You boys are shallow."

Dave gave Ben a quizzical look and asked, "What's she mean by that?"

"I dunno. Probably that Ashley's got a great personality." The men chuckled and went to scrape pizza off the picnic table and clean the children's faces.

Monday, April 22, 9:05 A.M.
Smith-Palmer & Co., Detroit

"Welcome aboard, Rick." Three words finally freed Rick Blaine from the yoke of unemployment.

Who would have thought that he'd end up working for a regional brokerage firm as a stock analyst, specializing in 'banks and financial institutions' no less? It was fortunate the opening hadn't been for a specialist in a field foreign to him, like aerospace, automotive, biotech, tobacco or any number of other industries which Smith-Palmer & Co. followed closely.

The starting pay wasn't enough for his family to break even, but he and Stephanie had set aside sufficient funds to make up the difference . . . for a while. Besides, they wouldn't have to move. Who could stare a gift horse like this in the mouth?

It all started shortly after Rick's' first meeting with the support group recommended by Reverend Ryan Sladden. He had scheduled an appointment to see the minister to discuss faith. It was a subject he was out of touch with, and he also felt apprehensive about the possibility of being embarrassed. But as Ryan had pointed out he had little to lose.

The session turned out to be more than merely enlightening. Ryan didn't condescend, nor talk in sanctimonious tones . . . quite the contrary. Rick was amazed at the minister's depth, as well as his understanding and nonjudgmental acceptance of human nature. Rick left Ryan's cluttered office feeling better about himself.

His new attitude showed and the renewed optimism gently led him into more productive directions. By coincidence, that same week a friend of a friend called to tell Rick of a recently vacated position at Smith-Palmer. He went for the initial interview with a confidence he hadn't felt for weeks, and when he was ushered into the office of the company recruiter he almost passed out. Sitting across from him was an old college classmate. They shook hands, laughed and caught up on old times . . . Rick breezed through the requisite first interview.

Next, he was introduced to his potential boss, the firm's director of research. Incredibly, years ago the man had transferred all his personal banking accounts to Rick's prior employer, First State Bank of Michigan, where he couldn't have been happier with the service. He told Rick that the tellers still spoke highly of him, crediting Rick's administration with the bank's success. The research director held out his hand and said, "Welcome aboard, Rick."

The Smith-Palmer job seemed tailor-made for Rick. As the bank and financial stock analyst he was to prepare in-depth research reports on numerous assigned companies, and render judgments on same. The sales staff would circulate his reports to their clients as part of the full-service concept at Smith-Palmer. Evidently, the reports were taken very seriously. Smith-Palmer's stock analysts were the account executives eyes and ears to the inner workings of each firm reviewed, and a vast number of investors bought and sold stock solely upon those recommendations. The more accurate Rick's reports proved to be, the more the clients would follow his advice and the more sales would increase. By no accident whatsoever, as sales increased, Rick's compensation would too.

Luckily, he was an excellent numbers guy and knew how to dissect financial reports and uncover hidden weaknesses or strengths. Best of all, he was expected to interview senior management at the firms he was researching. Rick was superb at one-on-one meetings.

Someday, he knew he'd have to do a report on his ex-company, but he was less inclined to use his new office to trash them as he would have been a few short weeks ago.

Friday, April 26, 11:00 A.M.
Taylor-Bishop Offices, Manhattan

The Fallen Angel had narrowed her list of potential targets to seven. Before her were the individual company summaries spread across her desk. She drew her hand lightly across the material touching each file almost reverentially. The myths and tall tales these seven had perpetuated were truly amazing to Ashley. Yet recent press releases and research reports described them all as having bright futures . . . maybe yes, maybe no.

The phone rang, jarring her concentration and she picked it up without enthusiasm. Her secretary's voice was low and trembling with excitement. "Antonio Veron is on line one," she said. "Ashley, you *know* he's called every day this week. Aren't you going?" Joyce's voice was rising to a level suggesting hysteria.

Impatient to return to the summaries Ashley tapped the end of her pen against the phone, wondering if Antonio could be put off again. She really didn't want to be bothered, not now. "Uh, Joyce, this just isn't a good time. Just get a number where I can reach him."

From the other end of the phone she heard a groan. "Please! I've lost track of how many times you've told me to say that. Look, Ashley . . . I don't get you. How *can* you turn down an invitation to his premiere?" When there was no answer the secretary screwed up her courage and added, "I'd kill to go with him . . . the man is *gorgeous*."

"Fine, then you go. I've got work to do."

"*Ashley!*"

She sighed. Unlike Joyce, men were not life's be-all and end-all. Obviously, Ashley appreciated and understood men for what they were . . . objects for her amusement or commercial exploitation. "All right, Joyce. But I can't talk to him now, okay? Tell him I'm in conference, that I'd love to attend his premiere and then find out—"

"*Oh, thank you, thank you, thank you!*" Joyce shouted.

Uncomfortable at the outburst Ashley held the receiver away from her ear, and stared at it before placing it firmly against her chest muffling all sound. Counting slowly to ten she leaned over to smell the actor's most recently delivered roses . . . their bouquet was marvelous. Presuming her effervescent secretary had finally come down off the ceiling, she raised the phone only to hear Joyce adding, "You'll be the best looking couple there, Ashley, you always look so stunning. *God, this is great!* Wait'll I tell my friends. They'll die!"

"Joyce. *Joyce!* Can you get a grip on yourself?"

"Huh? Oh sure. Sorry, but I'm just so excited. A film premiere! Awesome! Red carpets, stars, paparazzi, Champaign & caviar. Are you going to wear a slinky dress?"

Lowering her voice to force attention Ashley replied, "Actually, Joyce dear, I probably won't be going after all. That's because your heartthrob will hang up if you keep him on hold much longer. Now, would you kindly get the particulars and a number where he can be reached this weekend?" Ashley broke the connection and immediately reflected on Antonio and her personal life.

Had Antonio met her on a regular weekend, she mused, rather than at a must-attend celebrity affair, there would have been no connection to begin with. Few besides Ben and Molly or the kids saw Ashley on weekends, and the transformation from

Sunday night to Monday morning would have astonished each and every one of them.

The weekends were supposed to be exclusively her own, providing her a chance for complete solitude and rejuvenation. She relished spending time in her apartment where she lived rather than merely slept, a critical distinction bespeaking the effect of early horrors she still struggled against remembering.

Her private domain, which she often thought about during the week, was a prewar co-op with high ceilings and eccentric moldings. It was also eclectic and probably didn't lend itself to any particular design label. Nonetheless . . . with one exception . . . the overall feel was contemporary, uncluttered but definitely not sterile, indisputably affluent without a trace of nouveau riche.

Ashley's entry foyer was the exception. It was as interesting as any clue to her fiercely self-protective nature. An 8x8 cubicle partitioned to block any possible view to the rest of the apartment, the stone cold space made the intended keep-your-distance statement and, indeed, few were allowed to cross the threshold and invade Ashley's privacy.

Unadorned textured walls were painted a deep and very dark chocolate, by no coincidence the exact color of Ashley's hair. The floor was a white terrazzo so highly-lacquered that the effect was a startling reflection, light drawing upon darkness and vice versa. A black Oriental visitors' chair stood beside a glass on metal end table, which supported a tall heavy glass vase filled with clear-glass flowers. Three identical brushed silver frames housing black and white photographs of bleak winter scenes hung on the walls. The room was without warmth . . . without life.

Beyond the nearly disguised door leading to Ashley's inner sanctum the mood changed drastically. Twenty-one hundred square feet containing kitchen, dining and living areas, a master bedroom and a den office were painted beige and tan throughout. Accents were rust and an abundance of white, with occasional sunshine yellow splashed here and there. The furniture was classically simple in design, sofas and chairs were comfortably upholstered, and a mélange of accessories gave insight into personal tastes.

In the living room an oversized sofa with luxuriously tufted seats was further padded by a collection of huge pillows covered in Thai fabric. Behind and a short distance to the left of a massive Japanese silk screen stood an unusual pyramid, taller than Ashley and composed of what appeared to be four blocks of colored granite, one stacked atop the other in order of size. Over in the corner, a leggy green plant overflowed its tall brass vase. Scattered about were acrylic accent tables containing accessories ranging from a large Ming ginger jar to well read books, woven basket trays and small pieces of crystal including a geometric Steuben clock.

Like the stark contrast between foyer and living area, between past and present, Ashley's work week appearance was totally unlike that of the weekend. On work days Ashley was as meticulous with hairdressing, make up and apparel as she was with her dissections of investment strategies. She never considered how the carriage-to-pumpkin routine would strike people like Ben and Molly, who saw her as a tall slender young woman with large eyes and a broad mouth unenhanced by makeup. Sort of a grown-up urchin covered in shapeless sweats and T-shirts, with thick hair tumbling to her shoulders.

During the week though, Ashley's features were blazes of sophisticated color set against a flawless light-olive complexion. Her wardrobe was a mixture of every imaginable style, and selection was made mostly by mood: Severe black Chanel's or soft hazel cashmere sets, each accessorized to draw attention to deep-set saucer eyes framed by elongated oval brows and lashes a shade deeper than the shiny dark mane she normally swept back and slightly up.

Ashley also spent as much time on wardrobe fittings as on actual choice, each outfit tailored without apology for the accentuation of the perfectly shaped breasts while exaggerating her slim waistline. Her long slender legs indisputably complimented shorter skirts, although she was capable of wearing any length. Understandably, second-glances from casual observers were common but they really didn't register any more than a passing fly would attract the attention of a web-spinning spider.

Well, for Antonio she would make exceptions to both her philosophy of men and self-absorbed weekends. His Manhattan premiere mandated it. The Spanish-born actor was on course to becoming a major star. He was also enchanted, possibly even obsessed, with Ashley Taylor-Bishop. He called incessantly and her office was forever filled with a dozen fragrant red roses.

But now it was time for reality, not sentimental reflections. For the next two hours she studied the seven summaries and made notes before breaking for a brief walk outside to clear her head. Surprisingly, her thoughts drifted back to Antonio. He was an attractive man, no doubt about it. At the charity event where they had met he had been surrounded by young starlets and bleached blond wanna-be's. Then the minute Antonio laid eyes on Ashley he stepped from the adoring throng and made his way to her side. The man was smooth, original. He offered an introduction complete with the fact that Ashley reminded him of paintings, which once graced the pages of *Playboy* magazine . . . portraits of women by the Peruvian artist Varga.

Ashley hadn't known whether to feel offended or complimented, but she smiled at the memory. Yet, notwithstanding how she felt about him nothing would come of the relationship. It was something she'd learn over and over. Harsh lessons had drained her of any passion . . . no more tears. If the truth be known Ashley couldn't remember the last time she had cried, not that it mattered. Anyway, without passion it was near impossible to sustain a relationship beyond a few dates.

Reentering her office she turned back to the summaries lying on her desk. Her staff members had spent countless months poring over financial statements, research analyst reports, industry articles, press releases, and personal interviews, anything they could get their hands on. Reams of graphs and spreadsheets were attached to thick dossiers describing each company's key management team. A good start and she was proud of her people . . . an excellent crew that Ashley had put together from scratch.

Until today she had harbored plenty of secret doubts concerning her mission to find a mega "Virtual Reality Corporation." Just getting this far was taking longer than she'd ever expected, and this was only phase one. The project seemed so endless that months ago her staff had suggested quitting, yet she wouldn't let go. A small voice kept egging her on and she'd discovered long ago to trust that voice. It was still coaxing her forward.

Thursday, May 2, 6:30 P.M.
Hilborn Residence, Ann Arbor

For the past two hours Charles had been tromping back and forth from one room of the house to another, unable to sit still or concentrate. Peering out the dining room window for the umpteenth time, he held his breath and watched as a car slowed and stopped. *"Jenny. I think he's here."* Jenny came rushing up beside him and pushed to get a better view. Nudging his wife back, Charles said, "You're crowding me."

Shoving him again an excited Jenny confirmed, "It is him! Go answer the door."

Doing as his wife commanded Charles quickly opened the door and welcomed the tall man into his home. "Jenny, this is Mr. Adam Sanchez, the business consultant I hired to enlighten us about Brett Hollister and the boys down at LoneStar." They'd both been anxiously awaiting this meeting for over a week, like a couple of high school seniors sweating out the results of midterm exams. Having Mr. Sanchez make the presentation at their home had been Charles' idea, it seemed less threatening somehow.

The dark haired, swarthy man shook her hand firmly, "I'm very pleased to meet you and yes, Mrs. Hilborn, I'm a full blooded Mexican."

"I'm so sorry, was I staring?"

"A little. I'm aware of how unusual it is for someone of my ethnic background to be a business consultant. So I'm not offended in any way. I was born in the United States; my parents live in a small border town. They thought that being the first American in the family warranted an American name so they picked Adam, taken from another 'first born.'"

"Actually, that's why I hired Mr. Sanchez," Charles explained. "The dean of our business school said that Adam was twice as smart and charged half as much as anyone else. That sounded pretty good to me."

A good-natured chuckle emanating from Adam put them all at ease. "Mr. Hilborn, I have to be twice as good as my competition. A fact I've learned to live with. I do appreciate the chance to consult for you. Well, shall we begin? What I'd like to do is to go over my general conclusions first then we can go into specifics as you desire. Anything of consequence that I'll be telling you tonight is also in this report. Since you hired me the report only goes to you. Is this acceptable?"

Husband and wife looked at each other for an instant and then Jenny said, "Before you tell us your conclusions, could you tell us something about your protocol with the LoneStar executives?"

"Yes, excellent, Mrs. Hilborn. I met with ten executives over a two-day period. Many of the interviews were conducted with Chester Bennett, their general counsel, in attendance. Although, I must admit toward the end he got a little bored and excused himself to do something else. Almost all interviews took place in the executive's own office. I requested that by the way since it's less intimidating. Perhaps that's also why we are meeting at your house tonight?"

"Touché."

Chuckling again, Adam remarked, "Good. Then we can proceed." Drawing out a sheet of paper with bullet points, he glanced at it momentarily and then began, "First of all, Brett Hollister runs that place with a single mindedness. He calls the shots, he sets the agenda, and it's his company. Second, financial discipline is absent. Cash is being spent on country clubs, car allowances, sporting events, lavish office decorations, generous pensions, several condominiums for executive use only, charities, corporate chauffeurs . . . the list is almost endless. Third, there is open hostility between the business units and the systems group. Evidently, this high-tech area is supposed to develop and maintain a state-of-the art software system interlinking each unit. Word is that it's losing money, has no competent management, no marketing plan and continually screws-up the most basic job request. Quite a few of the business units have actually purchased other software systems they know they can rely on . . . so there is no interface between groups. The existence of this bootlegging has been held back from Mr. Hollister."

Charles looked at Jenny, waiting for the familiar refrain of: "I told you so." Adam continued, "Fourth, the senior managers as a group are not coordinated and do not communicate well with each other. There are no formal management meetings. Hollister simply meets with whom he wants whenever he wants, and whoever else has a problem just goes it alone. Hollister is certainly open to receiving anyone who wants to see him, but most managers try to avoid him. I understand he has quite a temper. Fifth, the investment community is viewed as the enemy. No one but Hollister can talk to any reporter or research analyst, and he won't. The only communications out of the company are those required by law, like quarterly financial statements and an annual shareholders meeting. Sixth, the senior managers themselves are for the most part undisciplined, lifeless and self-indulgent. Preserving the status quo is their chief concern."

Clearing her throat, Jenny said, "Don't sugarcoat your findings for us, Mr. Sanchez. And if those were the good points, I don't want to hear the bad ones."

"Mr. Sanchez," Charles puzzled, "is any of what you've said just cause for me to refuse a directorship?"

"In and of themselves? No. However, due to the limited scope of the assignment I was unable to determine if there were any material underlying issues for you to be concerned about. For instance, large impending losses or evidence of fraud or legal issues, things of that nature. Also, they do have ample liability insurance protection for officers and directors, so you should not have to worry personally. Earnings last year were above expectations, although most of that came from nonrecurring items. I made some inquiries and LoneStar's reputation on the street is quite good and Brett Hollister has been a well-respected business leader for years."

"Anything else we should know?" Jenny was still skeptical.

"Only that LoneStar is an enigma. I, like the rest of the world have no idea what's going on inside that fortress. The managers either do not know or will not say. Hollister is also one smooth talking Texan. To tell you the truth, after interviewing the man I really wanted to call my stock broker and buy a few thousand shares of LoneStar. But twenty minutes later I could not remember one concrete thing he said."

Charles wrinkled his forehead, "Well, I've always enjoyed a challenge." Studying his hands he considered his next statement, and finally added, "Besides, if I could help correct some of these problems, give guidance to the company, isn't that what a director is supposed to do?" Charles looked at Jenny and Adam, who had to admit he was right. "Well, thank you for your insights, Mr. Sanchez. You've been most thorough . . . most impressive. Perhaps I'll have need of your services again."

As Adam left the house Jenny tugged on her husband's sleeve and prophesied, "You're going to take it." She knew him too well.

PART 4
PREPARATIONS

CHAPTER 8

Monday, May 13, 10:15 A.M.
LoneStar Offices, Dallas

The pace at work was maddening, nerves were frayed and details seemed unending. LoneStar's Controller, Emmet Griswald, along with a handful of others were spending inordinate amounts of time preparing for the annual meeting and his phone never ceased ringing, as it was doing now. Can't somebody else pick-up my phone? he pouted to himself. After ringing incessantly for a full two minutes, he answered his own question: Apparently not! Grabbing the receiver Emmet curtly answered, "Yes?"

"Oh, hello. Mr. Griswald? My name is Rick Blaine, I'm a stock research analyst with Smith-Palmer. I'm sorry to be bothering you this morning but I can't seem to get Mr. Hollister to return my calls. Your name was in last year's annual report as the company's controller, that's why I'm calling you."

"What can I do for you?" Actually, Emmet knew exactly what this guy wanted, the same as all the other guys who couldn't get through to Brett wanted. Mr. Blaine wanted to know what was going on at LoneStar. Emmet also knew that any other firm would fall all over itself trying to help this analyst, wanting to ensure their company received as much positive spin as possible in a research report. A single 'buy' recommendation could move a stock up ten, twenty percent. LoneStar on the other hand was staffed by a bunch of monks who'd taken forced vows of silence.

"Mr. Griswald, I'd like to update the last research report we did on LoneStar, which was three years ago. What I'd really like to do is spend some time with you and Mr. Hollister going over a list of questions I have. Do you think you could arrange that?"

"I'm afraid any meetings of the nature you're describing have to be approved by Brett . . . ah, I mean, Mr. Hollister. To be truthful, Mr. Blaine, I think we'll all be pretty busy here for the next few weeks getting ready for the annual stockholders meeting. You should attend; there'll be a question and answer session at the end." No way in hell was Emmet going to invite Brett's wrath by setting up an interview without permission, no sir. He'd had enough of Brett's screaming and yelling lately, especially when all he was trying to do was report facts. Emmet certainly wasn't the one who created the messes and he wasn't the one pissing away money . . . too bad Brett didn't see it that way.

For twenty-six years, Emmet had been at LoneStar and had seen it all. In the beginning, Brett had taken Emmet into his confidence and they'd made numerous trips to New York together, talking to bankers, lawyers and research analysts. That was during Brett's early years as chairman when LoneStar was expanding and Brett needed Wall Street's indulgence and deep pockets. Now it was as if Brett thought they were out to personally screw him.

Still, LoneStar was as much Emmet's company as Brett's and he'd do whatever he could to see it endure, even if it meant bringing up issues that weren't popular. You'd think Brett would've known Emmet's loyalty by now. It was a shame how circumstances kept pushing them further and further apart. Emmet wasn't invited to strategy meetings anymore even though he was senior vice president and controller, a rather substantial position at most firms. In fact, he was now relegated to filing the SEC's required financial statements . . . a keeper of history, period. Other executives had taken to avoiding him too, so he usually spent his lunch hour jogging along the Turtle Creek bike path - alone.

"Mr. Griswald, I appreciate how busy you all must be but I really need some private time with you and Mr. Hollister. I doubt that an annual meeting will be sufficient." There was a pause and then the stock analyst added, "Listen, Mr. Griswald, I'm considering coming out with a buy recommendation on your stock but I can't do that unless I speak to senior management. Do you think you could just ask Mr. Hollister to meet me?"

"A buy recommendation?" Well now, that's what we need all right, Emmet admitted as he twisted his tie. Someone plugging LoneStar's stock, putting it back into the investors' eye, getting some positive momentum going. Sure, and other analysts could follow along and really energize the price. Why not suggest a quick meeting to Brett? Brett and Gary Nash could sit down with this guy and dazzle him like they did in the old days. It was worth a try. "Mr. Blaine, I can't promise anything but I'll sure talk to Brett about your request. Why don't you give me your number and I'll get back to you?"

"Thank you, thank you very much. Whenever it can be arranged will be fine with me. We could meet before or after your annual meeting. Either way, I'll leave my calendar open."

"Can't make a promise but I'll see what I can do." Finally, he had something good to present to Brett. A buy recommendation. Even Brett couldn't bellyache about that.

Thursday, May 16, 3:45 P.M.
LoneStar Offices, Dallas

Life was good. No, life was great! Gary Nash was at the pinnacle of his business career. Never before had everything gone so right for him. Brett was constantly beaming at him, praising him, and congratulating him in front of others. The SWAPs were in the money, throwing off hundreds of thousands of dollars a week. Riches beyond belief were there for the taking and visions of glory danced in his head.

Bob Bell, the managing director of Pagent & Associates, had suggested to Gary that given the current market conditions LoneStar should double their SWAP position. Like a shooter on a streak at the craps table, Gary just couldn't say 'no.' To perpetuate his grandeur in the eyes of one and all he casually mentioned to Brett that there was a way to double their SWAP winnings. Brett needed the cash badly and didn't hesitate supporting such an ingenious plan. More accolades were heaped upon Gary for his initiative. Like that pink bunny on television his luck just kept going and going and going.

Then an extraordinary idea hit Gary: Why couldn't he play this same game with his own money? The returns were far superior to money markets, or stocks and bonds for that matter. He didn't even have to tell his wife . . . that was the best part. He could keep all the profits in a new account and then surprise her on Christmas morning with a six digit bank statement, all done up in a fancy package with a bow on top. Why not include a couple first class tickets to Rio or the South of France? The look on Pamela's face would be priceless.

A few calls to Bob Bell confirmed that he could indeed participate in the SWAP market. Now the only question was with how much? Being new at this he followed LoneStar's lead and doubled the amount he initially considered. That should just about do it, he concluded. Aw Pam, honey, we've made it this time. Nothing but the best.

Sunday, May 19, 2:35 P.M.
A Public School, Manhattan

Streaks of lightning periodically lit up the gymnasium's block glass windows but the kids didn't notice. Scores of tiny eyes were glued to the magician. He'd just put a live pigeon into a small box that was sitting on a four-foot high pedestal. He waved his magic wand and said some ancient words found in a long forgotten sorcerer's spell book. Then without warning he slammed the top of the box with his hand, collapsing it with a 'crunch' to the thickness of a pancake.

The kids sitting on the hardwood floor in front of the magician squealed and shrieked, some covering their faces to prevent the inevitable sight of smushed pigeon. But with a flourish he swiped off the pieces of box onto the floor (no carcass observed) and pulled the same feathered creature out from behind his cape. The kids yelled and applauded.

The adults sitting further back on the lower bleachers were clapping too. Molly McHenry leaned over to her husband, Ben and said, "This is so wonderful. I was worried the kids would be disappointed with the rain keeping them indoors today."

Ben whistled with two fingers stuck in his mouth then said, "Yeah. Whose idea was this?"

She shook her head. "Don't know. I guess the hospital set it up. Too bad Ashley isn't here. Bet she'd enjoy it. She called the hospital yesterday, very apologetically. Said she had to work again today. Some big project, she said. I was concerned a little at first that we wouldn't have enough volunteers to watch the kids, but with this magic act entertaining them we don't even need to be here ourselves." She leaned over and kissed her husband on the cheek.

Ben turned and grinned. "Wouldn't miss this for the world."

"I just hope Ashley's boss isn't taking advantage of her. I think she lets people walk all over her. I worry about her sometimes, you know?"

Watching the next trick Ben didn't immediately respond, but he finally said, "Yeah." It was obvious he wasn't paying her any attention.

Same day, 2:45 P.M.
Taylor-Bishop Offices, Manhattan

Ashley had long ago accepted the fact that work came first and might infringe upon her free time. But she was inordinately annoyed whenever the reason turned out to be a waste of her time. Lowering the brief, she glared at her staff sitting uncomfortably around the conference table in her office. They too would rather have been almost anywhere else.

"This is useless, ladies! Not what I expected from you at all!" She crumpled the pages and spoke in a firm, controlled tone. "Redo it!"

Lauren Washington, the most senior staffer shifted in her chair until finding enough courage to say, "We've put a lot of hours into that analysis. How 'bout . . . we take a breather. You know, let our heads clear."

A few nodded in agreement as Ashley scanned their tired expressions. "Fine. If anyone wants a break, take it. Just don't come back!" She stood up and walked to the window, keeping her back to the employees. Peering through the glass she continued, "You're supposed to be the best. That's a tremendous asset to me. But if you're suddenly willing to accept anything less . . . then I can't afford you." Turning towards them she added for emphasis, "Is that understood?"

No one said a word but as soon as Lauren stood up the others did too. With a wave of her arms Lauren began ushering the weary women out of the office. "You heard the boss, ladies. Let's get back to work." Once the others left Lauren walked closer and quietly said to Ashley, "Sugar works sometimes."

Shaking her head Ashley leveled her gaze and replied, "Not here." Then she tilted her head towards the office's plate glass window. It captured a panoramic view of the skyscrapers marking New

York's financial district. She lowered her voice so that Lauren had to strain to hear, "Not there, either."

Tuesday, June 4, 11:30 A.M.
Chairman's Office, LoneStar International

"Gentlemen, I expect your full cooperation and total attention to every detail and I will NOT accept mistakes or excuses, is that clear?" Brett's eyes bore into each man sitting around his private conference table. If there was one time to avoid screwing up, the annual shareholders meeting was it. "I want to insure that no question is asked that I don't have a ready answer for, and I don't want some dissident stockholder group getting control of the proceedings. So I want each of you to come up with ten questions about your own department, and then ten answers. Chester, I want you to run the meeting strictly by the book, don't let anyone sidetrack us. If for whatever reason we get into trouble I want you to call out some rule or point of order and stop it. Clear?"

Chester and the other senior managers had been here before, they knew the routine. "Yes, sir."

"Also, after I get your questions I'll pick eight that I want to be asked. Emmet, you distribute my eight questions to a group of your accountants and make damn sure they're at the meeting and make double damn sure they're ready to ask the questions. You got it?"

"Ye...yes, sir."

"Emmet, I also want two more of your people who know the others to be our moderators. You know, the guys with the hand-held mikes who walk around and pick people from the meeting to ask me questions? Make *sure* they only pick our people. And for God's sake don't use the same people as last year. No fuck ups, you hear me?"

"Ah, no, sir . . . I mean, yes, sir."

"Okay, are there any other comments or questions? No?" Looking at his notes to make sure he missed nothing of importance Brett closed his eyes and deliberated whether or not to ask the next question. Regrettably, it had to be asked and he had to ask it of Emmet Griswald. "Emmet, you getting any more calls from nosey stock analysts or bond holders that we should know about?" Brett cursed having the bobble head at this meeting but the controller knew more about LoneStar than anybody else. Brett pleaded silently for Emmet to just answer the question and not reach for his tie.

Immediately grabbing at his tie Emmet tried to relieve the pressure building up around his neck. The other participants watched helplessly and waited for the string of babbling that was sure to commence. "Ahh, well, yes . . . sir." Emmet cowered instinctively as he spoke, like a faithful dog slapped once too often. "Some analysts . . . well, some are saying that, um, they're thinking of, ah, giving us 'buy' recommendations, but only if . . . only if they can meetsoidjprivatelymovnsodhn0nlmanagement."

Gulping sorely needed oxygen, Emmet composed himself.

No one else dared to speak even a word. Emmet continued, "The Wall Street guys, um, who bought our bonds, they'll, ah, they'll beohereonealneo. They're not happy about . . . ah, well, they um, think that . . . maybe weanmzowneostockpriceup. But sonlnocjlnei ldiownleljop."

The Chief Information Officer, Sidney Spence was perplexed and without thinking he asked, "Emmet, why do bond holders care about our stock price?"

A consensus grown from around the table made it clear no one wanted Emmet answering any further questions. Saving the situation Brett jumped in and said, "It's not all bond holders, it's just a New York group called Cypress who bought all two hundred million dollars of our convertible debt last year. See Spence, other debt only pays interest. Convertibles give them the right to trade in the bonds for *five* million shares of stock anytime they want, at a strike price, or cost to them, of forty dollars per share. So if we're able to increase our earnings and get the stock up to say forty-five dollars, these guys will convert the two hundred million of bonds and end up with two hundred and *twenty-five million dollars* worth of stock. That's *twenty-five million* reasons why they'd care."

The glaze in Spence's eyes indicated that he hadn't fully grasped the situation. Brett tried another approach, "The real problem Spence, is what happens if Cypress converts and keeps the stock. Look, we have twenty million shares outstanding now, but once they convert we'll have a total of twenty-five million shares. No big deal, right? Except Cypress will control five million shares, twenty percent of our stock. That's a pretty powerful voting bloc. We'd have to let them have representation on our board.

"Such being the case, and knowing their only goal would be to ramp our stock price up even higher so they could sell and make a fast buck, they'd force us to forfeit our future for instant profits. I'd just as soon keep the stock price under forty awhile longer and not give them a reason to convert. That'll also give us time to get our house in order and think of a way outta this mess."

A tinge of crimson suddenly materialized on Brett's neck and face, indicating the conversation was about to take a turn for the worse. "That's also why I don't want any of you talking to any reporter or research analyst. Too much good news about us would be bad, understand?" Not to mention, Brett said to himself, those New York bastards would stick their noses into everything. Hell, those black-hearted butchers would tear up every employment contract and start giving *me* orders. Can't let that happen.

To protect his sovereignty and independence Brett knew he had to keep these bastards off the board. Why the hell he ever agreed to issuing convertible debt in the first place was beyond him. But all he could do for the moment was shake his head in disgust. Who the hell's side was God on anyway?

Thursday, June 6, 6:45 P.M.
Taylor-Bishop Offices, Manhattan

Not wanting to disturb her boss from reading, Joyce quietly entered the office and said, "Ashley, here's what you've been waiting for." With that, Ashley's personal secretary gingerly placed two folders on her desk and slipped back through the door.

Reaching out Ashley touched both thick files with no small degree of deference. One of them was about to die a glorious death and make her fabulously wealthy, but first things first. Holding a file in each hand she balanced them as if weight alone would make a difference, but she knew better. The winner had to be able to hold itself together long enough for her to spread a rumor or two, pushing its stock into the stratosphere. Then she'd sit back and wait for it to blow itself into bits, just like *Virtual Reality*.

Opening the file in her right hand and flipping to the first section she scanned the Executive Summary. Well that's interesting, she admitted. LoneStar's having their annual shareholders meeting next Tuesday. No reason not to attend is there? I'll probably learn more being there than here. How about candidate number two? Nope, nothing happening in the immediate future. Okay, that's settled then.

Pressing her phone intercom Ashley spoke rapidly to her secretary, "Joyce, book me a flight to Dallas, I'll leave Monday and return Tuesday evening. Arrange to have me picked up at the airport and get me a room at The Mansion. Then send in Jackie and Vanessa, I want them to tell me about LoneStar's senior management. Also, have Lauren find out what the current market value is for those SWAPs." Ashley glanced at her watch and cursed the time. She'd have to cut her workout short tonight.

Monday, June 10, 9:50 A.M.
Hilborn Residence, Ann Arbor

His wife was fussing with his tie, brushing his lapels and checking the shine on his shoes. "Charles, no matter what, I want you to know how pleased I am for you." Jenny still wasn't sure about LoneStar, Adam Sanchez had seen to that, but she had to admit that this type of opportunity didn't come along very often. And she was so proud of him.

Give me the name of another man, she thought, who sent himself through college by working all sorts of bizarre jobs, started teaching, was drafted into the Army, spent a tour of duty in Vietnam, got back in one piece, went back to teaching, married the most beautiful woman in the world, received his PhD, applied to and was hired by the University of Michigan, appointed department head, fathered two children, wrote numerous articles and two books, helped Dream Makers get off the ground, and was now being asked to join the board of a national company!

She reached around and hugged him again.

The only complaint she had with Charles was his total lack of regard for politics, her pet passion. Even when they were invited to the White House for last autumn's Presidential reception, he'd somehow managed to find a television set and flip it to a college football game. He was so engrossed he didn't even notice the President standing behind him, rooting for his own alma mater. There she was at a major black tie function with her hubby razing the nation's chief executive officer because of a fumble recovery. Thank goodness he hadn't asked a waiter for beer nuts and pretzels. She almost killed him that night.

For more years than Jenny cared to remember she'd been embroiled in getting someone elected to public office, or pushing one proposal or another through the governmental maze. It was far more than a hobby, it was her life. Not the kind of work for the impatient or faint of heart though, as the wheels of government didn't just spin slowly, they ground you down.

"Jenny, I've never been to an annual meeting before, any suggestions?"

"Yes, sit up straight, try to look important, make sure your socks match and forget your light-up tie. Other than that you'll do fine. Give a call as soon as you can. I love you."

"Love you too. Say, do you think my old blue double knit leisure suit would look better?" Jenny grinned and shook her head, "You're incorrigible. Good thing you're cute is all I can say. Now go, and leave me to my own devises."

"I'd rather stay and watch."

"Go!"

Same day, 10:45 A.M.
Smith-Palmer & Co., Detroit

"Any luck getting that meeting arranged with Hollister?" Rick's boss was a little preoccupied but he still knew what was going on with the people who reported to him.

"No. I've placed about five calls to their Controller, Emmet Griswald and a couple more to Hollister, but nothing yet. For whatever reason LoneStar doesn't want to talk to me. I'd like to think while I'm there something will happen and I can get a quick interview. I'll let you know."

"Fine. Hey, if you get the chance take in a game at Arlington Stadium. Well worth the price of a baseball ticket."

"Thanks, I appreciate the advice."

"Rick, don't get down on yourself because these guys won't talk to you. You're doing a fine job; we've no complaints about your work. Hey, even the sales staff likes you and that's kind of unusual. Just do the best you can without compromising yourself. Okay?"

Rick nodded his head, "Yes, sir. Thanks. I'll check in when I get a chance."

"Great. Here, take this baseball . . . get me a couple autographs."

PART 5
BABYLON

CHAPTER 9

Tuesday, June 11, 8:50 A.M.
LoneStar Offices, Dallas

Tension hung in the air like thick wet fog making it difficult to focus on normal routines. Nerves were raw and anxiety permeated each floor at LoneStar's world headquarters. Today was 'D-Day.' At 10:00 A.M. sharp the show would start. Every employee not required to attend the annual meeting busied themselves with whatever was at hand, hoping that burying their heads into work would make the day end faster. Senior managers were dashing about shouting last minute orders, technicians in the media center were frantically trying to find a replacement microphone, Brett was rereading his opening message and changing key points, copies of Robert's Rules of Order were being selectively highlighted by a half dozen legal staffers for Chester's use (if necessary), and final proxy voting results were being rechecked by the outside accounting firm of Russell, Powell and Young.

Shareholders started arriving around 9:00 A.M., giving them one hour to mill about the lobby, checking out the art work and antiques. Stiff faced senior managers started to drift into the media center around 9:30 A.M. More stockholders arrived around 9:40 A.M., and then a couple business reporters from area newspapers showed up, along with Rick Blaine of Smith-Palmer, and another research analyst named Steven Golding from a major New York investment house. The newest director-elect, Charles Hilborn was talking to Arthur King by the podium as Treasurer, Gary Nash swaggered into the gathering and seated himself in the front row.

The chatter and general noise from close to two hundred people huddled together waiting for the program to begin only served to heighten the tension, and there was plenty to go around. Emmet Griswald was still checking out some last minute numbers in his office feverishly trying not to be late, while eight accountants rehearsed asking the 'impromptu questions' just handed them, each now wishing they were home with the flu.

At 9:50 A.M. Ashley Taylor-Bishop entered the small auditorium filled mostly with men. She stopped at the doorway to survey the layout and literally stopped the show. Those around her immediately quit talking. The sudden quiet caused others to turn. She stood for a moment longer then glided into the gathering, parting the sea of men much like Moses and Joshua did to water. Eyes widened, hearts thumped, elbows poked ribs of those not paying attention, and low guttural noises emerged from the populace.

Never had they seen such an absolutely ravishing creature, short of a fashion model waltzing down the runway at Versace's spring collection showing in New York. She was dressed like a model too: A claret colored business suit with fitted jacket, sans blouse, leaving a tantalizing view of cleavage, with matching tight slacks covering her shapely legs and offering a grand view of a perfect rump.

Necks craned to catch another glimpse of her, while fantasy filled dreams ran unchecked and wishful comments were uttered to anyone and to no one in particular. She glided down to the front row turning heads of both men and women and picked the empty seat next to Gary Nash, who momentarily lost his smugness as well as his ability to form coherent sentences.

With all eyes focused on the unbelievably attractive woman making small talk with the lucky treasurer of LoneStar, Brett entered the media center and wasn't paid any attention to at all. Somewhat resentful, he bulled his way to the stage area and took his position on the left side of the twenty by forty-foot visual display screen.

Just as the doors were closing Emmet Griswald stumbled in and continually apologized as he made his way along the back wall until he lodged himself in the farthest corner. At exactly 10:00 A.M. the lights dimmed, and brightened, then dimmed again. There was a general rustling as seats were taken and a full color logo of LoneStar International was projected onto the entire screen. Hidden projectors then began quickly flashing different pictures of employees at work, all with heartwarming smiles. Background music was piped in, starting with Lee Greenwood's *I'm Proud To Be An American.* It's Showtime, Brett said to himself. Looks like a full house.

The visual display was now showing various clients and customers shaking hands or discussing some important aspect of life with their LoneStar account officer. After a few more minutes of film headlining another forty or fifty happy campers, a spotlight was turned onto Brett standing at the speaker's podium. The screen went back to the LoneStar logo and the music gently ended.

"Ladies and gentlemen." Brett paused for a few moments until all attention was refocused on him. Satisfied, he flashed them a down-home friendly smile and began. "My name is Brett Hollister, I'm the Chairman of the Board, President, and Chief Executive Officer of LoneStar International Corporation. Welcome to Dallas. On behalf of the board members, the employees and the customers of LoneStar, I wish to extend to you our warmest greetings. It is our intent today that you walk away from this meeting with as much pride and commitment to LoneStar as we have.

"This is a dynamic company, possessing solid foundations and a vision to grow in a highly competitive world. In my ten years at the helm we've doubled our size, then doubled it again. Our stock has increased in value . . ." not much lately he admitted to himself, but it *had* increased, ". . . and cash dividends have always been paid. Yes, we have been challenged and we will continue to be challenged. But let me assure all of you of one fact. We have never and will never let you down." Brett really liked that last line. Ranked right up there with "ask not what your country can do for you . . ."

Rechecking his notes, he continued, "While creating meaningful jobs for thousands of Americans and giving our shareholders a fair return, we've never lost sight that we're also here to help the community. To put back into the community some of the fruits we've harvested. To help the less fortunate who cannot help themselves. In this regard a major piece of my time and effort has been devoted to doing just that. Also, I'm pleased to report that during the last twelve months, over one million dollars has been donated to twenty-eight different charities and community organizations making their lives a little bit better." There was a smattering of applause as Brett beamed. Who could find fault with charities?

"Now, I'm sure some of you have never attended an annual meeting before and you may not know what to expect, so here is our agenda. First, we'll have the results of the shareholder's proxy voting reported to us by Mr. Chester Bennett, our general counsel. Then we'll introduce our new board members and then Mr. Gary Nash will go over our financial reports. Lastly, we'll have an open question and answer period. Let me set the rules up for that ahead of time so we can get as many questions answered as possible in the allotted time.

"We have two gentlemen wearing matching green sport coats . . . stand up please, thank you. These two gentlemen will walk around the room and randomly pick those of you who are signifying a desire to ask a question by the raising of your hand. Please do not shout or get out of your seats. That will only cause a disruption in the process and result in fewer questions being asked. Do we all understand? Fine, now without further ado I present to you General Counsel, Mr. Chester Bennett."

Not a bad opening all things considered. The crowd was pretty good too, everyone was behaving themselves. Thankfully Chester didn't have anything confrontational to say, only that the proposed slate of candidates for board members had been approved along with the retention of the outside auditors for another year. Who could have a problem with that? Checking his watch Brett duly noted it was 10:25 A.M. They were right on schedule.

Steven Golding, analyst from New York mumbled, "What a bunch of horseshit. What's he running for, honorary chairman of Charities R Us?" Steven was incensed. This was the same crap pulled last year. Hollister doesn't talk to anyone in the media or any research analyst for a year and then all he says is everything's hunky dory? Does he think he can just pat us on the head and send us back home? What is this shit? I didn't fly from New York to listen to this garbage. Last time he didn't say squat and I never even got a chance to ask a question. Well, today I'm gonna grab one of those green jackets when they walk by.

Ashley was appalled, too. Mr. Hollister, she mused to herself, I don't think this crowd is going to let you get away with it. She'd already noticed Paul Victor, a senior partner of The Cypress Group, the convertible bondholders, nervously whispering amongst his entourage. Those guys were as cold blooded and ruthless as they came. Now that their option to convert into stock was almost in the money they'd stop at nothing to push the price higher. A bland annual meeting, the only public forum permitted by LoneStar, with no revelations of planned revenue enhancements, no strategic goals and no mention of key areas of opportunities for the future, just wasn't going to set Wall Street on fire and give those boys what they wanted.

Turning to Gary Nash seated next to her, Ashley displayed a dazzling smile. If nothing else she now knew this company was her Holy Grail. Brett Hollister was a windbag who hadn't a clue on running a major diversified company, particularly if this ass Nash mumbling and drooling next to her was an example of the forward thinking senior management team. Still smiling at the man, Ashley surmised Nash knew zip about options, SWAPs or anything else. Maybe he'd learn something if he'd stop peeking down my jacket, she thought drearily. Can't wait to hear *his* speech. Lord help us all.

Rick Blaine couldn't keep his eyes off of the woman in the front row. Who was she? Did she come alone? The drone of the next speaker was simply a background noise; no intelligible words were getting through to his consciousness.

Too bad I can't get her attention, he thought, just smile at her. No harm in smiling is there? That's the type of woman you want on your arm walking into a restaurant, all those envious eyes locking on you. Wish she would've sat next to me. Just my luck. Face it; no one's been attracted to you lately have they? No second looks from flirty girls? To be truthful, they don't even know I exist. I'm not hard and lean, and I'm not young looking anymore. So where did these extra pounds come from? Why do I have bags under my eyes? Why can't I climb a flight of stairs without puffing or having my knees ache? What happened?

"Thank you, Mr. Nash, for reviewing our financial results. I trust all will agree we are performing as well as can be expected given the current economic environment." Brett looked out into a sea of blank stares. Yes indeed, this meeting was going just the way he had planned, even though hardly anyone seemed pleased with Gary's speech. But Gary had filled the required eight minutes and that was just as important. Now all we have to do is open the floor to a few questions and we can all get back to work for another year.

Brett motioned with his hands, "Will the two gentlemen in the green coats please stand up. Thank you, now if you will kindly locate someone in the audience who has a question we can begin." A flurry of anxious hands shot into the air.

One of the green coats quickly spotted and wove his way over to a coworker, as he'd been instructed. "Do you have a question for Mr. Hollister?"

In a dull monotone, Mrs. Frome, the elderly accounts payable supervisor with salt and pepper hair done up in a bun, said, "Yes . . . thank you. Mr. Hollister . . . as such a key figure at LoneStar, I was . . . wondering if you were considering retreating, no, ah, I mean . . . um, *considering retirement,* that's it . . . ah, anytime soon? That's what I meant to say . . . retiring." She hurriedly retook her seat.

A beaming Brett hesitated for effect then responded, "No, no I don't have any immediate plans for retirement. I feel that while we have come a long way, we still have a great deal of road ahead of us. I wouldn't want any of our shareholders to ever think that I would walk out of a job that was unfinished. I plan on being the chairman and president until the board drags me out in a pine box." A smattering of chuckles rose from the audience, mostly from LoneStar employees attending incognito. Brett was smiling too. Wasn't that a great question to start with? Hey, could he stage a meeting or what?

While Brett was answering Mrs. Frome's question the other green coat had been passing scores of outstretched hands to reach a familiar face. As soon as Brett finished speaking, per instructions, green coat number two put the mike in the face of another cohort and said, "Yes, sir. Do you have a question for Mr. Hollister?"

A tall, pencil thin data entry clerk took one last look at the written question in his hand, stuffed it in his pocket and said, "Yes, I do. Mr. Hollister, with all the growth going on here do you feel that you have enough capable senior management?"

Brett scrunched his face as if contemplating the limits of quantum mechanics, "That's a good question; let me respond to it this way . . ."

Steven Golding was furious. What kind of dumbass questions are these? Who are these guys asking questions anyway, his kids? I've got to do something before he adjourns this meeting. Where are those little green suits? Oh yeah, there's one, and he's walking my way.

Charles Hilborn, the newly installed director, didn't know quite what to make of these proceedings. Seemed tame enough so far. Although, there were a lot of waving hands and what sounded like murmurings beginning to reach above the normal crowd noise. Still, Brett was handling himself well, albeit pure fluff. Charles wondered if all annual meetings were so self-serving. These questions were like softball pitches that anyone could knock over the fence.

He was in the zone, like a salvation preacher caught up in his own rhetoric, ". . . so while I have total confidence in my staff today we must always cultivate new blood with fresh ideas for tomorrow." Brett was really pleased with his answers, although there was an irritated look on many of the attendees. What's their problem? he wondered.

The general counsel, Chester Bennett also perceived that the crowd was getting restless. Didn't it seem like every year the meeting was more hostile than the year before? Well, its 11:25 A.M., he confirmed, another half hour of questions and they could adjourn. A half hour is about six more questions; trust Brett to have figured that out before hand. Six more canned questions and we're outta here.

A green coat with microphone was on his way into another section of seats when he was abruptly jerked around and physically held. Before he could squirm his way free, the mike was yanked out of his hand. "Mr. Hollister, Steve Golding here, could you tell us why you're using sophisticated interest rate sensitive SWAPs and who's your internal expert on SWAPs, particularly since so many other companies with highly trained and knowledgeable traders have gotten burned using SWAPs?"

Brett wasn't totally prepared for this sudden change of events but what was there to hide? The SWAPs were doing better than expected. "Mr. Golding, I want you to know, I want all of you to know, that LoneStar would never enter into a financial transaction unless we had every confidence that it would be well managed and be of substantial benefit to all of us. Just to bring you up to date, we have made over three million dollars since we initially began hedging ourselves with SWAPs, that's less than three months ago.

"Also, I want to emphasize that we have on our staff a very, very capable senior officer who knows the SWAP market like the back of his hand. I can only say that we are indeed fortunate to have a man of Mr. Gary Nash's caliber with us. You should also know that Wall Street and the entire business community holds Mr. Nash in their highest regard. We know what we are doing, Mr. Golding. We are increasing our shareholders value which is our job." Whoa, Brett was pleased with that answer. Just no more surprises, that's all.

"A follow-up if I may," Steve added quickly. Might as well because Mr. Green Coat wasn't going anywhere. Not without his microphone.

Gary couldn't believe his good fortune. Not only did the most beguiling creature he'd ever seen in his life choose to sit next to him, but now he was being publicly praised as well. She knew it was him receiving the accolades, because they had been politely chatting right before the meeting and had exchanged names. Her name was Ashley and like most naive women she was easily impressed with his commanding knowledge of financial markets and securities. Well, why shouldn't she be? I'm a pretty impressive fellow, he acknowledged with all due modesty.

". . . the follow up question, Mr. Hollister, is why LoneStar has to sell assets in order to get enough cash to make debt payments. What are you doing with all the cash this place makes? Who's using it? Where's it going? Why aren't you paying down your debt with it?"

Dead silence. Brett froze. This wasn't supposed to be happening. The questioning was getting out of order. Order? . . . Yeah, that's it, order. "You're out of *order*, Mr. Golding. There are other shareholders who would like an opportunity to ask a question and you already did. So please give the mike back to the gentleman you so rudely took it from and we'll continue." Control is not airtight today, Brett conceded. He turned his head a bit and glared at Chester.

One of the green coats had found another employee with a question ready to go. "Mr. Hollister, how do you view the general economic environment?" The accounting trainee quickly sat back down, while those around her cast deadly looking stares in her direction. Probably wasn't the best question to ask.

As Brett began his canned answer a clamor of voices began shouting to be heard. "Hey, what about the cash, why can't you pay bills around here?" "Yeah, where's our money, what are you doing with it?" "Say, you're not broke are you?" "It's that damn software system you're trying to build isn't it? It's a bleeding money pit!"

Losing his train of thought along with his temper, Brett replied, "Will you all just calm down? There's no cash problem here, we have plenty of cash. We're not not paying bills. I mean we are paying bills. Look, this is a major financial institution; I can get money whenever I want. This is all foolishness." Why wouldn't they just sit down and listen? Then they'd understand.

The boys from The Cypress Group were undergoing seizures. Not only weren't they going to get the stock price uptick they'd been expecting from this meeting, but now this bumbling idiot was about to dropkick them all into oblivion. They pleaded to one another, "Someone help us." "What's he doing?" "Can't we shut him up?" "We've gotta do something."

Chester Bennett was tongue tied and furiously flipping through pages of Robert's Rules of Order, trying to find the correct objection to put an end to this chaos, and he didn't have much time. Brett was beginning to turn regal red. Chester looked over at him again. No, no don't lose it Brett, Chester urged telepathically.

The confusion and clamor was becoming more than Brett could take. No one was paying attention to him, they were shouting at him and each other. This had to stop, now! "Quiet! *Quiet everyone. We will not continue until I have order. Is that clear? Until I have order. Now take your seats immediately.*"

Dumbfounded, that's how Ashley felt. This management group was completely incompetent. The jerks were about to blow the whole deal for her. Having the stock drop like a rock was exactly what was supposed to happen but only when she was ready for it, not now. Not today! Somehow she had to do something but that cash question was a good one. Hollister couldn't answer it without opening himself up to harder questions. Well, the only thing to do when you've been dealt a losing hand is to kick the card table over and call for a re-deal.

It wasn't hard for Ashley to walk over to the closest green coat amidst the confusion, smile seductively at him and take the proffered mike he'd been clinging to just moments before. In her loudest voice she said, "Mr. Hollister, Mr. Hollister? I wonder if I might ask a question." The crowd promptly began to simmer down and compose itself. Within seconds they came to order and seats were retaken. Brett beheld her gratefully, like a life line thrown at the last possible moment.

Ashley waited for almost total silence . . . she needed everyone to be paying attention. Clearing her throat while Hollister dabbed his forehead with a handkerchief, she said, "Mr. Hollister, why do you continue to refuse to admit you've been, and even now are in secret negotiations with the Blackstone Group, J.P. Morgan and Goldman Sachs for the express purpose of selling LoneStar to the highest bidder?"

That did it. Visions of large conglomerates fighting each other over LoneStar and paying top dollar for its stock was infectious. New questions were blurted out, the people and the press wanted to know all about the details of the secret buyout meetings. Brett stood speechless, confused . . . totally out of his element. He was simply incapable of making a response to such a ludicrous statement. The crowd took his silence to mean 'no comment,' the internationally recognized ploy for not wanting to admit the truth.

The Cypress boys were ecstatic. Victory had just been pulled from the jaws of defeat. Who cared if the rumor was true or not? The fact that the street now believed LoneStar was in play and was about to be acquired was all that mattered. By the opening bell tomorrow LoneStar stock would begin to reflect a buyout premium. Who would have thought Ms. Ashley Taylor-Bishop had some stake in LoneStar? But there she was, lovely as ever, probably holding insider information again and ready to make a killing.

Paul Victor, the tall, lanky west coast ex-surfer with long blonde hair combed straight back and a ready eye for the ladies smiled at his adversary and thought: Well, you go right ahead Ms. Bishop. Make your killing. But you won't be alone this time. No, you bitch. I'm going to be right beside you riding this stock all the way. You won't burn me and my boys again, and there's not a damned thing you can do about it.

Same day, 12:20 P.M.,
LoneStar Office

"Hi, Jenny, it's me." Charles felt like he'd been run over by a truck. This was the first and hopefully the last annual meeting he'd ever have to attend. All those noble thoughts he'd held about helping LoneStar, all those honorable ideals. "Aw, I don't know anything about the corporate world," he confessed. "Who am I kidding?"

"Where are you?" The voice of his best friend.

"I'm in an empty office at LoneStar. The meeting just finished."

"Well, don't keep me in suspense. How did it go?"

"Okay, I guess. I'm not sure. It's the first one I've ever been to so I don't know what they're supposed to be like."

"You don't sound like it went 'okay.' What really happened?"

Charles took a deep breath and answered, "It started off well enough but along the way Brett lost control. I mean he *really* lost control. Started yelling at the stockholders. Everyone was shouting at each other. Mass hysteria. Chester stood up and officially adjourned the meeting, while people were still screaming out questions. Then some technician starts playing marching band music and this enormous movie screen lights up and displays flags of America, Texas and LoneStar all waving in the breeze. The crowd was incensed. So Brett just stomped off never to be seen again."

"Not exactly a textbook ending, huh?"

"No, not exactly." Charles felt bad for Brett, real bad. He also felt bad for himself. What did he get himself into? "You can say 'I told you so,' if you want."

"Oh, I am so sorry for you, Charles. I can just imagine what you're going through. Is there anything I can do?"

"I don't think so, other than to having a double scotch waiting in your hand when I get home."

Same day, 12:25 P.M.,
LoneStar, Lobby

"Excuse me, I'm Rick Blaine, I work for Smith-Palmer as a research analyst. I noticed you in the meeting; you caused quite a stir with your question." Rick, along with the other two hundred plus people had poured out from the media center. Those who either didn't have cellular phones or had dead phones and needed to make a quick call headed for a bank of three telephones along a wood paneled corridor. Everyone else hurried outside to relay what had just transpired to whatever individual or group they represented. Spotting her in the four deep line waiting for a telephone Rick was star struck. On impulse he walked over to her. Hey, he was a research analysis, right? Just part of the job. She was even more attractive up close.

"Hi, I'm Ashley Taylor-Bishop. Yes, I suppose I did, didn't I."

Her smile melted him. She was so . . . so desirable. He felt younger just talking to her, being close to her. "Ah, I've really only just started doing research reports. I used to run a pretty good sized bank but I was on the wrong side of a merger." What on earth made him say that? Why was he spouting off like this?

Ashley laughed and offered, "I know all about getting on the wrong side of people. They can be infuriating but you've got to deal with it. No choice in the matter."

Her laugh was delightful to listen to. Screwing up some courage, he said, "Look, I was about to call a cab. If you're going to the airport, I'd be happy to share a ride." That was awfully presumptuous, but since part of his job was learning what others think it was actually in the line of duty . . . right?

"Oh, I've already made other arrangements."

Struck out with the first pitch. It was a crushing defeat and Rick was crestfallen. "Sure, well some other time." At least he had gotten a chance to talk to her.

"If you don't mind riding in a limo, I can give *you* a lift to the airport."

What did she say? She'll give *me* a ride? Oh, thank you, thank you, thank you, Lord. "Well, ah, yes, that would be fine, thanks." He tried to look dignified and not seem too anxious.

"My pleasure. Look, I've got a couple calls to make, why don't we meet at my limo? It's outside. Black Cadillac with a woman driver and a car phone that doesn't work, to match my own cell phone that's dead. Say in about twenty minutes?"

"Yes, yes that'll be great. Right, okay, twenty minutes. Thanks." Rick forgot all about checking in with his boss.

Same day, 12:35 P.M.
Chairman's Office, LoneStar International

The surrounding walls reverberated as Brett slammed his office door shut. Never had he been so humiliated, never had he been made to look the fool. Where the hell was all my help? he cursed silently. Yeah, where the fuck were they? I give explicit instructions and that halfwit Griswald can't even carry them out. No one was supposed to ask me questions except those *I* wanted. Dumb son of a bitch can't even do a simple fucking job.

Cracking open a new bottle of Jack Daniels at his private bar Brett poured three fingers into a glass, added a couple of ice cubes and tossed the liquid back against his throat. The burning sensation felt wonderful. Another round it is, he said to himself. Walking with a fresh drink over to the sofa in front of the fireplace he wearily sat down. This wasn't fun anymore, he confessed. Used to be when he said something it was gospel. Now everyone did just as they good and well pleased. No respect, that's the problem . . . no respect.

"Brett, mind some company?" Chester entered his office. Brett didn't move or speak so Chester walked over to the bar, poured himself a stiff drink and took a seat next to Brett.

After a few minutes Brett said, "I really did it this time, didn't I?" Chester was the only one he could open up to.

Contemplating his response for a few moments, Chester finally replied, "It could have gone a little better I suppose, but when you think about it, it wasn't so bad. Look Brett, you took a couple hits today, okay, it happens. But you've done nothing to be ashamed of. Look at what you've built up here over the past years. You've got every right to be proud. I am."

"Yeah, I'm proud all right. I'm proud that I've got thousands of people working for me and they can't do the one damn thing I ask. Chester, they ignored me. That ain't right."

"So what are you going to do?"

"I don't know. Did you talk to any of the board members?"

"No, they all left after you did."

"Okay, on your way out tell Suzanne to hold all my calls for the rest of the day. I'll make a few phone calls myself, see what damage I've done. I'll talk to you later." Taking the proffered hint Chester got up and walked away from a friend who looked considerably older than he had just a few short hours ago.

PART 6
DECEPTION

CHAPTER 10

Tuesday Morning, July 2
Lower Manhattan

Wall Street buys on rumor and sells on fact so during the weeks immediately preceding Brett Hollister's revelation about LoneStar being in the throes of secret merger negotiations, the price of LoneStar stock broke through the forty dollar per share level with ease. Steven Golding issued a 'buy' recommendation on LoneStar if for no other reason than it was still cheap compared to what an acquiring company would end up paying in a free-for-all bidding war. Other analysts followed suit.

Paul Victor and the boys from Cypress thought the stock was such a bargain they considered adding to their current position by buying LoneStar stock on the open market, but there was no sense in getting too greedy . . . at least not yet. Rick Blaine of Smith-Palmer also issued a 'buy' recommendation on LoneStar. Actually he was the first analyst to publish a 'buy' opinion and his firm's sales staff and clients loved him as their portfolios prospered literally overnight.

Back in Texas, the local newspapers graciously kept the color out of the business section when reporting on LoneStar's annual meeting, in deference to long time resident and community leader Brett

Hollister. But it was safe to say there was very little 'warmth' emanating from the Dallas headquarters of LoneStar International. Everything Brett had worked so hard to build was suddenly crumbling before his eyes and he felt powerless to stop it. Could things get any worse?

Same day, 10:15 A.M.
LoneStar Offices, Dallas

Gary Nash hung up the phone and gazed out of his tenth floor office window. His view took in Love Field a smaller airport than D/FW International to be sure, but Southwest Airlines didn't seem to notice. Every couple minutes or so another one of their planes appeared in the air. It was mesmerizing watching airplanes take off and land, and sometimes twenty minutes or more would pass before Gary snapped back from his daydreaming.

Moments ago his Wall Street buddy Bob Bell informed him that the SWAPs were doing fine. In fact, Gary had personally made close to a quarter million dollars. This was almost too easy, Gary told himself. This was the free lunch everyone always said wasn't possible. Well, they were wrong. Why not double up again? That way he'd have enough money for early retirement plus that vacation home in Colorado. And saying 'goodbye' sooner than later was now an obsession.

Over the last few weeks Brett had become a butt kicking, loud mouthed, screaming tyrant. Only the feeble minded wandered into Brett's line of fire. Conferences or outside meetings usually scoffed at as being totally worthless where religiously attended by those lucky enough to be invited . . . simply to get out of harm's way. Brett was clearly not in the mood for anyone's comments, questions or concerns.

Not that Gary Nash needed to talk to him for guidance or anything. No, Gary could handle his own areas just fine. But some of the other managers really depended on Brett for counsel. Without Brett they were left to their own faculties, which too often went lacking. Back stabbing, bickering and finger-pointing were also on the rise. Not to mention that little Napoleon in systems, Sidney Spence, was still sucking cash without anything to show for it. Spence's area had probably drained more than a hundred million dollars.

Gary also recently heard that the credit card division was having a rough time. Not too surprising when you consider whom they sent pre-approved credit cards to. He'd heard they'd lowered credit standards enough to include rescue mission regulars. That's not the way he'd go about increasing sales, but when all those managers' bonuses were tied to sales volume rather than profitability it sort of made sense. Well, that wasn't his problem. He was doing his job and just wanted to be left alone.

Okay, not totally alone. He could still feel Ashley's hand on his knee, a burning sensation unlike anything he'd experienced before. She had leaned over to congratulate him on his accomplishments right after Brett had announced to everyone at the shareholders meeting how proud he was of his treasurer. She even said that she'd like to learn more about those 'SWAP things,' as she called them. Why yes, he'd be happy to teach her. How about after the meeting? Unfortunately, she couldn't then but here was her card, please call her in a few weeks.

Looking at his calendar he confirmed that it had been more than a couple of weeks since the annual meeting. No time like the present, right? The rolling in his stomach said so.

Same day, Same Time.
Lower Manhattan

"Ashley, it's for you. Some man named Gary Nash on line two, says you're expecting his call?"

"Joyce, tell him I'm in a conference, that I really want to talk to him, and that I'll call him back." Ashley had found it was better to let the overconfident one's squirm a little, it made them more vulnerable. The call did remind her however, of all the disorder and anarchy caused by Brett Hollister.

That sure was one hell of a meeting she conceded, what with old Brett up there like some big sugar daddy spouting all that self-serving bullshit. I thought Steve Golding was going to go for his throat, along with those other hyenas from Cypress. What a day. What a stroke of luck making the acquaintance of Gary Nash . . . such a twit. And then running into that guy who issues stock reports. Yes, you Mr. Rick Blaine. I'm going to need your help more than you know.

"Joyce, see if you can locate a Rick Blaine for me. He's a research analyst at Smith-Palmer. Somewhere in Michigan I think. The number's got to be on the internet somewhere."

Ashley leaned back and talked in a hushed tone to the silent telephone, "Ricky baby, you don't stand anymore of a chance than numb nuts Nash.

"Got it, Joyce? Yeah, thanks. Put it through for me."

Same day, Same Time
Smith-Palmer & Co., Detroit

Pouring over the annual report of a company he was going to interview soon, Rick Blaine heard his phone ringing. Without taking his eyes off the report he picked up the phone and answered, "Rick Blaine speaking."

The connection was clear like they were next door to each other and the silky voice filled his ear, "Hi Rick, this is Ashley Taylor-Bishop. You probably don't remember me but we shared a ride to the airport. LoneStar's annual meeting?"

Damn! Double damn. His heart surged to full speed ahead and his hands started quivering. "Oh, ah, why, hello. Ah, sure I remember you, Ashley. How 're you?"

"I'm doing just fine Rick and thanks for remembering me. Say, I'm going to be in Detroit the week of the fifteenth and I was wondering if we could meet for a business dinner. I have a few clients who might need a strong regional investment house like Smith-Palmer."

She's coming here? Holy shit. "Um, yes, yes I'd love to. When do you get in and where will you be staying?" Little beads of perspiration peppered his forehead and nose. He quickly wiped them away to better concentrate on the conversation.

"I'm flying in Thursday the eighteenth so how about dinner at say seven-thirty? I'm staying at that charming hotel in Birmingham, what's its name?"

"You must mean the Townsend. I know it. Look, I'll make dinner reservations and see you then." Sweaty palms were leaving splotches on whatever he touched.

"You're so kind, Rick. I'm not imposing on you am I? You weren't planning on taking a vacation or anything were you?"

"No, no. You're not imposing at all, really you're not. Ah, I'm looking forward to seeing you again." Oh yeah, did he want to see her again.

"Thanks. See you soon. Bye."

"Uhh, right. Bye." Okay, get a grip, he reproached himself. It was just a phone call. She's not coming here to seduce you, it's just business. Oh, but the memories of that limousine ride back to the airport with Ashley were powerful. He could still picture her sitting next to him, the most desirable woman he could envision. Her top two buttons on her jacket were unbuttoned and there was no undergarment, only soft swells of firm breast. Rick remembered how the curve of her breasts showed particularly well whenever he'd arched his neck and looked straight down her front. What a sophomoric thing to do. But if she noticed him leering she didn't seem to mind, and that was even more exciting.

They talked of his new job and of Smith-Palmer. They laughed at the spectacle they'd just witnessed. He found out she was from New York and that she was fairly well connected to the street. She also mentioned how she'd been tipped off of possible merger talks and wanted to find out if they were true. "Apparently they were," she concluded.

She asked him what he was going to write about LoneStar and he spelled out his yet to be released report that investors should 'buy' LoneStar if only for the merger premium. She seemed delighted and urged him to beat his competition by publishing early. God, she was beautiful.

With wings on his feet he flew home that night, reminiscent of when he bore his first schoolboy crush. Rick recalled how carefree he was that evening when he entered his house, as well as being sexually aroused. His mind staged vivid images of what tonight's homecoming was going to be like: Okay kiddos, daddy's home, here I am, give me big hugs, quick dinner, homework and then off to bed.

And as for you Stephanie Blaine, what say we turn in early? He opened the door expecting such a reception but was slammed in the face with a cold dose of reality. Stephanie was teary eyed from yelling at the kids. Without so much as a, "How was your trip, dear?" she launched into one complaint after another. "The kids did this, the kids did that, this broke, that broke, something else wasn't right." She followed him upstairs and continued to bitch while he changed clothes. Then when he shut the door on her to go to the bathroom she really blew a fuse. "Don't you dare leave the room when I'm taking to you," she shouted through the door. Angry himself, Rick quickly discarded all prior romantic notions. All he remembered thinking about was how come Stephanie couldn't be more like Ashley?

Sunday, July 7, Early Afternoon
A Playground in Manhattan

Dave Hanson was lying face down on the grass, gasping for air. A soccer ball then shot past his head followed by eight tiny pairs of scampering feet. Two pairs of tiny feet actually ran straight across his sweat soaked back. "Ouch! Hey, watch it!"

Ben McHenry yelled from the sideline, "Dave. Lie still. Don't get up! Take the full count!" Ben threw a towel onto the soccer field indicating surrender and laughed hysterically.

Molly poked her husband in the ribs. "Will you stop teasing Dave? Honestly. I have to watch you more than the kids!"

Picking himself slowly off the ground, Dave brushed his grass stained T-shirt. After catching his breath he wobbled off after the ball. Ben was still grinning when he noticed a small red Mercedes pull up and park beside his old Ford pickup truck. The female driver exited and walked over to Ben and Molly. She was an attractive younger woman carrying a dark leather briefcase.

"Hello. Are you here with the children from the hospital?"

Ben nodded, "Yes ma'am."

The lady smiled, "Oh good. I was hoping I could find Ashley Bishop. Is she here?"

Molly noticed the expensive watch, rings, designer clothes and Italian shoes of the visitor.

"She's on the other side of the field." Unconsciously, Molly hid her own plain wedding band behind her back and tried to straighten her discount store bought blouse with her other hand. "I'll go get her if you'd like." The lady was obviously someone important.

"No, thank you. I see her." She nodded and walked off.

Without thinking Ben's gaze followed the lady's swaying rear-end. Another sharp pain in his ribs quickly ensued. Molly's elbow was at it again. "Watch it, Mister."

Ben grimaced from the jab and retorted, "That's what I was doing." Noting the tactical error he'd just made he held up both hands and said, "Ah, just kidding, honey."

The McHenry's observed the woman cross the soccer field to where Ashley was shooting baskets with another group of kids. One of the children pulled on Ashley's baggy sweatpants and pointed to the other lady walking towards them. Ashley handed the ball to the small boy and walked straight over to the other woman.

Molly and Ben couldn't hear the conversation but body language informed them that it wasn't good news for Ashley. The well-dressed woman handed over some papers, said a few words, shook Ashley's hand and left. The lady smiled and nodded as she passed the McHenry's, got back into her car and drove off.

Sitting on a picnic table alone Ashley looked dejectedly at the documents. Molly left Ben and hustled over to her. "Hey. Anything wrong?"

Ashley shrugged, shook her head and shrugged again. "Oh, no. Not really. It was a long shot anyway. It wouldn't have worked."

Moving next to her, Molly whispered in a confidential tone, "What wouldn't have worked?"

Ashley appeared lost in thought but finally said, "I ah, wanted to see if I could . . . Oh, it wasn't a very good idea. I . . . if I maybe could adopt one of the kids. Sara. She doesn't have anyone and is going through a pretty rough time. So I thought it would be . . . but it won't work. That was a lawyer. She just told me my chances of adopting anyone is less than zero."

"Why? Because you're single?"

"I suppose getting married again might help, but that's not it."

"I'm sorry." She was married before? Molly patted Ashley's hand while one of the kids came over to check on them. Molly told the child to run back and play.

Casting her eyes down at her finger bearing the plain wedding band Molly said, "Too bad your lawyer had to mess-up your day off."

"Huh? Oh, she's leaving on a business trip in a few hours. Wanted to give me these personally. Dug up some pretty convincing arguments too. Still, I thought whatever happened so long ago wouldn't matter so much." Ashley waved the papers in the air then added, "But they're wrong, you know?" Getting to her feet, she roughly folded the papers and jammed them inside her sweat pants while a sudden flash of anger appeared. "None of that was my fault! I was just a kid!"

Molly had never seen her angry before. "Is there anything I can do?"

As quickly as the anger appeared it disappeared. Ashley's thoughts seemed off in another world. There was a new sheen of perspiration on her face and a tremor in her hands. A couple moments later she started walking back to the playing children. Suddenly stopping she turned around and said, "I'm sorry. I didn't ask how Ben's new job was going."

Ashley now seemed okay, but talk about a conversion shift . . . it was sort of spooky. Molly reflexively gazed at her husband grilling hotdogs and hamburgers. "He loves it. It came right out of the blue. First our hospital bills get paid off then he gets a better job. You sure called that right." Molly froze. Quite a string of coincidences happening around here, she thought. Too many coincidences. "Ashley, I'm wondering." She walked over and looked Ashley square in the face and asked, "Should I be thanking you or anything?"

"What for? Look, you and Ben are nice people. Sometimes good things happen to nice people. That's just the way it is."

"But you're a nice person. So how do you explain those papers stuck in your pants?"

Ashley seemed to want to say something but wavered. After a few moments, she said, "You know what? You're right. I'm never going to be able to explain them. I should just move on." Pausing to stare at baldheaded Sara off by herself, Ashley half-heartedly began shooting baskets.

Tuesday Afternoon, July 9
LoneStar Offices, Dallas

Emmet Griswald was in a panic. Brett had called him up late yesterday and demanded an updated budget by three o'clock today. Saying he didn't care if the entire accounting staff had to spend the whole fucking night working on it, Brett made it clear that failure would be dealt with swiftly and severely. So Emmet and his staff pulled an all-nighter, and they were still working on it at noon when Brett's secretary called informing him of a senior management meeting at two o'clock, and it would last at least one hour. No agenda was given.

Working frantically Emmet and his people shuffled, printed and assembled the new budget into a presentable form. "No telling what this meeting's going to be about," he told them as he stuffed several copies under his arm and flew out the door. Charging up the stairs and running along the halls Emmet finally entered the conference room at 2:02. He'd made it.

"You're late, Griswald."

Like a deer caught in oncoming headlights Emmet stood paralyzed. Everyone in the room was staring at him like he'd just committed the unforgivable sin. The chairman's voice spat fire: "Wasn't I specific enough for you, Griswald, or are you someone special? I call a meeting at *two o'clock* and you don't show up on time. Who the fuck do you think you are? I'm the chairman here, *not you.*" Emmet held out the budget packages for Brett to see why he was a little late, but Brett wasn't interested.

The enraged ex-lineman shook his head as a raging bull does before it charges, "I am sick and tired of not getting what I ask for. I'm sick and tired of being second guessed by all of you. Every one of you shows me a total lack of respect. Now WHAT do I have to do to get your attention?" He slammed the table, *"Well? Tell me."* The silence in the room was deafening, just the way Brett liked it. "From now on each of you is on notice. You piss me off once more and you're fired. *Do I make myself clear?*"

Brett looked around the table daring anyone to stand up against him. "All those employment contracts you have won't be worth shit, and I'll make damn sure you never get a job again. *You understand me? You getting this?*" Ten pairs of eyes focused on the papers in front of them, while Emmet remained quivering in the doorway. No one ventured to look at Brett.

"Good, sit down, Griswald." Brett was finally getting his message across. He could tell that these guys were now hanging onto his every word. About time, he told himself. "I want to talk about why we don't have enough cash to pay the fucking debt payments. Who the hell is using it, where's it going, and who's responsible?" Brett glared at Emmet and added, "And how come I have to find out about this all by myself?"

Seeing his secretary outside the conference room waiting with a fax, he threw on a smile and waved for her to come in. Entering quickly, Suzanne placed the piece of paper in front of her boss and retreated. Brett skimmed the letter quickly and said, "Shit. Bennett, you stay here with me. The rest of you get back to work." A group of very grateful senior managers packed up and vanished.

Once alone, Brett said, "Those pricks from Cypress faxed over this letter. They're gonna convert their bonds into common stock. Said they also want board representation. They want to replace four of our current directors with their own people. If we don't go along they'll take legal action. Said they want to meet with me next week to agree upon the strategic initiatives for LoneStar. They want me to acknowledge their 'requests' by tomorrow." Brett had been slapped hard and he didn't like it.

"Who do they want off the board?"

Brett had made Chester's job pretty shitty lately but the pay and perks were still better than the lawyer could get anywhere else, so he was stuck. Besides, being on the board gave Chester more perks than most so he obviously didn't want to be one of the 'four' destined to be removed. Brett crumpled the message and tossed the paper over Chester's way. "Read it yourself."

Chester quickly smoothed out the message and scanned it. "They want us to get rid of Arthur King, Ben Walker, Whiteside and Wilson?" Relieved his name wasn't mentioned he looked up from the paper and asked, "What are you going to do, Brett?"

Brett's face was buried in his hands, not exactly the picture of a confident commander-in-chief. Sighing loudly, he said, "Tell me again what my alternatives are."

Actually, there weren't any. "As we discussed before, with a twenty percent block of voting stock Cypress will be our largest shareholder. As the largest shareholder they'll have the ear of our board, since the board is supposed to represent shareholders. It would be Cypress' contention that with the largest block of voting stock under their control they have a vested interest in the workings and happenings of LoneStar, and they deserve representation on the board.

"All things considered, it would probably be in the best interest of the board to approve such a request. The board could always reject this proposal, but if Cypress gets really mad they could drag us to court or publicly solicit the other shareholders. You know, start a proxy war. That would set the media off. Not good for business or our stock price. We don't have too many options when you come right down to it."

Rubbing his eyes Brett said, "Damn it all to hell. Might as well arrange a conference call with the directors tomorrow. Ten in the morning. Tonight, send each of them that letter with a cover sheet reminding 'em it's confidential. I'll call the four being shit on this afternoon and give 'em the bad news. Bastards." Waving Chester away Brett covered his eyes with white-knuckled fists. He had some heavy thinking to do.

CHAPTER 11

Friday, July 12, Early Morning
Fort Worth, Texas

It had been three days since Brett called with the bad news and Arthur King was still devastated. To be kicked off the board just wasn't right . . . just wasn't right. But as angry, grieved and offended as he was, Arthur's wife found the situation even more damning. This was a personal humiliation to her, "How could they do such a thing? What's mother going to think?" For three days she'd berated him unmercifully. This morning it was, "Do you know what our friends are saying behind our backs? They're saying you're a failure just like your daddy. Didn't he warn you about Hollister? Now I won't be able to show my face at the club anymore."

Arthur had been pushed off his pedestal both at home and at work. Bizarre rumors of why he suddenly departed from the board of LoneStar ran amok at his small Fort Worth bank. Everything from using drugs, to being gay, to beating his wife were offered as plausible reasons. It was stupid and senseless but he could do nothing about it. Rage continually grew inside him. This was all Hollister's fault, Arthur reasoned. Brett had that board in his hip pocket and could do anything he wanted. Someday, he vowed . . . someday he'd get even.

Same day, 10:30 A.M.
LoneStar Offices, Dallas

Thumbing through his address book Gary Nash was trying to decide who he should call to have lunch with, when the call came in. "Mr. Nash, there's an Ashley Bishop on the line for you."

Gary's pulse quickened. "Please, put her through." She'd already called once in the last week, although it had been just a quick, perfunctory call. But a *second* call? I think she likes me, he thought with equal amounts of conviction and hope. Straightening himself in his chair in an attempt to act more stately, he said, "Hello, Ashley, glad you called."

"Oh, it's so good to hear your voice. Sorry I didn't have much time to talk last week but I'm sure you know how things can get."

"Oh, indeed I do. Things have been pretty hectic around here too."

"I'm sure it's nothing that you can't handle."

"Well, no, you're right. Actually my areas are doing fine but there are a few holes around here that need attention. So we'll see what we can do for them." Gary's chest puffed up a bit at the bravado.

"Are those jackals from The Cypress Group still hanging around? You mentioned they were threatening Mr. Hollister last time we talked."

"They're a bunch of heartless, back-stabbing terrorists. All they want is money. They're going to convert their bonds into stock you know." That'll impress her that she's not talking to some dumb fencepost. "I'm sure they'll be putting pressure on us to increase profits, to get our stock up. That's what I'd do if I were in their shoes." Yes, that's right, little lady. I'm worldly and I can see both sides of a complex issue.

"Well, Gary, since you know what kind of people they are you can help them get what they want."

"Huh? What?"

"I know you've already thought of this, Gary, but with all your knowledge of those 'SWAP things', ah, couldn't you just do more of them? They want more profits and Mr. Hollister said how well you understood SWAPs, and how much money they're making."

Glorious lights exploded within Gary's mind. Sure, what a great idea. He'd be the hero of LoneStar. This could be the best thing ever. "Yes, I've thought about that, ah, but you know Ashley, well of course you don't but let me tell you that SWAPs are highly technical synthetic instruments. Only a very few people really understand them. Those of us who do, know you can't just double up whenever you want. You have to understand durations and convexities, things like that." That had to impress her. Hell, it impressed him! Gary acknowledged he'd have to get Bob Bell to explain those terms to him again, before someone asked what they really meant. Talk about potential embarrassment.

"Gary, you are so fascinating to talk to. I don't think I've ever met anyone quite like you before, and I really want to learn more about securities and stuff. Will you be coming to New York anytime soon?"

Pay dirt, I just hit pay dirt. Gary was jubilant. She wants to see me? "Sure, I get to New York pretty often. Always dealing with Wall Street, you know."

In a very soft, suggestive voice, Ashley uttered, "Oh, right, I forgot. Listen, Gary, please give me a call before you come next time. I really want to get to know you better. You could be a tremendous help to my business career."

"Sure thing. I'll be happy to teach you a thing or two. Bye." He had her eating right out of his hand.

Monday, July 15, 11:25 A.M.
LoneStar's Boardroom

They were all silently looking at one another, sizing each other up. Cypress had four representatives and two lawyers sitting on one side of the conference table, while Brett was on the other flanked by Chester Bennett, Gary Nash, and Emmet Griswald. The meeting wasn't going well.

"I said you don't sound too sure of your numbers, Mr. Hollister. In fact, I'm suspect of all your numbers."

That son of a bitch can't talk to me like that, Brett thought as he did a slow burn. "We know exactly what we're doing, Mr. Victor. I'm not sure I like your implication."

"I'm not sure I like what I see either, Mr. Hollister. You don't seem to have a firm grasp on all these various departments, divisions and companies you've concocted. Can't say I blame you much, with all the inter-company allocations and billings going back and forth. I don't know how anyone could know what's going on. You have over fifty separate companies all reporting their results on home grown software systems that don't interface with each other. I can't figure anything out in this maze, but that shouldn't be my job."

Veins stuck out of Brett's neck and forehead and his color was turning a decidedly deep hue of red, "The fact remains, Mr. Victor . . . "

"The fact remains, Mr. Hollister, that as a major creditor, soon to be a major stockholder of LoneStar International, we are entitled to expect the best possible presentations from senior management. If this is your best, don't bother wasting our time making another." Dabbing at his nose with a white linen handkerchief, Paul Victor, dressed in a custom made suit, pale blue shirt with white collar and cuffs, and a boldly colored silk tie, added, "Let me make myself clear. We are investors. Investors who want to make an acceptable return on their investment. We also want to feel comfortable with the people responsible for ensuring the safety of our investment, in this case you. So why don't you tell us how you're going to kick some life back into this quagmire you've created and jack up profits?"

Brett was beyond being irritated, he was about to go ballistic. Chester whispered in his ear, "Don't do it, Brett. Keep your cool. We have enough problems already."

It was to no avail. Brett's fingers tightened on the table top and he sputtered, "You may be the largest stockholder but don't you ever talk to me like that again! I'm the one and only chairman here! Without me you don't have any investment . . . you got nothing! Don't push me Victor, *I don't like being pushed!*"

Paul Victor elevated his left eyebrow, gave Brett a look that would freeze water and stood up. "Very well, Mr. Hollister, we won't tell you how to run your business, at least not yet. But I expect the profits of this institution to take a dramatic turn for the better and not in a few quarters. I mean now, right now. If you can't do it we'll find someone who can." With that, Victor and his earnings advocating entourage exited. So one meeting was adjourned and another meeting convened with all division heads five minutes later in Brett's private conference room.

Still fuming, Brett said to the assembled group, "I've never been so insulted in all my life." Chester could think of nothing to say, and neither Gary nor Emmet were any too anxious to impart words of wisdom either. In fact, everyone was looking out the window or at whatever was in front of them. Finally, Brett cleared his throat. "Okay, it's pretty damned obvious what those pricks want, just like I said all along. They want quick profits and they want 'em now. So, who around this table has any ideas? Chester?"

"Well, I'm not in line management so . . ."

"Don't give me that crap, Chester. You know as much as anybody what's going on around here. *So don't play dumb now.*"

"Ahh, no sir. I was about to suggest we do another mailing of pre-approved credit cards, lower the standards a bit more so we'll be sure to get to people who'll use the credit lines."

Brett shook his head, "No, that'll take too long. By the time we get the forms sent out, the applications signed and returned, the card mailed and actually used, and the monthly statement issued, it'll be six months from now. We don't have six months. Emmet?"

At the sound of his name Emmet flinched in his seat. Fear was clearly visible in the harried controller. For years Emmet had been excluded from strategic meetings and hadn't a clue what opportunities were available. The exception being one everyone but Brett seemed to grasp. The systems group under Sid Spence was a black hole sucking immense quantities of cash. If it was shut down they'd save a couple million a month. The question was how would Brett react? Systems had always been the fair-haired child and Brett was enamored with high-tech gizmos . . . it's the future, he always said. Brett even dismissed a board member for disagreeing, which was why nobody ever voiced opposition.

"Emmet, I'm waiting."

Tugging on his tie and searching for the right words, Emmet said, "Ah, can we sellanypropertyiabnhdin, or anyassetsmcojan, umm, with gains nononjdinthem?" Better to leave the fair-haired child alone.

"Did you say sell assets? I don't know. Not a bad thought, Emmet. Gary, we have anything lying around that we can sell?"

It was a well-known fact Gary possessed an uncanny ability to recall specific information concerning LoneStar. Gary closed his eyes and quickly skimmed a list of corporate assets handily stored in his memory banks. "No, no we don't. Anything of any value has already been sold."

Brett's head was downcast, shoulders slumped. Anyone who knew anything about him could tell he was a very desperate man. "I'll listen to anybody. Anyone have any ideas?" Brett was pleading to them.

Agonizing seconds ticked away until Gary Nash cleared his throat and said, "Well, there might be a way."

Looking at the corporate treasurer like he'd just been thrown a life jacket, Brett said, "I'm listening, Gary."

Savoring the moment of glory, Gary said, "What I mean is, if I were to go to New York, talk to some of my contacts there, we might be able to increase our SWAP profits enough to get Cypress off our backs." Gary leaned back and waited.

Brett pounded the table, "Yes, *yes*, that's the ticket. Good work, Gary. Leave as soon as you can. Tell me what we have to do and I'll push whatever it is through the board. Damn, damn, this'll work, this'll work." Brett was beaming. "Gary, you pull this off for me and you'll get a fat bonus."

The other senior managers were starting to believe the legend that Gary Nash was truly blessed. He'd just gotten Brett off their backs, Cypress would love him, and his bank account would be overflowing. So what made him so smart all of a sudden?

Friday, July 19, Early Morning
Birmingham, Michigan

Rick felt terrible, and ecstatic, both at the same time. He'd just let his wife down in every sense of the word, but had the greatest time of his life doing it. These conflicting moral and physical sensations were bouncing around inside his brain as he drove home at three o'clock in the morning. What are you going to do? he asked himself. What, are you going to say? How on earth did it happen? How could you let it happen? But I'm so glad it did happen.

He remembered counting the hours before his private meeting with the haunting Ashley Taylor-Bishop. Their dinner started off as most business dinners. Ashley ordered white wine, he had a scotch. She was lovely as expected; everyone at the Townsend gave her second and often third looks. Wearing a double-breasted black brocade evening suit that showed off her cleavage, Rick was permitted to leer anew. Some patrons even stared at Rick, presuming that he must have something on the ball to be sitting with this captivating creature.

She laughed at all his jokes, her smile was dazzling, her wit charming and his heart was on his sleeve. Even the dining room's old world ambiance contributed nicely to their intimate dinner . . . the hotel catered to the rich and famous, and elegant dining in hushed tones was the canon. Still, there was a twinge of guilt. Probably because he twisted the truth to his wife regarding this 'business dinner.' He conveniently left out the part about who he'd be dining with and where, only that it was an out of town customer and he was expected to attend.

Sometime during the dinner, about the time of his fourth scotch, Rick began to take offense at his wife. Why had she let herself go like she had? Her weight was up, the circles under her eyes were more pronounced, she never exercised, seldom looked alluring, whenever he walked through the door from a hard day's work she'd be more than likely crying or angry. Hell, the list could go on and on, but the main point was: Didn't he deserve better?

That's when he glanced at Ashley who was everything he always wanted, and somehow it happened. One moment they were having after dinner drinks, then they were in an elevator walking to her room, then they were inside the room for a nightcap, then they were touching, kissing, holding each other, and then . . . it just happened.

She was adorable after they'd made love, still in the bed, under the covers, listening to the sweet melody of light classical music. She told him how he made her feel so safe and warm inside. How he was so romantic and considerate, and what a gentle lover he was, not demanding like some others. How lucky the women in his life were and how Ashley envied them.

Lightly drawing her fingers along his skin, Ashley confessed she wanted their friendship to continue even if they were never intimate again, and could they continue calling each other? This passionate goddess almost begged him to say 'Yes,' and he did with every fiber of his being. They kissed as he left the room and Rick never felt so vibrant, so young . . . so alive.

The best course of action he finally resolved, pulling into the three-car attached garage, was to say nothing, at least not until he had a chance to clear his thoughts. He'd simply explain that the customer was flying out in the morning and they had to settle some major business issues before he left. Sorry it took so long, honey, but once I realized how late it was I didn't want to call and wake you . . . something like that.

There was no sound in the house as he entered. Rick crept up to his bedroom, into the bathroom, changed clothes and as quietly as possible slid into bed. Stephanie moaned, turned over and patted him on the leg. Feeling a rush of relief at not being confronted, Rick rolled over and closed his eyes. Yeah, in the morning she'd buy his story. Why shouldn't she? It was a good story. Hell, he almost believed it himself.

CHAPTER 12

Wednesday, July 24
Financial District, Manhattan

The Lower Manhattan offices of Pagent & Associates inhabited three entire floors of a venerable skyscraper that offered a magnificent view of Ellis Island and the Hudson River. Two of the floors were used exclusively for offices and conference rooms, while the third was dedicated to trading operations. Gary Nash always enjoyed visiting Wall Street, particularly the trading floors, no matter whose. Rows and rows of tiny prefab desks with eye level shelves were home to both sales staff and traders. Each small station was usually void of desk drawers but contained anywhere from one to six monitors arrayed in seemingly haphazard order, all flashing numbers, codes, letters and charts. How the individual salesman or trader ever figured out what they were looking at was beyond him.

Most trading floors were divided into sections, although the casual observer would never know it. One section might be for equities (stocks), another might be municipal bonds, mortgage backs, Treasury's, options, whatever the investment house specialized in. The activity varied from section to section. On any given day there would be sales staff leisurely reading newspapers, jotting down something on a form, drinking coffee or talking to coworkers, while others a few yards away were standing up and literally yelling at their respective trading desk, trying to execute some transaction.

Managing Director, Bob Bell had reserved a conference room for today's meeting with Gary Nash. Coffee, Danish, rolls, orange juice, fruit and an assortment of soft drinks were all laid out on the buffet table. The dapper attired Larry Hendricks had rushed in late and was now munching away on a bagel spread lightly with cream cheese. Gary watched Bob who was in deep thought, absent mindedly stirring black coffee with a ball point pen.

After he finished relaying the broad facts of the Cypress meeting in Dallas, Gary had expected Bob's immediate concurrence to increasing the SWAP position, but the man was taking a long time to reply . . . too long. Wanting to move the conversation along, Gary said, "Bob, you know we need a quick injection of earnings. We need to do something to give us breathing space." Gary mulled things over for another second and then added, "That's why I personally flew out here, because it's so vital to LoneStar. We're expecting your help." No need to tell him the other reason was to have dinner tonight with the most gorgeous creature he'd ever met.

Bob finally answered. "Gary, you guys already have a ton of SWAPs, more than firms twice your size. Adding more could become an issue with your auditors or your board."

"That's not the point, Bob. We need earnings and we need them now!"

"Well, rather than add to your position I suppose you might consider removing the collar on your SWAPs. You know, strip off the interest rate protection program. You'll bring in more cash today but let's be frank; your exposure to interest rate swings would be considerable."

Without hesitating Gary said, "How much more could we make?" Why should he care about what may happen months or years from now? Paul Victor was gonna break their balls next week!

Still not convinced it was a smart play, Bob Bell offered, "I'll have Larry run some numbers for you, but in today's market you'd probably pull in a total SWAP income of five million a month. Maybe more"

"*Five million.*" Gary couldn't believe it. He could personally add sixty million to LoneStar's bottom line annually? Hot damn, he'd be famous . . . rich . . . rich and famous.

Bob was shaking his head, "Listen. We're gonna need more collateral. In order to take the collars off we'll need to increase the amount of pledged assets. We have to protect ourselves, you know?"

All Gary could think about was the five million a month. Christ, that's all they'd need. Why didn't he think of this sooner? "Ah, what did you say, Bob?

More collateral? Sure, sure. Just tell me how much."
Who gives a damn about collateral?

"I don't know yet, but we'll probably want to double the amount you've pledged already. Is that going to be a problem?"

If it was, Brett would figure something out. "No, no that's not a problem." Gary was practically drooling. "When can we do it?"

"As soon as we get some new agreements and disclosure forms drafted and signed. Probably next week."

Gary nodded, "Okay, let me make some calls. How about you two come back in an hour or so?"

As Bob Bell and Larry Hendricks both stood up, Bob added, "Gary, really think about what you're doing."

This from a guy wearing enough gold jewelry to buy a small Caribbean island? "Always do Bob, always do." What was the matter with these guys?

Same day, same time,
LoneStar Offices

"So that's the deal, Brett. You need me for anything else?"

"No. You've done great, Gary. I'll find out about the collateral and then I'll contact the board's executive committee. That way I'll only have to get a few directors involved, and since they can act on behalf of the whole board why bother the rest?"

Moreover, Brett didn't have the time or inclination to explain himself to the whole board.

There was a lilt in the treasurer's voice as he said, "Brett, it's getting late and I've got to wrap up a few more things so I'll spend the night. I'll be back tomorrow afternoon."

"Sure, no problem. Thanks, Gary. You really came through for me. Bye." For the first time in a while, Brett relaxed. Now let's find out what kind of collateral we have around here, he said to himself. "Suzanne, get me Emmet Griswald."

Seconds later he heard, "Mr. Griswald is on line one, Mr. Hollister."

"Emmet, I need collateral to pledge to Pagent, the New York investment house for my SWAPs. What've we got around here?"

"Ah, well, I'm afraid we don't have much. The, ah, treasury securities are already pledged, and the only, umm marketable properties were just sold to make thelastdebtpaymentonovwoainv."

Brett gripped the phone and shook it, "That's not a good answer. Think man, think. Where can we come up with collateral by next week?" This has got to work, Brett muttered silently. I won't let that scum Victor push me outta here.

After a pause, Emmet came up with an idea, but by the tone of his halting speech it was plain he didn't enjoy sharing it. "Ah, Brett, the only, umm way we can lay our handsonthatkindonvoe of money, ah, by next week, is to . . . draw down on our bankworkingcapitallinesomawoweihveo. Umm, It's not what we're supposediownuio use the line for, but we can probablypullitoffomweu. I can start drawing a few million every day, so ah, they won't noticesomuchweoivmoe."

About damned time that pain in the ass said something useful. They could draw down on various bank lines of credit. As long as the banks didn't catch on to what they were using the funds for it would work. "Right, do it, Emmet. Begin immediately. Now you call me back if you have any problems, but I don't want to hear any." Brett disconnected the line. One down and one to go. "Suzanne, put in a call to the executive committee members. I don't care where they are, I need to talk to them."

Within two minutes his secretary announced, "Mr. Hollister? I have Mr. Kelly on line one."

Excellent. "Afternoon, Warren. Sorry to bother you but we have an opportunity here and we have to move fast."

Same day, 5:10 P.M.
Lansing, Michigan

"Almost time to go home, you have any big plans tonight?" Jenny Hilborn was just finishing signing some paperwork at her party's office in Lansing, Michigan. The bright eyed, wide bodied, Sandy Skamansky stood over her waiting for a response.

"We're having dinner tonight with Senator Whippel and his wife if traffic will cooperate." That was true enough, the traffic in the state capital could be atrocious at day's end. "I'm not looking forward to hearing about Charles' commute either," Jenny grumbled. "He hates driving and it'll take an hour for him to get here from Ann Arbor."

"Say, how's Charles liking his new role, board director isn't it?"

"Yes. I guess you can say it's a challenge. Definitely not for everyone, but I think he's finding it interesting."

"It's not local I hear."

"No, it's in Dallas. A company called LoneStar."

Sandy hesitated a moment then said, "LoneStar, LoneStar. Something familiar about that name. Have I seen it advertised on TV?"

Jenny shrugged, "Could be, they're into an awful lot of things, credit cards, insurance, real estate, mortgages, property management, construction . . . a man by the name of Brett Hollister runs it."

"Brett Hollister? That sounds familiar too. Where have I heard of him?" Sandy couldn't place it, and added, "It's like I overheard an offhanded remark in a hallway or someplace like a restroom. Somewhere that wasn't private and that's why it stuck me, because what I heard should have been discussed in private. But I just can't remember." She shook her head and shoved the last of a Twinkie into her mouth. "I'm sure it's nothing, Jenny. Listen, you give Charles a big hug and kiss for me. He's such a stud muffin."

"Watch it, woman."

Swallowing, Sandy confided woman-to-woman, "Don't let Senator Whippel choose the wine tonight. The man doesn't know the difference between a cork and a screw." Both ladies laughed and were still chuckling as they left party headquarters and headed in different directions.

Same day, 9:55 P.M.
Mid-Town, Manhattan

On top of the world. What else could he possibly ask for? Breaking a piece of bread Gary waved it around and said, "I hope you don't mind a good steak for dinner. I try to eat here every time I come to New York." Gary really did like a good steak and while the atmosphere at Smith & Wollensky's was far less elegant than the Double Eagle in Dallas, the food was every bit its match.

"No, this is wonderful, Gary. I actually love the waiters in those coats and white aprons. Gives the place a certain turn-of-the-century charm."

Pouring more red wine for both of them Gary continued explaining about his day in the city, "Anyway, it looks like those Pagent boys and I will be able to restructure our SWAPs to take advantage of the yield curve. Could be worth millions a month to us." Gary could tell that Ashley was hanging on his every word.

"I sure envy your knowledge about the financial markets. It's so interesting what you do. All those power lunches you go to and working with Wall Street investment bankers. You're one very impressive man and I'm learning so much from you," Ashley's stunning smile turned sensual as she continued. "Gary, I was wondering if we might go to your hotel, you know, we could have a drink in your room and talk more about SWAPs."

The feeling of jubilant lightheadedness that bowled him over when they first met reemerged, and he had to fold his hands to keep them from shaking. "Why yes, yes. That's a wonderful suggestion. Yes, a bit too noisy in here to have a decent discussion, anyway. Let me get the check." No doubt about it, this lovely vision was head-over-heals for him.

Riding in a cab up Third Street, Gary was bubbling with anticipation. He could only imagine what thoughts were going through Ashley's mind. The cab turned west on 55th Street and he firmly placed his hand on her knee.

* * *

The cab bounced and changed lanes about fifty times in the span of six blocks. Ashley was lost in thought too and didn't even notice the hand fondling her kneecap. Come on girl, she urged herself, this won't be so bad. Look, he's going to be so easy to handle that it'll be over in twenty minutes. Who knows, he may even surprise you. Besides, he's a fountain of information and you need him. So smile at the horse's ass like you mean it.

Ashley smiled like a cat about to lap milk. The cab made a few quick turns and deposited them at the Parker Meridian hotel on 56th Street between Sixth and Seventh Avenue. They walked through the lobby and around to the second bank of elevators. Gary pushed his floor, looked around and said, "I like this place. Very continental. A lot of European guests come here. I hear people speaking French all the time. The service is excellent. I understand there's a gym next door but that's something that I've never paid much attention to." He patted his stomach and added, "I should start though, huh?"

Guiding her arm through his Ashley winked and said, "Oh, I don't know. You look pretty good to me."

After being deposited on his floor they entered the hotel room. Straightaway, Gary poured them both a drink from a fresh bottle of Jack Daniels. "Here's looking at you kid," He drained his glass like Humphrey Bogart once did in an old movie.

Draining her drink too, but more to numb her senses than anything else, Ashley said, "Gary, if I go put on something that I brought along would you think me wicked?"

"No, no, not at all. Ashley, you're the most beautiful woman I've ever known." She knew that Gary was feeling like a kid, a kid ready to explode, and she knew from experience that men said the most darned things when they got all whipped up into an emotional froth.

"Why don't you make yourself comfortable, pour us another drink and I'll go change." After ten of the longest minutes Gary probably ever spent in his life, Ashley floated back into the room. His eyes bugged out and his mouth dropped open. She was wearing a sheer black strapless bodysuit with push-up cups and a plunging V-centre, and lace top thigh high black stockings. "You like?"

His cracking voice failed to produce any intelligible sound and he was clawing the armchair's upholstery. It was all he could do to mutter, "I'm gonna die." She smiled seductively. He was hers, totally, passionately, and unequivocally. Whatever she wanted from him, she'd get. No way was he going to disappoint her tonight.

Long before the estimated twenty minutes she'd allocated for shop talk and hasty sex, Gary was rolling over to wrap himself into the folds of blissful sleep. He hadn't disappointed Ashley, not verbally at least. As she put her street clothes back on she was thunderstruck by the absolute incompetence of

Hollister and his senior staff. Paul Victor forcing the four board members out couldn't be helped, although it sounded like Arthur King took it pretty badly. A call to Arthur was in order . . . couldn't hurt. But imagine, dropping the collars on the SWAPs without understanding the consequences.

She'd wanted them to add to their SWAP position, which is why she suggested it to Gary in the first place. But her motive was to quickly inject earnings and get the stock price up. Now a sharp move in interest rates could literally wipeout LoneStar. Regrettably, the timing wasn't right. The stock needed to go a lot higher before blowing up. Silently closing the hotel door on the sleeping Mr. Nash, Ashley walked back to the elevators. She checked herself in the hallway mirror and asked her reflection why couldn't life be simple anymore?

Thursday, August 1, 9:05 A.M.
Cypress Offices, Manhattan

Corporate offices have portrayed status in the investment community since the late 1800's, with rich furnishings, original art pieces, glitz and glamour. Being egotistical trend setters themselves, each Cypress partner continued the tradition of outdoing the others in amassing not only extravagant objects for display but enormous profits for their clients. These principals helped establish an unspoken creed at Cypress: Nothing was off limits as long as you weren't caught, and that included paying for insider information.

"Dammit. I should have known that stupid son of a bitch would try something like this." Paul Victor had just found out from his 'snitch' at Bob Bell's company that LoneStar had dropped the collar protection on the SWAPs. He rubbed his sore nose and muttered, "Those assholes must think I'm some sort of fucking idiot. I can't believe Hollister. Hell, one upward spike in interest rates and he'll lose the whole fucking company . . . taking us with him." Paul's three subordinate portfolio managers at The Cypress Group, and soon-to-be board members of LoneStar, weren't happy either. With the stock price at forty-four dollars Cypress' original investment had quickly turned into a twenty million dollar profit, and each man had a good percentage of that twenty million. "Well, that's it," he continued, "I'm not going to have some knucklehead pissing away my money. Who's got his fucking phone number?" There were going to be some drastic changes.

Same day, Same time,
LoneStar, Chairman's Office

"Go to hell!" Brett slammed the phone down, stood up and started pacing around his desk. Seething from head to toe he shouted, "Shit, damn, son of a bitch! I won't take that crap from anybody!" His gruff voice blasted out to his secretary, "Suzanne, get Bennett in here and I don't care what he's doing." He slapped the back of his chair and added, "Nobody's going to tell me what to do. Who does that little prick think he is anyway?"

"*Where's Bennett for Christ sake?*" Walking over to the bar he poured himself half a glass of Jack Daniels. Looking at his image in the mirrored wall he noticed for the first time deep lines spreading out from the corners of his eyes. Moving his face closer more wrinkles appeared, along with more gray hairs then he'd ever seen before. Used to be he looked younger than his age, but now . . . It was all the stress he was under, mostly from that bastard Paul Victor. Sure as shit that last phone call hadn't helped matters one damned bit.

"He's coming now Mr. Hollister. Here he is."

Hurrying to accommodate his boss Chester hustled into the office and said, "Hi, Brett, what can I do—"

Brett motioned for him to shut up and sit down in the chair facing his desk. "I just got off the phone with that s-o-b, Paul Victor. The scum doesn't like the way we're going to increase his revenue. Too damn bad I told him. He wanted to know if I gave the orders myself, so I say no, the goddamned Executive Committee of the Board approved the transaction. Then he gets really pissed, says they can't do something like that and I tell him that it's their right under our by-laws to act on behalf of the full board.

"So he asks me who's the chairman of this committee and I say it's me. Then he really explodes, says that having me being president, chairman of the board and now the chairman of the Executive Committee is a pure power play on my part without any checks or balances. Victor says he's going to have his lawyers explain the facts of fiduciary responsibility to our other directors and if they don't take some action he'll sue us all.

"He also wants those SWAP collars back on immediately and then he wants to close out the entire SWAP position. To top it off he says we should try earning our paychecks for once in our life. That's when I told him to go to hell." Brett's breathing was labored but not enough to stop him from draining his drink.

Chester, the levelheaded litigator spoke calmly, "Brett, the last thing we need is a shareholder suit filed against us. The publicity would damage you and LoneStar, and everything that means anything to us. We can't let that happen. Even if we haven't done anything wrong the press would muck this around for months, driving away customers."

Sitting back down Brett nodded and said, "Okay, I see your point. So what do we do?"

Chester thought for a moment and answered, "Well. I suggest you give up your chairmanship of the Executive Committee. Then he won't be able to say or do anything."

Brett turned on his general counsel and exploded, "Who the fuck is gonna take my place? Victor? *You?*"

Chester quickly responded, "No, Victor won't stand for me taking it and you won't stand for him taking it. What we have to do is propose someone neutral. Someone that he's not going to gripe about being in your hip pocket."

Glaring at Chester, Brett stated, "I *want* someone in my goddamned hip pocket. Listen, the chairman of the Executive Committee can do just about any damn thing he wants. He can get in my shorts and poke around all damn day."

Chester shrugged, "So what's left, Brett? A shareholder revolt? Cypress is our major shareholder and Victor knows he can push us to the wall on this one. You don't want to get into a public pissing match with the man over this issue, do you?"

Brett considered the arguments while simmering. Finally, he asked, "So who do you suggest?"

"There's only one director at LoneStar who's new enough not to be tainted, at least in Victor's eyes. Victor would have no grounds for refusing Charles Hilborn."

Squeezing his eyes together Brett blurted out, "Aw no, not Hilborn. Christ, he just gets done with that consultant bullshit and now I'm supposed to reward him? I'm supposed to smile and say no hard feelings, we need your wisdom, please take this position 'cause you're a hell of a guy?"

Looking hard at Brett, Chester answered, "Yes, that's exactly what you say. And you hope to hell he takes it. Because if Victor can't be made to back off we'll be in a hole deeper than you could possibly imagine, particularly if he exploits that last committee resolution on the SWAPs. Look, it wasn't the smartest thing for the Executive Committee to do. No decision of that magnitude should've been voted on over the phone without any documentation or supporting facts."

Sensing that Chester knew what he was talking about Brett relented as he always did on legal matters. "All right, all right. But as soon as we straighten out this mess, Hilborn's gone along with Victor. I don't trust either of 'em."

CHAPTER 13

Friday, August 2, 2:45 P.M.
Smith-Palmer & Co., Detroit

Rick Blaine was in a reflective mood sitting at his desk, staring blankly at his computer screen that was flashing little red or green rectangles signifying various stocks decreasing or increasing in price. So far everything at Smith-Palmer & Co. was progressing splendidly. Rick liked his new job, the research reports came naturally to him, the sales staff had crowned him guru of the month for his 'buy' recommendation on LoneStar, and he'd just been told his paycheck would be healthier due to the increased sales commissions generated by his reports.

Life at home was still the same, but fortunately there was never a hint of his recent indiscretion. Rick had to admit however, it wasn't easy walking past the good Reverend Ryan Sladden at last Sunday's church service. Ryan had asked him why he'd dropped out of sight, was everything going all right? Oh yes, everything was just fine, got a new job and the family didn't have to move . . . no problems at all.

Just one problem really, though he couldn't very well talk to his minister about it. Rick just couldn't keep Ashley out of his mind. She was with him constantly. Her face, smile, hands, legs, voice . . . everything. He wanted to see her again more than he ever thought possible, which wasn't exactly the kind of behavior typically embraced by church clergy.

Reaching for his phone he decided to give her a call. Nothing wrong in seeing how she's doing, right? She's going to have to fly through Detroit again sooner or later. Hey, wait a second. I feel like a hormone plagued kid going out on a first date. Look, my hands are sweaty from just thinking about calling her. Okay, so just do it.

"Taylor-Bishop Company. Can I help you?"

"Yes, please. Is Ash . . . , I mean is Ms Bishop there, ah, available, to um, talk to me?"

"I'm sorry; Ms. Bishop is on another call right now. Would you care to leave your name and number?"

"Ah, no, no. Just tell her that . . . no it's all right, I'll call back later. Goodbye." Rick shook his head at himself as he quickly hung up the phone. Just like my first date, he groaned. I couldn't complete a full sentence then either.

Same day, Same time
Hospital, Ohio State University

"Hi Courtney, what's happening? I'm not interrupting anything am I?" Stephanie Blaine often called her little sister, especially since their dad had taken early retirement and was off island hopping with mom. But it was odd for her sister to phone the hospital. Courtney Keller rubbed the back of her neck as a nurse placed a mug of steaming black coffee in front of her. Some days were worse than others, this was one of them. "Hey, Steph, good to hear you. No, this is fine. I'm not due in surgery for awhile."

"Any doctors sweeping you off your feet or are you still playing hard to get?"

Stephanie always enjoyed poking fun at the carefree singles lifestyle of her little sister. Courtney scrunched up her nose and replied, "Most of the doctor's around here are more infatuated with themselves than they could ever be with me." Ain't it the truth, she sighed to herself. Oh, they'd still hit on her, drawn by her strawberry blonde hair, gold tinted eyes, trim figure and shapely legs. But she'd given up pursuing shallow affairs ever since graduating from college. Being thirty-something changed one's perspectives.

The inquisitive older sister persisted, "So what *are* you doing for a love life?"

"Actually, I've just started going out with someone new. You won't believe how we met. There's this charming old woman who lost her husband a little while ago. Anyway, she comes by to see me at the hospital. We sort of bonded while her husband was here. So she tells me what a darling girl I am and that I'm just about the prettiest thing she's ever seen, and how much she appreciated my kindness to her husband. All very nice I say, and thank her. But you know what? Seems that she knows this single young man who invests money for her. Apparently, he's been doing really well and recently asked for some referrals.

"So with my permission, she's such a dear, she calls the guy up, his name's Mike Kilpatrick, and arranges a blind date, only he thinks we're meeting for a financial planning session. Well, turns out he's kind of cute, runs his own business and needs some exercise. So I'm playing tennis with him twice a week. Beating the pants off him . . . but he doesn't have that macho need to win, so we're getting along fine."

"He's a lucky fellow. I'm really pleased for you."

"Thanks. So how's Rick's new job going?"

"Oh, okay I guess. But, well, I've gotta tell you we seem to be drifting apart. I think he expects me to look like a model or something every night. I drive the kids around all day, keep the house up, run errands, attend school and church meetings, get things fixed, solve the boys' problems, clean up after everyone, wash dirty clothes . . . the list is endless."

"Sounds like you're both going through mid-life crisis or something."

"Yeah. He seems more distant lately, like . . . , oh, I don't know what."

"Hey, you're a terrific girl, Rick knows that. I'm sure you'll both work this out. You each just need a little more time together, you know, maybe without the kids."

"Good idea, but who am I going to get to watch the kids? Mom and dad are who knows where, you're out of state . . . and besides who's got the time?"

Courtney's voice was firm, "Don't screw up, Stephanie. Single life isn't all it's cracked up to be." A frantic nurse was pointing to a wall clock and waving at her from behind the doorway. Ignoring the gesticulations Courtney sipped the hot brew and said, "Listen, I gotta run pretty soon."

"Sure, me too. I'll call you again. Best of luck with Mike. Goodbye."

"Bye now." The activity outside the small office was bordering on chaos. Doctors, nurses and administrators were all jockeying for her attention. Tuning them out Courtney let her eyes wander to the framed photographs on her desk, settling on the family picture taken two years ago. Mom, dad, Steph and herself all dressed to the nines for dad's early retirement party. Rick was there too . . . a very handsome man. Her eyes then casually flickered to the other photograph and a big smile broke across her face. There they were, she and her college roommate, best buddies, sorority sisters and consummate flirts for two glorious years. She really had to give her a call.

Same day, Same time
Taylor-Bishop Offices, Manhattan

Deception was a constant ally of hers now, after learning about it long ago the hard way. This was just business, nothing personal. The call was being put through and Ashley waited, noticing that her other line was flashing. Whoever was calling Joyce could handle. This call was too important to postpone. Finally she heard, "This is Arthur King, how can I help you?"

"Thank you for taking my call, Mr. King. My name is Ashley Taylor-Bishop. I have my own financial services company in New York. I was recently made aware of your resignation as a director from LoneStar International. To be honest with you Mr. King, that's why I'm calling."

She could almost see him clenching his jaw as he said, "I see. You know young lady, you're not the first one to contact me. I'm only sorry I took the call. I don't want to hear any more rumors or suppositions about myself on why I left LoneStar. Now if you will excuse me –"

"Please, Mr. King. I have no intention of saying anything like that. Quite the contrary. I have been following your career for many years."

There was a pause, followed by: "I don't understand."

"Mr. King, I'm trying to expand our investment services into the southwest, which includes Texas obviously. I need someone who's familiar with that territory to help make introductions for me. I'd heard about you some time ago but knew you might feel awkward, since you were already on the board of LoneStar. I know your bank has decided not to offer upscale private financial services and that you're referring those clients to LoneStar. Well, those are the same clients I'm after. Do you see what I'm getting at, Mr. King?"

Arthur would know exactly what she was getting at. The question was whether he'd like it. "Yes, yes I do. Please call me Arthur and forgive me for my little outburst. It's been a little frantic around here lately, Miss . . . I'm sorry, I didn't get your name."

"Oh, please call me Ashley."

"Yes, of course, Ashley."

"Arthur, we're a multi-million dollar international company. We need people who have vision to not only help us grow now but to propel us into the future." She knew he didn't care about any of that. That's not why her offer would intrigue him.

"To tell you the truth Ashley, nothing would please me more than to help you pull business away from LoneStar."

"That would be wonderful, Arthur. What I'd like to do is to send you some information on us. I'm sure we can work out a suitable arrangement."

"I'd like that, Ashley."

"Arthur, I'd like to offer you a seat on our board. I think you'd be impressed with who we have on it and our board meetings are held in different locations throughout the world. Last quarter we met in London, before that . . . Tokyo. Naturally, all expenses are picked up by us, for both you *and* your wife. Her name is Doris isn't it?"

Doing research on the intended prey had always been Ashley's strong suit. She could tell Arthur was giddy with what she was offering. It was just the ticket to get his bitchy wife Doris back into that snobby country club of hers. Free trips around the world were good perks and sounded a thousand times better than stale meetings in Dallas.

Arthur cleared his throat and said, "Yes, her name is Doris. Ashley, I just know we can work something out. I'd like to start discussions as soon as possible."

Gazing out her office window Ashley beamed at Arthur King's exuberance to her make-believe offer. Score for the home team, she mused. I guess that twenty minutes with Nash was worth the effort. Now Arthur, if my female intuition is on target you must know some pretty juicy tidbits about Brett and the boys. So here's your chance to give. "That's great, Arthur. Now, not to beat a dead horse but we've been hearing some rather unpleasant things about LoneStar. I guess nobody really blames you for resigning. My good fortune, that's how I look at it."

A bitter voice replied, "You don't know the half of it. Hollister and his crowd have done some pretty unbelievable things over the years."

Ashley nonchalantly replied, "Really, Arthur? I can't believe that Mr. Hollister ever did anything that I haven't heard of before." The moment had arrived. Come on, come on . . .

Arthur's bitter voice now sounded a little offended. "No? You know anyone who engineered having his own employees send in political contributions to certain candidates and then padded the employees expense reports so they'd each get reimbursed?"

Making a note of it Ashley grinned and said, "He did?" This was a new one for her. Illegal as hell, but new.

Arthur continued, "He sure did. He's got a rookie congressmen in his pocket because of it."

"Amazing."

"Know what else? He's been able to cook the books, you know, overstate earnings."

She shook her head in disbelief, "Whoa, wait a minute. How can he do that with an outside accounting firm checking everything? Isn't Russell, Powell and Young the certified public accounts for LoneStar?"

"You just don't understand the way Hollister works. Ever wonder why LoneStars' had the same public accounting firm forever? Ever wonder why no one else ever gets a chance to bid for the business? Ever wonder why the accounting fees are twice as much as they should be? Brett's bought them off."

She was still skeptical, "I can't believe that, Arthur. How could any accounting firm knowingly put itself into that kind of a position?"

"Easy. Look around, notice all the mega-mergers going on in all major industries. Every time two big firms merge one of the outside accounting firm's ends up being one too many. That's a tremendous loss of revenue for the loser. See, public accounting firms are getting squeezed like everyone else. Now suppose you're guaranteed a sweetheart deal and all you have to do is be a little less aggressive in researching a few transactions over here, and pass over a few entries over there. Who's going to know?"

She thought about it for a moment, "He's really quite a character, isn't he? Listen, I've got to run but I'll make sure we send out that information. Goodbye, Arthur. I look forward to working with you."

"Wait, make sure to attach your business card with the package, Miss, uh . . ."

Having no intention of ever talking to him again Ashley quickly replaced the receiver. Her mind was already racing.

Monday, August 5, 8:25 A.M.
Cypress Offices, Manhattan

The door to his office was partially open so he heard his assistant answer the telephone on the second ring. "Cypress Group. Mr. Paul Victor's office. Can I help you?" There was a short pause and then, "Paul, a Jackie from Taylor-Bishop for you."

With no hesitation Paul picked up the line. "Yeah?"

"It's me."

The voice calling was familiar and he instinctively lowered his own, "Are you alone?"

She followed his lead and lowered her voice too, "Yes, for the moment."

Maintaining the hushed tones, he asked, "So have you found out anything? What's she up to?" There was nothing like having someone right in the enemy's camp sending out smoke signals.

The female voice responded in a whisper, "All I know is that Ashley hasn't purchased any LoneStar stock yet. I'm too new to be in her strategy meetings so all I can do is look over shoulders and wade through waste baskets."

"Right, right. Look, you're doing fine, just keep your eyes open. She's up to something. Why else would she have said what she did at the annual meeting?"

"I have no idea. By the way, about my money . . ."

"Yeah, I know. I'll have five thousand delivered tomorrow morning."

"Thanks, I'll call you when I get something else. Bye."

"Bye." Paul replaced the receiver and leaned back in his chair. Now what was The Fallen Angel up to? She'd just about singlehandedly saved that dumbass Brett Hollister from flushing LoneStar's stock down the toilet . . . coming up with that 'for sale' proclamation. Now the price was up to . . . to what? Let's see . . . holy shit! It's hit a forty-six dollar handle. That's six bucks above the forty-dollar strike price. That's thirty million bucks we're up . . . son of a bitch. But why isn't she buying the stock? Where's her profit, what's her angle? She never does anything without an angle.

Paul doodled on a scratch pad by multiplying the five million shares they now owned by six dollars, then ten and then twenty. Those were the profit potentials from LoneStar's soaring stock price. But why wasn't Bishop jumping in? He puzzled on that for the next half hour and couldn't figure it out.

Wednesday, August 7, Early Afternoon
Hilborn Residence, Ann Arbor

During summer recess without any classes to teach, Charles typically immersed himself into books and research reports. Unlike bygone years however, the stacks of scholarly manuscripts and papers overflowing the living room tables and chairs today weren't retelling anesthetizing history lessons, but rather offering modern business management theories, strategies and case studies. "Here, let me read that." Jenny Hilborn held her hand out and was not to be put off.

Charles handed her the piece of paper and walked over to the idle fireplace. "Okay, you read it. That's the description of the executive committee's responsibilities." Charles had told his wife of Brett's call and surprising request. Chester had emailed over some information to make the decision a little more informed.

Jenny looked at something called "The Resolution Establishing and Defining the Duties of the Board Committees." She read it once then said aloud, "And I quote, 'The Executive Committee shall have and shall be entitled to exercise all the powers of the Board of Directors of the Company in the management of the property, business and affairs of the Company and may authorize the seal of the Company to be affixed to all papers which might require it, the only limitation placed upon the powers of the Executive Committee being that it shall exercise the powers of the Board of Directors only to the extent permitted by law.' Charles, you could run the company with these powers if you wanted."

He nodded in agreement, "So it would seem."

"Why do they want you to chair this? You've never run a company before."

"Brett says it's because I'm such a worldly guy, you know, I've been around. Besides, I'm intelligent, he wants to rely on me more and more, so on and so forth. Chester says it's because they're in a tight spot with a major stockholder. Seems this stockholder doesn't want Brett to be the president, chairman of the board and chairman of the executive committee. Thinks it's too much power for any one individual. Can't say I disagree."

"Fine, so put someone else there, why you?"

"I'll forgo what Brett said and only relay what Chester said, it'll save time. Chester said most of the board members are beholden to Brett and everyone knows it. The only member who isn't in that category is me."

Jenny looked hard at Charles and said, "Are you going to accept?"

Charles paused and answered the question with a question of his own, "Should I?"

She started to wave her finger at him, thought better of it and in a stern voice said, "Do you know what you're getting into? Remember what that consultant Adam Sanchez said and what happened at the annual meeting. You have to admit Brett seems to have his own agenda and you don't know what it is."

Plopping himself down on the overstuffed sofa in their living room Charles leaned back and gazed at the ceiling. "The chairman of the executive committee is supposed to be a check and balance. You know, get in the way when it's called for, and protect the shareholders' interests and all that. It's what I'd expect my students to do in similar circumstances."

Jenny inhaled deeply, "Yes, I suppose it is. Okay hotshot it's your life. Only don't be surprised if they don't play nice."

CHAPTER 14

Friday, August 9, 10:10 A.M.
LoneStar Offices, Dallas

Another plane took off from Love Field. Gary Nash sat at his desk gazing at his personal bank statement that now totaled six hundred and thirteen thousand dollars. Every month the money seemed to flow in, which caused him no small amount of second guessing. If only I would have done this sooner, he thought. If only it was double or triple this amount then I could retire and get that vacation home at Copper Mountain. Face it, you're blessed, everything's going your way. Everyone says so. When you're on a lucky streak you don't cash in and go home. No way. Grabbing his phone he dialed the managing director of Pagent & Associates, New York.

"Bob Bell, speaking."

"Hey, Bob. Gary Nash."

"How's it going, Gary?"

"Great. Couple of things. First, I need to know what we'd have to do to unbundle the SWAPs. You know, cancel them out."

There was a slight gasp on Bob's end of the line. "I, uh, I'll have to get in touch with the trading desk. But why would you want to know that?" Bob was suddenly very agitated, probably worried about losing a steady stream of commissions.

"Hey, nothing to worry about. The guys from Cypress just want to know, that's all. They've been asking a lot of questions lately." Gary glanced out his window, he'd also been asking himself the same question: Why indeed? No one explained it to him. Brett just called and said he needed the information. That was Brett for you, playing everything close to the vest.

Bob's tone was noticeably depressed, "Okay, I'll find out and call you back."

It was obvious Bob wasn't taking this news too well but Gary could help ease the pain. "Thanks. By the way, what would you say if I wanted to personally increase my position? You know, double or triple it?"

"Are you serious?"

"Yes, I am. I don't want any of those collars either."

"Are you on a death mission or something? Gary, we'd need a ton of collateral to do that. I don't think you have enough. Besides, this isn't riskless."

"Look, you tell me how much it'll cost and I'll figure out if I want to do it, okay?" What's the matter with Bell, doesn't he want more business?

"Fine. I'll find out and give you a call back. But Gary, you remember this conversation. You're making a bet on which way interest rates are moving. Rates change."

Gary didn't pay much attention as his mind was elsewhere, somewhere in Colorado at his soon-to-be new vacation home. "Yeah, whatever. Call me as soon as you can.

Tuesday, August 13, 10:30 A.M.
Political Party Offices, Lansing, Michigan

A looming shadow suddenly appeared over her desk. Jenny Hilborn looked up from her workstation at Sandy hanging over the top of the partition, dropping donut crumbs into Jenny's space. "Have something on your mind, Sandy?"

"If you have a minute why don't we take a walk outside?"

That was odd. For as long as she'd known Sandy Skamansky they'd never hesitated to talk shop in the office. Why the mystery?

The women left the building and walked aimlessly around the Capital's street on a day that was warm and overcast. Gazing upwards at the rolling clouds Jenny recalled that rain was in the forecast. Not wanting to be caught too far away in a sudden downpour she slowed her pace and asked, "So what's up?"

Sandy looked around making sure they were alone and replied, "Remember when I said that LoneStar and Brett Hollister were vaguely familiar? Well, I remembered why."

Stopping, Jenny turned and studied Sandy. "Okay, so what do you remember?"

Noticeably uncomfortable, Sandy whispered, "I overheard some staffers in Washington talking about how Hollister had stuffed an elected official's stockings with illegal campaign contributions. It was about a year ago. Could be I'm just not remembering right but I don't think so."

"Do you know how he did it?"

"No. That's all I heard and I wasn't even supposed to hear that."

"Did you ever check it out?"

"You kidding? It was just a conversation and I didn't even know Hollister or LoneStar at the time. Who'd have believed me anyway?"

"I appreciate you telling me this Sandy. Sounds like a little snooping on my part is in order. Can you help?"

"Well, I suppose. But I think we should just forget about it. Listen, I've made a few phone calls regarding Brett Hollister. Believe me, he's not someone you want to cross swords with."

"All right, I'll be careful. He won't even know I exist."

Thunder rumbled overhead and a smattering of heavy raindrops began leaving small dark splotches on the pavement. The two women scurried back to the office building as the raindrops intensified. Between labored breaths, Sandy said, "You know. This could be God's way of telling you to stay away from Hollister."

Wednesday, August 14, 11:35 A.M.
Smith-Palmer & Co., Detroit

The two boys were screaming in the background and Stephanie sounded upset, "You have to go out to dinner? Why didn't you say something this morning?"

Because Ashley only called me up ten minutes ago, that's why, Rick said to himself. He squeezed the telephone tight in his hand and stated, "I'm sorry, Steph, but I wasn't even supposed to be going. That's why I never mentioned anything. One of the other analysts got sick and I was told to fill in." It was getting easier for Rick, the lying part.

"When will you be home?"

"I don't know. Just kiss the boy's for me and don't wait up. I'll try not to make any noise when I get home." Come on, let's cut the small talk. I gotta get going.

She replied in a voice edged with disappointment, "Well, have fun. I guess I'll see you whenever."

"This isn't fun, Stephanie. It's work," he quickly replied, surprised at his own righteous indignation. "I'm late. Goodbye." She was becoming more and more irritating. But he wasn't going to let her ruin tonight. Rick replaced his phone, packed up his briefcase, shot out of the office and drove like a bat out of hell to the Townsend Hotel twenty miles away. He'd just as soon wile away the hours there as anywhere else. Ashley wasn't due to arrive until six o'clock but he didn't care. Look at those hands . . . shaking again.

Same day, 12:35 P.M.
Taylor-Bishop Offices, Manhattan

The offices of The Taylor-Bishop Company were deserted and would remain so for at least another twenty minutes. The staff usually took an extra long lunch break whenever Ashley was out of town, sort of a mini-vacation for the troops. Since Jackie Wells hadn't had much luck finding anything of interest for Paul Victor, she planned to use this opportunity to search Ashley's private office.

The relatively young Jackie Wells joined The Taylor-Bishop Company after numerous unsuccessful attempts at other companies. Since leaving Florida to seek fame and fortune all she could say with any certainty was that well paying jobs were scarce, and living in New York City was unbelievably expensive. Shortly after Jackie first arrived in the Big Apple looking for work and after many polite 'I'm sorry' responses, she interviewed with The Cypress Group. With a senior partner named, Mr. Paul Victor no less. Paul didn't have any immediate openings but he was aware of one over at the Taylor-Bishop Company. So he gave her some useful background information and faux references to help smooth the interview process with Bishop, and then added, "Please let me know if you get the job."

Okay, so the interview went great and out of courtesy for his help, and because he was very cute, Jackie did contact Paul once Ashley hired her. "Excellent, I'm really happy for you, hope everything works out. Oh, by the way, if you ever need some extra cash, call me up." Well, it didn't take Jackie long to realize she was desperate for 'extra cash,' as she found herself spending way more than her paycheck afforded. So she called Paul. After an intimate dinner and a night of exquisite albeit totally meaningless sex, Jackie became his 'snitch.' That was four months ago.

Checking her watch one last time with excitement and fear heightening her senses, the tall willowy redhead walked over to Joyce's secretarial desk. She opened the top drawer and rummaged around, finally locating keys to Ashley's private office. Taking a deep breath and listening once again for any noise, Jackie unlocked the door and scooted inside.

The contemporary office greeted her indifferently. Jackie's eyes swept over Ashley's white marble topped desk, a matching credenza with her personal computer, a white leather high back desk chair, white leather sofa and easy chairs, a glass coffee table and end tables, accent chairs, conference table, some rather interesting sculptures scattered here and there, and several brightly colored paintings.

Now where would I hide something special? she wondered. There weren't any file cabinets so that left the desk. Sitting in Ashley's chair Jackie began unlocking drawers. She hunted through stacks of papers, files and folders, but nothing looking remotely interesting. Everything seemed normal, no secret documents, no microfilm or files stamped 'Confidential,' and no compromising photographs . . . hey, wait a minute. There at the bottom of one of the drawers were several round CD disks and a handful of thumb drives. Retrieving the disks she turned each over in her hand and her heart skipped a beat. One of the disks had the name 'LoneStar' printed on it.

You found it, you did it! Son of a . . . Okay, let's see if you can make a copy. Running back to her own workstation Jackie hurriedly inserted Ashley's disk into her computer and typed a command. No file names showed on the directory. You hid the names, she seethed. You protected all the files . . . bitch.

Without knowing the password Jackie couldn't access the information on the disk or make a copy. Worse still, passwords could have any number of characters, how the hell could she figure the right sequence? Oh, look at the time. The others are coming back any minute. Think, think. Let's try typing in: LoneStar. No luck. How about: Bishop? Nope. Ashley? No.

This was useless. And if she waited much longer someone was bound to catch her.

Disappointed and dejected she returned the disk to its proper place, locked all the drawers, closed and locked the office door and then returned the keys to where she found them. Well, at least she had something to report to Paul. She'd even ask for more money—had to. There was a mounting stack of unpaid bills at home.

Same day, 10:45 P.M.
Townsend Hotel, Birmingham, Michigan

The heavy drapes were drawn in Ashley's luxurious hotel room. Soft light came from a single brass table lamp. A half empty bottle of champagne was chilling in an ice bucket on the coffee table along with a serving dish offering a wide assortment of fruits, shrimp, cheeses and crackers. Ashley smiled at Rick, placed her now empty champagne glass next to the ice bucket, stood up, wet her lips with her tongue and slowly unzipped her skirt letting it fall deftly to the floor. Rick was sitting in an overstuffed occasional chair, drink in hand trying to act calm.

Smiling seductively, Ashley purred, "Sorry I couldn't give you much notice, Rick. But I didn't know until this morning myself." One of her clients in Chicago had called for an urgent meeting. Detroit happened to be an opportunistic stop on her way back to New York.

Having a hard time speaking Rick cleared his throat and stammered, "Ah, don't be sorry, not on my account, anyway. I'm just glad you called." Rick's mouth was extremely dry, so he gulped the clear, bubbly liquid . . . draining the glass then quickly refilling it. Ashley finished unfastening the last button on her blouse and let it slide off her shoulders, allowing it to float gracefully on the floor atop her skirt.

With sultry voice she asked, "So, what have you been hearing from our friends at LoneStar?" She unhooked her black strapless push-up bra and held it in place, waiting for an answer.

Awed by the softness and firmness of her body he wanted to tell her everything . . . anything . . . he couldn't help himself. "Ah, um, I haven't heard much, ah, lately. It's um, not, a company known for their, ah, communication efforts." Talk about communication efforts. "Why? Have you heard, um, anything?" The bra drifted slowly to the ground.

Putting her fingers around her high cut matching bikini bottoms she rolled them down over lithe thighs, letting them catch briefly on her knees before dispatching them the rest of the way. "Oh, I've heard that a couple of major firms are getting ready to make a run at them through a stock tender offer. You're still going to keep the 'buy' recommendation on them, aren't you?"

The pounding in his ears was like a thunder of drums. How was he expected to talk shop at a time like this? "Right, sure, yes, a 'buy' recommendation.

Yes, it's not going anywhere, I mean, it's staying." Ricks' eyes were wide with anticipation and hunger. His shaking hands slopped champagne out of the glass and onto his slacks. He felt weak all over.

"That's good." The totally naked Ashley glided towards Rick until she was right in front of him. Reaching out she undid his tie and gently pulled it from around his shirt collar. As she was unbuttoning his collar button she asked a question his wife never had: "What would you like, lover?"

Thursday, August 15, 4:55 P.M.
LoneStar Offices, Dallas

There was no joy for those sitting around the conference table, especially for Treasurer, Gary Nash. But for the moment Brett's eyes bore into Chester Bennett, to the relief of everyone else. "Chester, I want this next board meeting to go without a hitch. Nothing off the agenda, no unsolicited comments from anybody. I want it to be neat and quick. No screw ups. This'll be the first time Paul Victor and his New York lackeys are going to be at my meeting and I don't want to be embarrassed again. Got it?" That was a rhetorical question for Brett was in no mood for any arguments.

Everyone was feeling the pressure and Chester was no exception. "Sure thing. We'll have the approval of the prior minutes, the Hilborn appointment to chairman of the executive committee, the replacing of the SWAP collars, a couple of junior officer promotions and the reporting of our last quarters financial statements. All are noncontroversial . . . shouldn't take more than an hour."

"Hmm. Let me remind you gentlemen, I'm not gonna put up with any more surprises."

Gary Nash along with the other managers nodded, but Gary's mind wasn't on Brett at the moment. How could this have happened to him? It certainly wasn't what he'd expected. Bob Bell called ten minutes before this meeting saying the security required by Pagent & Associates to increase his own personal SWAP position was substantial. A lot more than he'd ever imagined. Gary had no doubt he could triple his gains, retire and get that second home, but those Wall Street shysters were putting the screws to him. Gary knew they were trying to squeeze him out because he was winning.

The only way Gary could pledge enough collateral, though, would be to take a loan out on his home. It had taken him and Pamela twenty-one years to finally pay off that mortgage and now he'd have to get another one? That wasn't right.

Well, why burden Pam? Why did she have to know anything about it? Gary could probably get her to sign some legal looking papers, tell her they're for some investments, and slip in a 'power of attorney' giving him the right to sign on her behalf. Then he'd have LoneStars' own mortgage lending division rush his application through without any of that extra bullshit they make everyone else put up with. That way, in less than a month he'd have enough money for Mr. Bell's precious collateral. Then as soon as his trading account hit one million dollars in profit he'd close it out and tell Bob Bell, Larry Hendricks, and all the other Wall Street bastards to go screw themselves.

Oblivious to Gary's personal dialogue the pre-board agenda meeting continued unabated with Brett dictating orders and everyone else furiously scribbling notes, nodding enthusiastically, and saying nothing. Happy campers need not apply.

Same day, 6:25 P.M.
Taylor-Bishop Offices, Manhattan

One major drawback from a day or two of business travel was returning to find your desk piled high with a day or two's worth of work. Plowing through yesterday's mound of paper and reports Ashley was interrupted by a knock on her door. "Ashley, you real busy?"

Looking up reluctantly from an unread memo Ashley resisted a sarcastic retort and instead said, "What's up?" Her private secretary, Joyce looked frightened as she slowly walked into the office. A couple years ago Ashley had pulled Joyce out of a hell hole, giving her and her young daughter a fresh start.

More important, Ashley had handed them back their dignity. Joyce's loyalty to Ashley was absolute, she was a tireless worker . . . and she never looked so troubled. "Problem?"

"I'm having a hard time saying this because I really have no proof, but I think someone was searching your office." Joyce really didn't like this at all.

Ashley looked dubious and asked, "My office? When?"

"Yesterday, while you were in Detroit."

"Who'd want to come in here? What makes you think so?"

Joyce took a deep breath and said, "The keys to your office that I keep, they were in the right drawer of my desk but in the wrong place. I always keep your keys separate from the others so I won't mix them up, but this morning they weren't where they were supposed to be. Ashley, I've never mixed the keys before. I think someone used them yesterday, probably during lunch."

Knowing her secretary wasn't prone to fabricating stories, she replied, "Okay, Joyce, I appreciate you telling me. I'll check around, see if anything's missing or looks funny. But let's keep this between us for now." Another complication to handle before getting any meaningful work done. Ashley waited until Joyce left.

She couldn't believe someone had snuck in here, although she was obligated to give the place a "once over." Ashley scanned her office looking for anything odd but all appeared normal. Her attention next focused on the desk. Everything's fine on top of my desk, she confirmed, so let's just open these and take a peek. Nope, nothing looks moved or missing in this drawer. This one looks fine too, files are in order, and no papers appear to be missing. No one can access my computer files because I put everything on protected disks, and the disks are right there at the bottom of the drawer just like . . .

Whoa, wait a moment, she puzzled. My disks. They're right side up! The labels are showing. I always turn them over so the back is face up, so no one can accidentally see any names if the drawer happens to be open. Joyce must be right. Someone has been in here. But looking for what?

Pressing a button on the phone console, Ashley said, "Joyce, could you come in here?" Let's think this one through, she admonished herself. Don't make it worse than it is; just take it step by step. "Close the door and sit down. Joyce, you were right, someone's been in here. Obviously, they wanted in here pretty bad since they had to steal keys to do it. I have no clue who it could be, you?"

Joyce considered the possibilities, "Most of the girls have been here since you first started the company. I've never heard them bad mouthing you, just the opposite really. Jackie Wells is the newest but it's not right to blame someone just because they're new."

Ashley nodded, "You're right. But we can't go on living like this, not knowing who to trust or constantly looking over our shoulders. Okay, here's what we'll do. You try to monitor as many of their phone conversations as you can without anyone catching on. First time you hear something suspicious, get me."

Joyce's eyes widened, "I don't think I want to eavesdrop, Ashley. Isn't there another way?"

"I'm open. We could try a security camera but the mystery person my not sneak back for months. You have any better ideas?"

Biting a fingernail, Joyce answered, "No, no I don't have any. I . . . I guess it's the only thing we can do right now. But I don't like it."

"I don't like it either but I need to know. However, let's understand one thing. I don't want to know anything that you hear of a personal nature no matter what. Is that clear?"

"Yes, sure. Then I guess it's all right. I'll let you know if I hear anything."

"Joyce. The sooner we find out who's not with us, the sooner we can wrap this up." Ashley leaned back in her chair and wondered why one of her girls would do this.

CHAPTER 15

Friday, August 16, 10:10 A.M.
Smith-Palmer & Co., Detroit

Every time he thought of her, he'd become aroused. Rick could close his eyes and see her face with those enchanting eyes, and those firm round breasts, and flat stomach, and long legs. She was a perfect woman and he couldn't keep her out of his mind. Never met anyone like her. Had to see her again, tell her that he. . . he what? Exactly what would he say to Ashley?

Would she want to hear that his relationship with Steph was deteriorating? Well, it was. All Stephanie did was complain about this or that. Unless everything was just right, meaning the kids were behaving, there were no financial concerns looming, nothing was broken, wasn't too tired, or didn't have one of those convenient sinus headaches, unless the entire day had been absolutely picture perfect he could forget about any late night intimacies. On the other hand, with the extra thirty pounds she'd allowed to settle around her hips and thighs he wasn't all that interested anyway. Why couldn't she be more exciting? He didn't want to become old and boring, and that's the road Stephanie was dragging him down.

The telephone rang abruptly ending his mental discourse. "Hello. Rick Blaine, speaking."

"Rick, it's Steve Golding, we met briefly at the LoneStar annual shareholder's meeting. I'm a research analyst like yourself. As a matter of fact we both issued 'buy' recommendations on LoneStar right after that meeting."

"Sure, I remember you, Steve. What can I do for you?"

"Well, I know your sources are confidential and I'm not looking for any insider information, wouldn't want it to be truthful. But I was wondering if you could tell me if you're still as committed to your 'buy' recommendation as before."

Rick was startled and asked, "How's that?"

"Look Rick, I'm not trying to scoop you. I just know that without the story of a potential buyer LoneStar's stock would be trading in the thirty's, not the mid-forty's. Rick, I can't find any trace of a buyer, not anywhere. I just don't want to be set up for a fall, that's all."

Rick recalled what Ashley told him during their last meeting at the Townsend Hotel. She said how a couple of very large companies were about to make tender offers for the stock of LoneStar. Remembering the vivid scene a smile crossed his face and he suddenly found it difficult to remain seated. "Steve, I can't say anything other than I'm convinced a couple major firms are pursuing the acquisition of LoneStar. I'm keeping my recommendation."

"Fair enough. Guess your sources are better than mine. Thanks a lot, Rick. Let's keep in touch. Bye."

Rick adjusted his slacks and leaned back. Ashley, he mused. I'm sorry to be using you like this, and I know it's not fair of me. But I'll make it up to you . . . promise.

Same day, 1:15 P.M.
Taylor-Bishop Offices, Manhattan

Joyce rushed into Ashley's office. "Ashley, you won't believe it. The second call I listened to today was it."

Putting down the file she was working on Ashley motioned for her to come in. "Well, close the door and tell me."

"Huh? Oh sure." Joyce quickly closed the door and sat down.

"This is amazing; I almost said something on the phone. My God, I don't believe it."

"Joyce, get a hold of yourself, take a deep breath and *talk to me.*"

Joyce nodded and blurted, "It's Jackie. I saw her extension light up on my console during lunch so I hit it. She was calling The Cypress Group."

Ashley wasn't sure she heard right. "The Cypress Group. The Cypress Group?"

"Yes, she asked to speak to Paul Victor."

"*Paul Victor?* That snake?"

"Yeah, Mr. Heart-throb himself. Anyway, she tells him about going into your office yesterday, says she didn't find anything except some computer disks. But on one of the disks was the name LoneStar. Says she tried to copy it but all the files are protected and she doesn't have any idea how to access them. Victor tells her never to go into your office again, it could jeopardize the whole thing. She says she's just trying to do a good job. Victor tells her to go back to work, keep looking in waste baskets like she has, but also to look for something that could be a password."

Ashley's face turned to stone. "That lousy son of a bitch. Buying off one of my girls. Why can't those bastards just leave me alone? Well, we'll just have to think about this won't we?" She paused, opened her lower drawer and took out the LoneStar disk. "Listen, Joyce. Call a strategy meeting this afternoon. Jackie is about the only one who doesn't attend them so I'll mention something to the others, like we've all got to be extra careful about leaving work out on our desks because the janitorial service doesn't know what's trash and what's not."

Continuing to finger the disk, Ashley added, "But above all, Joyce, I don't want Jackie or anyone to know that we're onto her. We've got to act as if nothing's happened, understand?" Ashley closed her hand around the disk. As for you Paul Victor, I don't know how yet, but I'm gonna take real pleasure cutting off your balls and mounting them on my wall.

Tuesday, August 27, 12:45 P.M.
LoneStar Boardroom, Dallas

The luncheon dishes were swiftly removed by tuxedo wearing waiters. The gourmet prepared Italian feast complete with thick rich sauces and assorted pastries had been enormously enjoyed by everyone . . . everyone except Charles Hilborn and the four Cypress men, who seemed a little testy with all this pomp and circumstance. Brett didn't appreciate the obvious snub, it meant they weren't duly impressed or properly prepared for his staged performance. Cautiously, he said, "Gentlemen, it's time. Please come to order. The first order of business is the approval of the minutes from the last board meeting. You'll find said minutes behind Tab A. Is there any discussion? All right, then may I have a motion to accept the minutes as presented?"

"So moved."

"Is there support?"

"I'll support."

"All in favor, say 'aye' . . . Mr. Secretary, please note that the motion passed unanimously."

"The second order of business it the proposal to appoint Dr. Charles Hilborn as chairman of the Executive Committee. I think you all appreciate the checks and balance any major company needs at their most senior levels. It is my opinion that Dr. Hilborn is eminently qualified to provide LoneStar the additional oversight, which up to now has rested solely upon me. Tab B will provide you with more information on this topic. Now, is there any discussion?" Brett was bound and determined to have this meeting run on schedule and without incident. He scanned the other nineteen board members and said, "Since there is no discussion may I have a motion."

"So moved."

"Thank you, and is there support?"

"Support."

"Thank you. All in favor say 'aye' . . . Mr. Secretary, please note that the motion was passed by unanimous consent. The next topic is the promotion of three individuals to the office of Vice President. Their accomplishments and resumes are behind Tab C. Is there any discussion?" Let's keep moving this along gentlemen, Brett uttered under his breath.

The three promotions were approved without any issues being raised. Likewise, Gary Nash's presentation of the financial statements was politely listened to by all the directors. Just as Brett was thanking Gary for such an in-depth analysis and only a few seconds before the treasurer excused himself, Paul Victor raised his hand and spoke.

"Mr. Chairman, I'd like to ask Mr. Nash a question."

Brett didn't want any interruptions and he made sure Victor knew it. "We've got an agenda Mr.

Victor, and I will not allow the proceedings to be sidetracked with extraneous dialog. Is that clear?"

Paul nodded, "Yes, perfectly clear. Now, Mr. Nash, I am unable to determine from these reports you handed out the actual losses at the credit card division. Could you enlighten us please?"

"The losses of what . . . ?" Gary was unaccustomed to having questions put to him at a board meeting, especially regarding departments or divisions he didn't control.

The newly appointed director from New York prodded the obviously uncomfortable treasurer, "The losses of the credit card division, Mr. Nash. Aren't they increasing? Aren't they rising more than ever before? Aren't they higher than our competitors? Haven't we been lowering our soliciting standards?"

The chairman thumped his gavel and interjected, "Mr. Victor, those questions will require a thorough review and analysis of the credit card operation. Such a review is not on our agenda today. If you want to propose a topic for our next meeting, please contact our board secretary, Mr. Bennett."

Paul Victor cocked his head in disbelief. "You mean you don't know, that you really don't have a clue, and unless it becomes a board item you'll never take the time to find out?"

"That's enough, Mr. Victor." The gavel thumped a second time as Brett's anger started to kindle.

Victor persisted by asking, "So I suppose that also means that since the systems group isn't on the agenda we can't find out how much money they've been pissing away?"

Brett was moments away from losing control, "I've had just about enough, Mr. Victor. You're out of order and you will be quiet. This is a structured meeting not some New York free-for-all." He gritted his teeth and clenched both fists, fully realizing there wasn't enough room for both of them and he didn't plan on leaving.

Continuing in a voice dripping with contempt for Mr. Victor, Brett said, "The next topic gentlemen is the replacing of the SWAP collar. As you know, the Executive Committee removed the collar on voice vote. However, after the insistence by Mr. Victor and the three new directors from The Cypress Group, the board is being asked to reconsider an earlier decision and place the collars back on the SWAPs. Any discussion?" Brett held the gavel like a weapon ready to strike out at the enemy.

An ensuing debate on whether-or-not to employ SWAPs at all was initiated by Victor, but once again suppressed by Brett as it wasn't an agenda item. Paul Victor and his three associates wouldn't be silenced with a silly gavel and ended up shouting at Hollister. Brett Hollister, to his credit, took it all and then screamed back louder than all others combined. The meeting was adjourned fifteen minutes later amid spiteful threats and counter threats. Not exactly the well orchestrated meeting so typical at LoneStar International.

Same day, Three Hours Later

The unappetizing meal sitting on the tray in front of Paul Victor did nothing to mitigate his anger, and the first class seat on the return trip to New York didn't sooth the savage beast much either. Nothing short of getting rid of that pompous ass Hollister would help. He looked over to one of his traveling companions and said, "When we get back, find out from our legal staff what we can do to get that jerk off the board and outta my life. What a fucking incompetent. What an ass. If we can't fire him I wanna buy him off, pay him to leave. Find out what the price tag is for triggering his employment contract. Damn, I wanted to kill that son of a bitch." Unable to clear his mind he ordered a double vodka, blew a sore nose and pleaded to a troublesome stomach ache to go away.

Saturday, August 31, 1:55 P.M.
Sports Club, Columbus, Ohio

Sweat dripped down Courtney Keller's forehead and rolled into her eyes, stinging them unmercifully. She brushed her forearm across her face, allowing the thick cotton wristband to soak up a broad swath of perspiration. This was their third set of tennis and

Courtney had taken the first two: 6-3, 6-2. She was now serving for the match. Her opponent looked more than a little exhausted. Actually, Mike Kilpatrick looked about ready to collapse. Courtney was a solid player and had been slamming shots from one corner of the baseline to the other. Mike was able to get to most of the balls but could never put much pace on the return, so she just kept humming them back . . . making him run all over the court. She loved it.

Serving from the deuce side she decided to try a serve down the middle, right at his backhand. She tossed the ball into the air and smacked it. Mike lunged awkwardly, swung late, and sent the ball high into the rafters of the tennis club.

Raising her hand in victory, Courtney yelled out, "Ta Da." She couldn't help gloating as she pranced to the net.

With great effort the independent financial advisor lumbered over to the net and stammered, "Have any oxygen on you?"

"That was really fun Mike, thanks for the game." She was beaming.

Taking in deep lungs full of oxygen he barely managed to say, "I'm going into cardiac arrest. I'll need mouth to mouth resuscitation."

Grinning, Courtney replied, "Nice try, but we don't resuscitate for heart problems. We use electric paddles."

"Oh, well in that case I'm fine."

"Come on, I'll buy you a beer at the club diner. That should perk you up." She and Mike had been seeing each other for the past few weeks. Happily, both wanted the budding relationship to continue. Somehow Mike helped Courtney leave behind all problems from the hospital and her sister's waning marriage.

The defeated combatant fell into one of the silver speckled, gray plastic, lounge chairs and put a towel over his head. The 1950's jukebox was playing *I Did It My Way*, by Frank Sinatra. "How appropriate," Mike conceded between heaving gasps. "I've just been pounded into the ground, but I did it 'My way' . . . with dignity. Ooh, I'm in pain. Don't you know you're supposed to be the weaker sex?"

Courtney patted his shoulder, walked over to the counter and bought two beers, then rejoined him at the small round table. "Here you go big fella, this should make it feel better."

Speaking from under the towel, Mike offered, "My mom always kissed whatever was hurting me, to make it feel better."

Now that's a sly move, she admitted. "Well, your mom's not here, so all you get is a cold beer."

Sighing, Mike replied, "Okay, you're the doctor." He chuckled at the little joke then wheezed again.

Yes, Courtney Keller was a doctor. She'd been part of the medical community ever since graduating from Penn State University. Right after Penn State she entered Ohio States' School of Medicine, loved it and settled down in Columbus. She was now in her early thirty's, with a well deserved reputation.

Removing the towel from his head Mike took a long swig of cold beer and declared, "Yeah, that's much better." Dropping the wet towel to the floor he added, "Tell you what. Since I still can't talk yet, why don't you tell me about yourself? Any Brothers or sisters?"

"Uh-hmm, I have one sister, Steph . . . Stephanie Blaine. She lives up in Michigan, the Detroit area. She and her husband Rick have two boys, middle school and high school. We grew up in Michigan. She stayed and I left."

"Any brothers?"

"Nope, only the one sister. Although her husband Rick is kind of like a brother, at least sometimes."

"Hey, wait, I know a Rick Blaine from Detroit. Well, I don't personally know him but he writes stock reports for a brokerage house."

Courtney was visibly impressed. "That's him. He's with Smith-Palmer, joined this year. I think he's called a research analyst or something."

"No kidding? That guy did me a huge favor. Came out with a stock recommendation that I followed. Sure would like to thank him sometime."

Obviously proud of her brother-in-law, Courtney said, "No problem. I'll pass your message along. Small world isn't it?"

Gently taking her hand in his, Mike's demeanor suddenly changed and he said, "You know doc, I'm falling for you."

"Good. I must say it's about time." Courtney kissed his hand and considered herself about the luckiest girl in Ohio.

Monday, September 2, 9:25 A.M.
Chairman's Office, LoneStar

The weekend had been marvelous, grandkids can do that. Brett and his wife had played host to their three rambunctious offshoots gratefully dropped off by a harried mother. For two days they dashed them through the Fort Worth Zoo, Six Flags, and Wet 'n Wild. The theme parks entertained one and all to the point of near exhaustion, but they loved every minute. It was just the tonic Brett needed to push all thoughts of Paul Victor out of his mind and put him in a better mood.

Then as always, the momentary serenity was rudely interrupted by a buzzing from his secretary. "Mr. Hollister. It's Congressman Lodge on line one."

Lodge? This was unexpected. Taking the call from the man beholden to his creative campaign financing, Brett bellowed, "Hello, Congressman. Good of you to call a devoted constituent. Now, it's not time for re-election so you can't need money. Therefore, I can only conclude you need keys to my weekend retreat."

"Nothing like that you old horse thief. I'll keep it in mind, though, next time the wife's away. Ever hear of a Jenny Hilborn?"

Caught off guard it took a few seconds to register. "Yes, I know her, not really well though. Met her a couple of times over the last few years. Why?"

"She seems to know you pretty damned well. She's been asking a lot of questions, poking around."

Brett was confused. "Questions about what? Poking into what?"

"LoneStar employees contributing to my election campaign, that's what."

"I don't believe it. How the hell could Hilborn's wife . . . oh, shit, that's right. She's tied up in politics. Damn. How far has she poked?"

"Far enough that one of my staffers heard about it and told me, but not far enough to alert the Ethics Committee. I don't know what's going on Brett but I . . . we don't need this woman going any further."

Assessing the situation, Brett counseled, "The best thing we can do is divert her, even discredit her. Make it so no one will believe anything she has to say."

"Brett, Jenny Hilborn's been around these hallowed halls of politics for over twenty years. She's well respected on both sides of the aisle. How can we discredit her?"

There was only one way Brett could think. "Have one of your staffers go public that she's been misusing public funds, reallocating them to her own personal account. As long as the papers pick it up she'll be hamstrung from mucking into your affairs. If she does, you just go on the morning news circuit saying how regrettable it is that she's attempting to smear others simply to evade a thorough investigation. The media will eat it up."

Lodge chuckled and said, "Brett, you're one devious son of a bitch, I'll give you that. Okay, I'll start the ball rolling. Any chance anyone else knows what she's up to?"

"Her husband most likely but I can cry vendetta too, if it gets to that. Just remember you gotta go public before they do."

"Understood my friend. Keep in touch."

Brett hung up the phone, conceding that Dr. Charles Hilborn was undoubtedly the worst choice he ever made for a director.

CHAPTER 16

Wednesday, September 4, 9:30 A.M.
Cypress Offices, Manhattan

Sitting around the eight-foot oval, thick glass and chrome conference table with the other senior partners of The Cypress Group, Paul Victor contemplated what he wanted to say about LoneStar. Over six billion dollars from very affluent and influential investors were being managed by this imposing body of seven men. Cypress catered to the super rich, providing investment alternatives and returns unavailable to common mortals.

Nothing but success was tolerated so understandably the self-imposed pressure was nearly unbearable. No senior partner, no matter who, was absolved from a serious error in judgment. Understandably, each partner was a pure shark unwilling to give anyone a break, but more than willing to wring whatever cash they could out of any situation. Paul had no intentions of being the next failure, particularly not with LoneStar. Although, he was currently on the hot seat.

"Paul, perhaps we should just cash in the LoneStar stock, take our profit and move on."

Another partner offered, "I tend to agree, Paul. LoneStar's too big and too complex for you or anyone else to get their arms around. This guy Hollister sounds like a loose cannon. He'll likely destroy the ship as save it."

Paul raised his left eyebrow and dabbed his nose with a handkerchief. "I share your concern. But for the record, since we converted our bonds into five million shares of LoneStar stock we've made around thirty million dollars. For each dollar that stock climbs we make another five million. Everyone here knows the street has pegged an acquisition price north of sixty. Right now it's trading at forty-six, so that's a potential fifteen point increase or an additional seventy-five million dollars.

"This is why I am so adamant about kicking that ass Hollister off the board. I want LoneStar sold and it won't be with him there. I want him out, I want to find a buyer, and I want the stock trading over sixty. So what if it costs us five million to pay Hollister off? Whatever it costs is chicken shit compared to what we'll make. On the flip side, that idiot will cost us five million bucks each time he does something stupid and drops the price a buck."

That's reason enough, Paul admitted to himself, but if he could also structure a merger before that whore Ashley Bishop bought any stock he'd shut her out from her own damned game. It would be so sweet shoving this back into her pretty face. Still, he'd like to know why she hadn't bought any stock.

"Paul, who'll watch over the store in Hollister's absence?" asked a skeptical partner.

Swiftly returning to the discussion at hand, he answered, "Ah, the chairman of the executive committee, Dr. Charles Hilborn. He's a college professor and won't stand in our way or give us any problems. Actually, I suspect everything's way above him, which is exactly what we want." Paul blew his nose noisily and apologized, "Excuse me, lousy cold."

"Have you talked to Hilborn?" the man persisted.

Paul shook his head, "No, not yet. I wanted your concurrence first."

The senior partners looked at one another and spoke amongst themselves in hushed tones. Finally one of them said, "All right, Paul. Go ahead. You've wetted our appetites with those profit projections. We're sure you know what you're doing. Now, let's everyone get back to work."

Friday, September 6, 3:50 p.m.
LoneStar Offices, Dallas

The atmosphere at LoneStar was reminiscent of the fortress-like mentality of Germany's General Staff during the last days of World War II. Executives practically barricaded themselves behind their office doors refusing to be seen or make decisions that could provoke a summons from Brett Hollister. Productivity slumped and moral nosedived, but far be it from anyone to carry that message to the chairman. No, it was better to let events take their course as they always did, and in a little while when survival was no longer an issue, then they could reemerge as if nothing had happened and go back to business as usual.

It was no secret however, that more than a few calls were going out to executive search firms as senior managers attempted to market themselves to other companies. Much to their dismay the harsh facts of life were that LoneStar's compensation packages were well above industry norms. They were stuck.

Given the circumstances, Gary Nash clung to his SWAPs as if they were his lifeline, which gave rise to scrutinizing the Wall Street Journal every morning and gluing himself to CNBC.com. Unlike most days when he relished reading reports of declining interest rates, which by some complicated formula translated into more money for him, today he wasn't so happy. Interest yields were suddenly heading up. Nothing significant, but still . . .

His telephone rang and picking it up he said, "Gary Nash."

"Hi, Gary. Bob Bell. How ya doing?"

Talk about coincidences. "Fine, Bob"

The Pagent & Associates managing director said, "Gary, interest rates are turning a bit. You should think about pulling back. At least enough to give my oversight group some comfort."

"Are you suggesting LoneStar pull back their position too?" Gary was beginning to have doubts about Bell's loyalty.

"No, not at all. The company's SWAPs are still throwing off cash. Maybe not as much as before but they're doing fine."

"So what's all this about my own position? I've told you I'd have the collateral in another couple weeks if that's what's bothering you." What's with these guys? They know he's good for it.

"Look, Gary, you're still in the money. Just remember it's a pure speculative play. You're betting on which direction interest rates go. So far you've been right, but some people over here are getting concerned. We just want you to trim back your exposure a little, that's all."

Like hell I'll trim anything back, he silently swore. I'm winning, I'm playing with their money and they don't like it. "Thanks for the heads up, Bob. But I'm not folding and I'll get your precious collateral next week. Goodbye." No way was he letting those vultures scare him away. He wasn't some green kid they could jerk around, either. Still, he'd have to make sure his mortgage was approved before Bell used it as an excuse to cut him off.

Same day, 4:50 P.M.
Chairman's Office, LoneStar

It was about time those New York bastards started treating him with respect. Still, it was out of character. Brett looked at the now silent phone and tried to understand what had changed. Nothing was different as far as he knew, which could only mean they were up to something. "Suzanne, have Mr. Bennett see me immediately."

"Yes, sir."

Brett walked over to the bar area and helped himself to half a glass of Jack Daniels. He then wandered to a massive built-in shelving unit displaying numerous Chinese or Japanese artifacts . . . he could never remember which. Picking a hand painted plate off its holder he stared at the intricate faces. It sure didn't look special, at least not to him. Imagine paying ten thousand dollars for it? But just like those other trinkets proudly exhibited throughout the executive offices it was a bold testimony to the occupants good taste and status, or so said the decorator who had purchased all these treasures. Carrying the plate along with his drink over to the sofa Brett sat down and waited.

In a few moments the general counsel entered and said, "Brett, you wanted to see me?"

"Yeah, come in, Chester. Get yourself a drink."

Pouring a couple shots from the same open bottle into a glass, Chester added ice and sat down next to his boss. "Okay, Brett, I'm prepared. What's happened?"

"Victor happened. Mr. Paul Victor of The Cypress Group called. I thought he was going to start bitching about one thing or another but he was as pleasant as could be. Said he appreciated the work I'm doing. Says he's sorry for the wrong foot we've gotten off on. Hell, he even wants me to fly to New York, visit his offices to get better acquainted." Brett drained the last of his drink and turned his head towards Chester and added, "That's one silver tongued, lying son of a bitch. So what do you think he wants?"

Chester considered for a second and then answered, "Oh, I think he wants you out."

"What do you mean, 'He wants me out'?"

"I mean that you two are like oil and water, you'll never be able to work together. You have no patience for each other. Seems to me he wants you out . . . gone. Without you he figures he or your replacement can pretty up this firm, invite some suitors over, let them sniff around and then buy the place. Once LoneStar is sold he'll make himself what . . . another fifty, sixty, seventy million dollars?"

Sounded about right to Brett. "Okay, so what's your advice?"

"Go meet the man, see what he's offering. Who knows, it might be an offer you can live with."

Brett inclined his head to the ceiling while rubbing the plate. "Well, I'm not letting that bastard make a fortune off of my dead bones."

Chester stood up to leave. "Okay, suit yourself."

"I will. Tell Suzanne no calls for awhile." Brett needed some time to figure out a few twists of his own.

Monday, September 9, 9:45 A.M.
Smith-Palmer & Co., Detroit

One of the sale staff at Smith-Palmer & Co, stuck her head into Rick's tiny office, which was overflowing with stacks of papers, files and reports, and offered a bright and chipper, "Morning, Rick. How's it going?"

He looked up from his computer screen and wondered about people who were so cheerful Monday mornings. Was it something they did over the weekend? "Oh, hi. Ah, great, thanks."

"Just thought I'd drop by, tell you that your reports are pretty good. Some of my customers have been complimenting them so I'm passing it along."

"Thanks. I do my best."

"Sure do. Hey, I've noticed that LoneStar has fallen off its recent highs. It's down to forty-four, anything that we should be worried about? Should we tell our clients not to accumulate?"

Reciting Ashley's insights as if they were his, Rick said, "I've checked them out with a pretty reliable source recently. The word is a couple of major firms are about to buy them. I'll make some calls again but for now keep the "buy."

"Okay, you're the expert. See you." Thankfully, the perky face disappeared.

A two dollar move in a stock's price was insignificant in today's volatile market. But, if nothing else it gave Rick a reason to call Ashley, see how she was doing, find out if her sources had any late breaking news on LoneStar, and when she might drop by again. He sure missed her. It was like the longer they were separated the stronger his feelings grew. Yeah, he wanted Ashley to . . . to what? Love him? Naw, he simply wanted to be with her, that's all, nothing more to it than that. Again and again he promised himself it would never become anything more than that.

Same day, 10:10 A.M.
Taylor-Bishop Offices, Manhattan

That certainly wasn't the kind of news she was expecting. Ashley hung up the telephone, grabbed her LoneStar disk and inserted it into the computer. Only last night she'd reflected on how well her plans had been going . . . perhaps too well? Based solely on rumors of a pending takeover from "unknown" companies, LoneStar's stock had rallied to a fifty-two week high of forty-six dollars before correcting itself back to forty-four. If the truth be known, their management team was in chaos, debt was staggering, revenue was deteriorating, profits were eroding and there wasn't a strategy in place to avert financial disaster. It was *Virtual Reality* reincarnated.

But an anxious Gary Nash had just called her with news that he and Brett were coming to New York next week. Brett was going to visit Mr. Paul Victor of The Cypress Group, while Gary ran over to Bob Bell's firm to check how his SWAPs were doing. What else was there to do but say, "Oh, be sure to let me know the date, I'll keep whatever night it is open." That made Gary's day.

Cypress called Brett, hmm? Ashley knew Victor wasn't the chatty type, especially where Hollister was concerned. So while Gary was still in a good mood, she asked, "Any idea why Paul Victor wants to talk to you?" That's when the shoe fell. Still trying to impress her, he answered, "We think they want to offer Brett some kind of package for him to resign. Don't know if there's anything to it, least not until Brett hears the whole offer."

Ashley was outraged. What right did Victor have sticking his arrogant nose into her scheme? Hollister was the key ingredient, she needed him running LoneStar. While Ashley contemplated this latest revelation, Joyce interrupted: "Ashley. Rick Blaine's on line one."

Without realizing it, Ashley smiled as she reached for the phone. "Rick, oh I've missed your voice."

"Ah, really? I've, ah, missed yours."

"You coming to New York anytime soon?"

"Ah, no. You flying to Detroit?"

"Mmmmm, not for a while I'm afraid. We'll just both have to be strong, I suppose." Funny, she did miss him. To be sure she'd spent plenty of evenings entertaining men far more powerful or attractive than Rick. But there was something special about this unassuming research analyst.

Stammering on the phone, Rick remarked, "Yeah, strong. Well, I ah, can do that, as long as I know I'll see you again."

"Rick, you're such a sweetheart. We'll work out something . . . promise. Did you have anything else on your mind?"

"Well, yes, I do. Ah, I've noticed that, ah, LoneStar's stock price dropped from its recent highs. You know any reason why?"

Ashley knew there were generally three possible stock recommendations: 'Buy' which means to accumulate more of the stock, 'hold' or 'neutral' which means don't accumulate any more of the stock, and 'sell' which means get the hell out of the stock. Ashley considered Rick's question in light of Gary's call.

If Victor was the bastard she knew him to be, he'd push Hollister out with money or by manipulation. Without Hollister the remaining ineffectual top management would be in turmoil. Investors would probably wait until a permanent replacement was brought in, to see if LoneStar was truly serious about being acquired or not. Victor might even attempt to find a buyer for LoneStar. But finding a legitimate buyer could take months, if at all. So for the foreseeable future the stock price would probably trade in a narrow range.

"Ah, hello? Ashley? You there?"

She went through her logic once more before saying, "Sorry, Rick. Listen, due to a potential change in senior management it would be my advice to issue a "hold" on LoneStar."

There was silence on the other side. Finally he said, "A change in management? Uh, how do you know?"

"Trade secret."

"Oh. Well, okay, thanks a lot. I ah, don't know how you know but I'm sure glad you do. You're making me look awfully good over here."

Ashley's response was warm and sincere. "Rick, I couldn't think of a nicer guy to share my secrets with. You keep in touch, you hear?" She strolled over to gaze at the panoramic view her office windows afforded. Tilting her head and starring down at the swarming masses engulfing Lower Manhattan she wondered how different life would be in a quiet, peaceful Michigan town.

Wow! Where did that come from? Better knock it off, she chided herself. He's not your type!

Thursday, September 12, 4:30 P.M.
Hilborn Residence, Ann Arbor

Charles and Jenny were home, sitting next to each other on the sofa in front of the empty fireplace, holding hands. Jenny's initial shock had already passed. Now a full array of emotions burst forth. First she couldn't believe it, then she refused to believe it, then she felt sorry for herself, and when she finally accepted what had happened she broke down and cried.

In an odd twist of irony, the day had started off rather pleasant. To be truthful, it was better than most for the sun was shining and the commute to Lansing was uneventful, no traffic jams, no highway construction . . . just a beautiful day all around. Jenny and coworker Sandy were editing some committee reports when one of the party officials asked to speak to her. Once inside his office the day quickly turned into an unforgettable nightmare.

Jenny was informed that a certain Texas congressman's office was inferring that she may have inadvertently . . . or with malice and forethought . . . no one was sure just yet, misappropriated funds. The details of the assertion were sketchy. Actually, details of any kind were sketchy. However, being a United States Congressman did give the accuser a degree of instant credibility. So in this situation, and to avoid further embarrassment while the matter was under investigation, it would be in everyone's best interest for Jenny to immediately take a leave of absence . . . without pay.

She was furious. How the hell could they even believe such an outrageous claim? "Doesn't over twenty years of service count for anything with you people? How could you do this to me? Where's due process of law? It'll take months, years to sort out a baseless assertion like this." Then the repercussions really set in. During the long investigation she'd lose her contacts and connections, the lifeblood of any political operative. *How could they do this to me?* But they did it. They sent her packing because a Texas congressman said she had stolen taxpayer's money. It was so unfair.

Charles knew Jenny lived for politics, it was her essence, her being, and from what he could tell she was good at her job. "Why would a freshman Texas congressman even know you're alive?" he puzzled. Something was horribly wrong.

Between sobs she said, "I'll tell you why. Because a little while ago, Sandy told me about a conversation she'd overheard. It, it seems your Mr. Brett Hollister skirted campaign finance laws to get one of his cronies elected. I was just about to tell you when I was sent packing. Now if I say anything publicly it'll look like I'm trying to get back at him. Damn that man. I hate him, hate him, hate him."

Charles was numb. He couldn't move, could hardly breathe. After what seemed like hours, he said, "Jenny, I'm so sorry. If I would have known any of this . . ."

Tears rolled down her cheeks as she replied, "I know Charles, it's not your fault, I'm not blaming you. It's the system I work for . . . correction, worked for. I just can't believe it. But it's not your fault."

Charles knew better. He knew full well that he was the one really responsible, and it wasn't like Jenny hadn't warned him.

CHAPTER 17

Friday, September 13, 6:15 P.M.
Hilborn Residence, Ann Arbor

A jet of water suddenly sprayed onto his face, and he bumped his head trying to stand up. "Just a minute," he called out to the ringing phone as he pulled himself out from underneath the kitchen sink. Wiping wet hands on his pants, Charles cursed the clogged pipes and picked up the phone. "Yes?"

"Dr. Charles Hilborn? Paul Victor here. Sorry to bother you. Is this a good time to talk?"

As Charles stood by the phone dripping wet and holding his throbbing head while his wife, who'd been royally screwed by Brett Hollister's inflated ego, wouldn't come out of the bedroom, he seriously considered saying, "No, it's a god awful time to talk." Instead he said, "What can I do for you, Mr. Victor?"

"Please, call me Paul."

"Okay. I'm Charles."

"Thank you, Charles. The reason I'm calling is confidential. I'd like it to stay that way, just between us for the next few days anyhow."

"Okay, you've got my attention, Paul."

"Charles, we at The Cypress Group are not pleased with the recent conduct of Brett Hollister. In fact, I would go so far as to say that we have no confidence in him being the leader of a major financial institution. He's erratic, paranoid, temperamental, illogical, vindictive and thoroughly untrustworthy. We have no desire to allow him to stay in any position of power or influence at LoneStar, not with the amount of money we've invested there."

Charles' could not have agreed more. "I'm listening."

"I've arranged a meeting with Brett here in New York next week. It's my intention to present him with a severance package, attractive enough so that he'll take it and run. His current employment contract is very generous but I plan on sweetening it to ensure his quick departure."

"Go on."

"With Brett gone we'll need a caretaker, an interim president if you will. Someone to hold the ship together until a permanent replacement can be hired. I don't expect the process to take more than three to six months. A sizeable compensation package will go along with the job, complete with stock options."

"Paul, you're presuming Hollister will leave for more money. I doubt it, I really do. I don't believe for a moment he's motivated by money. That's his company, not yours, not mine, not the shareholders."

"Well, it's been my experience that people can be bought, Charles. As a board member and a major shareholder I'm going to do my best to push LoneStar into increasing its shareholder value, and that'll only happen if we get rid of Hollister."

Charles nodded, "Okay, you've got my blessing to talk to him. Not that you really need it, but you've got it."

"Thank you. Actually, there's something else I need from you."

Here it comes . . . here it comes, Charles steadied himself. "What might that be?" He waited for the zinger.

Paul hesitated for a moment before answering. "I ah, need you to run LoneStar, as interim president."

"Are you crazy? *Me*? Run LoneStar? There are over three thousand people there."

"It's just for a couple months. Look, Charles, you have common sense and integrity, and the senior managers know what they're doing, so all you have to do is show up for work and tell everyone good morning."

"Have one of the senior managers run it."

"Can't, they're all Brett's boys. We'd never know what they'd be telling him, or what thoughts he'd be putting in their heads. No, it's got to be someone we can trust, someone who doesn't owe Hollister anything, and that's you."

Well, it was true enough he didn't owe Hollister anything, quite the contrary. Charles would just as soon strangle the stocky Texan. Paul's thought process of taking away what Brett loved most seemed fitting after what he did to Jenny. In fact, the idea sounded pretty good all around. Paul gets what he wants, I get what I want, Brett retires into the lap of luxury, and I suspect most of the board would secretly applaud a change at the top anyway. But Brett would never go for it, not for money. No, he'd have to be persuaded another way. He'd have to be put into the position of having to give up his job to preserve something more important, like his reputation—then he'd cooperate.

In spite of several gnawing concerns, Charles felt a rush of excitement. "Tell you what, Paul. I think we're getting a little ahead of ourselves. You have your chat with Brett. Now I'm not saying 'no,' but unless Brett agrees to your offer there's really no decision on my part to make. But I do wish you well."

"Good enough. I'll let you know one way or the other, bye."

Saturday, September 14, 10:40 A.M.
The Abbey, Birmingham, Michigan

The personal computer still had all those yellow sticky notes plastered all over the monitor and the sofa was still piled high with books. Rick Blaine had just sat down, and the Reverend Ryan Sladden was shoving a stack of papers to one side of his desk in a feeble attempt at tidying the place up. "Good to see you again, Rick. I was really pleased to hear about you landing a job so quickly."

"Yes, I have to admit it seemed like someone was pushing all the right buttons for me." Rick had dropped by The Abbey in hopes of catching Ryan alone in his office.

"Well, congratulations again."

"Thanks, seems like such a long time ago that I hardly think about it. As if it never happened."

"So, Rick. To what do I owe the pleasure of this visit?"

"Ah, it's a little hard to say, I mean to put into words. You see, I've this friend, and this friend has a problem."

"A friend in need, huh?"

"What? Oh yeah, right. Anyway, this friend is married, happily married, but he's being drawn towards someone else. This friend asked me to help him, so I figured you must have run across this type of situation before, so here I am."

"Here you am, what?"

Rick was startled at the retort. Was Ryan making a joke? "Ah, here I am asking you what to tell this guy who's falling in love with someone else."

"Is your friend looking for approval?"

"No, advice."

Ryan sat back in his chair. There was absolutely no indication if the cleric had already penetrated the flimsy deception. Who did he think he was kidding anyhow? Sure he knew the "friend" idea was lame, but it was all he could think of. His feelings towards Ashley were growing more powerful daily, he didn't know what to do, or who to talk to. He was also growing more distant from Stephanie, and he'd caught himself intentionally avoiding her. But who could blame him? She was always so busy, so tired, so boring. It's no fun making love to someone you almost had to splash with cold water to wake up.

"Ah, you see, Ryan, well, my friend said he thinks he's in love with this other person." Rick couldn't believe he'd just said that. Did he really "love" Ashley?

"Is he truly in love, or is it infatuation?"

"How's that?"

"Is your friend really in love, or is this a crush of some sort. Those are quite common. Well, not too common I'm happy to say."

"No, my friend said love, so I guess he meant it." Come to think about it, I guess I do love her. It feels so right.

"What does love mean to your friend?"

"Huh? What does love mean?"

"Yes, exactly. What is your friend's definition of love?"

"I don't know really, guess its feeling like you never want to leave the person, and always want to be with them, something like that."

Reaching behind himself, Ryan pulled a book off a shelf full of other books and began flipping pages. "It's important to know that love cuts both ways. Both parties have to feel the same way about the other. Oh, yes. Here we are. I've always liked this definition of love. Never been able to improve upon it. Here goes . . . Love is patient; love is kind; love is not envious or boastful or arrogant or rude. It does not insist on its own way. It is not irritable or resentful; it does not rejoice in wrongdoing, but rejoices in the truth. It bears all things, believes all things, hopes all things, endures all things. Love never ends." Ryan looked up and added, "Not bad, huh?"

Rick was going to have to think if love by that definition fit better with Ashley or Stephanie. But Ryan was right, "Yeah, that's pretty good."

"All I'll add is to tell your friend not to rush into anything. It's curious, but a lot of adults in similar circumstances have told me: Having is not as exciting as wanting. Usually they figure this out too late."

Rick didn't want that to be true. "Ah, right. That quote you just read. Was it a poem or something? I'll tell my friend to pick it up at a bookstore. I'm sure he'd like to read it himself."

"It wasn't written by a poet, well, not exactly. It was written by a man named Paul, to the faithful in a city named Corinth, quite a few years back. You'll find it in any Bible, *First Corinthians, chapter thirteen, verse four.*"

Talk about being blindsided. Rick stood, shook hands and then left without knowing what to do next.

Having his heart torn like this had never happened, and he was ill prepared to deal with it. Up till now his family always came first, he never had a wandering eye. If one year ago someone had suggested he was going to have an affair, he'd have laughed in their face. But not now . . . not anymore.

Monday, September 16, 10:00 A.M.
Hilborn Residence, Ann Arbor

Jenny continued believing the world had collapsed around her, and there was precious little Charles could do to ease her suffering. His love for Jenny was boundless; they were a team, partners, friends. Never would he have joined LoneStar if he knew this would be the result.

So he sequestered himself, and after hours of deliberation Charles decided he could help her most by exposing Brett Hollister and that sleaze ball Congressman Lodge, and then getting Jenny her job back. In order to do that however, he needed leverage on Brett, and he knew just the man who could help.

"Dr. Hilborn, of course I remember you. I must say I'm surprised that you're calling me."

"Thanks for taking my call, Mr. King. I'll just start by saying how very sorry I am at the way you were pushed off the board at LoneStar. It was poorly handled." Arthur King was the one person Charles could think of who might have damaging information on Brett and who wasn't beholden to, or afraid of, or intimidated by the man.

"Yes, I wasn't pleased either, Dr. Hilborn. Is that why you called, to offer me your condolences?"

"No. Not in the least, Mr. King. I'd like to be honest with you—"

"You're the second person to use that phrase with me, Dr. Hilborn. I don't think I like it much anymore. A while back a fast talking lady led me like a newborn steer, fed me a business proposition and then never called back."

"I'm sorry to hear that, Mr. King. I meant only that I'd like the two of us to speak frankly with each other." Who else called him? Charles wondered.

"If you must." The "and make it short" went unspoken, but was clearly implied.

"Mr. King, there are certain members of the board at LoneStar who are not at all pleased with the way Brett Hollister is conducting himself. In fact, there will probably be some pressure applied on him to resign."

"Why would Brett resign?"

Charles could tell the conversation had suddenly caught Arthur's attention. "Certain board members believe he can be induced to resign with a generous severance package."

The reply was laced with sarcasm, "Bull." Arthur sighed and continued, "No, Dr. Hilborn. Brett will not be bought off. Take it from me; he'll stay there until he dies. It's his company. You can tell those New York hot shots that it ain't gonna work that way, no matter what they offer him."

"I tend to agree with you, Mr. King. But certain actions taken by Mr. Hollister have compelled me to assist the dissident directors. Now, I'm not sure how many others are as totally committed to removing him as I am, but I can tell you that he is not on a pedestal any longer. I doubt there would be too many mourners."

"Okay, so what do you want from me?"

"I, like you, Mr. King, don't believe Brett can be offered enough money to leave voluntarily. He has to be presented with a deal, something he understands, where the best course of action for him is to resign. Then he'd have no alternative but to take a package and go."

"Yep. That's how I see it, Dr. Hilborn."

"What I need is something that he did. Something that if brought to the public's attention would damage his credibility and tarnish his name. I need something that's provable to the board, to Brett, and his lawyers."

"You've seemed to have given this a great deal of thought, Dr. Hilborn. What's your reason, if I may ask? You haven't known him all that long."

"My reasoning is that he's lost his grip on reality. He believes that the ends justify the means, his means. He's inflexible in his thinking and has surrounded himself with a bunch of yes men who do nothing but feather their own nests and heap hollow praises upon each other, feeding their already overinflated egos. Add to that, I think he takes pleasure in humiliating people, it somehow makes him feel, I don't know, important."

"I see."

"Mr. King, can you help me? I can't promise you anything, but I'll do what I can to make it up to you."

"I think I'm going to like working with you, Dr. Hilborn."

Feeling his first surge of excitement in a week, Charles said, "Call me Charles."

"Thank you, I will. Please call me Arthur. Now this is no reflection on you, Charles, but I've decided recently to insist on face-to-face meetings to discuss LoneStar, or any new business interests. No telephone arrangements. As I said before, I was recently played the fool and I've learned my lesson."

"Sure. Well, why don't we meet at D/FW airport? How about the Admirals Club? I can call to confirm the time early next week."

"Wonderful. I look forward to that, Charles. Goodbye."

Running his hands through his hair, Charles decided to make his wife a pot of tea as he replayed the conversation with Arthur in his head. It appeared most promising.

278

Tuesday, September 17, 11:45 A.M.
Cypress Offices, Manhattan

Brett was being treated like a member of the royal family. The limousine driver was waiting for him at the baggage area, holding a white cardboard card with "Mr. Hollister" written in bold, black letters. The ride to Manhattan was beset with stops and starts caused by clogged intersections and narrow streets, which was quite normal and expected. What wasn't expected was the bowing and scraping of the Cypress staff, attempting to meet the fiery Texan's every whim.

"Please come in, Mr. Hollister, thank you so very much for visiting us." Paul Victor had on his best, warmest smile for Brett. "Please help yourself to the buffet. Can I offer you something to drink?"

"Yes, coffee. Black would be fine. I'll just poke around here and take a few canapés, maybe some salad." Brett was almost enjoying himself. Did these dumbfucks think he'd be taken in by all this charm and hospitality? Horseshit. I've stomped cockroaches with more smarts than these boys have, Brett mused.

"I've invited our other three board members of LoneStar to join us. They'll be here momentarily. Lovely day isn't it? How was your flight?"

"The flight was fine, although I have yet to fully appreciate your quaint driving customs."

"Ha ha, yes, I know what you mean. Oh, good, here they are now." The other three recently installed LoneStar directors entered. They all shook Brett's hand, and then grabbed plates and began filling them with luncheon delicacies and desserts. For the next ten minutes the five men ate, drank and immersed themselves in small talk. At the appropriate time, Paul Victor cleared his throat indicating that the chitchatting was formally at an end.

"Thank you again for visiting us on such short notice, Brett. I'd like to start by saying that we at Cypress have been very pleased with our investment in LoneStar, ever since we purchased those convertible bonds."

A black day indeed, Brett murmured to himself, while still smiling at his host.

"Now that we are significant shareholders, we look for even greater rewards from LoneStar. It goes without saying, Brett, that without you at the wheel LoneStar would still be a small time, two-bit outfit, struggling to make a buck. But with your leadership, well, LoneStar is now a highly prized company and other firms are bound to see the inherent value for a strategic alliance." Paul was smiling, the three other directors were smiling and Brett was smiling. What a marvelous meeting this was turning out to be. Brett noticed Paul eyeing his comrades and slowly nodding his head at them as if to say, "We've got this pig herder right where we want him."

Paul continued, "Brett, what we want to discuss is how we can best leverage LoneStar, to join it with another firm and make it a truly great company. Now we all appreciate how difficult it might be for you to be part of that scenario, how a change like that could be awkward and how you might want to pursue other alternatives or options, particularly while you're still at the top of your game. Now we don't have any intention of holding you back, actually we'd like to help you, you know, for all you've done for us.

"With that in mind we'd like to have you read these documents. I think you'll find them most acceptable. In fact, we can have you talk to one of our private investment consultants if you'd like, seeing as how you might need one shortly." That last statement induced the Cypress team members to respond with good-natured chuckles and smirks. "However, we'd like to hear what you have to say too. I'm confident we can work out an agreeable separation package." The four Cypress employees all sat back in unison, all smiling, all silently praying.

Taking a few minutes to look over the documents, Brett finally looked at each man and then Paul Victor. "Let me tell you what I think of you and your proposal . . ." Oh, you're a good man Chester Bennett, he said to himself. You were right on. You figured out exactly what this scum was up to. Well, Mr. Paul Victor, I can play this game better than you.

In a nervous reflex action to Brett's pending reply, Paul pulled out a handkerchief and blew his nose. Brett waited a few extra moments for effect and then concluded his statement, ". . . after a brief review, your proposal does merit further consideration on my part." Brett couldn't help but smile. These boys had no idea who they were jerking with. Suddenly, he remembered a few lines from an old Jim Croce song: ". . . You don't spit into the wind, you don't pull the mask off the old Lone Ranger and you don't mess around with . . . me."

The high-strung Mr. Victor appeared totally relieved and absolutely elated by Brett's answer. "I'm really glad to see we can work together. I told these guys you were smart, that we could do a deal, that we both want what's right for LoneStar and the stockholders. See, guys? Yes sir, Brett. We're going to work real good together."

"I'm looking forward to it too, Paul. It's time for me to stop beating my head against a wall. After we settle on a suitable partner to buy LoneStar, and once we've completed negotiations with them, well, could be I'll just take my package and retire." And if pigs had wings they'd fly.

Paul grinned from ear to ear, and concurred, "You got that right, Brett. My friend, you're going to make millions, millions." Smiles broke out all around the conference table, hearty handshakes ensued as were fond goodbyes, and Brett was ushered back into the limousine to redeposit him at La Guardia. Weaving their way through traffic Brett picked up the car phone and called his general counsel in Dallas.

After a ten-minute conversation with Chester Bennett, Brett made a local call to Gary Nash who had tagged along to visit the offices of Pagent and Associates.

* * *

Gary had been rather impatient for his bosses' phone call. Finally the debriefing came. "Okay Brett, I understand, sure, sure. Look, I think you did the right thing. Why don't you just catch the next plane back home? I've still got some work to do here, so I'll probably fly back tomorrow. That's right, good, un huh, right, okay, see you then." Gary Nash had been force-fed the next series of plays by his chairman. His head was still spinning as he left Bob Bell at Pagent and Associates, flagged a taxi and made his way uptown towards the Parker Meridian. Ashley was to meet him for dinner at some fancy French restaurant a few blocks away from the hotel.

True to form, Gary's cab became stuck in rush hour gridlock complete with horns blaring, carbon monoxide pouring out of ancient delivery trucks, robot like pedestrians doing battle on the sidewalks, bicycles and roller blades spinning around endless seas of yellow cars . . . all part of Manhattans' charm. "The games afoot," Gary announced under his breath.

Thirty minutes later he was let off at Le Cygne, on 54th street, between Park and Madison. Ashley was already there sitting at the small bar with men stacked about two deep around her, plying her with drinks and lavish praise. Gary muscled his way through, whispered in her ear, kissed her on the cheek, received a great big hug in return, grabbed her in tow, and bullied his way through the crowd to the waiting Maitre d' and their table. Oh, those envious eyes that bored into Gary's back.

* * *

Ashley could tell Gary was a bit preoccupied. Their polite conversation through most of the dinner was just that, polite. She'd been trying to loosen him up, but her undivided attention, flirtatious body language and tracing his inner thigh with her bare foot under the tablecloth hadn't worked. Even after four stiff bourbon and waters, Gary would only say that Brett's meeting with Paul Victor went about as expected. Gary was being coy, she decided. Imagine, trying to delude himself that she couldn't coax the truth out of him! Pretty damn sure of yourself aren't you, Mr. Nash? Well, I accept the challenge. Ashley beamed her most radiant smile at him.

* * *

Gary *was* pretty pleased with the day's events. Brett's plan seemed to be coming together and Bob Bell had informed him that his own SWAP transaction had stabilized, and he was back at six hundred seven thousand dollars to the good. That sure eased his mind. But to top it all off, during dinner Ashley had fallen all over herself, hanging on his every word and trying her best to seduce him. Then too, take a look around the dining room. Every male patron was green with envy wondering how a guy like Gary could have such an angel. Eat your hearts out.

Admittedly, a handful of female diners gave the impression they'd just as soon watch Ashley choke and die; but quite a few also looked longingly at Gary, obviously recognizing his highly desirable attributes, just as Ashley had. Yes, all in all, it was a pretty fair day.

"Gary, let's get out of here, I don't think I can wait any longer," Ashley moaned suggestively.

To be sure, having her foot massaging his thigh and groin area took the luster off hanging around for dessert. "Whatever you say, love?" Did he have this tart eating out of his hand or what? With a snap of his fingers the check appeared, was paid for and a cab hailed. Once inside the cab Ashley's hand found its way to his inner thigh, taking over the duties previously performed by her foot. No complaints were forthcoming.

Welcoming Gary back to the hotel, the registration clerk handed over a room key and pointed them to the elevators around the corner of the lobby. Like kids, they held hands and giggled until the elevator doors opened on the thirty-third floor, at which time they rushed down the hall to the waiting room. Barely had they entered when Ashley practically broke his neck with a passionate kiss.

* * *

Coming up for air, she rubbed her hands all over Gary's back and bottom. Now we'll see who cracks first, Ashley said to herself. Purring like a kitten, she suggested, "Gary, I think you should sit down on the bed." She couldn't help but notice the dumb smirk on his face. Think you're pretty smart don't you? Think you've got me wrapped around your finger, huh? Well Gary Nash, you're gonna tell me everything. Everything!

With a sultry voice honed over the years, Ashley whispered, "Gary, I want to dress up for you again, but I can't make up my mind what to wear. So I brought three of my favorite outfits and what we'll do is this: I'll describe them to you, and after I'm finished you tell me which one you want me to put on. Okay?" She could tell Gary liked this game, liked it a lot.

Knowing exactly how to manipulate the man, Ashley added, "But first, you have to get comfortable and relax a bit. Yes, that's right, untie your tie, take off your suit coat, slip off your shoes, lean back against the headboard, and put some pillows behind you . . . good. All right, now we can start." Gary was transfixed, she had his undivided attention.

Standing at the foot of the bed, Ashley began, "The first is called a merrywidow . . .," Ashley used her hands to outline on her own body what she was describing, " . . . it's a white, stretch mesh bodice with lace insets, so you can see my nipples right through the fabric. It has underwire cups with a little ruffle at the hem. Oh, and I can wear it with or without garters. The bikini bottoms are the thong type, you know, the ones that travel right up my cheeks, like this, and shows off most of my behind?" Gary was starting to hyperventilate. "So how does that one sound to you?"

Words were difficult for him to form, but he anxiously nodded his head and uttered, "Okay," in a weakening voice.

Ashley pouted. "Only okay? Well, we'll just have to do better won't we?" Ashley guessed that he'd last through one more description. "Next, I brought along a real intimate black number. There's a lace bra with scalloped cups, so you can get a good look at my breasts. Then there's a lace garter-hose that's one piece, but looks like a lace garter belt and stockings. Oh, and the stockings are black and have a lace top, they come way up here on my thigh. There's a matching thong bikini bottom too, you know what those are now, right? Would you like to see me wearing that?"

Gary was a quivering mass of manly flesh, practically drooling from his mouth like a little boy overdosing in candyland. Ashley feigned annoyance and said, "Now, Gary, you'll have to tell me if you'd like me wearing that or not. I can't understand you."

"Yesss, yesss. I'd really like to see you wear that. Just please hurry."

Ashley congratulated herself as she went into the bathroom to change. Why is it women find dealing with men so difficult? They're so predictable.

CHAPTER 18

Wednesday, September 18, 8:15 A.M.
Chairman's Office, LoneStar

LoneStar was typically deserted this early in the morning. Only the security guards and housekeepers were about making sure everything was as it should be, and that all of the coffee makers were fully loaded and brewing. Chester and Brett were sitting in Brett's private conference room alone, looking at the papers Paul Victor had presented Brett during yesterday's meeting.

"You know, Brett, this severance package ain't half bad. You'd walk out of here with close to seven million dollars."

The chairman peered at Chester with surprise in his eyes and said, "Those pricks can choke on their fucking money for all I care. They're not getting my company and that's final. Hell, I'd rather blow this whole damned place up, sell it for scrap, than let'em have it."

Brett suddenly grinned and added, "But you should have seen the look on their faces when I almost said 'yes' to their scheme. Shit, they must think I'm the dumbest son of a bitch to come their way in a long time."

Chester shrugged and said, "Brett, I've been thinking over your plan and I gotta tell you, it's awfully risky."

"Sure it's risky. No guarantees. But if we can report really poor earnings this quarter and then I announce something like, oh, like I'm not sure how long it'll take us to get back on track, hell, the investment community will drop our stock like a hot rock. If we can help knock the price back under forty bucks a share, then those Cypress assholes will start booking losses. One thing I know, they sure as hell can't afford to report losses. Their clients will start pulling money out so fast it'll make Victor's head spin. I figure Cypress will cut and run, maybe even before we hit forty. Then no more Cypress and no more Paul Victor. Besides, whoever buys their stock has gotta be better than them, right? Then we can start inching the stock up again. Anyway, what've we got to lose?"

Chester slowly nodded his head, "Okay, what'll we do next?"

"You, me and Nash need to have a meeting with our public accounting firm, a real private meeting. Probably only with the managing partner, Joel Freedman. We have to make sure he'll look the other way, let us record some extraordinary losses so we can panic Wall Street a little. I'll set up the meeting in the next couple days. Now I've already said this to Nash and I'll say it to you, no one can know what we're up to, no one. Not your wife, your secretary, your girlfriend, shrink, nobody. Got it?"

Chester shrugged at his boss and answered, "Brett, if there's only you, me and Gary Nash, you've got nothing to worry about."

Same day, 9:35 A.M.
Taylor-Bishop Offices, Manhattan

Ashley didn't sleep well and had risen early . . . Gary's revelations prior to having sex had seen to that. Hitting her intercom she said, "Joyce, no more calls for a while." The morning sun brightened the world outside and the coffee was fresh and hot, other than that it was a bleak day. She had to give Hollister credit, his plan as divulged by a blubbering Gary Nash last night was a good one, well, sort of good. If Brett was successful in surprising Wall Street with terrible earnings, LoneStar's stock would plummet. Every financial newspaper would print the story of unexpected losses, every research analyst following the stock would issue 'sell' recommendations. Victor and the boys at Cypress would be forced into panic selling, sending the stock further down and forever screwing up her own plan.

But, and this was a big 'but,' no public accounting firm would ever knowingly allow the management of a major publicly traded company to 'cook' the books as was being implied. A tweak here and there as Arthur King mentioned could be overlooked, but nothing so blatant as what Hollister had in mind. However, even if this idea didn't work,

Brett would try to pull something else. Ashley had to look at this from every possible perspective, and choose her next moves very carefully. She turned on her computer, inserted a disk titled 'LoneStar' and began typing.

Thursday, September 19, 10:20 A.M.
Dallas/Fort Worth Airport

Certain privileged travelers get a choice of lounging in one of the Admirals Club's at D/FW International Airport. Charles Hilborn and Arthur King shook hands in the club's lobby in the 3E terminal across from gate thirty-three. They ordered a couple cups of coffee at the bar, found their way to a deserted spot and sat down in comfortable chairs.

Ensuring no one was eavesdropping, Charles began in a confidential tone, "As I said on the phone, Arthur, I need something that I can pin on Brett. Something that he won't be able to squirm out of, something his lawyers can't poke holes through." Charles had never wanted to nail someone so badly, but then no one had ever hurt his Jenny like this either. She still wouldn't leave the house; she just sat there most of the day staring at a television screen.

"Charles, I talked to my father, who's not a Hollister fan either. We think Brett's intimidation of the public accounting firm is as good a place as any. I know he's had the managing partner overrule junior auditors and browbeat them into altering their 'work papers' so no one will be the wiser. You know about work papers? Those notes written in longhand where the lowly accounting scribes spend hours and hours painstakingly recording their findings? They're usually on legal size yellow sheets of paper. Anyway, these papers are used as proof of an audit's integrity and independence. It's the backup, the outline, the diary if you will, used to support their conclusions."

Accounting was not Charles' strong suit. "So how can I use them?" For a handful of reasons he had decided not to bring up his last conversation with Paul Victor regarding the severance agreement for Brett Hollister and presidency for him, mainly because he just didn't believe it would happen. No matter how convinced Paul was, Charles felt sure Brett had other plans. He'd never simply walk off into the sunset. But kicking ass and screaming all the way? Yeah.

Arthur lowered his voice and said, "Emmet Griswald, the controller is the man you need to have a chat with. Emmet's been there for years. He's worked with all the auditors of Russell, Powell and Young. He also has knowledge of Brett's 'irregular' accounting changes."

"Can I trust Emmet?"

"Can you trust him for an honest answer? Yes. Can you trust him to tell you everything? Probably. Can you trust him to keep this private between the two of you and not tell Brett? I don't know."

"Hmm. So do you have any suggestions? Emmet's gotta know he'll lose his job if he's ever caught helping me."

"Yes, I agree. Listen, you tell Emmet he has a job at my bank anytime he wants."

Charles was taken aback by the gracious offer. "Thank you; I really appreciate that, Arthur."

"Hey, good controllers are hard to come by, so don't go getting mushy on me. This is strictly business."

"Sure, but I still appreciate the offer. Any thoughts on the best way to approach Emmet?"

"I suggest you don't just drop in for a tête-à-tête. Brett will find out and eat you both for lunch. You can't call Emmet either, because he'll probably say he's busy and he'll call you back, only he'll go straight to Brett first. So the only way I can think is for you to buy a good pair of running shoes and go jogging along Turtle Creek around noon tomorrow."

"What?" Charles must have heard wrong.

Tugging on his bow tie, Arthur grinned devilishly and answered, "Emmet runs every day, weather permitting, along Turtle Creek Boulevard. I think he puts in about ten miles. That should give you plenty of time to strike up a friendly conversation, presuming you're in fairly good shape."

Charles didn't see much humor in this situation. Instead he said, "Wait. This isn't what I had in mind. I was thinking more like meeting him for lunch, or maybe after work for a couple of cold beers." He had to admit he wasn't in the best of shape.

Reaching over and slapping him on the back, Arthur laughingly replied, "Charles, you'd better check into a hotel and get some sleep. You're gonna need it." Charles was not happy.

Friday, September 20, 8:15 A.M.
Taylor-Bishop Offices, Manhattan

The hired 'snitch,' Jackie Wells was desperate. She needed money and Paul Victor was the only source she knew for getting quick cash. Unfortunately, she still couldn't find anything of value at Taylor-Bishop . . . no disk codes, no secret strategies, no diagrams, and no nothing on why Ashley hadn't bought any LoneStar stock. It was like a security curtain had been suddenly dropped. The other employees no longer left sensitive papers or files laying about either, and paper shredders had been recently installed, which rendered her wastebasket treasure hunting routine pointless.

I want something, anything. A hustling Lauren almost bumped into Jackie and that gave her an idea. Why not ask an innocent question? What've I got to lose? She'll just think I'm inquisitive, trying to learn more about the business.

Lauren Washington was heading back to her own office when Jackie caught up with her. "Excuse me, Lauren. Do you have a minute?"

"Oh, hello, Jackie. Uh, sure, a minute. What can I do for you?"

"I've got a question about the stock market. Suppose you knew some information about a certain company, and suppose that you wanted to make some money off that information by buying the company's stock. Okay, now suppose you don't buy any of the stock of that company. So, the question is: How can you make money without buying any stock?" Jackie replayed that question in her mind before saying to herself: Yeah, that's what I want to know.

Lauren seemed to consider the problem for a moment and then answered, "Hmm, well, since this is a hypothetical case, I'd probably look into selling the stock, not buying it."

Doubt crossed Jackie's mind. "What do you mean sell the stock? I said you didn't own any."

"I heard what you said, Jackie. My answer to your question is to sell the stock."

Probably didn't understand the question. "No, you can't do that. You can't sell something you don't own."

"Sure you can. First call a broker. Then you borrow shares from the broker's own inventory at today's price, say ten dollars, and then you enter into an agreement with the broker to sell them for you, also at ten dollars. Then the proceeds are credited to your account. Then you wait for the stock price to go down. Say it goes to eight. Once the stock price is down, you have your broker go out into the market and buy back the same number of shares to 'cover' the ones you originally borrowed and sold. That closes out your position and the broker has the same number of shares he initially started with. See, your winnings come from replacing the stock you sold at ten with stock that you bought later at eight. It works great if the stock falls, not so great if the stock rises."

All Jackie could think of was: Why haven't I ever heard of this? "I only thought you could win if stock prices go up. Betting stock prices will go down seems, well, un-American."

Lauren smiled and said, "Yeah, I suppose it does. That's how most investors think too. Selling short, that's what it's called, isn't used all that much. I guess it's traditional for investors to pick out stocks they think are about to skyrocket, you know, like a lot of the technology stocks did in the 90's. What average guy sits around trying to figure out which stock is about to sink?"

Jackie pursed her lips and then asked, "But if you sold short, and then the stock price increases—"

"Yep, you're right. Then you'd be caught buying back shares at say twelve dollars to cover the shares you've already borrowed and sold at ten. That's a two dollar loss to you. Obviously, it can get real expensive if the market rallies significantly and you're holding onto short positions. It's a great way to go broke fast. Most brokers require you to keep enough security with them to cover potential losses, just so they won't end up paying for your mistake."

Jackie nodded and said, "Learn something new every day, but I don't think that's what I'm looking for." Now she wasn't even sure what she *was* looking for. All she knew was, this selling short was way over her head and she just couldn't make herself think that way. It was like betting against the home team. Besides, everyone wanted LoneStar's stock to rise.

Looking at her watch, Lauren said, "Uh, Jackie, I've got to get going . . ."

"Oh, sure. Thanks for your time." But now what? She still needed something for Paul Victor.

Same day, 12:15 P.M.
Turtle Creek bike path, Dallas

Ya know, this isn't any fun. Actually, I hate this. I'm hot, tired, my lungs are gonna burst and my legs feel like jello. I'm gonna die, I know I'm gonna die. I can't go any farther. Hey, maybe a cadence would help. Yeah, that's it, I'll do a cadence. Let's see . . . I-want-to-be-an-Air-born-Ran-ger, I-want-to-live-the-life-of-dan-ger . . . Whoa, where'd that come from? Nope, sure don't like that one. For the love of God, Emmet, slow down a bit.

Charles had spotted Emmet Griswald ten minutes ago about a quarter mile ahead, but the miserable little controller ran like a deer. Charles had

scarcely managed to keep himself within eyesight. Emmet was now circling a large garden of red flowers, Azaleas, Charles guessed. Hey, here's my chance, he thought. Without hesitation, Charles took a shortcut straight through the flowerbed leaving a path of death and destruction in his wake, but finally ended up in front of Emmet.

The surprised controller reduced speed and said, "Dr. Hilborn? Hi. Didn't know you were in town, or that you were a runner." As the good doctor was unable to verbally respond, Emmet slowed down to a mere walk to match Charles' wobbly trot.

Coughing and sweating, Charles gasped out, "Love it. Great for the heart." After that last burst of energy, Charles was laboring for every breath.

"You don't look so good."

"I'm gasping for air at the moment. Say, can we walk slower for a bit?"

"Sure. You okay? You want to sit down? I can flag a cab."

"Don't rub it in." They were both walking along the river, although only one of them was holding his sides and moaning. Charles coughed again and muttered under his breath, "I'll get you King."

"Excuse me?"

"Oh, nothing. Just remembered that I owe someone something. Listen, Emmet, I didn't just happen to be jogging along the same path as you today. My intention was to find you, talk to you privately." Driblets of sweat covered his face, and Charles' attempts at using his equally wet arms to swipe them away failed miserably. Much to his discouragement, Emmet wasn't even perspiring.

The controller gazed around the area as if to see if they were alone. "I see. So what do you want to talk about?"

Arthur had warned Charles about Emmet's speech problem, so Charles was prepared for a litany of strung together words. But so far, nothing. Emmet noticed him staring and said, "I only have difficulty speaking when I'm nervous."

Embarrassed, Charles said, "I'm sorry, Emmet. I didn't mean anything—"

"Forget it. What can I do for you?"

"Right, let me get to the point. A few of us directors are no longer comfortable with Brett Hollister running the show. For a lot of reasons we feel he's unqualified. Now, we don't want a public execution, in fact, a very generous severance package has been offered. I'm inclined to think he'll reject it, but you never know. In the event he refuses the package I need something that by merely letting Brett know that I have it, he'll resign, with dignity and full benefits I might add.

"I need your help. I understand that he's been involved with altering auditors work papers, which violates the spirit if not the actual intent of quite a few governmental rules and regulations. If that can be documented, I can force him out."

Emmet stopped walking and said, "You expect me, after twenty-six years to turn against my chairman? Even if I wanted to, at the mere hint of what you're . . . proposing, um, Brett would fire me. Look doctor, I needmyjobinidn. I need the pension, the health insurance, life insurance . . . I've got more than just myself to thinkaboutopvp. I've a wife and three kids. It's not fair to them."

"I know, Emmet, and if there was another way I'd take it. But you're the only one who can give me what I need. If you require reasons . . ."

Shaking his head, Emmet interrupted by stating, "No, no I don't need reasons. I'm aware of what Brett's become. He's changed you know. I, I don't like going to work, don't like getting up in the morning. I even stay up late on Sunday nights, to delay Monday from coming. Each time I'm called into his office, or each time my phone rings, my stomachturnsintoknotsoiwehj. He yells and screams. Look, I'm, ah, sputtering again. So no, you don't have totellmeaboutoewno Brett Hollister."

"I'm very sorry for you, Emmet." What a wretched existence.

"I don'tneedoevnw your sympathy, I ah, said all that so you'd understand that I'm here becauseIneedajobpiwvppw. Have to think of my family." Emmet started to walk again.

Raising his voice a notch, Charles said, "Okay, but what if I told you that you have an alternative?"

Emmet stopped and asked, "What alternative?"

"Arthur King needs a controller. He's holding that position open for you."

An assortment of emotions crossed Emmet's face. Finally, he said, "Thanks, it's good to know someone thinks well of me. Please tell Arthur I'm very flattered, but I'm the controller of LoneStar. I'm, I'm sorry, Dr. Hilborn, I can't help you." With that, Emmet broke into a trot leaving Charles far behind, standing in a pool of sweat.

Monday, September 23, 9:30 A.M.
Chairman's Office, LoneStar

All weekend long, Brett had gone over his plan for maneuvering Paul Victor into unloading his five million shares of LoneStar. Today's meeting with Joel Freeman was probably the most important one he'd be calling for quite a while, which was why he was more than a little upset that Chester and Gary weren't showing more enthusiasm. They just sat there, like bumps on a damned log. What's their problem? he wondered.

Placing his hands on the conference table, Brett wrapped up his solo speech by saying, "Okay, Joel, now you know our problem. What we need from you is a solution." Brett leaned forward and waited for the reply.

The long-time auditor, managing partner and major contributor to numerous Brett Hollister sponsored charities and political campaigns, Joel Freedman let his gaze drift past Chester Bennett and Gary Nash, and then settle on Brett. "Gentlemen, I've enjoyed our relationship and I understand the consequences of my next statement. But I have to tell you what you're suggesting is insane."

Brett eyes sharpened on Joel and his voice was a low rumble. "Watch what you say, Freedman."

Talking the thick glasses off his big bubble nose, Joel stroked his walrus-sized mustache and replied, "Brett, you cannot significantly alter the books of a publicly held company. The Securities and Exchange Commission would nail you and me and everyone else to a wall."

Sitting rigid, staring the man down, Brett said, "We've done it before."

Sweat began beading on Joel's face. It took effort to retort without whining, "No, not like this we haven't. Listen, I know you've tickled with the books a bit, you know, pumping up earnings by screwing around with reserves, or keeping inflated values of properties on the books for an extra quarter or two to avoid taking write-downs. But this, this is too much, we can't substantiate a forty or fifty million dollar surprise. We'd be sued by anyone who owns one share of stock for misleading them. Then we'd be jailed for falsifying records of a publicly held company. Everything bad that could possibly happen to us, would!"

"Balls", Brett exploded. "I want Cypress off my back. I want them out of here. I need to drop my stock price and I don't wanna hear I can't."

Wiping his face with his coat sleeves, Joel was quick to offer, "Nobody said you couldn't book losses Brett. I said you couldn't book fabricated losses." Brett looked at him with newfound respect and said, "Go on."

Taking a breath, the accountant whispered, "If you need a quick loss, go buy a company that can provide you one. Buy a company that's losing money, and in all likelihood will continue to lose money. The investment community will think you're nuts and your stock price will drop. Now you'll have to do some pretty fast talking to the other board members, but there's nothing illegal about being stupid. Ah, sorry, I didn't mean . . ."

Not bad. That wasn't a bad idea at all. Brett perked up and said, "Then when the time's right, after Cypress has unloaded their stock, we can sell the loser, say we goofed, then everything goes back to normal. Damn, Joel, I like it. I like it a lot."

Chester cleared his throat. "Ah, I'm not sure we want to jump into something like this without checking out the details. Besides, how can we find a lemon that we can resell when we want?"

Brett waved off Chester. "You just let me worry about that. I'm going to start making some calls. Chester you research anything you want . . . but you do it yourself. This has got to stay confidential. Anyone have any last comments? No? Okay, just one more thing. Who else do we have to tell, who else needs to know what we're doing?"

Motioning with his right hand Gary Nash said, "Griswald. We'll need Emmet, you know, to do the tax work and consolidating entries."

Brett nodded, "Okay, Gary, you talk to Emmet. Make damn sure he understands that this is top secret and no one else is to know anything. Got it?"

"Clear."

"Fine. That it?" Brett noticed Chester still wasn't very happy so he asked, "You got a problem, Chester?" The tone of the question left no mistake that the only acceptable response would be "no." The general counsel understood the situation all too well. "No problems, Brett."

CHAPTER 19

Tuesday, September 24, 4:05 P.M.
Cypress Offices, Manhattan

The stock market had closed five minutes ago and it didn't take long for the senior partners to come calling. "Paul, I'm sure you know that LoneStar is at forty-three a share. That's three dollars down from recent highs, which is fifteen million less profit for our investors and us. This isn't setting well with the rest of the membership."

What is this, a fucking echo? Paul murmured to himself. Two other partners voiced similar concerns about LoneStar and Paul was getting a little sick of the constant oversight and nagging. But instead of reacting indignantly, he simply said, "I appreciate your apprehension. Just let me assure you that once I've been able to bring in some serious bidders, this stock is going to shoot right through the roof. Hollister is probably counting his severance money, so he won't be a problem. Hilborn doesn't know enough to be a problem. We're going to make a killing on this one. I know it. That's a promise."

The partner didn't even flinch, but replied, "All right, Paul. Just remember we bayonet the wounded around here." Paul knew his associate wasn't kidding. Shit, I don't need this, he thought, grabbing for a tissue, blowing his nose and reaching for a couple antacid tablets.

Friday, September 27, 4:50 P.M.
Taylor-Bishop Offices, Manhattan

Something was amiss. Gary Nash hadn't called her since their last evening together and Ashley was getting worried. He was a far too valuable a source of information for her to lose. She needed him and would do almost anything to keep the relationship flourishing. Placing a call to Dallas herself, she waited until they were connected. "Hello, Gary. It's Ashley. Have you been avoiding me? Don't you want to see me anymore?" Ashley was using her best, softest, silkiest voice.

"Ashley! Oh no, nothing like that."

"So you're just too busy to call me, huh?"

"That's right, really. We're all jumping around here like chickens with our heads cut off. Brett's pushing all of us."

Oh? What new plan could Hollister be up to? "You'd rather work on Brett's silly plans than talk with me?"

"No, no. It's just that we don't have much time. Ever since our auditors said we couldn't book losses that weren't real, Brett's been having us scour the nation looking for a company we can buy that's a real loser."

Holly shit. That's how he's going to pull it off? Have to give the cretin credit, he's one devious son of a bitch. Holding her breath she asked, "So who's the lucky winner of your nationwide talent search?"

"Don't really know yet. Looks like it could be either General Systems out of Oregon or Conductor Images out of Southern California."

Bless you Gary Nash. That's what I needed. Thank you very, very much. She looked at her watch and said, "When do I get to see you again?"

"As soon as I can get away. Maybe in a week or two."

Better lay it on thick, she told herself. Don't want him straying. "I'm not sure I want to wait that long. Can't you call me in a couple of days?"

"Ah, absolutely. Um, but now I've got to run, goodbye dear."

Dear? Now it's dear? Well, I suppose I can live with that. Getting up from behind her desk, she strolled to the window and thought: Brett's going to buy a loser, huh? Good plan, bad timing. Too bad I can't let him do it, at least not yet. The stock's nowhere high enough for me to start shorting. I want it in the sixties. Then Brett can blow the place up if he wants and send the price screaming down into oblivion.

A flash of inspiration smacked her, sending her running out the office door. She caught Joyce's attention and in a hushed voice said, "Call Jackie, tell her to get over here, say I have to go over something with her. As soon as you hang up, get in here." Yesss, this is going to work out just fine.

After making the call Joyce hurried into her boss' office and said, "Jackie's on her way."

"Great. You sit down, take this note pad and start scribbling."

"Start scribbling?"

"Yes! Just do it." Ashley moved some files around on her desk. Okay, she thought, now I'm ready. Where are you Jackie? Hurry, I need to tell you something . . . something you're not supposed to know.

After a few seconds Jackie poked her head in the office. "You wanted to see me Ashley?"

Looking up from a file that happened to be upside down, Ashley quickly slammed it shut and said, "Yes, yes I do. But I'm right in the middle of dictating a letter, why don't you just sit down. I'll be right with you. Now where were we, Joyce?"

Joyce hadn't a clue where they were. "Huh? Um, I'm not sure . . ."

Jumping in before Joyce had a chance to blow the charade, Ashley said, "That's right, I remember. So to continue . . . I'm concerned that the contemplated purchase by LoneStar at this time could be detrimental to the overall strategic plan as envisioned. Please forward any information you have on General Services out of Oregon, and Conductor Images out of Southern California to my attention A.S.A.P. I cannot stress strongly enough that I am gravely concerned. Okay, Joyce. Did you get all of that?"

Ashley looked straight at Joyce and repeated slowly for Jackie's benefit, "Did you get their names? That's General Services and Conductor Images."

Did it work? Let's hope so. "Now get that letter off as quickly as possible. That's all for now, thanks." Joyce got up with a very perplexed look on her face, but thankfully didn't say a word. Once they were alone, Ashley said, "Sorry to keep you waiting, Jackie, just some unfinished business."

Jackie's face turned ecstatic but she tried not to show it. This was the kind of information Paul Victor would pay plenty for. This was her lucky day. "Sure, no problem, what can I do for you?"

"Well, I've been meaning to talk to you about setting up some new files, you see . . ." Oh, Jackie. Dear, dear Jackie. I can tell what you see. You see dollar signs dancing in front of your eyes. Want to know what I see? I see you telling that insignificant bug Paul Victor exactly what I want you to tell him. Come into my parlor . . .

Same day, Seven minutes later
Cypress Offices, Manhattan

It had been a miserable week for Paul Victor, but all it took was one call to change everything. He was suddenly whispering, "Okay, Jackie, I hear you. Let me do some research on the companies and if there's anything to this, I'll get back to you with another check. No, I promise. Bye." Paul Victor was confused. What could Hollister be up to? Why would he be trying to buy another firm when the plan was for him to sell the one he was running? Just didn't make sense. Odds are that Jackie made it up, or heard wrong. Well, a few phone calls would clear it up.

Sensing a growing tremor in his stomach, Paul tore open a packet of antacid tablets, dropped them in a glass, added water and drank. A good thing to remember was to keep Jackie on a short chain. She was the newest of his "snitches" and was desperate for cash, giving him concern that she could fabricate a tidbit just to get a check. The other six had been supplying him sensitive information for years and were like family. It was a great set up. For essentially peanuts he'd managed to scoop his competition and beat them to the punch time after time. Well, that's what makes the world go around, right?

Monday, September 30, 9:01 A.M.
Chairman's Office, LoneStar

Sipping his first cup of black coffee of the day, Brett ran his thick fingers across the leather bound desk calendar, paused every so often, and jotted down names of people he needed to contact. With any luck, initial negotiations would commence with Conductor Images by mid-October. Turning a few more calendar pages he circled November 15. That was the target date for signing the final papers, and by early December . . . Paul Victor would be history. Reaching for the phone he began to dial Chester Bennett. He'd noticed a certain lack of enthusiasm on Chester's part, and that had to change.

Before completing the call his secretary buzzed him. "Mr. Hollister? Mr. Paul Victor is on the line for you." Stopping his finger in mid-flight, Brett hesitated and then hit the blinking light. Victor probably wanted to stroke him a few more times and then talk about that damned separation agreement. The man was dumber than a box of rocks. "Hello Paul, what a pleasant surprise. I was just . . ."

"Save your horseshit for someone else, Hollister. Who the fuck do you think you're screwing with? Who the fuck do you think you are?"

What was this all about? Who the hell did he think he was talking to? "Don't use that tone of voice with me, Victor. I don't have to listen to it."

"You pompous ass. Did you think you could pull off something like this without me knowing about it? Are you that fucking stupid?"

Brett's sensors went on full alert. "What seems to be the problem?"

"I'm talking about you going behind my back and fucking me. I'm talking about you thinking you're so damned smart that you can go and buy a fucking loser of a company to fuck me."

Damn the man. How did he know? "Look, Paul, you got this all wrong. Why would I want to buy a company that's losing money?"

"Now you're insulting my intelligence? Shit, Hollister. You think I'm some kind of a dumbass? I know all about the companies you're sniffing out and it don't take much smarts to figure out you're trying to trash your stock. You want the stock to tumble, right? You're trying to force me to sell, right? Well, you're fucking inept. Now you listen real good. Call off all discussions with General Services, Conductor Images and anyone else. And don't ever try something like this again. I want a full report on this incident by the next board meeting. *It's now an official agenda item, here me?*" Paul slammed down the phone.

"*Suzanne, get me Nash and Bennett. I mean now!*" Someone talked. One of those two ingrates talked, and Brett was going to skin the bastard. No one was going to screw him again, no one. Damn that man Victor. Why couldn't he just die?

Both Gary and Chester hustled into Brett's office, being forewarned by Suzanne that an ill wind was blowing their way. "What's up?"

"I'll tell you what's up, the deal with Conductor Images is up, that's what's up. Someone talked. One of you talked to Paul Victor, he just got off the phone. He knows. He knows everything and he wants my ass. Shit, this is the absolute worst thing that could happen. Not only is he not gone but now he'll be digging deeper than ever!"

The color of Brett's face was flaming red, a bad sign. He glared at the two men and said, "All I want to know from you is, which one talked? Who did it? I want a goddamned name and I want it now."

Gary and Chester looked at each other, blood draining from both their faces. Neither had any clue. Who could possibly have talked to Paul Victor? Whoever it was, Brett was going to roast over hot coals. Not a career-enhancing move.

Pounding on his desk Brett yelled, "*I want a name.*"

Gary grasped at a straw, "It wasn't us, honest. Maybe Emmet knows something."

A cruel grimace slashed across Brett's face. "Griswald? Yeah. Suzanne get Griswald here, now."

Pacing back and forth, Brett seethed and muttered under his breath. Gary and Chester were as far away from him as possible, seeking shelter but finding none. Walking over to his shelving unit Brett grabbed the fragile hand-painted plate that cost ten thousand dollars. Unable to control himself, he flung it across the room. The plate shattered, sending splinters ricocheting off the wall. Seconds later Emmet walked in. "You wanted to—"

Brett blurted out, "Who the fuck told you to talk to Paul Victor? Who the hell do you think you are?" Emmet, Gary and Chester were speechless.

Brett walked over and shoved his face into Emmet's. "I said why'd you talk to Paul Victor about Conductor Image? Don't play stupid with me, Griswald. I just got off the phone with him. He knows everything and the only way he could know is 'cause you told him. I think you're a lying bastard, Griswald, always have. Think I'm playing around? Well, you're fired as of now. *Fired*. Get outta of my sight. Did you hear me? I said you're fired!"

Both Gary and Chester were cowering together in a corner of the office, which suited Brett just fine. He turned back to Emmet expecting the same reaction but something was wrong. Brett was amazed at how utterly calm Emmet appeared. Like he didn't care about his job and didn't care what Brett said.

The controller never backed away, he simply returned Brett's stare and said without stammering, "You sure you want to do this Brett? After all the years we've been together? You might want to think about it."

What? Was this guy brain dead? Brett was incredulous and spit back, "Who the hell do you think you're talking to? Get out of my office and get out of my company. I've just fired you, or are you too stupid to realize it? My only regret is I didn't do this years ago. You've been a pain in my ass too damned long."

Emmet nodded, turned to Gary and Chester, paused, smiled to himself and walked out of

LoneStar. There seemed to be a little spring in his step.

* * *

From his car Emmet called Arthur King in Fort Worth. Arthur was most gracious and extended him every courtesy. Emmet could start work tomorrow, all compensation issues and benefits would be taken care of by the personnel department. Emmet thanked him profusely, pressed 'end' and made a second call.

"Hello."

"Dr. Hilborn?"

"Speaking, who's calling?"

"It's Emmet Griswald. Ten minutes ago I was fired by Brett Hollister. Two minutes ago I was hired by Arthur King. I wanted to call and thank you for that."

"I'm glad I was of some help."

"More than you could ever imagine, Dr. Hilborn. You know, I didn't even stutter. Anyway, I was wondering if you'd like those work papers, the originals and the edited versions we talked about before?"

"Mr. Griswald, I'd love them."

"Okay, I'll send them tomorrow from my new office."

Emmet hung up the phone and thought: You're more than welcome, Dr. Hilborn . . . more than welcome.

* * *

It was a little past nine-thirty in the morning. There wasn't enough antacid tablets in the world to calm Paul Victor's stomach. Didn't Hollister get the picture? Didn't he know millions were at stake? Why the hell would that fool walk away from a seven million dollar severance package and then turn right around and sink his own stock? Dumb son of a bitch.

Ever since he called that ass, he'd been rubbing his nose and sniffing. Paul picked up the phone, dialed and wondered why Hollister couldn't just up and die?

"Hello."

"Charles? Paul Victor here."

A cheery voice greeted him. "Good to hear from you, Paul."

There's nothing worse than a guy in a good mood, when you're not. "Listen, Charles, I think you were right about Hollister. You know, about him not accepting a severance package. I don't think it's in the cards any longer." Paul knew the other partners were going to hang him by the balls. He'd already promised to pull this deal off, but the stock was falling, Hollister was still in charge, and he was screwed. What else could go wrong?

The happy go lucky professor said, "Paul, what if I can get him to accept your severance package?"

Was this guy for real? "I'll kiss the ground you walk on. I'll make a donation to whatever charity you want. I'll name my kids after you. I'll do anything you want."

"Fine. Look, I'm going to talk to the other members of the executive committee and then fly down to Dallas. I suspect that Brett will be reasonable when he sees me."

"You're serious aren't you? I won't believe it until it happens but if there's anything I can do, you just name it. Holy mother. Oh, and call me as soon as you can. Thanks, goodbye." What a morning. Paul inhaled slowly, while trying to reassure himself Hilborn's confidence was well founded. His stomach felt like he'd spent all day riding the Magnum at Cedar Point, and his nose was flowing constantly. Gotta take better care of myself.

CHAPTER 20

Thursday, October 3, 9:50 A.M.
Chairman's Office, LoneStar

Whichever employees had vacation days remaining, took them. Others who weren't so fortunate started calling in sick with much more frequency. Only the very loyal kept up appearances and insisted all was fine, but it wasn't. The headquarters of LoneStar was nicknamed 'hell on earth,' and Brett was regarded as the rider on the pale-colored horse. Among the general corporate populace there was plenty of grinding and gnashing of teeth, and the once sheepish directors were suddenly resisting Brett's iron grip on policy issues.

"Mr. Hollister, Dr. Hilborn is here to see you. I told him he's a tad early for the appointment."

"Thank you Suzanne, have him wait a few minutes. I'll call when I'm ready." Since insisting a few days ago to a face-to-face meeting, Brett had wondered what the man wanted. Most likely he was coming to cry and moan about the way his wife was mistreated. Well, life's a bitch. Besides, she started it by sticking her nose where it didn't belong.

But the topper came from that blithering idiot, Congressman Lodge, who just got himself caught sexually harassing two staffers. After all the time and effort Brett put into getting that clown elected, he wasn't worth a damn anymore . . . damaged goods.

Fuming at the recent turn of events Brett felt his blood pressure rising. Son of a bitch, Hilborn better be damn quick 'cause I've got better things to do than wet nurse him.

"Suzanne, show the good Doctor in please." Might as well get this over with, he reasoned. But I swear if he starts in on me I'll . . . "Oh, Good to see you again, Charles." Brett stood up and offered his hand in mock friendship.

Shaking the hand in a perfunctory manner, Charles said, "Hello Brett. Sorry to interrupt your day."

"Not at all. I've always got time for a director. What can I offer you? Coffee? A soft drink?"

"Thank you, no. Actually, I've come to have a serious dialogue with you Brett. That's why I requested two hours of your time."

Shrugging his massive shoulders in abject apathy, he said, "Okay, you got it. What's so important we couldn't discuss by phone?"

"I'm not very pleased with the way you've been running this company, Brett."

Without moving a muscle in his face, Brett spit back, "Tough."

"You've abused your power. You've overstepped the limits of prudent judgment."

Brett started to turn red. Who the hell did this teacher think he was? "You don't have enough experience or intellect to make any accusations like that, Hilborn."

"No? You've allowed your ego to dominate business decisions. You've surrounded yourself with 'yes' men, and you rule by intimidation. Then you wonder why earnings end up in the crapper."

A menacing smile crept across Brett's face. "What's this all about, Hilborn? You here whining to me because your pretty little wife got her butt in trouble? She stuck her nose into other people's business, you know? For God's sake, grow up. She started it. She's the one who launched an investigation. She's to blame, not me. Hey, I'm only protecting myself."

The normally stoic Charles Hilborn leaned across the desk and brazenly stated, "That's what I mean about your ego. Don't you see? You're the one who broke the rules on campaign financing, not her. You're the one who bought a politician, not her. You're the one who's responsible. But you refuse to accept responsibility for your own actions. You think that if it weren't for my wife, everything would be okay. But it's not okay. You knowingly broke the law. Yet you have the gall to infer you're the injured party?"

That did it! Brett exploded, *"I've had enough of your mouth.* I'm removing you from the board. You're nobody, Hilborn, you're nothing. You weren't shit when I found you and you ain't shit now. Why don't you leave while you still can?"

Charles stayed in the chair, "No, I don't think I'll do that just yet. Now that we've established that you're incapable of distinguishing right from wrong, I think it's time we ask you to step down."

Leaping to his feet Brett slammed his hands on the desk. *"Get the fuck outta my office or I'll throw you out."*

Slowly removing a few sheets of paper from his briefcase, Charles slid them over the desk in front of Brett's hands. "You should look at these. I found them quite interesting. Seems you don't care to play by *any* rules. I guess you figure that as long as you don't get caught, then you're in the right. That's the whole problem, Brett. You bend and twist rules to suit yourself. You've put yourself above the law and you laugh at the dumb bastards who play the game straight."

Brett's eyes were full of disgust as he studied the papers in front of him. *What the . . .* where did these come from? Every damn sheet of paper had been destroyed . . . he'd seen to it personally. How the hell did . . . "Where'd you get these? They don't mean nothing, you know."

"No? Hmm, that's not what the other members of the executive committee said. In fact, they were quite perturbed when I faxed them a set. It seems that they think you've lied to them, that you've altered reality, or caused reality to be altered to fit your own personal agenda. They said that you've acted contrary to your fiduciary responsibility as chairman and president of a publicly traded corporation. They're so displeased that . . . oh, where is it? I know I brought it along. Ah yes, here you go. Why don't you look at this?"

Brett looked down at the new sheet of paper as it was slid before him. It was a policy statement by the executive committee to immediately relieve Mr. Brett Hollister of all duties and responsibilities at LoneStar, until a full investigation into these matters was completed. In addition, it stated that, "Until such time as this investigation has been concluded to the satisfaction of this committee, or until the full board decides otherwise, Dr. Charles Hilborn is to assume all responsibilities as interim president of LoneStar International Corporation."

In measured words Brett's coarse voice reverberated, "You're not taking shit, Hilborn. You understand? This is *my* company." Brett's hands had clenched into fists, as his muscles tightened around his neck and broad shoulders, bunching under his suit coat. With shallow breaths he leaned over the desk, getting very close to Charles and repeated, "This is my company." It was a fine line between intimidation and threat.

* * *

Noting Brett's changing features, the glare of the eyes and the loathing they projected, Charles recalled the last individual who stared at him like that, and it unwittingly sparked a particularly bitter memory –

It was a bug-ridded jungle, and they were exhausted. Captain Charles Hilborn of the 82nd Airborne was returning from patrol with his platoon. Their mission was to find and capture as many Viet Cong as they could, and bring them back for interrogation. The weather was miserable . . . rain, mud, slop, nothing dry anywhere. Still, they managed to find one of the enemy rotting away in a filthy, rat infested hand dug tunnel. They forced him out, searched him, gave him something to drink and fed him. He actually smiled at his captors, thanking them by nodding his head vigorously up and down as he wolfed down the food and fresh water.

No one really knew how, but the little bastard had hidden a knife somewhere. With a flash of movement his stringy arm shot out in a quick arc catching a kneeling Sergeant right across the throat, severing the carotid artery. Charles stood helplessly watching as the life oozed out of his Sergeant. Quickly drawing his army issued Colt 1911 .45 automatic from his shoulder holster, he aimed it squarely between the eyes of the prisoner. Charles gazed at his dead comrade for the longest time. Sergeant Johnson . . . Sergeant Jimmy Johnson. He'd been under

Charles' command for five months, a lifetime in Vietnam.

Charles knew Jimmy lived on a farm with his mom and dad, somewhere around Chicago. Just the other day he was telling Charles about this muscle car he'd bought before getting drafted. It was his pride and joy, a black 1971 Ford Mustang Mach 1. Cost him forty-six hundred dollars. Jimmy said his dad was going to keep it for him until he returned. Well, he'd never return now.

The Viet Cong glared at Charles with pure hate and rage, plainly wanting to strike again. With stone cold gray eyes that pierced through the man's soul, Charles said in a pitiless tone, "Go on . . . try it."

* * *

There was no question, Brett was going to fly over the desk and nail Hilborn to the wall, like he'd done on the gridiron to those glory-grabbing quarterbacks. But standing firm and looking directly into Brett's eyes, Charles too leaned over the desk. They were literally face to face, and in a pitiless tone that Brett could hardly comprehend, Charles spat, "Go on . . . try it."

For one of the few times in his adult life, Brett was forced to rethink his own impulsive actions. So very few had ever stood up to him like this before, people ordinarily backed down. But the man on the other side of the desk, this college professor, wasn't someone to take so lightly after all. How could he have so misjudged the man? Restraint finally won, Brett sat back down in his chair knowing he'd best try a different approach. "Don't push your luck, Hilborn. Whadda ya want?"

Charles resumed his seated position as well and answered, "I, we, the board, all want your resignation effective immediately."

The whole board? Damn. Brett's mind raced, trying to talk his way out. "Just because I had some financial reports altered a little bit? I did it for the good of the company, you know. There were a couple of quarters that we needed more earnings. We had to show Wall Street we were growing or they'd trash our stock price."

"I'm sure you believe that, which is exactly why you've got to go."

The wind was snatched out of Brett's sails. He was dejected, defeated and demoralized. This bastard Hilborn and the fucking board weren't going to back down. There was nothing left to do but grab his golden parachute. "You going to honor my employment contract?"

"I'll do better than that. You can have the deal Paul Victor promised you."

Well, that was something. "How long do I have to consider your proposal?"

"Zero time. No time. It's resign with dignity to pursue other interests, or find yourself smack in the middle of a very messy investigation. It's your choice, but think what the news channels will say. A press release is going out early next week with one message or another."

"You'd do that wouldn't you?" It was a rhetorical question and Brett practically spat the words. "What'll you do about these altered work papers?"

"I'll let the new accounting firm review them and decide on the proper course of action."

"So you're changing outside auditors too? Don't long standing relationships mean anything to you?"

Charles sighed and shook his head. "It's a new ball game, Brett. They're second on my list to be removed."

Better to take what he could and regroup. "All right. All right. I'll have Bennett draft up a resignation letter for me to sign, and one honoring Victors' severance package. You can sign that, right, Mr. President?" Bile clung to his throat at the mention of the word "president." It signified the end . . . a humiliating end.

Monday, October 7, 2:50 P.M.
Cypress Offices, Manhattan

Paul Victor was moments away from listening to another rejection, he could tell by the attitude of the man. Not wanting to prolong the inevitable, he spoke into the receiver and said, "Well, if you change your mind, please call me." Paul replaced the phone, plopped a couple more antacids into a glass of water and gulped it down. This wasn't going the way he'd intended. Before the news about Hollister's early retirement became public knowledge, Paul was calling everyone who might have an interest in buying LoneStar. No luck. Mild curiosity perhaps, but nothing solid. It was almost laughable because after a while, Paul could recite the reasons for their apprehensions even before given: An unimpressive senior management team; questions of accounting integrity; a systems support group that was sucking money with no end in sight; credit card losses were rising; too much debt; compensation packages way above industry norm, blah, blah. It was fucking hopeless.

The stock was now down to forty-one dollars a share. The senior partners had lost another ten million dollars in a matter of days, twenty-five million from the high, almost their entire gain had been wiped out. Sure as hell they weren't going to wait forever for Paul to deliver as promised. Besides, it didn't take a rocket scientist to figure out that the longer he took to find a buyer the more the stock would slip. Another one-dollar drop in price and Cypress would be back to square one. Forlornly, he watched his silent phone. It was a bad omen.

He hadn't heard from snitch Jackie Wells either, so he was clueless what that bitch Ashley Bishop was up to. Talk about that slut being lucky or what. How come she didn't buy LoneStar when it was rallying? She probably had Hollister feeding her every damned iota of insider information, that's why. Well, two could play that game, except Jackie wasn't the most reliable of informers. Screw it, he had something else more important to worry about. He had to find a buyer for that Texas garbage heap.

Same day, 6: 10 P.M.
Upper East-Side, Manhattan

Ashley took off from work in the early afternoon and hit the gym. She did a circuit on the weight machines, jumped on a stair climber, ran for half an hour on a treadmill, hopped into a shower, piled into her car, drove home, changed into old flannel pajamas and fuzzy slippers, rolled her hair, smeared her face with cold cream, grabbed a pint of cappuccino chocolate chunk ice cream . . . her favorite . . . and flopped onto the couch.

Looking at her reflection in a nearby mirror, she had to chuckle. The image reminded her of the wicked witch on a bad hair day. Well, so what? Who was going to see her anyway? Ashley picked up the phone and dialed a now familiar private Dallas number. It was time to find out what was going on at LoneStar.

On the third ring the treasurer answered, "Hello."

"Hi, Gary, it's Ashley. I haven't heard from you." She pulled the top off the ice cream container and looked around for the misplaced spoon.

"Oh, hi, Ashley."

He sounded horrid. "What's the matter? You sound like a condemned man."

"Yeah, I guess I do. It's the changes around here. Hilborn's not the timid college professor I thought he was."

Hilborn? Changes? *What's he talking about?* "Ah, where's Brett?"

"Abandoned ship. Took early retirement. Never said a word to anybody, just left. I think there'll be a press release tonight."

"Have you seen it?"

"The release? No, Bennett's putting it together, but it'll just say that Brett's leaving for personal reasons and that Hilborn's the interim president.

"Brett's gone?"

"Yeah, well, sort of. I mean Brett's gonna officially resign this week, but Hilborn's already here."

"What? He's there now? What's he got you doing?"

"He pulled the senior managers in over the weekend. Told us we're switching public accounting firms . . . he's canceled a lot of perks too. He's personally reviewing any expenditure over five hundred dollars, he's stopped all overtime, he's making everyone review their budgets, but the worst is he's bringing in a damned business consultant. Some guy named Sanchez. Can you believe it? A Mexican!"

Sanchez? Adam Sanchez? This conversation was going from bad to worse.

"Look, I can't talk anymore and I'm not sure when I'll be coming back to New York either. I'll call you later."

Stop. Don't hang up. Think girl, think. "Say, Gary. Are you alone?"

"Yeah, why?"

Taking a deep breath, she refocused herself and said in a soft, sexy voice, "Please don't hang up. I was just thinking if you can't come to New York, let's do the next best thing."

"What are you talking about?"

At least he hadn't hung up. Ashley had to know everything that was happening there. "Did you know I'm calling you from my home?"

"No," he said testily.

"Well, I am. Do you know what I'm wearing?"

Again he said, "No." But not so testily.

"I have on a silk robe, no bra, just panties." She gazed into the mirror again and viewed her faded blue plaid jammies and fuzzy slippers, complementing nicely the globs of face cream and hair curlers. Yes, she was quite the sizzling sex toy.

Evidently, Gary's fertile mind was imaginative enough to create its own reality. He enthusiastically replied, "Yeah?"

"Um. I'll just open my robe a little. Oh, yes. That feels so much better."

"Your robe?"

"Can you see me, Gary? Close your eyes and picture me. I'm opening my robe wider now." Actually, she was scratching her rear-end, and putting another pillow behind her head. No telling how long this was going to take.

"Opening . . . wider?"

"Ah uh. Now I'm running my hands up and down my body, and all around." She was still holding the ice cream in her hand, wondering where that spoon had disappeared. Oh good, she found it.

With a crack in his voice, Gary said, "Yes, I can see you."

She purred, she whispered, "That's good. I'm going to pull my panties down now. Will you watch me?"

"Yesss."

"Good boy. Here they go. Ahh, much better. Oh, look, now I'm touching myself." Ashley scooped her first spoonful of heavenly sent ice cream and swallowed it. "Ohhh, that's so good!" the words just jumped from her mouth as the ice cream went in.

On the other end of the conversation, Gary couldn't believe his ears. "Oh, Ashley. You're making me so hot. I need you."

That was a close one, she told herself. "Ah, do you want me to talk to you some more. Talk dirty?"

"Yes, yes. Please don't stop."

"Will you tell me all about that nasty man Hilborn?"

"Yes, yes. Of course I will."

Ashley smiled at her reflection in the mirror. She rubbed her fuzzy slippers together and ate another spoonful of ice cream, moaning for Gary's benefit.

CHAPTER 21

Tuesday, October 8, 9:15 A.M.
Smith-Palmer & Co., Detroit

Going through the motions of a contented husband as he left his happy home for work, Rick Blaine said goodbye to a moody Stephanie, climbed into his car and drove away. He wasn't fooling anyone. At least at the office he didn't have to pretend. More and more each day he was preoccupied with thoughts of Ashley. Opening his desk drawer, he picked up a matchbook from the Townsend Hotel. Wonderful memories flooded back to him, bringing a glow to an otherwise dismal morning.

He thought how exciting it was to be with Ashley Bishop. Could it ever happen? He needed to talk to her, explain things to her. Who knows? Perhaps she felt the same way. She sure acted like she loved him, always calling him, and meeting him whenever possible. What else could it be? Reaching for his phone to make the call it suddenly rang, startling him.

Just like every time the phone rang, his heart leapt in the hopes she'd be the one calling, saying she was coming to him. He often played the scene over and over. She'd say her life was empty without him, that he'd spoiled her for any other man, and she missed his touch. He'd say he felt the same. Then sweeping her up in his arms they'd make wild love, and live together forever.

The phone rang again snapping his trance. Sighing, he picked it up. "Hello, Rick Blaine speaking."

"Hi, Rick. It's Ashley."

* * *

It had taken Ashley a long time after her telephonic "romantic interlude" with Gary Nash to call Rick. She was crushed after Gary's conversation. All her plans, all the untold months of plotting and maneuvering . . . everything was now ruined. Gary had lowered the boom. He told her about the new management team and what they were up to.

Between her compulsory suggestive gasping and his panting, Gary confirmed that 'Sanchez' was indeed Adam Sanchez, a name well known to Ashley. She'd never actually met the man, only knew him by reputation. He was supposed to be clever, insightful, resourceful, a no nonsense, straight forward individual and honest beyond reproach. His Spanish heritage only made him more determined at being the 'best.' He'd already cleaned up a couple of textile firms that were totally mismanaged, and while this was his first foray into the financial arena the problems weren't that much different.

How Hilborn ever latched onto Sanchez was beyond her. But combining that with hiring a new accounting firm, closing out the SWAP position, firing Sid Spence as head of systems, putting the whole high-tech division up for sale, instituting draconian cost reduction measures, placing the breaks on any questionable credit card solicitations, forcing everyone to explain why they weren't making budget . . . well, everything that should have been done a long time ago. But under Brett nothing would have been, which was why she chose LoneStar in the first place. Why did they have to axe Hollister just when everything was going so well?

Reclining on the sofa after hanging up on Gary, she dissected and analyzed the situation. The real questions were: Could Hilborn and Sanchez pull it off? Could they turn the company around? Could they get rid of the deadwood and revitalize LoneStar? Could they pare back the huge expensive debt and increase earnings legitimately? Could the stock price stabilize, preventing any quick meltdown?

After deliberating far into the night, Ashley's answer to all of those questions was: 'Maybe.' Or at least the odds were not in her favor. All her research into LoneStar said that it was a totally mismanaged company, but it could provide shareholders with a decent return if it was re-engineered, stripped down, and the place run properly. Her grand scheme of profiting from selling the stock short and then reaping huge profits as it plunged into the abyss, taking Paul Victor and his cohorts along for the ride, was suddenly gone, vanished. "I don't deserve this," she said aloud.

By the next morning, Ashley knew there was nothing to do but accept it as another regret, pack up, and move on. Then she remembered Rick Blaine. She couldn't just leave him hanging. Besides, she felt an obligation to let him know what was going on at LoneStar, and a small sliver of pride knowing she'd had a hand in his success. Might as well finish on a high note with the man. Knowing it was the right thing to do, she placed the call and heard a compassionate: "Ashley. I've missed you. How've you been?"

I've just been dealt a dead man's hand . . . that's how I feel, she said to herself. Yet finding no reason to burden him with her problems she answered: "Great, really great. You still walking on water?"

"Yes. They think I'm magical around here. I keep getting my buys, holds and sells right, and they're making a fortune off me."

"You deserve it, Rick. You're to be envied."

"Envied? I'm not so sure about that. What's up? You don't sound so good."

Really? She didn't think her voice sounded different. How could he tell? "I'm sure you've heard rumors about the shakeup at LoneStar. Well, I think you'll find that it's going to take a long time to put that house in order. Now while they're doing that, you'll probably see the stock price drift lower. Whether or not they can pull it off is yet to be seen. So you might want to consider changing your recommendation from a "hold" to a "sell," just until the dust settles."

"Ashley, are you giving me insider information? I know now's not a good time to ask after all the help you've been to me, but I've got to know."

"Rick, I have industry sources and contacts that you don't have, and you probably never will. As long as you state in your reports that you're getting your facts from industry specialists who you consider reliable, but in no way can guarantee authenticity, you'll be fine. If you're ever put into a jam where you have to give a name, you can give them mine."

"Okay, thanks. Really, I appreciate everything you've done for me. Are you going to be passing through Detroit anytime soon? I'd, ah, like to talk to you about something important." His voice was almost pleading.

Squeezing the phone, she thought about their relationship and admitted she wanted to see him again. But she also knew it would never work. The game was over, time to move on . . . and yet. Was she beginning to feel something special? "Not real soon, Rick, sorry."

"Oh, I see. Ah, Ashley, is there anything I can do for you? I'd like to help if I can."

She smiled. This was the first guy to ever offer her help with no strings attached. "No, but thanks for asking. It means a lot to me."

"Well, can I call you soon?"

Hesitating before answering, Ashley said, "I'd like that. Now I really have to run. Bye." Ashley was uncertain how she should feel, but one thing was for sure, she wanted Rick calling her.

Thursday, October 24, Noon
Country Club, Dallas

Gary Nash was having lunch with Chester Bennett at the posh country club where LoneStar executives now had to pick up their own tabs. Hilborn and Sanchez had repealed free club memberships, car allowances, free cellular car phones, free tickets to sporting events, free use of the company's condos and free lunches. Just about every perk they had was gone and that didn't endear Hilborn or Sanchez to the officers at LoneStar. Worst of all was having a Mexican running around dictating corporate policy. It was unbelievable . . . unthinkable.

"So what'd you think, Gary?" Chester Bennett was as dismayed and disappointed as anyone at the loss of all their executive perks.

"Hell, Chester. I think the whole deal sucks. It's not what I signed up for and I don't like being told to close out the SWAPs. What're we going to replace that lost income with? I suppose shutting down Sid's systems group and putting them up for sale was a good move, but still . . ."

"Yeah, I know what you mean," Chester sympathized with his cohort.

Gary was more than a little perturbed about having to close out the SWAPs. First of all, it sabotaged his best excuse for going to New York, and no New York meant no Ashley. Second, they'd made a ton of money off the damn things so why stop now? It didn't make any sense to him. Bob Bell wasn't any too happy either since his commission check would be taking a beating. Fortunately, Bob agreed to keep Gary's own position open, so if nothing else Gary could make a few more dollars and then retire in style. "Chester, you going to stick around or are you going to see if they'll cut you a deal to go, like they did with Brett?"

"Don't know. All I know is I have a lot of stock and a lot of stock options, and over the past months the stock has plunged from forty-six to thirty-nine bucks. I'm not thrilled about it and I doubt any other stockholder is. Who knows, maybe we should start a palace revolt."

Gary considered his own situation; relieved he had his own SWAP account. The secret bank balance was now six hundred and eighty-seven thousand dollars, and interest rates were still cooperating making his future bright indeed. Picking up the check, Gary signed his name. "It's on me today." As soon as his account hit a million.

Friday, October 25, 10:10 A.M.
Cypress Offices, Manhattan

LoneStar stock had tumbled to thirty-eight and a half dollars a share, and Paul Victor wanted to crawl away and hide. Not only had he managed to lose thirty million in gains, but now Cypress was seven and a half million dollars in the hole. Almost daily someone would remind him that Cypress lost another five million bucks every time the stock fell another buck below forty, the price being what they'd converted their bonds into five million shares of common stock. Too bad they couldn't start all over again, at least the bonds paid interest.

The senior partners were past livid. His credibility was about zero and any thought of a seven figure quarterly bonus was long dead and buried. Hell, any thought of keeping his job was 'iffy.'

Paul rubbed his eyes and told himself this had to stop. The stock price needed a major boost, but what could he do? He couldn't sell the stock now. They'd book a seven and a half million-dollar loss, and he'd never work on Wall Street again. Paul's phone rang, it was the switchboard operator.

"Yeah, what is it?"

"A call for you. Jackie Wells."

"Fine, put her through." Paul forgot to lower his voice, he just wasn't in the mood. "Jackie?"

"Hi. Ah, I was wondering if you could help me out. See, I'm a little short of cash, and there's some bills—"

Paul cut her off before listening to the same tired pitch. "I don't want to hear it. The only thing I want from you is the code to Ashley's computer disk. Hopefully she's got something up her sleeve that'll get me outta this fucking mess. You get that for me, then we talk."

Jackie had an inspired idea. "Maybe I can buy it from her secretary. You know, give her an incentive to deal with me."

"Fine, do it. I don't care what you do. I don't even want to know, that's your business."

"How much can I say you'll offer?"

"Listen, first you get me the disk and the code, and then we'll talk." If he could use Ashley to bail himself out, any price would be cheap.

"Great, Paul, I'll talk to her today. Bye."

Pouring himself another glass of water, Paul mixed in a few more antacids as another worried senior partner appeared at his door. Before the man could speak, Paul raised his hand and said, "Yeah, yeah, I know. It's under control, trust me."

Same day, 1:25 P.M.
Smith-Palmer & Co., Detroit

Scanning corporate reports, Rick looked at his monitor and scribbled some notes but his mind kept wandering. He should have done something for her, it was obvious she was upset. In fact, each of their recent conversations ended up being shorter and shorter. They were cordial, but not . . . special. Why not arrange a research interview with a New York bank? That way he could see her again. On the other hand, maybe he should just send flowers.

The phone rang interrupting his train of thought. "Not now," he groaned without moving. Calling out in a loud voice he said, "Hey, Linda, can you see who's calling me?" Perhaps he should send Ashley flowers and a card, and then follow it up with a visit. Yeah, he could compose a card that was romantic and sensitive . . . sure, that's what women wanted, right?

Linda yelled back, "Rick. It's your wife on line two."

"Tell her I'm busy. I'll call her back later. Thanks." Let's see, what should the card say? How about . . . the phone rang again. "Linda. Can you get that?" Where was I? Oh, right . . . ah, Ashley, You Mean More To Me Than . . ."

"Rick. It's some guy named Mike Kilpatrick. Says he's a friend of Courtney Keller."

Ah, what's the use? "Right. I'll take it." He tossed the pen down and picked up the phone. "Rick Blaine, speaking."

"Hello, Rick? You don't know me but we have a mutual friend, Courtney Keller, your wife's sister?"

"Oh, sure. Stephanie mentioned you and Court were an item. Said you'd be calling me. I understand you're an investment advisor. What can I do for you?"

"Nothing really. I just wanted to thank you for your research reports. They've been a life saver to me."

"Well, I'm glad to be of service. So how are you and Court getting along these days?" Courtney was a knockout of a woman and she kept herself in great shape, unlike Stephanie who always complained about never having time to exercise, but plenty of time to bitch. Rick liked Courtney a lot, she reminded him of Ashley.

"We're doing fine. Actually, I think I'm falling in love. She's smart, pretty, has her own job, her own house, her own car and can beat me at tennis. What more could a guy ask for?"

Rick chuckled and replied, "Yeah, I see what you mean."

Suddenly more serious, Mike Kilpatrick said, "I've always wanted a family, you know, house, kids, dogs, cat. This probably sounds corny to you, but a two-car garage, picnics, vacations, neighbors to talk to and someone to love you when you get home is like a dream to me. I envy you, Rick. I understand you have it all."

"You're the second person in the past few weeks to say they envy me." Ashley had said the same thing.

"Excuse me?"

"Oh, nothing. Look, I'm really very happy for you, Mike. What about a wedding? Any plans like that?"

"It's sounding better and better to me. Who knows? Could be we'll be related someday. Well, I just called to introduce myself and say thanks. Take care, and keep those reports coming. Bye."

"Goodbye." Leaning back in his chair he thought how come everyone envied him but him? Seems that everything Mike wanted was exactly what he wanted. Funny thing was, he already had it. So was he just being a big jerk, trying to be somebody he wasn't? Should he just forget about ever seeing Ashley again?

Taking the scrap of paper with his half written love message, Rick tore it up and tossed it in the wastebasket. What's the point? What could she possibly see in him anyway? Naw, better just forget the whole thing. Then the phone suddenly rang and his heart leapt into his throat hoping against hope it was Ashley . . . it wasn't.

Same day, 5:55 P.M.
Taylor-Bishop Offices, Manhattan

Jackie had scripted out exactly what she was going to say. She'd waited until Ashley had gone home and Joyce was locking up for the evening before approaching the secretary. Figuring if Paul was putting so much pressure on her to get that disk, then it was probably worth a lot of money to him . . . like fifty thousand dollars? Enough to finally get ahead once and for all.

Pretending she was on her way out the door, Jackie suddenly stopped in front of Joyce and said, "Oh, didn't know you were still here."

"Just packing up myself."

"Ah, Joyce. Can I ask you something?"

"Sure, what's on your mind?"

"I um, need a favor, a big favor. But you can't tell anyone about the favor."

Joyce's eyes opened and looked at her suspiciously. "So what do you want?"

"I'm taking a business course at night school, and for an assignment I'm to analyze a publicly held company. Well, I screwed up, I didn't think it was due until next month but it's due next week. I don't have time to do the proper amount of research and I don't want to fail the class. It's just a stupid research paper, not life or death or anything. Anyway, that's why I need your help."

"I'm not following you at all, Jackie."

"Look, Joyce. I know Ashley and the girls here did a major research project on LoneStar International. I think there's a disk in her desk drawer. Anyway, if you could just make a copy for me, I'm sure I could put it into the proper format for my class. It would sure save my butt."

Joyce was mystified. "You want me to copy one of Ashley's files, without telling her?"

"That's right, you can't tell her. That would ruin everything. What boss wants a flaky employee who forgets when major assignments are due? See, you can't tell her."

"I don't know Jackie. You'd better let me think it over. I'll talk to you Monday."

"Okay, and thanks." Jackie patted Joyce on the hand and added, "I just know you'll do it for me. Thanks again, you're a lifesaver." Jackie practically skipped out of the office congratulating herself for dreaming up such a convincing lie.

Sunday, October 27, 11:35 A.M.
Keller Residence, Columbus

The ghosts and goblins had been preparing themselves for Halloween and almost every nook and cranny of her hospital was decorated with pumpkins, skeletons, witches, black and orange streamers, balloons, bales of hay, and enough candy to send the geriatrics ward into cardiac arrest. Today thankfully, Courtney Keller didn't have to watch out for rubber mice or creepy spiders, it was her day off and she took advantage of the occasion by sleeping in late.

Tonight, Mike Kilpatrick would be picking her up and taking her out for dinner. Then this Thursday evening they'd be attending a hospital sponsored costume party where she was going as a belly dancer . . . had even taken some lessons. Maybe she'd even reward Mike with a private show.

Poised in the middle of her breakfast table in the fully equipped kitchen with serving bar, was a beautiful floral arrangement delivered this morning. Amongst the peach roses and baby's breath was a short note from Mike wishing her 'Happy Birthday' and confirming he'd pick her up at five o'clock. Opening the freezer, Courtney extracted a small, rock hard container that promised a delectable microwave gourmet meal in only four minutes. What was life like before microwaves? she mused.

Five minutes later, the piping hot concoction was steaming away next to the flowers as the phone rang. Timing was everything. "Hello?"

"Courtney, it's me. How you doing girl?"

"Steph? You just caught me eating a nutritious lunch of baked Lasagna and garlic bread. What's up?"

"Just calling to wish my little sister a happy birthday. How old are you again?"

Courtney feigned indifference and answered, "Just forget how old I am. That's not important nowadays anyway. It's how you feel."

Stephanie chuckled and said, "I see. Hey, did you hear from Mom and Dad?"

"Yes, they're somewhere in the Caribbean Sea, around Aruba. I got an email from them at the hospital yesterday. They're both doing fine and said to pass along their love."

"Early retirement seems to agree with them."

"Yeah. Well, you write a best seller and you can retire too."

"So what are you and Mike going to do to celebrate? I want all the juicy details."

Blowing on a hot fork full of Lasagna, Courtney leered at the phone and remarked, "You mean you want to hear everything? Even the part about the buckets of whipped cream and having him tying me down spread eagle on a mirrored canopy bed, and then—"

"All right, all right. I don't need to know everything. So how are you two getting along?"

Courtney grinned, and with euphoria lifting her voice replied, "Really fabulous. He's such a sweetheart. We're going to a romantic French restaurant tonight, music, candlelight, the works. Then it's off to a movie, the kind where women cry and men doze."

"He seems like a real catch. Any plans?"

"I think so. Oh, Steph, I'm so happy right now I could burst."

"That's great. You deserve the best." There was a sudden thud and screams in the background of the Blaine household. "Oh no, the boys are fighting again. Listen, I've got to run. So happy birthday again, we all send our love and we'll see you for the Michigan-Ohio State football game."

"That's a date. Give Rick a big kiss for me too. You two doing all right?"

"Ah, we're doing. Bye."

Swallowing a rather tasty mouthful of nuked pasta, Courtney worried about her sister. She should volunteer to watch the kids and let Steph and Rick have some time alone. Yeah, and she'd drag Mike along. That would prove if he really loved her.

Same day, 1:50 P.M.
A Public School, Manhattan

Lurching under the bulk of a large pillow tied to his back, Dave Hanson made guttural noises as he did his best to impersonate Lon Chaney in *The Hunchback of Notre Dame*. The children giggled and screamed in mock terror as he chased after them. Molly McHenry was prancing around the gym as the head of one sorry looking horse, while her husband Ben was . . . that's right, the horse's ass. Over in the corner was an old witch with a scary green face, white scraggly hair and pointy black hat stirring a smoking caldron.

The horse's head suddenly reared up and hollered, *"All right kids.* I think the witch is ready to serve lunch. Grab your bowls you little urchins and present yourselves."

Not surprisingly, very few children hurried over as instructed. That old witch was cackling, and crooking a long finger at them, beckoning for them to walk her way. Clutching a bowl, Dave 'Quasimoto' Hanson, lumbered over to the ugly witch and howled for some chili. Filling his bowl to the top, she cackled and said in a squeaky voice, "Come my pretties. I won't harm you."

One by one the children took a plastic bowl and spoon and shuffled closer to the witch. The horse trailed behind them, nudging any stragglers. With little hearts thumping, lunch was served and the kids scampered far away to huddle together for protection and eat. With moans and groans the horse broke in two, and sore backs belonging to the McHenry's were stretched and cracked. Giving Ben the evil eye while rubbing her rear-end, Molly said, "Just watch were you put that big nose of yours, Mister."

Checking out his nose for abrasions and contusions, Ben replied, "Sorry, but I didn't see your break lights go on."

The witch laughed and dished them up an extra portion of chili. "Here you go."

Molly gratefully accepted the bowl and sat down on the floor. "Where on earth did you find that getup?"

Taking the hat and white wig off, Ashley sat down next to her. "What getup? You mean this? I'll have you know I've been wearing this to work for the last month. That's why I'm called the witch . . . or is it bitch?" The last few weeks had been hard on Ashley and her staff. The LoneStar project had taken a lot out of them and they were still brooding and mourning its demise. Ashley continually told them that disappointments were the name of the game and to get used to them. It was a hard concept to accept or embrace for the uninitiated.

Finding a spot on the other side of Ashley, Ben settled himself and asked, "Did you do a lot of trick or treating as a kid?"

"No, not much."

"Hmm. I sure did. I remember bringing home a pillowcase full of candied apples, popcorn balls, pennies, nickels, M&Ms, Clark bars, Tootsie Rolls . . . makes my stomach gurgle just thinking about it."

Molly placed her hand on Ashley's hand and said, "Ah, Ashley, we've gotta talk to you. I don't know quite how to say this, but, well, you see . . . Ben's getting transferred. We just found out this week. Well, um, we'll have to be leaving soon . . . moving, you know? We'll write you of course and call all the time, and we'll miss you and the kids terribly. I just wish we didn't have to move." Ben was looking down at his hands as Molly sniffed.

The green make-up of the witch cracked into a wide smile. "I'm so happy for you. It's a much better job and you two deserve it. Anyway, the schools there are better for Tracy."

Eyeing Ashley curiously, Ben asked, "How'd you know it's a better job or that the schools are better?"

Gripping Ashley's hand harder, Molly said, "Ashley? Are you behind all this? Have you been behind everything? Did you pay our medical bills and get Ben his new job? Who are you?"

The green make-up hid all expressions and in a matter-of-fact tone, Ashley replied, "I'm not anybody." Standing up, she added, "I'll miss you both you know, so will the kids." Noting the children were about finished with lunch, she said, "Might as well go clean up."

Looking up at her, Molly pleaded, "Please, wait. Can't we talk? I want to know who you are, Ashley. I want to know more about you."

On her way to picking up the children's now empty chili bowls and spoons, Ashley answered matter-of-factly, "No. No you don't."

CHAPTER 22

Monday, October 28, 8:15 A.M.
Taylor-Bishop Offices, Manhattan

Joyce appeared the moment Ashley walked into her office. "Ashley, we need to talk." Without waiting for her boss to respond, she closed the door and stood in front of the desk as Ashley stowed her purse and opened the leather briefcase.

While turning on her computer, Ashley said, "Okay, so talk."

"Jackie wants that LoneStar disk of yours real bad. She wants me to make a copy of it for her."

"Really? Did she give you any plausible reason why?" Obviously, that bastard Victor had put her up to it. Ashley surmised he was probably ready to jump out of the window with LoneStar's price under forty, and was grabbing at anything to save himself.

"Kind of. She said she needs it for a night school project, says she'll fail without it. Almost had me believing her. But I happen to know she isn't taking any night school classes. She's quite a good liar, you know?"

"I had my suspicions. Did she offer you anything?"

"You mean for the disk? No, she just wants a copy of it."

Ashley reflected for a moment then said, "Well, let's see how badly she wants it. Tell her you've thought about it and you'll do it, but you want some money. Say you want . . . oh, ten thousand. See what she comes back with. We can't make it too easy for them."

There was a puzzled look on Joyce's face again, but she said, "Okay. I'm sure you know what you're doing."

"Oh yes, Joyce. I know exactly what I'm doing. Now if you'll excuse me, I have a lot of work to do and one very important phone call to make." Opening her bottom drawer she extracted the LoneStar disk and thought how opportunities present themselves when least expected. All you have to do is be patient.

Absent-mindedly, she inserted the LoneStar disk into the hard drive, typed in the appropriate password and scanned the screen. After a few minutes, she broke eye contact from the monitor and looked around her desk. Somewhere was her address book containing special phone numbers.

* * *

Brushing orange balloons out of her face, Courtney picked up the phone at the nurses station. An intern dressed as Spiderman scurried past, followed by a sword waving pirate and a size fourteen female squeezed into a junior miss fairy costume. The lunatics had taken control of the asylum. "Yes, this is Dr. Keller."

"Courtney, you old sawbones. How are you?"

"Ashley? Ashley Taylor, is that you? What's a tycoon like you doing calling up an old family type doctor?" Suddenly a pang of guilt hit Courtney. How long had it been since they'd seen each other?

Speaking with a lilt in her voice, Ashley said, "I'm wishing my old sorority sister a belated happy birthday, that's what. And I still go by Ashley Taylor-*Bishop*."

"Oh, that's right. I forgot, sorry. Your divorce doesn't seem all that long ago."

"I know, actually the marriage didn't last all that long either. But like I said, the whole thing was pretty painless."

"I felt so bad for you, I wish there was something I could've done."

"You were there for me when I called. That's more than most."

"I sure love hearing from you. Still watching the kids on Sundays?"

"Uh-huh. That's kinda the reason I forgot to call you yesterday. We were throwing them a Halloween party. Sorry."

"Don't be silly. Say, how's your adoption going?"

"Oh, guess I didn't get around to telling you. Seems my colorful past won't leave me alone. I'm too busy to be a parent anyway."

"Sure, I know." Why couldn't Ash get a break in her private life? Changing topics, Courtney said, "I was just looking at that old picture of us, seems like yesterday we were at Penn State, doesn't it? You were such a knockout."

"Don't go patronizing me. As I remember you had a fair number of boys hanging around. Anyway, I'm doing fine. In fact, a major disaster may just have been averted. Your practice okay?"

"Yes, it really is. Tell me, does anyone have your undivided attention yet?"

"Well, no, ah . . . well, who knows? I don't know. I can't tell. He lives in another state so you know how that goes. How about you?"

"I'm hooked. He's a financial planner, doing pretty well. Actually, he could be a cashier at a hamburger joint for all I care. Ash, he's gentle and romantic and funny and good looking and—"

"Whoa. Hold it right there. You're making me jealous. Court, I'm really happy for you."

"Thanks. You need somebody too. Especially after all those jerks."

"Well, who knows? Look, if you and Mr. Right ever decide to tie the knot be sure to invite me to the wedding."

"Invite you? You'll be in it! That is if you'd like to be."

Courtney knew her friend had never stood up in a wedding, other than with Jim Bishop . . . which was at a courthouse and didn't count for much. Ashley's excitement was genuine as she said, "Court, I wouldn't miss your wedding for the world. I know you're busy so I'll let you go. You stay in touch, okay? Love you."

"Love you back." Courtney hung up the phone. A smile broke across her face. They sure had shared good times at college. From mixers, football games, double dates, parties and cramming for tests by means of all-nighters, to a spring break in Mexico. The girls were inseparable. Probably their vastly different backgrounds helped forge such a unique bond.

Courtney Keller was from an upper middle class family. All the family members supported and loved each other. She and Stephanie were heavily involved in school activities, pulled down decent grades, tons of sports, went to parties . . . everything a kid could want and still walk away relatively unspoiled.

Ashley, on the other hand, never knew her father. It seemed the man didn't take his responsibility very seriously as he bolted before she was born. Ash once confided to Courtney how she was raised outside a coal-mining town by her mother, a very pretty woman . . . a very *young* pretty woman, who unfortunately crumbled after being abandoned with a newborn. The illiterate, school-less, weak-willed mother took shelter in the welfare system, handouts, unsalvageable boyfriends and finally alcohol induced prostitution.

By age eight, and after numerous charges of child neglect, the well intentioned community folk decided that an alcoholic mother whose only source of income was selling herself, and who carried out these deplorable acts while little Ashley waited outside the mobile home, no matter the weather, was far from the proper caretaker an impressionable child should have. Legal action was taken and Ashley began her journey through a maze of foster homes.

She must have been a looker even as a pre-teen . . . Ashley was raped repeatedly by her third 'foster dad' as her 'foster mom' stood guard at the bedroom door watching, telling her, "Be good for daddy." Ashley ran away from them but was caught and forcibly returned, since no one would believe her wild stories. Same thing happened again. All the time she thought it was because of her, it was her fault, something was wrong with her. . . little tears rolled freely. Courtney knew kids being abused think that way, that their opinion of themselves is lower than dirt.

Foster dad's five and six helped themselves to Ashley's adolescent body too. But a spark of independence welled up when Ashley was fifteen, and she managed to make good an escape in the rusted out car of a drug-addicted boyfriend who "loved" her. He was everything to her and she naively believed anything he said. Like when she was jarred out of a deep sleep in his car by blaring alarms coming from a convenience store. Her boyfriend quickly jumped in behind the wheel, slammed the car into gear and sped off. They were pulled over by the County Sheriff thirty minutes later.

The tragedy of the story was how he'd convinced the vulnerable Ashley that if she really loved him, she'd say it was her who killed the cashier. Since she was a minor they'd let her go after a couple weeks. Nothing to worry about. And when she got out they'd get married . . . after all, he loved her.

Never had Ash felt so needed and safe as with him. He always said how special she was, something no one else ever had. Without a thought for herself, she confessed to the crimes, assured that within a month they'd be back together again . . . forever. The courts had other ideas. After two years and four months in a vile, overcrowded girls correctional facility in Pennsylvania, a place that proved to be every bit as horrific as her foster homes, she was released.

On the first day of the rest of their lives, she ran out to the waiting arms of her lover, except the street was empty. No car, no boyfriend, no anybody. At an age when most girls were saying goodbye to orthodontists, learning to drive, studying for college entrance exams or worrying about who would invite them to the prom, Ashley was escorted by the police back to the wretched mobile home of an uncaring, soulless mother. More tears flowed.

The toll alcohol and prostitution had taken on her mother was shocking. Near destitute from a lack of obliging men, her gnarled mother grabbed onto Ashley like a shimmering gold coin, and plunged the unwilling daughter straight into the family business. "Don't let me down, hear?" she'd say. "Tonight's a real gentleman. So you do him right or I swear I'll send you back to prison." The mother controlled her, as well as the money tossed on the bed, which was used mostly for gin. Ashley got nothing but heartache, a longer police record, and a back-alley abortion, which left her withering in pain . . . and irreversibly sterile.

While others might have acceded to the downward spiral, she wouldn't. After scraping together ninety-seven dollars Ash hitchhiked her way to wherever, never looking back. She managed to put food in her mouth and clothes on her back by taking jobs as a cashier, waitress, gas station attendant, bartender, anything really. Limiting her diet to peanut butter sandwiches and sleeping in parks or the cheapest motels imaginable she roamed through small towns with no real plan other than survival. Any man who offered help ended up only helping himself, which was a hard lesson for a young girl to learn. Tears again.

Figuring she should finally use her looks for *her* advantage, she literally said, "What the hell," and turned to table and lap dancing where your past didn't matter as much as your titillating floorshow. Besides, she reasoned, her self-esteem was already trashed so what did she have to lose? It changed her life. She discovered all about cosmetics, wearing flattering and enticing costumes, and how easily money could be extracted from men as they hyperventilated in front of her.

It wasn't the most noble of professions to be sure, but it paid better than anything else she was qualified to do. As Ashley's performance improved she moved up to the higher-class establishments like Rick's or The Men's Club, where the customers were both washed and had all their teeth. Now money flowed freely. Once in a while a patron got a bit too physical, but she'd learned to take care of herself so it wasn't a big deal. Besides, clearing five to six hundred dollars a night bolstered her tolerance for wayward hands. No more tears - ever again.

Ashley had previously tended bar at a pub around State College, where Penn State University resides. Knowing she had more on the ball than most of those binge drinking, pampered, self-absorbed classmates, she finished a local high school program and applied to said institution of higher learning. Quite on her own merits she was accepted, excelled and joined a sorority.

The hardened brunette was fascinated by the prospects of college life. This was the means of gaining respect. With a bachelors degree she could open doors of opportunity and prove she was as good as anybody. College was expensive though and as her financial resources ran low it was back to strip clubs. As luck would have it one of the sorority sisters found out about Ashley's immodest moonlighting activities, and they ended up deactivating her. Courtney had pledged with Ash and couldn't believe the "sisters" self-righteous indignation, so she quit too. The two girls happily shared an apartment until they graduated.

Without question, Ash had her own value system. She even dated a handful of professors; one who knew influential people on Wall Street and another who eventually helped Courtney gain entrance into Ohio State's medical program. Courtney grinned as she remembered feebly attempting to explain to her suspicious parents the circumstances behind a certain glowing, overly enthusiastic recommendation sent on her behalf to the admissions office at Ohio State, from a Penn State professor she'd never taken a class from.

Courtney desperately wanted Ash to finally find someone. Why not someone like her new boyfriend from 'another state?' Just might be just the one. She truly hoped so!

CHAPTER 23

Tuesday, November 5, 11:20 A.M.
Chairman's Office, LoneStar

This certainly wasn't a bad way to exist, he admitted. Charles was enjoying the corporate life, particularly since it was on an interim basis. Paul Victor had seen that the board members approved fairly generous compensation packages for the outgoing Hollister and the incoming Hiborn. How ironic that Charles would make more money in a few months than he could from an entire year of teaching. It didn't seem right somehow, but he and Jenny weren't complaining.

Pressing his intercom, he said, "Suzanne, get me Emmet Griswald please."

Jenny was still putting her life back together, and talk about ironies! After Congressman Lodge was hoisted in front of the ethics committee on sexual harassment charges, the allegations against Jenny drifted without form, substance, or a hearing date. Then one day she unexpectedly received a call from a member of the opposition party. He offered her a better slot on their side of the aisle; also saying that since they're the majority party he'd guarantee those asinine charges against her would be dropped. Two minutes after thinking it over, she accepted . . . hell hath no fury like a woman scorned. Now she was busy making life miserable for her previous 'colleagues.'

Looking out at the Texas landscape from Brett's old office, Charles congratulated himself the hundredth time for hiring Adam Sanchez. What a catch. The guy was awesome. Charles would turn Adam loose in a department and the next thing you know there would be a long list of suggestions. And acting upon Adam's suggestions proved to be an awfully intelligent thing to do. Not popular, but intelligent.

Emmet came on the line and said, "Dr. Hilborn? Good to hear from you. Still slaying the dragons?"

"Emmet, all I can say is this is an adventure. I've taught classes and done case studies on mismanaged companies before, but until you're actually thrown into one and told to fix it, you just can't appreciate it."

"Hmm. Any conclusions?"

"The way I see it, Brett would borrow a ton of money for buying new companies and to overpay executives, then scramble around to sell assets and use the cash to buy more companies. The debt he accumulated is staggering. Emmet, it's a no-win situation. How long did you people think you could keep doing that? Didn't you see the handwriting on the wall?"

"Charles, sometimes reality can be what the chairman wants it to be."

"Right, right . . . I suppose you're right. So how's the new job coming?"

"I like it. I don't even mind Monday mornings."

"Well, I'm really happy for you. Look, I just called to see if everything was going okay. If you want, I could talk to Arthur about letting you come back here. We can use someone who knows which closets have the most skeletons."

"No, I appreciate that, but no. You're correct in your assessment of LoneStar. We were living in a fantasy world. I'm in the real world now and I like it. Besides, I feel I owe Mr. King."

The man was loyal. "Sure. Well, I wish the best for you."

"Thanks, and doc? Ah, I think you should know that Brett called me up the other day. Said he wanted to make sure we were still friends. Then he said he was pushed into firing me, that you and Paul Victor made him do it. I don't know what he's up to but you can be sure it isn't in your best interest."

Same day, 12:50 P.M.
Taylor-Bishop Offices, Manhattan

Seething as she picked up the phone, Jackie scanned the office to make sure she was alone and then dialed Paul Victor. The nerve of Joyce demanding ten thousand dollars for the disk and code. Where'd she come up with that? Shit, the uppity bitch was supposed to make a copy, not commit extortion.

Hoping it was a bad joke Jackie had approached the secretary again today. Same answer. Ten grand or forget it. "Damn, come on, Paul. Answer the phone."

"Paul Victor."

Jackie whispered, "It's me. I got Ashley's private secretary to agree to giving me a copy of the disk and password, but she wants ten thousand for doing it."

Paul tried to whisper, but failed. "Ten thousand? Dollars? You've gotta be kidding."

"So what do you think?"

Paul lowered his voice and said, "I won't be played with, Jackie. Let me think." After a few moments he replied, "Okay, you tell her she can have the money, but only after you look at the disk and make sure it's genuine. I'm not paying money for blank data."

"I already told her that. She said, 'Too bad, then you don't get the disk.' Seems she doesn't trust me either."

"Then I suggest you pay her and I'll reimburse you once I've had a chance to check it out."

Now it was Jackie's turn to raise her voice. "Where the hell am I supposed to come up with ten thousand? You come up with it, the disk is for you!"

Paul matched her voice level. "If you want me to pay you anything Jackie, you'll get that disk and code and send them to me. Tell you what, after I've looked at them I'll pay you, ah, um, twenty thousand dollars."

"Bullshit!"

"Excuse me?"

"Bullshit, Victor. That's a term you should understand. You'll pay me fifty thousand."

"What? Why you ungrateful bitch. Just why the hell should I do that?"

"Because you'll never get the disk if you don't. Fifty thousand is cheap Paul, real cheap. You think about it and call me back when you've decided." She had him and they both knew it.

Paul whispered again, "No. No, I don't have to think about it. Okay, you've got a deal. I'll pay you fifty thousand if the disk says what it's supposed to say."

In a hushed tone, Jackie said, "Deal. I'll need ten thousand right away for . . ."

"*No! You pay the ten thousand. It comes outta your pocket or I swear it's no deal.*"

"Okay, okay, take it easy. I'll scrape it together somehow. I'll call you tomorrow." Jackie dropped the phone and then her head into her hands. Where was she gonna come up with that kind of money? She'd have to hock almost everything she owned. But then there was the fifty thousand . . . tax free.

Same day, 2:45 P.M.
LoneStar Offices, Dallas

Gary Nash's desk had never been so cluttered with files, papers, reports and pie charts. Brett Hollister had never asked Gary Nash a tenth of the questions these new guys were asking. Every damned day it was something else. Now they wanted to know why certain banks weren't paying a higher rate of interest on deposits. Gary knew it was because those banks were friends. They hosted golf outings at Hilton Head, footed the bills for Caribbean cruises, and they looked the other way when needed. Without a doubt, there were lots of reasons why banks didn't pay up for deposits, but none he dared tell Hilborn.

As Gary was fumbling through some files, his secretary interrupted and said, "Mr. Nash. It's Brett Hollister for you."

"What? Oh, okay, I'll take it. Hello, Brett? How's it going?"

"Hi, Gary, just fine, just fine. Pamela doing okay?"

"Yeah, she's fine. Still spending more than I earn, but whose wife doesn't? What can I do for you?"

"Just called to see how you were. Anything interesting happening?"

"Interesting? You might say that. Hilborn and his sidekick 'Pancho' are running around like the Keystone Cops, screwing up everything in sight. Makes you wanna scream."

Brett seemed pleased with that answer. "How about we get together, have lunch at the club?"

"Fine by me. But you'll have to buy. Dues and business lunches were one of the first perks cut around here."

Taking a serious tone, Brett offered, "I don't know how you can work for a Mexican, Gary. Must make you feel like a damned dog."

"Yeah, sure does." Humiliated, that's the way he actually felt.

"Well, there's something we can do about that." Gary sat up in his chair. "Yeah? Like what?"

"I'll talk to you soon. Goodbye, Gary."

"Yeah. Bye." Scratching his balding head, the treasurer wondered what the hell that was all about. It was a question he didn't have long to ponder, for Gary's secretary interrupted a second time. "Mr. Nash? There's a Bob Bell from Pagent waiting on line two."

"Hum? Okay, fine. I'll take it . . . Hi, Bob. What can I do for you?"

"Gary, have you been watching interest rates?"

What was this, twenty questions? "No, I've been kind of busy, Bob. Why?"

"The Federal Reserve went and raised the discount rate this morning, trying to put the squeeze on inflation."

Gary didn't comprehend the significance of that last statement. "Federal Reserve? What discount rate?"

It was easy to tell Bob Bell wasn't fond of talking about the Federal Reserve. Sighing audibly the managing director spouted, "The Fed Chairman is screwing up Wall Street, well, him and his policy setting Federal Open Market Committee. First we think he's going to tighten money, but he doesn't. Then we think he's going to loosen money, but he doesn't. Then we think he's not going to do anything, but he does. Shit, why he can't just let the market decide where interest rates should be?"

Gary didn't understand a thing Bell was saying, but an ominous gloom descended into the treasurer's office.

Cautiously, Gary sought guidance by asking, "So?"

"Like I told you, today they increased the discount rate. It's the interest rate the Federal Reserve charges to banks when the banks borrow money. It's supposed to, and does to a certain extent, regulate the flow of money into the economy. They kicked it way up today and all the other interest rates are following suit."

Realization of what Bob was saying finally jarred Gary and he was petrified. "So what're you telling me? What's my account look like?"

"It's down to around a hundred thousand and change to the good."

"*What!* No way. It was almost a million dollars! *Why didn't you tell me before?*"

"*Before what?* I didn't know the Fed was going to change interest rates. They didn't call me up and ask my permission."

"*Shit. You can't do this to me, Bell.* You've screwed me outta a million dollars."

"Get real, Gary. You're the one who wanted the collars off and I practically begged you to get out way before, so you have nobody but yourself to blame. Now listen carefully. Don't wait too long before you decide what to do next. If rates go much higher we'll have to do something about your collateral to protect ourselves."

"Damn you. That's what you want isn't it? Well screw you, you lying prick." No longer interested in the conversation Gary slammed the phone down.

Same day, 4:35 P.M.
Taylor-Bishop Offices, Manhattan

Joyce knocked on the door and cleared her throat, "Excuse me. Ashley?"

Ashley looked up from the computer screen and waved her over. Joyce stepped in and said, "I've just spoken to Jackie. She's going to bring ten thousand dollars with her tomorrow morning and I'm going to give her the disk. We'll meet here at five-thirty in the morning, before anyone else arrives. She wanted some kind of assurance that she's not going to be handed an empty disk. I told her the LoneStar password was VR2 just like you said."

Smiling, Ashley said, "Did she ask what VR2 meant?"

"Yep, just like you thought she would. I said you picked it because of a similar transaction you did a while ago, some company called Virtual Reality."

A glow radiated from Ashley's face. "Yessss, that's great. I'll have a disk waiting for you in my desk by morning. Thanks, Joyce." Joyce closed the door as she left, and Ashley continued typing and humming.

Same day, 11:10 P.M.
Blaine Residence, Birmingham

The Blaine's weren't communicating and it was like pulling teeth to even start a civil conversation. They had just retired for the evening when Stephanie asked, "Rick, what's wrong with us? What's wrong with me?"

Not again, Rick moaned inwardly. "Nothing's wrong."

"But you're so distant. You act as if I'm not here most of the time. Well, I don't like being treated that way."

Why was it she was always too tired to have sex at night, but never too tired to spend half an hour yakking? "Look, like I've said before, it's the new job. I'm under a lot of pressure to perform. If I screw up it'll cost us big time, and you seemed to like the extra cash I've been bringing home."

"We never talk anymore."

"Fine, we'll talk tomorrow. Goodnight."

"Is it me? What's the matter, don't you find me attractive anymore?"

"Please! We've been over this a hundred times. This isn't about you; it has nothing to do with you. Just drop it." He rolled over and faced the wall. After a long moment, Stephanie turned away, too.

Wednesday, November 6, 1:25 P.M.
Cypress Offices, Manhattan

For the past half hour since Jackie dropped off the disk Paul Victor was glued to the computer monitor. Now he sat stunned, shocked and stupefied. He couldn't believe what he was reading. He'd been tricked, duped and screwed by that bitch Ashley Bishop. Shit, what an ass he'd been. Just look at this, every step of her damned plan was so well laid out. She'd figured out how to make a fortune while he crashed and burned.

Now he knew why she never bought any LoneStar stock, she never intended to buy any, at least not until it fell through the roof. That whore was going to sell the stock short when it hit sixty.

All this time he was banging his head against a wall trying to do anything he could to get the stock price up, and there she was sitting back and laughing at him, rooting him on, hoping he'd push the price up. Yeah, she probably had a real good laugh at the annual meeting too, making everyone believe LoneStar was in play, that someone was going to acquire them while knowing all the time the place sucked. Christ, just where the hell did she get her information?

Paul wiped his runny nose with a tissue. She probably got her information on LoneStar just like she did from Virtual Reality . . . one of their horny executives. He'd heard rumors that Bishop had made an absolute killing selling VR's stock short, now he believed it. It just figured she'd use that code for LoneStar's password. Boy, she had balls. Reluctantly, he had to give her credit.

Still mesmerized by the plan he read the summary again. How did she know LoneStar assets were overvalued? How did she know the credit card division was gonna explode? How did she know Hollister played with the books? He didn't know any of this and he was on their fucking board of directors!

Paul paged through her analysis wondering if she was only guessing. It just could be the company wasn't in as bad of shape as she believed. Nobody was all knowing. So, needing to convince himself, Paul placed a call to the newly installed president of LoneStar. The secretary answered and passed him through.

With little preamble, Paul asked, "Charles, how's it going?"

"This place is a nightmare. No one knows anything, no one is responsible for anything, and no one cares about anything."

"I'm sure you're doing just fine. Listen, Charles, I have a concern you can help me with. I'm talking about certain assets being overvalued. You know, land, buildings, companies that Hollister bought over the years at top dollar. Are they now worth a whole lot less? I'm also wondering if you feel that we're adequately reserved for say, credit card losses?"

Those were good questions, and Charles said as much. "Look, Paul. I'm afraid the new auditors won't be able to answer those questions for another month or two."

"*Another month? Why so long?*" One of his portfolio managers walked into his office, smiling. "*Get the fuck outta here!*" Victor screamed. The man darted out and Paul spoke into the receiver again. "Sorry, sorry for the interruption. Now, ah, why so long?"

"Paul, it took years to get us to where we are and it's going to take time for us to figure out exactly where that is!"

"But don't you have any ideas? Any gut feelings?"

Charles tried to be helpful. "I know Brett shaved the books while he was here. That's how we nailed him, remember? It wouldn't surprise me to find a couple major black holes left by him either. I just don't know."

Paul closed his eyes and slumped back into his chair. "I see. Listen, you've been a big help. Keep me posted of any new findings, okay? Goodbye." He replaced the receiver, opened another packet of antacids and chewed them whole, all the while pondering. The bitch was probably right, she always was. Hell, just look at LoneStar's stock. It had fallen from forty-six to thirty eight without breaking a sweat. If Ashley had set her sell order at forty-six instead of sixty, she'd have made six dollars per share. Yeah, and a ton more if it keeps falling. Well, that's a good lesson to learn. Don't go getting too greedy.

Why couldn't that tramp Jackie have gotten him this disk weeks ago? He could have sold out at forty-three or higher, just like everybody begged him. Now it was too late, he'd already lost everything. The only option left was to close out the position and take his losses . . . and lose his job. Scrolling through Ashley's plan again, a wild thought nudged its way to the surface. Maybe it wasn't too late after all.

Another head thrust itself into his office and said, "Say, Paul, did you hear that—"

"*Get outta my fucking office.*" He didn't have time to be bothered, not now. Got to figure this out, he told himself. Paging down the computer file he reread how Ashley figured once the new auditors found all the dirty laundry left behind, the stock would get trashed. She was right. With credibility problems, new management, new auditors, undisclosed losses, cash flow problems, too much debt, too little focus . . . Wall Street would dump the stock. Hell, her estimate of the stock falling into the teens could be generous.

That idea continued to take shape. So why couldn't he ride the stock down instead of her? Why couldn't he bail out now, unload everything they owed, and then sell short? If Cypress were short five million shares at thirty-eight, and bought them back even at twenty, that would be a profit of eighteen bucks a share . . . *eighteen*! Good Christ, that's ninety million dollars! But what if Paul could get the committee to double up? That would be one hundred and eighty million dollars . . . *one hundred and eighty million dollars*! Son of a bitch. They'd be rich! He'd be rich!

As a newfound confidence overwhelmed him, Paul picked up his phone and started the wheels in motion by calling an emergency meeting of the Cypress senior partners. If he could pull this off, he'd be famous. Not to mention leaving Ashley eating his dust. Actually, he would leave everyone eating his dust. Cypress would suddenly be "number one" and they'd be overrun with new clients wanting to ride the magic carpet . . . and Paul would be the driver. Just think of the money he'd make. Sure, the notoriety was great . . . being on talk shows, getting quoted in the financial papers. But who could remember the investment hero from two years ago? He sure couldn't. Cashing in quick was the key in this business.

Paul leaned back as his mind drifted further into its reverie, oblivious to his surroundings. With this deal, he could write his own ticket. Set himself up for life. Finally stop living with that drunken slut of a wife. He'd leave that bitch, and let her have the fucking house. At least it would keep her from renting motel rooms for humping anything wearing pants.

For him, it would be a classy apartment on the Upper East Side. He'd start going out more, splash some green around, get a new sports car, clothes. Then he'd screw his brains out with nightclub nymphos and get a little crazy with some hookers. But the best part would be getting some better coke for his habit. Surely, if there was a giving, merciful god he'd make this deal happen.

With ever increasing enthusiasm Paul considered his new revelation while dabbing at his nose. This was his salvation, had to be. This would not only redeem him but be his crowning achievement. No doubt about it, he'd be set for life. Damn, this was good. Now, all he had to do was convince his partners. Looking up at the ceiling at an unknown deity, Paul whispered, "It's all I'll ever ask and you'll never hear from me again. Just gimme this."

CHAPTER 24

Thursday, November 7, 7:45 P.M.
The Whitney Restaurant, Detroit

The waiter poured out another glass of white wine. Rick didn't care what type it was, he simply drained the glass and waited for another refill. He didn't even pay much attention to his co-workers scattered all about him as their small talk held no interest. Only when the chief executive officer of Smith-Palmer & Company stood up to make a toast did a hush fall upon the participants.

Money was really starting to roll in for Rick, seemingly he could do nothing wrong. True, the general economy was strong, stocks were mostly rising, and investors were bullish. So in this environment coming out with 'buy' recommendations wasn't exactly rocket science. Practically every analyst said 'buy.' But coming out with a 'sell' and then being proven correct, well, that's how research analysts' got noticed in bull markets. Rick was getting noticed.

It seemed like every couple of weeks an additional few extra thousand dollars was tossed into his paycheck. The sales representatives were now quoting Rick's commentary, to lure new clients into the fold. Rick was even being asked to tag along on customer calls, to impress the impressionable . . . a showcase of all the powerful resources available at Smith-Palmer.

Now that money wasn't such a problem, Rick found little use for it. His family had all that they needed, his savings account was replenished, cars were new and all credit card debt had been paid off. You only need so much, he decided. The Blaine's had made it but it was a hollow success for him. Each time his phone rang his heart leapt wanting it to be Ashley, saying that she was waiting for him at the Townsend. But it never was.

Time was healing nothing and his relationship with Stephanie was worsening. He didn't want to hurt her, he just didn't want to be around her . . . and he didn't want to go home tonight, and he didn't want to be at this insipid dinner. All he wanted was to hold Ashley.

* * *

Sitting next to her husband, Stephanie Blaine reminded herself how proud she was of his success. The way he was able to bounce back so quickly from that bank merger nightmare. While she didn't know how he was able to master his new profession so quickly, especially being able to predict accurately which way a particular stock was going to move, she was proud. Especially since tonight's dinner was in his honor.

The pre-dinner small talk centered around Rick's reports on a company called LoneStar. The sales associates were almost giddy, pumping his hand and slapping his back. Apparently, he was the only stock analyst to issue a "sell" warning, saving Smith-Palmer clients from significant losses. No one knew how he'd anticipated that but good-natured kidding included his calling the psychic hotline.

Smith-Palmer's chief executive gave a fine speech for twenty minutes, chock full of accolades and humorous one-liners. Toward the end of the evening everyone came over to congratulate Rick. While he smiled and tried to act appreciative, Stephanie could tell his heart wasn't in it. Something was bothering him. Well, something was bothering *her* too. While picking out a new dress for tonight's affair she bumped into a neighbor. They had lunch together and talked about all sorts of things.

The dear friend mentioned she'd seen Rick having dinner at the Townsend a while ago. Stephanie reasoned the dinner must have been the one he'd mentioned before, with some out of town business client. The neighbor offered how she wouldn't be as gracious as Stephanie if she knew her husband was having a late night dinner with an absolutely gorgeous brunette. They continued talking about children, vacation plans and cleaning services, then pecked each other on the cheek and went their separate ways.

Rick was seeing another woman.

Wednesday, November 13, 12:10 P.M.
Country Club, Dallas

Dining at the Dallas Country Club literally meant being smothered with southern hospitality. All the waiters and waitresses knew the patrons and addressed them by name. Favorite drinks were memorized and brought without asking. Special dishes were always available for the fussy palate. There was nothing too good for the membership.

Chester Bennett and Brett Hollister were just finishing a delightful lunch of smoked salmon when the waiter suggested dessert. Chester responded first, "None for me, Raymond." He turned to Brett, winked and stated, "I have to go back to work. Dessert always makes me sleepy and I wouldn't want Mr. Sanchez finding me taking a nap."

"Nothing for me either, Raymond. I'll sign the check when you get a chance." Raymond bowed slightly, turned and disappeared, leaving the two members to themselves.

"Retirement seems to agree with you, Brett. You look ten years younger."

"Yeah, can't say I miss all those headaches. You enjoying yourself under the new leadership?"

"Humph. Not at all. To tell the truth, I wish they'd just trigger my employment contract, pay me off and let me go. Unfortunately, it would cost them more to get rid of me than to keep me around. Guess I only have myself to blame, since I wrote the contract myself."

Brett laughed out loud. "Yes, you really did a good job didn't you? So what are you going to do?"

"Do? What can I do? I'm stuck with them and they're stuck with me."

Brett shrugged his shoulders and replied, "Could be there's a way for you to become unstuck."

Chester paused. He was about to find out why they were having lunch together. "Oh? What do you have in mind?" he asked innocently.

"What would you say to getting the chance to rewrite your own employment contract with a big up-front dollar amount, sort of a signing bonus? Also, how about a better severance package than you have now, one you could practically retire with. Then you'd probably want your contract to become effective if your responsibilities ever changed, or there was a change in management, or if the members of the board were reshuffled. That way, you'd be almost assured your contract would be triggered within a year. You'd be able to walk away from LoneStar with a small fortune. Sound good?"

"Yeah, Brett, sounds real good. Just how is this going to be accomplished? Hilborn isn't about to dole out more money. Hell, he's running around squeezing pennies and selling everything that's not nailed down."

Brett chuckled. "Oh, I know he is."

"So what's the reason for him to be so benevolent?"

"Tell him you'll quit if he doesn't rewrite your contract."

Was this some kind of dumb joke? "Brett, that's not exactly going to send the man into a state of shock. Hell, he'd probably say 'thank you,' pat me on the ass and escort me out."

"Not if others are going to quit too."
"Others? What others? What are you talking about?"

"I'm merely suggesting that if, say, the top ten or twelve senior managers of LoneStar all signed a document stating unless certain demands are agreed to by the board, you'd all quit—"

Interrupting, Chester quickly said, "Brett, I don't think the board is going to believe we'd all quit. Where would we go? How are a dozen LoneStar senior executives going to find comparable jobs anyway? This is nuts."

"Chester, trust me. All of you have jobs waiting for you, right now, with me."

"*With you? What the* . . . Okay, hold on for a minute." Chester swirled the remaining coffee around in his cup, thinking. "Why don't you tell me *our* demands? The ones we're gonna take to the board."

Brett giggled like a kid hiding a report card with all "A's" on it. "You're going to require that I be reinstated as the chairman of the board. You're going to require that a press release be issued stating that I was begged to return, that accepting my resignation was a terrible mistake. You're going to require they fire Hilborn and Sanchez, and then issue a separate press release stating these men were totally ill equipped for the job assigned to them by an irrational board. Then we're going to have the board admit publicly that since I've left the stock has dropped like a rock, the company has lost credibility, there is no strategic focus, managers are reevaluating their commitment to stay, and on and on and so forth and so forth."

Chester stared in awe. "You really want your pound of flesh, don't you?"

"To be frank, I want every director to come crawling back to me. I want to rub their noses into what they did. I want to humiliate them. But I really want Hilborn's career to cease, forever. No one screws around with me and gets away with it. No one."

"I can see that. Okay, if we do this and if your conditions are met, what happens to the ten or twelve of us?"

"Whatever you want. Stay or go. But whichever you do, you'll be the richer for it."

"How many do you figure you'll have to convince, in order for the board to go along?"

"I need at least eight. Eight senior managers leaving would cripple LoneStar, if for no other reason than the banks will pull the credit lines. What bank is going to lend hundreds of millions of dollars to a company where over half the top management just quit?"

"So how many do you have?"

"I've only just started, Chester, but if you agree I'll have four." Brett sat back smiling. "This is sweet. This is so sweet."

"I suppose you've talked to a lawyer to bless this plan?"

"Yep. Did that before I officially resigned. He told me to make sure there wasn't any non-compete language in the severance agreement. Other than that it's a free country, you can work for me or not. Also, I didn't take any proprietary information with me. Chester, there's nothing they can do."

"Ah, give me some time to think about it. I suspect you're trying to do this as quickly as possible?"

"That's right, the sooner the better. Don't let me down, Chester. Damn, I can't wait." As the two men were leaving, Brett sang to a familiar tune: " . . . You don't spit into the wind, you don't pull the mask off the old Lone Ranger and you don't mess around with . . . me."

Thursday, November 14, 10:15 A.M.
Chairman's Office, LoneStar

Calls of congratulations kept pouring in. Vendors, banks, shareholders, creditors, newspapers, stock analysts, industry executives and a few employees all faxed or emailed their regards. Charles knew most of the smiles and glad handshakes were without meaning, but on the other hand some seemed sincere. The commuting back and forth between Dallas and Detroit was getting a little old, although having his wife embroiled in kicking shins and pulling ears at the Capitol made his presence at home optional anyway.

As it did so often during the day, his phone buzzed. "Yes, Suzanne."

"Mr. Sanchez is here to see you."

"Fine. Send him in." Even after working side by side, Charles couldn't tell the man's age. Somewhere between low thirties to mid forties he guessed. "Hello, please come in Adam. Care for something to drink?"

"No, thank you." Adam sat easily into a chair facing the desk.

Holding several 'good luck' letters in his hand, Charles said, "Adam, you've been spending a lot of time with our senior managers, department managers, supervisors and clerks. What are the troops saying about us? Will they give us enough time to turn this ship around and find a buyer?"

Adam shifted in the chair a little before answering, "Generally speaking, there is still a fair amount of resentment against you . . . us. I suppose the clerical level is more supportive than most, because the perks we have canceled did not impact them. Actually, they have appreciated most of the moves made. I would categorize the middle managers as wishy-washy. They would like to work in a more stable environment but are not ready to support us.

"The senior managers on the other hand are convinced we are the enemy. We have taken away their playthings and made them accountable. This is all new to them and they do not like it. They think you pushed out Brett and stopped their gravy train, and they do not like me because reporting to a Mexican is not an acceptable working condition."

"Will they give us the time we need?"

"I have my doubts about the senior managers. If they could go somewhere else, they would. But that is the rub. Who else would want them?"

"You're not overly impressed with our senior management?"

Maintaining his characteristically stoic posture, Adam replied, "That statement is being kind. These managers are more a hindrance than anything. They accept zero responsibility, hide from authority, show no initiative, no vision, no management capability whatsoever, come in late, take long lunches and leave early. Yes, and get paid handsomely for it."

"Any suggestions?"

"No, not yet. I suppose they are better than nothing if only for appearance sake. Regrettably, they could become bitter and start throwing wrenches into the machinery. We need to be watchful."

"Can we take anyone into our confidence?"

"No."

"So we just wait for them to do something stupid? That doesn't sound prudent."

"Perhaps we should approach a couple executive search firms. Nothing specific, but find out what is available . . . as a precaution."

"Good suggestion. Let's do it." Wondering if he could probe further without offending Adam, Charles said, "This is a little off track, and if I'm out of line just tell me. But I don't hear much of a Spanish accent from you."

Adam smiled. "I do not mind. I suppose growing up in California smoothed most of my rough spots. Attending college in Oregon finished the task."

"Oregon?"

"Yes, the University of Oregon. You know, the Ducks?"

"Ducks? I'm thinking that's not a Big Ten school."

Chuckling, Adam said, "No. But now that I look back it is fairly remarkable. My mother and father wanted me to be an American, as they could see only despair living in a Mexican border town. Perhaps they were right."

"You've never married?"

"No, not even close. Charles, I am a very driven, ambitious man. I will not let a family get in my way, not yet. I simply have not found a women willing to put up with those restrictions."

"I can see why. What you need is someone every bit as obstinate as you. I'll keep my eyes open."

A grinning Adam nodded and replied, "Thank you. Yes, that is twice I should thank you. First for giving me this chance. It is rounding out my résumé nicely, not to mention my bank account. Second for your offer of matchmaking. You returning home for the weekend?"

"Yep. You?"

"Nowhere to go. I will stay around here, do a little more work." Adam stood up and offered, "I think I had better contact those search firms. I have a bad feeling, Charles."

CHAPTER 25

Sunday, November 17, 9:35 A.M.
The Abbey, Birmingham

The Church Choir had just finished singing a hymn and sat down in unison. The lights dimmed and the last note from the organ grew fainter and fainter, then ceased altogether. After a few moments of silence, Ryan Sladden stepped up to the main pulpit. Due to an early morning argument, Stephanie and Rick Blaine had arrived late and consequently were seated in the front row. Not exactly where Rick wanted to be today. He and Stephanie were going through a rocky period and having the good Reverend staring directly at him for the next twenty minutes wasn't doing his conscience any good.

During the drive to church this morning Rick took an objective look at his life. He had a wife, great kids, a fine home, friends, a good job, and money in the bank . . . so why wasn't his life overflowing with joy? Because Stephanie was making his life miserable, that's why. Ever since that dinner held in his honor, she'd become more impossible to live with. Nagging, bitching, crying, short tempered . . . she was pushing him right to Ashley. So, in a way this wasn't his fault! Yeah, it's not like he's to blame. A fresh sense of relief enveloped him, allowing Rick to sit through the rest of the sermon without squirming.

After the service and during the drive back to their house, Rick decided to attempt neutral conversation. "Doing anything special today?"

Gazing out the passenger window, Stephanie thought for a while and then announced, "I wonder why you never mentioned your brunette dinner partner at the Townsend. Nothing to hide from me is there?"

It was like a sudden blast of icy water smacked him, sapping his breath. Rick sat dumbstruck. He clenched his hands tightly around the steering wheel, focused on the road ahead and didn't say a word. If she knew anything, she'd have said something by now. So the smart move was to pretend like there was nothing to talk about . . . don't dignify the accusation with any remark. But Rick could sense her eyes fixed on him. If there were a hole handy, he'd have gladly crawled into it.

Monday, November 18, 9:56 A.M.
Cypress Offices, Manhattan

The sun blazed brightly into the New York conference room of The Cypress Group. The emergency meeting called by Paul Victor was set to start in four minutes. Sitting by himself at the head of the table, Paul was nervous . . . exceedingly nervous. None of the other senior partners appreciated emergency meetings, particularly one called by someone who'd lost a small fortune. Several major clients had already called wanting to know what the hell was going on. "We're in a roaring bull market," they fumed. "How the hell can you assholes lose money in a bull market?" Unfortunately, no one had any good answers.

Paul rubbed at his nose and tried to dry his sweaty palms on custom tailored pants. He went over his opening remarks a couple more times in his head. This was as big a meeting as he'd ever attend, and could easily make or break him. Outside the window, a thick cloud suddenly blocked the sun and the room became considerably darker. Finally, Paul looked up from his notes; all the other partners were there now, waiting. He took another sip of coffee and placed the cup back into the saucer. Now or never.

Clearing his throat, Paul began. "Thank you for rearranging your schedules for me. I appreciate it. Rest assured that I would not have called this meeting if I was not convinced that a recently disclosed, major opportunity has befallen us." Paul was looking at six very unhappy men. Evidently, he'd lost a lot of credibility with them over the LoneStar episode.

"I know that my performance with LoneStar has not been acceptable. We all know that on my suggestion two hundred million dollars worth of bonds were converted into five million shares of common stock at a price of forty. I know that as we speak today our five million shares have fallen from forty-six to thirty-eight. I know that we've lost some ground to our competition because of this.

"While this is all fact, I submit to you that I've never failed this firm yet. No matter what the circumstances, I've always been able to pull profits out of seemingly total disasters. Looking around this table, I can recall a few of you coming to me over the years asking for assistance and receiving it." Paul noticed a few sets of eyes wavering. That's the reaction he'd wanted.

"We are all risk takers. We are all motivated by making more money for our clients than the next guy. When an opportunity presents itself, it's wrong for us not to grab hold and seize it for the benefit of our clients, not to mention ourselves. Such an advantage is here with us today." Well, he'd gotten their attention. That's all he could ask given the circumstances.

"It's come to my attention that the value of LoneStar stock is about to plummet. A private analysis says into the twenties. Now . . ." A pack of panic stricken men immediately besieged Paul with wild questions.

"Into the twenties?" "Shit. We'll all be ruined." "How could you let this happen?" "Where the fuck are your brains?" "Damn you, Victor."

Holding up both hands he urged them to relax, "*Please* gentlemen. Please. Let me continue." The six men resettled themselves into their chairs but all were glaring at him.

"Thank you. As I was saying, the stock is going to fall into the twenties. That's about a fifteen to twenty point drop from today's level. But it is this very fact that we will turn into an unparalleled victory for Cypress." Glassy stares were all around the table. They were too stunned to even blink.

One of them managed to form a few words and say, "Victory? A twenty-point drop is a victory? Are you fucking crazy?"

Quickly capitalizing on the question, Paul said, "No, not at all. In fact, what I propose is that we immediately sell our five million shares, at thirty-eight or whatever we can get for them. I then propose we sell the stock short."

Another partner shook his head in disbelief. "You want us to take a hit on five million shares, and then sell short? That stock's already cost us a fucking fortune, Victor. And you want to sell it short? Why, so you can bankrupt us, take us down with you?"

Evidently, they held him in little regard and Paul was getting irritated. Raising his voice a full octave he said, "No one's going to be taken down. Don't you see? Listen, if we sell this stock short at say thirty-eight and it falls to twenty, that's an eighteen-dollar profit. If we sell short a million shares it'll return eighteen million. Five million shares, we'll make ninety million. But if we short ten million shares we'll earn *one hundred and eighty million.*

"Another thing, this'll be happening fast 'cause the stock's gonna crater in a matter of weeks. We can play loose with the three-day settlement rules, and sell naked like we've done before. We'll spread the trades among a couple dozed brokers and use that 13-day mandatory closeout rule to our advantage."

Naked short selling was froth with risk. "That could cause us problems with the SEC, Paul. We'll need plausible deniability like before."

"C'mon, it's only illegal if we get caught. Besides, the SEC has bigger worries than us." He was losing a few of them. "Okay, okay, I'll only do it if it's really crucial to the bottom line."

One of the more visibly angry partners hit his fist on the table, "Why the fuck should we believe you? How in the world do you know the stock's going to tank? You're on the fucking board of directors and don't know shit. What happens if the damned stock suddenly takes off and we're short millions of shares? We'd be wiped out, that's what."

Another partner joined in, "Even if you're right and you know something we don't, we can't use it. You're a board director, remember? That makes us all prime targets for an SEC investigation. I for one don't want the SEC on my ass, 'bigger worries or no bigger worries.' Think, Victor. Cypress would be nailed to a cross. This is stupid. Look, I want us to get the hell out of that damned stock too. But not at the losses we're looking at today. Our client base would abandon us and I can't say I'd blame them. The best thing you can do is to get back to Dallas and fix the goddamned place, then find a goddamned buyer so we can make a goddamned buck on this deal."

In his zeal for profits, Paul had totally forgotten about his own conflict of interest, everything was just happening too fast. If only he could excuse himself, run back to his office, take a small hit of cocaine . . . his whole future was about to be pissed away. These guys were giving him the "black ball," telling him to fix the problem and go away. "You don't understand, I know the stock's going to fall. We've got to take advantage of it. Look, I didn't get a chance to finish. I'm going to resign from the board and I didn't mean we should be using Cypress funds. I meant that we'd use your funds. I mean, you guys can use your own personal funds through dummy limited liability companies. That'll remove any direct connection between us and LoneStar."

Six pairs of seasoned eyes registered total dismay. The eldest partner, the very dapper dresser Theodore 'Teddy' French, stroked his neatly trimmed beard and said, "Victor, I can't believe what I'm hearing. Have you lost all your senses, or do you think we have? You've got to be out of your mind." As a group they started to get up to leave.

Paul could only save himself by admitting he was a thief. Well, so what? All these guys were thieves too. Hell, they might even respect him all the more. "Listen, just *listen.* I stole somebody's private disk; a disk that says LoneStar is going to crater. I've read the disk. I believe the disk. We can all make a fucking fortune. I'll even personally guarantee your short positions with my own collateral."

Teddy's eyes suddenly turned from dismay into a dark shade of greed. "What do you mean, you stole a disk? Who from? Where?"

Licking his lips, Paul blew his runny nose and grabbed at the rope thrown him. "I have a snitch, she works at one of our competitors. She stole a disk from them and gave it to me. You can all look at it if you want."

Another set of avarice eyes searched Paul for some plausible sign that this was genuine. "Who's disk did you steal, Victor?"

Paul's heart was thumping, his mouth was dry and his forehead was sweating. "It's from the Taylor-Bishop Company. It's Bishop's herself. She was at LoneStar's annual meeting and has been planning this all along. Just like she did with Virtual Reality, that high-tech stock outta California that went bust a few years ago. She made a killing on that one, remember? Well, she's going to do it again, only this time bigger and better, and she's gonna do it with LoneStar."

The partners all retook their seats. Teddy French re-stroked his beard and said, "Paul, why don't you go get that disk and bring it back here, so we can all take a look at it." Six skeptical men leaned back into their chairs and waited for that disk. A myriad of thoughts flew through their collective minds, but a constant theme among them was the chance for quick profits and to pummel that damned woman.

Paul ran to his office almost giddy with excitement. He picked up the disk and flew back. Just as he entered the conference room the sun poked from behind a barrier of clouds, bathing the entire room in bright light. Surely, it was a sign from above.

* * *

The sun had set several hours ago in New York, and the seven partners of Cypress were exhausted. Each had gone over the stolen disk painstakingly and in the end each had come to the same conclusion . . . Ashley was brilliant. She was a wizard, or was that a sorceress? In any event Victor was proven right . . . this was a rare opportunity. All of them would soon be filthy rich.

Paul coughed and wiped his nose. "Are we all in agreement? Do we all agree that we'll immediately sell our five million shares of LoneStar stock at whatever price we can get for it? Tomorrow, I and my three portfolio managers will immediately resign from the board of LoneStar, and to avoid any 'insider' taint between LoneStar and Cypress, we'll form a series of new limited liability company's owned by 'significant others.' Then each of us will begin investing as much cash as possible by liquidating current personal holdings, and by inviting only our closest, richest, most influential friends and clients to invest with us, is that right?" All men present leered and nodded in agreement.

Paul continued, "Fine, then these new entities will begin selling LoneStar short. Like I said we can even sell naked depending upon circumstances. No reason to arrange for shares to be delivered if we don't have to, right? Then we can really trade some heavy volumes. Once the stock drops below twenty we'll close out everybody's positions and everyone rakes in millions."

That's the only part of this whole deal Paul didn't like, not one damned bit. He'd be selling everything he owned and placing the proceeds into a new company legally owned by his sister-in-law, but he had no other choice. Using Cypress accounts was out of the question because they would be considered indirectly associated with LoneStar, and any gains could be seized by the Securities and Exchange Commission if push came to shove. That was also true for an account in his wife's name. So a 'safe' account had to be used. This way the trail of cash and profits would be far enough removed that if the SEC ever did come sniffing around, they'd end up mired in a sea of legalities for years. Odds were in his favor.

Another plus was the fact that Terri Rothman, his sister-in-law, was dumber than his wife, Cindi. He should have no problems convincing the witless woman to sign some papers and then butt out. He'd just feed Terri and Cindi some line of bull that they'd be too dense to figure out. Still, it was a sad commentary that the only person he could think of was Terri. Paul vowed to get some better friends.

The six other men were still beaming as Paul continued speaking. "Now it'll take each of us a few weeks to set up companies, sell the family jewels and deposit the proceeds into our new LLC's. So I propose that we start selling short as soon as any cash becomes available. That way we won't flood the market all at once, and we'll get better execution on our trades. Any questions?"

No questions. A couple of the partners shook each others' hands and patted Paul on the back and packed up to go home. Paul was on top of the world. This was going to be good . . . really, really good.

Tuesday, November 19, 12:55 P.M.
Country Club, Dallas

Today's guest for lunch with Brett was the Treasurer of LoneStar, Gary Nash, who happened to be in a very somber mood and merely played with his food. His personal trading position with Pagent and Associates wasn't getting any better. The last call from Bob Bell informed him that all his prior gain had been wiped out, and then some. Gary replayed the conversation over and over . . . So where am I, how much do I have left? Gary, you're at least two hundred thousand dollars in the hole.

Gary was still in denial, wondering how he could have gone from close to a million dollars to down a couple hundred thousand. It's just not right. They could've gotten him out sooner.

Brett clinked his glass with a spoon to wake up Gary. "Say, Gary. You're awfully quiet today. You okay?" Brett on the other hand was in a very good mood.

"What? Oh, sure. I'm okay." Gary's blank eyes left Brett and looked down at his plate.

"Look, Gary. We can postpone our talk till another time if you'd like. But if the reason you're so down is because of the changes at LoneStar, well, I might be of some help."

Since they already canceled their lunch last week because Gary was too behind in supplying answers to Hilborn, he wasn't going to postpone again. Refocusing his wandering attention on Brett, Gary said, "I'm sorry. What help are you talking about?"

"Listen, I know everything Hilborn and Sanchez have been pulling lately. I know how they've been treating you. I know that you're stuck working for them and you think there's no way out. Well, I'm here to give you a way out." Brett flashed Gary one of the most fatherly smiles imaginable.

"Okay, Brett, what do you want from me?" Gary wasn't in any mood for guessing games. It seemed that lately everybody was using him for something, so why should Brett be any different? But two hundred thousand dollars in the hole? He could only hope interest rates dropped again. He promised himself to get out as soon as he was half a million up . . . no, a quarter million. He'd learned his lesson about being greedy.

A somewhat impatient Brett continued, "I don't want anything from you. Look, Gary, we can shake hands, say have a nice day and leave right now, but I think you might want to hear me out. Actually, I want to give you something. Will you listen?"

"Sure, I'll listen." So he did for the next ten minutes.

As soon as Brett finished his well-rehearsed speech, he signaled Raymond to bring over coffee. Gary's head was swirling again. He looked at his watch and silently swore. This luncheon had taken up most of the afternoon. He could only hope Hilborn or Sanchez hadn't been trying to contact him. "Okay, Brett, when do you need to hear back from me?"

"Like I've told all the others, the sooner the better."

"Have you talked to everyone now?"

"Yep, you're the last."

"How many confirmations you receive?"

"If you come back with a 'yes,' I'll have six. Five others are still thinking it over."

Gary nodded, but he was already rethinking about his trading losses. That big signing bonus Brett alluded to seemed the best way to get a large hunk of cash. Maybe it was enough to offset the trading losses. He sure as hell didn't feel any obligation to Hilborn. Of course, what Brett was suggesting would destroy everyone if it went awry. It was a delicate situation.

Fortunately, with the holidays approaching, nothing was gonna happen until next year so Gary could take his time to reply. Moreover, just think what would happen if Hilborn found out. The mutineers would be fired on the spot. There was also the possibility that interest rates would plummet, fixing this whole mess. So there wasn't any upside to making a hasty decision, and every reason to procrastinate.

"Well, Gary. What do you say?"

"Brett, I'm really interested. Let me think on it, I'll give you my answer as soon as I can."

"Just don't wait too long. I have a score to settle and I'm getting real tired of waiting."

Same day, 3:30 P.M.
Taylor-Bishop Offices, Manhattan

The pink messages were piling up on her desk. Idly thumbing through them, Ashley noted several from Rick Blaine. She'd have to take a stand with him fairly soon, one way or the other. Odd how his face kept popping into her thoughts more and more lately. Was it some sort of sign? Her senior associate, Lauren Washington entered Ashley's office and said, "You wanted to see me?"

Ashley put down the messages. "Yes, I'd like you to do me a favor without asking too many questions."

"Okay, shoot."

"I want you to send Jackie Wells out on some kind of assignment. Something that will keep her out of our office for about four or five weeks."

The surprised Washington asked, "When is she supposed to go?"

"Tomorrow would be fine, today better."

"Any idea what the assignment I'm sending her on might be?"

"Nope. I'll let you decide that one."

Scratching her chin, Lauren said, "All right. I'm sure you'll tell me why I'm doing what I'm doing when you can." Lauren knew from experience her boss had a good reason for everything she did.

Ashley's eyes drifted over to the window . . . it was another cloudy day. An omen? But there was no other choice; Jackie had to be sent off. She couldn't be allowed to roam around the office, poking around for secrets. On the flip side, Ashley couldn't fire Jackie. It would be an immediate tip-off to Victor that the snitch had been found out . . . and he might think twice about the pirated LoneStar disk. No, Ashley needed the opposition to go right on believing they had a snitch. "The games afoot, gentlemen."

CHAPTER 26

Wednesday, November 20, 2:15 P.M.
Taylor-Bishop Offices, Manhattan

"I'm sorry, Miss Wells. Paul Victor is in a meeting and cannot be disturbed. I'll leave him another message if you'd like."

"No, forget it." Discouraged, Jackie replaced the receiver. Just this morning Lauren told her to go home and pack a suitcase and hustle back to work because she was booked on the five o'clock flight to Seattle. No warning . . . and over the Thanksgiving Holiday too! Lauren explained there were a handful of potential companies out in that region that Ashley was thinking of investing in, and someone had to visit them and interview the various management teams. "Go and make sure everything checks out okay. Call in daily with status reports. Just remember we might need you to visit a couple of other firms while you're out there, so pack accordingly."

Jackie supposed this was a vote of confidence, but it sure came at an inconvenient time. Lauren said she'd probably be out on the road for weeks, and Paul hadn't reimbursed her the ten grand for Joyce's' bribe. That payment had forced Jackie to hock nearly everything she owned at a pawnshop. Now she was broke and desperately needed the fifty thousand payoff . . . per their agreement. So where the hell was he?

Monday, December 9, 9:40 A.M.
Taylor-Bishop Offices, Manhattan

The sidewalks were covered with icy, dirty slush, and a bone-chilling wind was howling down the streets, while the airwaves were flooded with Christmas music and commercials. The weeks between Thanksgiving and Christmas were the most uncomfortable for Ashley, just as they were for a lot of people. But because of the LoneStar transaction she couldn't take her customary warm weather vacation, so she purchased her first Christmas tree . . . a white artificial tree . . . and decorated it with silver and gold ornaments. It really did look pretty. It also looked pretty isolated standing alone in the corner of her office. Perhaps she should hang some twinkle lights around the windows, and wrap several empty boxes with colorful paper, suggesting real presents under the tree. That would give her office a more festive atmosphere.

Suddenly, her investment manager, Vanessa Garoon ran past Joyce's desk and into Ashley's office, skidding to a stop as she shouted, "The volumes up! The volumes up!"
Ashley looked away from her tree and inquired, "I presume you're talking about LoneStar?"

"Yeah, right. You told me to watch the trading activity, remember? Well, most days there's only around a couple hundred thousand shares traded. But today . . . the markets just opened and volumes at three hundred thousand already."

"Finally!" Ashley gave Vanessa a pat on the shoulder and said, "You did great, now go back and start plotting volumes and prices. Oh, tell Lauren I want to see her." Vanessa was gone in a flash.

Picking up the phone, Ashley hit memory four and waited while the other end of the line rang twice. "Yes?"

"Mrs. Stanfield? It's me, Ashley Taylor-Bishop. I think Mr. Victor and his friends are starting to sell their stock. Are you sure you want to jump into this?"

A blue-blooded voice replied, "Absolutely. Shift as much of my holdings into cash as you see fit. Let me know if you need more."

"Thanks. You're the greatest. Goodbye." Ashley punched memory five. She only had to wait one ring this time. "Barth residence."

"Hello, may I speak to Mrs. Barth, please. Tell her it's Ashley Taylor-Bishop calling. I'll wait." Now that Victor had made his move, Ashley could begin making hers.

"Hello, Ashley. How are you dear?"

"I'm just fine, Mable, thanks for taking my call."

"Not at all, I always love hearing from you. You're my favorite investment counselor you know."

"Yes, well, thank you. Mable, I think it's time for you to move out of some of your bonds and buy that stock we've talked about. Remember? LoneStar?"

"Yes dear, I'm not senile you know. Of course I remember. You just go ahead and do whatever you think is best. I'm sure Oscar would have wanted it that way, he did so like you while he was here."

"Thank you, Mable."

"Make me another fortune, I want to sponsor more children for summer camp. Dear me, there seems to be so many children who can't afford summer camp. Well, I'm going to want to send at least a dozen more next year so you'd better get to work."

Ashley smiled to herself . . . a dozen indeed. Mable Barth owned the whole summer camp, and every year gave free four-week enrollments to about one thousand disadvantaged kids. She was one in a million. Even Ashley contributed.

Lauren Washington entered her office. "Want to see me?"

"Yes, just hold on for one minute." Ashley hit memory six and waited.

"Hello?"

"Hello, Mrs. Blackburn? It's Ashley Taylor-Bishop. How've you been?"

"Oh, hello, Ashley. I've been just fine, just fine. Although I must admit, this house is just getting too big for me. Are you calling about that stock you think I should start buying?"

"Yes, that's right, Eleanor. I believe that you could do very well investing in LoneStar at this time. It has new management who're cutting costs and rocking the boat. But I have to be honest with you, this is more a speculative play than a sure thing."

"Yes, so you've said. Well, I certainly did very well with that Virtual 'whatever' stock you suggested, and I would like to add on another wing. Okay, let's do it."

"Thank you. I'll be in touch, Eleanor, goodbye." Ashley finished the call and looked at Lauren.

"Were you just talking to Eleanor Blackburn?"

"Yes, I was."

"She's the one who runs that children's hospital isn't she?"

"Well, she's the one who keeps the doors open, if that's what you mean."

"Great lady, huh?"

"Yeah, I understand she and her husband have always been that way."

"Kind of funny. I mean, most of your clients are older, wealthy . . . women."

Ashley shrugged her shoulders and replied, "I guess so. Never thought about it much, but I suppose I prefer dealing with gracious, appreciative clients." The "and men aren't" was acknowledged without needing to be spoken.

"Well, I can't fault your standards. So, what'd you want to see me about?"

"I want you to take this client list and begin cashing in the securities that I've circled. I'll tell you when we're okay with the other names. We'll be reinvesting the cash proceeds shortly. Notify our brokers that I'm interested in buying LoneStar stock, in sizeable blocks. But I don't want anyone on the street to know it's us buying, at least not yet. Make sure the brokers buy in their own name."

Lauren's jaw dropped opened and she stared at Ashley in utter amazement. "Wait. Wait a minute. What'da ya mean *buy*? We're supposed to be *selling* LoneStar. That's the plan . . . sell short. The stock's gonna drop into single digits. We've spent months figuring out how to get the price up to pull this off and now you're changing everything at the last minute? Why?"

"Lauren, I trust you completely but I'm afraid I wasn't able to take you completely into my confidence. You see, Jackie's a plant . . . a spy. She's been passing along information on us, what we're doing here. So I turned the tables. I've been feeding her only what I wanted her to know, and I couldn't risk her overhearing you or the other girls talking."

Sitting down with a thump, Lauren said, "Jackie's a spy? You're kidding. For who?"

"Cypress. Paul Victor."

"Victor? That son of a bitch? What a prick. Man, who'd of thunk . . . and can you believe Jackie that little tramp? So that's why you wanted me to get rid of her, right? Okay, so what happens next?"

Ashley winked and said, "Next, we screw Paul Victor and his buddies. Now go tell our brokers we're buying, I've got a few more calls to make."

Same day, 11:25 A.M.
LoneStar Offices, Dallas

Gary Nash's job wasn't fun anymore. He wanted out. Then again, Brett had promised him a way out, well, him and nine or ten others. If only he could turn back the clock back to when he was six hundred thousand dollars up. Why didn't he sell? Gary sighed as his telephone rang. "Mr. Nash? Mr. Bell is on the line."

At the name 'Bell,' Gary's stomach gave an involuntary churn. That New York slime could rot in hell for all Gary cared. Why couldn't they all just crawl back into whatever holes they crawled out of? All the man ever did was remind Gary he should have folded months ago. Well, screw him and all his kind. "Mr. Nash? Do you want to take the call?"

"Yeah, I'll take it," he said without enthusiasm.

"Gary? Things going okay with the new management team?"

"Yeah, fine. What'da ya want?"

"I hear someone is trying to sell your stock, any idea who?"

"No, is that what you wanted to talk to me about? 'cause I'm busy."

"Well, no. I was just wondering, that's all. Look, I called because your trades are really tanking. The Fed is still huffing and puffing about runaway inflation, so they're keeping the pressure on interest rates. Rates are shooting up and I don't see any change in sight."

Aw, for the love of . . . "How much?"

"Look, I told you to get outta this a long time ago. Don't you remember?"

"Oh, fuck you. *How much?*"

"Five hundred thousand."

"*What? Can't be. I don't believe it.*"

"Hey, I'm sorry. But that's where you are. Remember when you doubled up? Well, that cuts both ways. Anyway, the guys in credit wanted me to tell you they're going to need a lot more security, and they suggest you end your trading with us. Gary, can you come up with at least three hundred thousand of collateral? If you can't, we'll have to close you down."

"Five hundred thousand? I've lost five hundred thousand?"

"Yes, and we need another three hundred thousand of collateral. But remember that's just for now. No telling about tomorrow. Interest rates are a bad play in today's environment. It's not a good time to be speculating."

Gary's mind couldn't comprehend all this, so he lapsed into an emotional response, "Go fuck yourself. You did this to me, you made me use my house as collateral."

"Yeah, right. That's exactly the way it happened, Gary. You're not responsible, right?"

"Go screw yourself, Bell." Gary's mind wasn't focusing on anything; it was just sort of bouncing around in shock.

Bell was persistent and asked, "So do we close out your trades?"

Gary was having a hard time concentrating. All he could think about was the money he'd lost.

The managing director tried again. "Gary. Do you want to close out the trades?"

"Huh? Ah, not sure." Gary was numb.

"Gary, you gotta do something pretty damned soon. The guys in credit don't care who you are. All they care about is protecting the company. They're pounding on my door and I don't know how long I can keep them from pulling the rug out from under you. Do you hear me? Are you listening to me?"

What had happened? It seemed like yesterday Gary was moments away from retiring to a winter retreat in Colorado. How could he tell Pamela about secretly mortgaging their home, or losing half a million dollars? Thank God Brett could bail him out. "Huh? What'd you say?"

"I said are you listening to me? The guys in credit aren't going to wait. I've shuffled paper work on my side and stalled them as long as I could. Understand?"

"Call you later." What had they gotten him into?

Thursday, December 12, 1:45 P.M.
Cypress Offices, Manhattan

The office complex housing the Cypress Group was a flurry of activity, with Paul Victor's own room being dubbed "command central." Never had he felt so invigorated, so alive. Millions and millions of dollars were at his disposal, all he had to do was pick up the phone and execute trade after trade. Life was fantastic.

A handful of major investors had been contacted by their Cypress representative, given a confidential rundown of the situation and urged to jump in. Jump they did. Like hungry wolves who tasted blood. And Victor's name was prominently mentioned. That was the best part. Even the high rollers now knew him by name and his future was assured. Any of these boys would gladly hire the man who masterminded this sure thing.

"Paul, we've just hit a bid from Merrill for another twenty thousand shares at thirty-six."

Jotting the information down, Paul said, "That's the best you could do? Shit, okay, fine. Keep the pressure up, I want to sell a million shares today." Paul opened his desk drawer, took out a small packet filled with fine white powder, dipped a small silver spoon into the packet and snorted. Now was *not* the time to lose focus.

One of the senior partners stuck his head into Paul's office. Practically gloating he said, "I just got off the phone with my Atlantic City friends, they want in for twenty five big ones. Can you believe this?" He left laughing and shaking his head. The smell of new money was infectious.

Paul blew his nose and downed a couple antacid tablets. This was going better than he could have hoped. After convincing his partners, dozens of 'special' clients were coming over the transom with no letup in sight. He'd hoped to sell everything for around thirty-seven but the price was falling faster than anticipated. The stock was trading at thirty-six and he had millions of shares to go. Well, if he could get the rest done in the mid thirties and then close out the positions at fifteen, the profit would still be around twenty dollars per share. So even if they only shorted seven million shares, they'd reap a hundred and forty million dollar windfall. Damned good return for a few weeks work.

Another cohort shouted into Paul's office, "I just hit a hundred thousand shares at thirty-five and a half. Market's getting awfully soft. Do we keep selling?"

The drug now coursing through his bloodstream made the decision easy. Without hesitation Paul raised an eyebrow and spat back, "Short it."

Same day, Same time.

"Ashley?" Lauren poked her head into Ashley's office. "We just received confirmation for another hundred thousand shares at thirty-five and a half. The price has been falling all day."

Ashley smiled and said, "Yes, I know."

"How much more are we going to buy?" Lauren wasn't as confident as her boss. Any small miscalculation now would sink them. "Are we going for broke?

"We'll stop when the money runs out."

"Ah, don't you want to stop now? I mean the stock doesn't seem to have much support. We're the only buyers in town. Don't ya think we should pull back?"

"Lauren, you just keep buying and keep me posted." Ashley opened a desk drawer and gazed at a nestled 'victory' bottle of Dom Pérignon, 1897. Come into my parlor.

CHAPTER 27

Friday, December 13, 4:10 P.M.
Smith-Palmer & Co., Detroit

The offices of Smith-Palmer were gaily decorated for the Holidays. Red and green lights twinkled along the tops of modular partitions, fresh wreaths were hung on doors, Christmas cards were Scotch taped to walls, and everyone was in festive spirits. Why not? The year had been a good one and there would be plenty of extra cash to stuff employees stockings come bonus time.

Adding to the gaiety of the season was Rick Blaine, the unsung hero. Well, not exactly unsung. While he was yet to become a household name in the investment community, Rick's research reports were read by more clients than any other analyst at Smith-Palmer. So he received plenty of accolades from co-workers, particularly because of his timely 'sell' on LoneStar. The stock was dropping like a rock and Rick was their superstar.

Unfortunately, the slayer of dragons also had to cope with a bitchy wife. She even went so far as signing them up for marriage counseling sessions. Not too surprisingly, every day seemed like they were arguing more and enjoying it less. Where once a little annoyance would go unnoticed, now it was thrown into the face of the perpetrator. Rick found himself working longer hours just to avoid being around her.

Work really was piling up too. Each morning new requests for his personal appearance at business luncheons or dinners were all neatly stacked on his desk. Some days, with all the phone calls and meetings, he didn't get around to looking at his messages until late in the afternoon. Sipping on a diet Pepsi, Rick looked at his watch and noted that today was one of those days. Grudgingly, he went through his messages.

There was an invite for lunch, another lunch, a dinner, another lunch, a quick morning meeting, oh, a breakfast . . . good, at least he could start the day off on a full stomach . . . *holy shit! Ashley called?* An errant elbow inadvertently smacked into the Pepsi can as he reached for the phone spilling the contents onto his desk and reports. He began furiously blotting up the dark carbonated liquid with a handkerchief, while fumbling to punch in the correct digits. Sweat formed at both temples, his mouth was suddenly dry and the right ear strained to hear the connection. How long had it been since they'd last—

Joyce picked the receiver up on the second ring and said, "Taylor-Bishop Company. How may I direct your call?"

"Uhh. I need Ashley Bishop. This is ah, Rick calling . . . I mean Mr. Blaine, Rick Blaine from Smith-Palmer. I'm ah, returning her call . . . she called me first." Lord, why couldn't he speak like a normal person? A tongue-tied twit, that's what he was. How's that? A tongue-tied . . . could he say that five times really fast? Tongue-tied twit, tongue-tried twit, tongue tid tweed . . . nope, guess not.

"Mr. Blaine? I've located her, one moment please." Like a little kid on Christmas morning, Rick was bubbling over with excitement, anticipation, fear.

"Hi, Rick."

His heart burst open. "Hi, yourself. Ah, how are you?"

"Really doing well. Thanks for asking. You still king of the hill over there?"

"Yes, yes I am. I'm a bloody idol because of you. Have you seen LoneStar? It's dropped under thirty-six." Actually, all he wanted was for her to say she was coming for a visit.

"Yes, I've noticed. Listen, I may be coming your way before Christmas . . . business trip."

Yesss! Thank you, oh, thank you. Barely controlling himself, he replied, "That's fantastic. I've really missed you."

"Me too, lover."

"To tell you the truth I'm always thinking of you Ashley, can't get you out of my mind." He'd bought her a very special piece of Christmas joy, a delicate silver necklace. It had taken him over three hours to pick just the right one, hardly comparable to the five minutes standing in line for Stephanie's bottle of perfume.

"Oh, you're so sweet. Rick, I don't deserve you."

Should he? Should he commit himself? Better think twice. "I've ah, um, been meaning to tell you . . ."

It could have been the festive atmosphere at his office, or the holiday season itself. Perhaps it was the three Old Fashions he had with lunch, he couldn't say, but all of a sudden Rick blurted out, "I . . . I love you. I'm sorry, but I really do." There, he'd said it. Within seconds a giant lump lodged in his throat, making it impossible to speak further.
There was a deafening silence on the other end, too.

Finally she said, "I've never had anyone say they loved me, not like this. I don't know what to say. Thank you. You've just made me the happiest girl in New York."

That's all he wanted to hear. "I mean it Ashley, I really mean it. I want us to spend the rest of our lives together."

"Rick, you're probably the most charming man I know." Ashley's voice quivered as she added, "I'll see you soon and we can talk. Promise."

"Ashley, I know this sounds stupid especially over a telephone, but you mean more to me than anything. I love you. You're passionate, patient, intelligent, sensual, everything a man could ever want."

"Oh, Rick darling, I'm a long ways from Mary Poppins. Before we get too far ahead of ourselves, I need to tell you I'm not who you think I am. In fact—"

"I don't want to hear it, Ashley. It doesn't make any difference to me what you were or what you did. I love you for the person you are now."

"I've waited a long time to hear someone say that to me." An emotional groundswell was suddenly released. "Oh, see what you've done? I'm actually shaking . . . legs are jello. Just hold a moment." Rick could hear her taking several deep breaths before saying, "Okay. Listen Rick, we really have to talk, but not now. I'll call you soon."

"Great. Thanks, thank you. I miss you. Bye." He was in love for the first time in his life . . . real love.

Same day, 5:10 P.M.
Hollister Residence, Dallas

Brett Hollister strode into his book-lined study, his private sanctuary. There were all sorts of tomes stacked along oak shelves covering three walls. The fourth wall consisted of a wood burning stone fireplace flanked by pictures of him with famous or semi-famous personalities, and a few original *Remington's* and *Russell's*. A six-foot wide set of longhorns pointed out from high over the mantle, and several nineteenth century Winchester rifles and Colt revolvers were featured in glass enclosed display cabinets. Authentic southwestern hand-woven rugs, one in front of a large dark oak desk and the other in front of the fireplace grouped with a dark green leather sofa and two wingback chairs, were partially covering the highly polished hardwood floor.

Picking up the desk phone, Brett pressed the button next to the blinking light and said, "Hollister here."

"Hi, Brett. Bob Bell from Pagent in New York. How's retirement?"

"Worse things could've happened to me, Bob. How's the rat race on Wall Street?"

"Shitty, and as cut throat as ever. Lucky we were able to work a couple large mergers this year. Those fees really help."

"Still gouging your clients, huh?"

"Oh, we don't gouge, we simply help ourselves to the spoils of war. Admittedly, they're usually wars we've helped create." Both men chuckled knowing the truth within that statement.

Absentmindedly, Brett picked up a silver letter opener and rubbed his thumb along the sharp point. "What can I do for you?"

"Actually, I called with something you may find interesting. I know you and the Cypress group never got along too well. I hear they're selling out."

Brett snapped to full attention poking his finger with the opener in the process. "Ow, selling out?"

"Yeah. They've been selling their LoneStar stock, unloading it. Could be they already sold it all."

"You don't say." After all that grief Cypress put him through. In short order Victor and his three stooges would be resigning from the board.

"I do say. Ah, Brett? You wouldn't know why they'd be doing that do you?"

Brett thought for a moment and answered, "No. Can't say as I do."

"I mean, if something was really wrong with LoneStar, you'd know about it wouldn't you?"

"What are you driving at, Bob?"

"Let me be honest with you Brett, we're carrying a pretty big position with Gary Nash. I've been trying to get him to cash in, but so far he's riding it out. Anyway, we've needed a whole lot of collateral from him so he's pledged all his LoneStar stock and took a mortgage out on his home. Now all that recent Cypress selling has pushed down the share price even further, I think it's trading around thirty-five. Our credit people are going berserk and they want me to cancel him. I like Gary and I've done all right with LoneStar, so I'm willing to cut him some slack. But if his collateral is gonna drop in value . . ."

Quickly analyzing the turn of events, Brett offered, "Bob. In my opinion Charles Hilborn is a good teacher but the man has no business sense and I'm not surprised this is happening. I have to tell you the truth; I never wanted Hilborn in such a key position in the first place. That was Paul Victor's idea and he forced it over my objections. Perhaps Victor has come to the same conclusion and has decided to cash in before the bottom falls out."

An agitated voice replied, "So you're saying the stock's going down more?"

"I sure hope not. Remember, I still have an awful lot of that stock myself. I just said that's what Victor might think. Look, LoneStar's strong enough to weather whatever Hilborn messes up, so I'd say don't cut Gary off."

A somewhat relieved Bob Bell said, "Okay, and thanks, Brett. If I can ever return the favor, just give me a call."

"I'll do that, Bob. Now you take care, hear?" Brett rapidly punched Gary Nash's private office number and rubbed his still bleeding finger. It had been almost a month since the two had talked and Nash still hadn't thrown in with him. It was high time to push the little bugger, and Bob Bell had just handed him the leverage he needed.

Same day, 5:50 P.M.
Taylor-Bishop Offices, Manhattan

Stretching like a Tabby just getting up from a nap, Ashley flipped off her computer and began tossing files into her briefcase. Suddenly, she remembered a promised call to Gary Nash. Cursing her forgetfulness she called Gary's private line hoping he'd still be at the office. It was only four-fifty in Dallas, but there were no guarantees with Texans.

Ashley felt nothing for Gary, even though they'd made love and were in constant communication. He was simply a tool to be used; much like she'd used others . . . much like she'd been used. Luckily, the phone was answered so Ashley immediately flipped an inner switch and purred, "Hey, lover. I've missed you."

Obviously in a good mood, Gary answered, "Howdy, girl. So what're you wearing today?"

Ashley giggled in spite of herself. "I'm at work, Gary, and I don't wear silk pj's to work. Anyway, I'm saving my best outfit for the next time we meet. When's that going to be?"

"I don't know, honey. How about I just hop on a plane and come visit you."

"You sure are chipper today. Does this mean you and the new management team are getting along?" She sure hoped so. Ashley was betting millions they would turn the company around.

"No, actually I don't think much of them. The good news is Brett wants me to join him in some new venture. Or he even thinks he can get Hilborn to pay me big time to stay, if that's what I want."

Hollister again? Couldn't that bag of wind just stay away? But why on earth would he want to hire Gary? "Well, Brett always looked to you whenever he had a problem. Makes sense he wants top people. What's the new venture?"

"Sorry, can't talk about private conversations."

Ashley pressed her lips together in frustration. What could Hollister be up to now? "Gary, when can I see you again? I really miss you." Ashley looked at her watch; there was a good half hour before the next appointment. Plenty of time to debrief the reticent Mr. Nash.

Playing the game of 'I've got a secret and I'm not going to tell you,' the cagey treasurer answered, "Oh, I really don't know when I'll get to New York."

She heard the sparkle of hope in his voice . . . more like expectancy. "Really? Are you too busy to close your door? I'm awfully lonely and I need someone to help cheer me up. Do you think you could help cheer me up, Gary? I need a man, a man who knows how to please a woman. I want you so bad I'm going to explode."

That's what Gary wanted to hear. "Ah, my door, it's . . . it's already closed."

Ashley's voice was cool and sexy, and she had Gary mentally and physically drained in less than fifteen minutes. He told her everything and anything she wanted to know, including Brett's plan to intimidate the board into reelecting him as chairman. She also learned what Hilborn and Sanchez were doing, and how Gary was getting pressured by Bob Bell at Pagent to settle up. Lucky for Gary, Brett had offered him a sizable chunk of cash. Gary said the cash was without strings . . . Ashley knew differently.

After saying their "Goodbye's," Ashley lapsed into deep thought. Somehow she had to warn Hilborn and Sanchez about Hollister. That thickheaded cowboy was about to queer the works, again. Too bad she couldn't use Arthur King to intercede, but the ex-director would never believe her after that telephone scam. In retrospect, her abruptness and cavalier attitude was a miscalculation. Live and learn.

Given time she could work through another board member but she needed access to Hilborn now. Cold calling the man was a long shot because he might not take her seriously. Somehow she had to gain his confidence without having her true motives questioned. But how?

CHAPTER 28

Monday, December 16, 11:25 A.M.
Chairman's Office, LoneStar

Adam Sanchez and Charles Hilborn were drinking coffee, going over the agenda for Wednesday's board meeting. "Charles, has Paul Victor contacted you?" Adam had been alerted to Cypress' selling through an acquaintance on Wall Street. Evidently, it wasn't a closely guarded secret since everyone seemed to know they were dumping LoneStar shares, almost as if they wanted everyone to know . . . and that was rather curious! Why would they want the street to know they were sellers? That only causes the stock price to fall faster and deeper, giving them less than they could have gotten if they'd done it quietly, without fanfare.

Charles shook his head and answered, "No, not a word. But if what you've told me is true, then I suspect we'll have four board resignations on my desk this week. I just don't get it, Adam. Why would they first push, shove and gore us to get our stock price up, and then drop it like a hot potato? It just doesn't make any sense to me. Aren't they screwing themselves out of millions of dollars?"

Shrugging his shoulders, Adam replied, "Sorry. My expertise is not capital markets or banking. All I can do is relay the story as told."

Charles got up and walked around the office. "Okay, we'll figure that out later. What do we have so far?"

"The agenda has the sale of our software division, and a report from the search committee on Hollister's replacement as president. We want to go over the preliminary budget and highlight the cost savings we have managed so far. I suppose we will also want to bring up the Cypress situation and the four probable resignations."

"What's the latest on the credit cards?"

"Those last few solicitations are likely to be painful. Losses are going to run three times as high as normal. We simply do not have any focus there. There is no marketing plan and no method of replacing customers, short of mass solicitations to the wrong groups. But changing their bonus structure away from sales to bottom line profit should help correct the situation."

"All right, let's inform the board. Anything else?"

"Yes. The senior management team is becoming openly hostile, arrogant, as if we report to them and not the other way around. I feel something is in the air, but I have no idea what."

"I've noticed that too. Did you contact those executive search firms?"

"Sure, and they all said the same thing. Give them a fat retainer; sign on the dotted line and in six to nine months they'll be able to fill all our slots. I have a few of their boiler plate retention contracts, nothing unusual in them."

"Good, let's show 'em to the board. The sooner we get moving the better. That it?"

Smiling, Adam countered, "You want more?"

Charles shook his head 'no.' Recently, he didn't feel an iota of guilt cashing those extravagant paychecks. This job was murder.

Same day, 1:55 P.M.
LoneStar Offices, Dallas

All weekend long Gary had been reliving his last phone conversation with Ashley. She sure could make him drool like a baby. Her call, mixed with Brett promising him enough money to cover the SWAP losses had put Gary into a marvelous mood. Everything was going his way again. "Mr. Nash? Mr. Bell is on the line for you."

Good. He had planned to call anyway, tell him to close out the position. Armed with Brett's cash bonus, he could cover the losses. True, his personal financial picture had seriously deteriorated, but as treasurer of LoneStar he made pretty decent money. Nothing time wouldn't heal. "Okay, I'll take it." Picking up the receiver, Gary said, "Afternoon, Bob."

"Gary. Have you been watching your stock? It's cratering. Falling through the roof."

"Take it easy, control yourself. What do you care about our stock price? You've never invested in it have you?"

"Me? No, never. But we have your stock as collateral for your trades and the value's dropping. The guys in credit say we need security or they'll pull the plug. I can't hold them off any longer. Your position is now over two million in the hole."

What? That couldn't be. He must have heard something wrong. "Hey, stop kidding around."

"I wouldn't kid about a two million dollar loss. The Fed Chairman is still keeping the pressure on interest rates so they keep going up, and you keep losing. You got the security?"

No. Please . . . no. This couldn't be happening. Sweat beaded up and then ran down Gary's forehead and the back of his neck, soaking his starched white collar.

"Gary?"

The stunned treasurer shouted back, "Gimme a minute." He had to think. What should he do? Brett? Yes, that was it. Give Brett a call, he'd figure a way out of this mess.

An impatient New York securities dealer said, "I need an answer, Gary."

What other choice was there? "Fine, close out the fucking position." Two million dollars? Gary's house wasn't even worth half of that. This had to be a bad dream, couldn't be real.

Much relieved, Bob replied, "Okay, consider yourself out. I'll come back with the final toll. Maybe we'll get lucky and it won't be so bad."

Like the son of a bitch really cared. Hanging up, Gary called his best buddy, Brett.

"Hollister residence."

"Jackson? This is Mr. Nash. Is Mr. Hollister available?"

"One moment, sir. I'll go see."

Gary closed his eyes tightly, trying to squeeze the terror out of his mind. His shirt was drenched, his head throbbed and there was a foul taste in his mouth. "Hello? That you, Gary?"

Thank God, Brett was home. "Yes, hi. You doing okay?"

"Sure, fine. What can I do for you?"

"Brett, I need that cash we talked about. Can you help me get it?"

"Oh, well, how much you think you need?"

Relief was instantaneous. How glorious those few simple words were, and what a friend. Gary sighed audibly and said, "It's, ah, around two million."

A shocked Brett hurriedly answered, "You need what? Two million dollars? What on earth for?"

"I was on the wrong side of a trade. I feel terrible about this Brett, but I'm desperate. With LoneStar's stock down my whole net worth is maybe a few hundred thousand. I've already mortgaged my home. That's why I need your help. It'll give me a clean slate."

"Oh, it'll give you a clean slate all right. Christ, Gary. We never said anything about two million dollars."

Gary wiped his hands through thinning hair as his pulse quickened. The conversation had just taken an abrupt turn for the worse. "Look. Make it a loan and I'll back you against Hilborn like you want. I'll tell'em I'll quit if you're not the chairman. Then with my new contract I'll sign over the up-front bonus you promised. All we gotta do is make sure it's for two million dollars."

"Gary, let me put this as delicately as possible. You're not going to get a signing bonus of two million dollars, you're not worth it, no one is. The board would never approve that amount."

Uncontrollable panic gripped him. "So . . . so what will they give me?"

"Hell, I don't know. I was thinking maybe a hundred thousand."

"*A hundred thousand?* Christ. I need more than that, a lot more. Brett, that won't work. You've gotta help me."

"Okay, Gary. Tell you what. If you join me, that'll give me nine senior managers. So you sign my letter and I'll loan you . . . a hundred and fifty thousand."

Gary was stunned. That wasn't enough, not nearly enough. If he liquidated everything, all his savings, all his investments . . . everything, he'd be nowhere close. What would he tell his wife Pamela?

Honey, somehow I've lost the house and all our savings. Oh, and I owe some fucking robber barons close to two million dollars. Oops, mistakes happen.

"Gary? Why don't you come to my house after work? I'll have your check and a letter for you to sign. I'll see you around seven. Goodbye."

Letting the phone drop from his numb fingers, Gary used his trembling hands to cover his face. What had he done? He'd ruined everything . . . lost everything they owned. "What happened?" he said to whoever was listening. Collapsing onto the desktop like a rag doll he was trembling uncontrollably.

Early Tuesday Morning, December 17
Columbus, Ohio

Holding her hand inches away from her face, Courtney gazed happily at the sparkling new adornment and then cried again. She wiped away the tears and dialed her sister's number. Stephanie Blaine picked up the kitchen telephone on the forth ring, and said, "Hello?"

"Steph? That you? I didn't wake you did I?"

"Oh, hi, Court. No, ah, I couldn't sleep, so I'm doing laundry. Boring stuff. What's up?"

Gushing with excitement, Courtney Keller blurted, *"I'm engaged.* Can you believe it? *Me."*

With an equal amount of joy, Stephanie shrieked, *"That's wonderful.* Congratulations. Mike Kilpatrick?"

"Yup, he popped the question this morning when we first woke up. Oh, I wasn't going to tell you that part."

Stephanie couldn't help but laugh. "That's okay, you're a big girl, Court. Have you set a date?"

"Well, neither of us wants to wait a long time, so we're planning sometime after the holidays. January or February. As long as it isn't Superbowl weekend . . . I want Mike's undivided attention."

Chuckling, Stephanie said, "I know what you mean. Rick won't let anyone talk while there's a game's on. I'm just so happy for you."

"Thanks. Say, you mind standing up with me? You know, matron of honor?"

"I couldn't think of anything I'd rather do. So where are you getting married?"

"Ah, that's open. Since time's short we're not going to be too fussy. Probably here in Columbus. Mike sort of belongs to a church here."

"Is Mike from Ohio?"

"No, he's from all over. He even has a couple relatives in Michigan, around Grand Rapids I think."

"Hey, why not have it up here? We can get The Abbey, it'll be lovely."

Courtney smiled from ear to ear. "Can you do that? Oh, Steph, that would be the greatest. Do you think you can?"

"Let me check. Now, you roll over and give Mike a big kiss for me and I'll call you back. Bye."

Same day, Four minutes later
Upper East-Side, Manhattan

The phone? Was that the phone? Who'd have the nerve to call at . . . what time was it anyway? *Five-twenty!* Ashley pried one eye open and reached for the ringing phone next to her bed. This had better be a matter of life or death. "Yello?"

"Ashley, are you asleep?"

The voice was familiar but she couldn't place it. "Not now. Who is this . . . Courtney?" Springing up in her bed Ashley had a horrible feeling something was wrong. Court never called this early. "Courtney? What's the matter?" With heart racing she braced herself for the bad news.

"*Ashley, I'm engaged. I'm going to get married!*"

"Courtney? *Courtney!* That's fantastic! When? Where? Who? Oh, this is just fabulous, Court. I'm so happy for you." Kicking the covers off, Ashley flipped on the lights and began pacing around the bedroom in circles.

"Isn't it marvelous? Mike proposed to me today. January or February wedding."

"Oh, this is wonderful. So where's the wedding?"

"I hope it'll be in a northern suburb of Detroit, where I grew up. The church is awesome. Looks like an English castle, you'll love it. My sister is trying to fix it for me. I'm so excited."

"Detroit. Hey, that's great. To tell you the truth I think I might be getting serious too. He happens to live in the Detroit area."

"You're in love? For real?"

"I think so. Oh Court, I've never felt like this before. I'm so happy, I feel like it's so different this time."

"I think I'm happier for you than for me. Will you invite him to my wedding?"

"Sure, why not? Who knows? You can convince him I'm not such a tart."

A sudden weightiness enveloped both girls. After too long a silence, Courtney replied, "You've never been like that. You've just had horrible luck, that's all. Any man would be a total fool not to want you." Good sounding words but they both knew different. Eligible men bolted when they found out about Ashley's past . . . convictions for murder and prostitution can do that.

In spite of everything, Ashley believed Rick would be different. Hadn't he said he loved her for who she was now? If only she could muster the courage to confront him with the truth. "No matter, I'll expect you to say nice things about me the first chance you get."

"Anytime. Did you sweep him off his feet at a convention or something?"

"Actually, we shared a ride in Dallas . . . a stockholders meeting."

"Oh, sounds romantic. Say, you'll be in my wedding party, right? I'm not having all that many, just my sister and her husband and Mike's brother and one other couple."

"I'd love to. Thanks for asking. You've just made my day, lady."

"Ash, you're the best. Listen, I've got a zillion things to do. I'll call you back with the details. Goodbye and congratulations yourself."

Ashley laid back down, closed her eyes and drifted into the same fantasy dream she'd had most of her life. She was inside a rustic cabin on a lake, with a sailboat gently bobbing in the cold waters, and a roaring fire from a cozy fireplace toasting her and her lover. She felt safe and warm, wrapped in the strong arms of a kind man. Only this time the nondescript partner had Rick's face.

440

CHAPTER 29

Wednesday, December 18, 10:45 A.M.
LoneStar Boardroom, Dallas

Most employees at LoneStar weren't aware it was board day. Gone were the heavy lunches, the staged presentations, the endless hours of preparation by housekeepers, cooks and chauffeurs. Instead, a far more Spartan forum was adopted. Charles and Adam took pains to ensure the board would be fully informed, and ample time was allotted for questions and answers, no pomp and no circumstance.

This was the first board meeting Charles had ever chaired, and he was more than a little nervous. Gazing at the other directors he noticed they all appeared calm, confident, composed . . . even Adam. Didn't they understand? The stock was plummeting, board members were resigning, rumors were rampant and managers were indignant. "Gentlemen, the first order of business is the acceptance of the prior minutes. Is there any discussion? If not, then can we have a motion to approve?"

"So moved."

"Is there support?"

"Support."

"All in favor . . . the Secretary will note that the motion was unanimously passed. Next, behind Tab B you will find four resignations from this board. As you know, The Cypress Group has sold all of their LoneStar holdings. Any discussion?"

Chester Bennett spoke up. "Why'd they sell our stock? It's trashed you know. The price is now around thirty-four dollars. I know you don't own any stock, but the other directors and I do."

That first salvo hit Charles hard. "I appreciate your concern, Mr. Bennett. Unfortunately, I cannot answer your question. My calls into Cypress haven't been returned. I don't understand myself why they did what they did. Does anyone around this table have any insight?" No one could volunteer anything. Dealing with Wall Street just wasn't one of their strengths.

Charles continued, "Actually, that is a pretty good lead into our next topic. There appears to be one investment group that has purchased most of Cypress' stock. This group called The Taylor-Bishop Company would like representation on this board. They have requested two interim seats, half as many as Cypress I might add. As you know, our By-Laws allow us to take such actions.

"They say they have no intention of interfering and only want an open line of communication to this forum. The two candidates are Ms. Ashley Taylor-Bishop and a Ms. Lauren Washington. Their resumes are behind Tab C. As you look at them, I trust you will be as impressed with their backgrounds in the capital markets. That's something we sorely need. Any discussion?"

Chester raised his hand and asked, "How much stock of ours do they own?"

"Actually, I haven't spoken to them, not yet. Adam took the call." All eyes shifted to Adam.

Clearing his throat, Adam addressed the directors. "Gentlemen. I spoke to Ms. Bishop yesterday. At that time her firm had purchased over five million shares of LoneStar. That would be for both their account and client accounts. It was her belief that additional shares would be added over the next few weeks. As you know, with twenty-five million shares outstanding, her company is the beneficial owner of over twenty percent of our stock."

Charles already knew the answer to his next question, but he wanted the other directors to hear, so he asked, "Why do they want to own our stock?"

Adam replied, "Ms. Bishop says it is a pure long-term investment for her and her clients. They expect our stock to appreciate in value primarily because of the new policies we are setting in place."

Charles glanced around the table and a few heads bobbed up and down in agreement. "Any further discussion? Then can I have a motion to approve the appointment of Ms. Taylor-Bishop and Ms. Washington to our board on an interim basis?"

"So moved."

"Any support?"

"Support."

"All in favor . . . Mr. Secretary please note that the motion was unanimously passed. Next . . ."

Chester Bennett's secretary opened the French doors, entered hesitantly, walked over to Chester and handed him a message. As quickly as possible she turned and fled.

All eyes were focused on Chester as he calmly read the message. Finishing, he looked up and said, "Excuse the interruption, but if I may say something, Mr. Chairman?"

"Yes, Mr. Bennett."

Chester held his breath, screwed up his resolve and continued, "I would ask for the other directors indulgence. A matter of grave urgency has just been brought before us."

Charles' eyes opened an extra notch. The second salvo, so soon? "What are you referring to?"

"I've just been handed a note. This note states that Mr. Brett Hollister is outside in our lobby. He would like the board's permission to enter and address us."

A collective 'gasp' could almost be heard from the directors. Charles was rightfully indignant. "Are you serious, Mr. Bennett? Why should we allow that? Mr. Hollister is not a director nor is he an employee. He is a shareholder, and shareholders are not granted private audiences with the board of directors. Mr. Bennett, I'm inclined to contact security and have him escorted off this floor."

Chester held up his hand in a semi-threatening manner. "I wouldn't do that, Mr. Chairman. Actually, I encourage you all to listen to him." Chester's voice was steady, but he was sweating profusely.

Charles Hilborn looked at the other directors and said, "If you will forgive me for a moment." Leaning over to Adam who was sitting next to him, Charles said very quietly, "Any thoughts?"

Adam considered the situation, and whispered, "I suppose whatever Hollister has up his sleeve will come out sooner than later. It also appears our Mr. Bennett is involved up to his neck. No telling what the rest of the board is thinking. Remember, most of them were handpicked by Hollister, but then again I'm sure he thinks they all screwed him royally."

Charles nodded and said, "So what are you saying?"

Adam tilted his head closer and whispered, "Charles, I would call security, have them standing by our doors ready to whisk Brett off at your command. Then I suppose I would invite him in, see what's on his mind. It's a given we will get nothing else done today, not until we find out what he wants."

Taking a slow pan of the other directors, Charles could see Adam was right. They were all chatting like school children, unable to direct their attention on anything but the Hollister issue. "Okay, Adam, you excuse yourself, call security and fetch Hollister here." With haste, Adam got up and left.

Tapping the gravel lightly, Charles said, "Gentlemen. I have asked Mr. Sanchez to escort Mr. Hollister into this room, to allow him to address us.

Does anyone have any objection?" No one said a word.

Charles looked at Chester and asked, "Do you have anything to say?"

A stoic Chester returned Charles' stare. "No, you'll find out soon enough."

Charles nodded and leaned back. Why couldn't Hollister just go away and leave them alone? He royally screwed up this company . . . practically sunk it. The man lies, cheats and then walks off with a multi-million dollar severance package. What more does he want?

The French doors opened and Adam entered followed by Brett. Adam took his chair after pointing where Brett should sit. Charles tried to read the man's face but there was nothing visible. He did notice that Brett exuded confidence, almost a kind of smugness. Also, upon first entering he saw Brett exchange knowing nods with Chester. Charles leaned forward and placed his elbows on the conference table, clasping his hands together in front of him, chest high. He looked at Brett, waited for a moment and said, "Mr. Hollister, I understand that you have something of importance to discuss with this board. May I remind you that it is only out of deference to your prior status we're allowing you to speak? Please be brief."

Brett let out a short grunt, a sound laced with contempt. "Then I'll get right to the point, Mr. Chairman. I have in my hand a document, a document that each of you will find most interesting." With that, he handed a stack of copies to the director on either side of him. "Pass these out, I'll give you a few minutes to read it." Each director took a copy and passed the rest on. Charles was the last to receive one. What on earth was this about? He started to read:

> Dr. Charles Hilborn
> Interim President
> LoneStar International Corporation

> Dear Sir:
> It is with deep regret that we the undersigned hereby tender our resignations as officers of LoneStar International Corporation. We do not do this lightly, but we feel you have left us no alternative. There comes a time when as senior managers of a publicly held corporation, we must put aside our own careers and futures to vigorously protest as strongly as possible our complete dismay, our total lack of respect and our unwillingness to ever serve you again. Our reasons are many, but foremost is your lack of leadership, and your inability to understand the complexities of a major financial institution.
> It is our sincere hope that by taking such drastic measures the board will come to realize the gross error they have committed by appointing Dr. Charles Hilborn to the office of Interim President. It is also our belief that the retaining of Mr. Adam Sanchez, an unproven, untested consultant to be Dr.

Hilborn's chief advisor, exemplifies his naivety and total lack of management qualifications. Witness the rapid deterioration of our stock price.

In the event the board of directors rightfully comes to the only conclusion possible for the preservation of our shareholder's value, we are prepared to reconsider our resignations under certain circumstances. However, in order to assure that such grossly negligent decisions are never repeated, a number of actions must be agreed upon. The specific actions we require are listed on the attached addendum.

Unless you agree to further discussions, our resignations will become effective as of noon, December 31. We await your reply.

Slowly raising his head from the letter that was signed by twelve senior managers of LoneStar, Charles caught Brett staring at him, actually gloating. Flipping the page to the addendum Charles continued reading.

ACTIONS TO BE TAKEN

1. The immediate removal of Dr. Charles Hilborn from all positions of responsibility and authority.

2. The cancellation of any and all contracts or agreements with Mr. Adam Sanchez.

3. The reappointment of Mr. Brett Hollister as President, and Chairman of the Board of Directors.

4. Public statements, acceptable to Mr. Hollister, acknowledging the boards' regret for

accepting his resignation and gratefully welcoming him back at a time of crisis.

5. A public statement, acceptable to Mr. Hollister, stating that Mr. Adam Sanchez will be sued to recover monies previously paid him for misleading Dr. Hilborn and causing irreparable damage to this company.

6. Revised multi-year employment contracts for all signatory's plus Mr. Hollister, including substantial up-front signing bonuses, stock options and improved severance packages.

7. The rehiring of Russell, Powell and Young to be LoneStar's outside accounting firm.

8. A letter from the Executive Committee to the directors stating that all prior (albeit questionable) financial reporting actions taken by any of the signatory's or Mr. Hollister, were conducted with the full knowledge of the Executive Committee.

Charles finished reading the demand letter and thought to himself, what a vain, conceited, egotistical man. No wonder the place was dying. Hollister was certifiable. But to top it all off, the man didn't even comprehend the precipice LoneStar was teetering on.

Turning to the none too happy Adam Sanchez he whispered sarcastically, "Well, now we know what he wanted. I'm really beginning to dislike him." Clenching his teeth until his jaw hurt, Charles said to Brett in a civilized tone, "Do you have anything to add?"

Brett gave his fatherly smile and answered, "I only want what's good for this company, please believe that. Imagine my surprise when these frightened souls approached me and told me of their concerns. I was heartbroken. I tried to talk to them, I told them to give you time but they wouldn't listen. They'd seen enough and been through enough. They simply no longer trust your judgment, Dr. Hilborn. They want me back and I'm afraid they are totally committed to this course of action.

"I don't have to tell anyone here the disastrous repercussions twelve senior managers leaving en mass would effect. The banks would pull all financing lines, vendors would cut off extending any credit, customers would flee and investors would dump the stock even more than they already have. I am afraid gentlemen, you have no other choice. I'm here today to personally offer you my services. Again, I only want what's best for LoneStar."

Twitching in his seat while ears burned, Charles said in a still controlled voice, "Thank you for your concern. Now if you will leave us, we have a board meeting to conduct."

Brett's smile dropped from his face. "I think we'd better discuss this right now."

Charles glared at Brett and repeated, "I said thank you for your concern. You can leave now."

Raising his voice, Brett said, "Your other directors might want to talk about this right now. They know when a real disaster's at hand."

Tapping the gavel, Charles said, "Apparently, you don't understand English. Please leave, now."

Brett was beginning to turn red. "Don't take this so lightly *professor*, I'm warning you."

"I appreciate the observation. Why don't you take Mr. Bennett here with you when you go? I'm sure you both have lots to gossip about." Now he knew why Bennett was so interested in who'd be replacing the four departed Cypress directors. They wanted first crack at telling them their side of the story.

At the mention of his name, Chester Bennett suddenly sat up in his seat and said, "You have no call to say anything like that."

Shaking his head in disgust, Charles replied, "Oh, knock it off, Bennett. If you were so concerned for LoneStar why didn't you ever approach me, or any of these board members? Why all this cloak and dagger stuff? Know why? Because you're just a spoiled little brat who got his hands slapped and now you're pouting. Face facts, you and Mr. Hollister damned near sank this company."

Addressing Brett next, Charles continued, "Believe me, it's not the situation I'm taking lightly . . . it's you two clowns I'm taking lightly. Now, if either of you needs help leaving this building there are some security guards who can assist."

Standing straight up and slamming his hands on the conference table as he ascended, Brett spat back, "Who the fuck do you think you're talking to? I'm calling the shots around here, not you. You're the one who's leaving, Hilborn. Not me. Not Bennett. You!"

Charles turned to Adam and said in a calm voice, "Go get the guards."

Brett exploded. *"Don't you dare tell that wetback to get the guards. I'm the fucking chairman around here! I want your sorry asses outta my boardroom or I'll remove you myself."*

That did it. Adam Sanchez quick stepped over to Brett and pressed right into the reddened face. Twenty men watched, unable or unwilling to move. Sending shivers through a corpse, Adam glared back. Finally he pointed a finger into Brett's face and said, "This *wetback* is gonna rip you apart, *gringo*, if you don't leave now!"

For the second time in the last two months someone was standing up to him. Brett twisted his face, thought about it, thought better about it, and said, "Come on Chester. Let's go before I break this twig in two." Brett and Chester pushed open the French doors and headed toward the elevators, a couple of guards in tow.

Closing the doors, Adam retook his seat and formally said loud enough for all to hear, "Sorry."

Charles looked at him and said, "Sorry? Sorry for what?" He turned and confronted the directors. "It seems we have a new agenda item. I'm open to any comments."

Most of the board members were limp, although one of them said, "He's right you know. No matter what, he's right. If twelve senior managers leave at the same time for the same reason, trumped up or not, it'll be hell to pay for the rest of us. I can envision class action suits, banks pulling out, clients leaving, revenues dropping, profits falling . . . just like Hollister said."

The others reluctantly nodded and grumbled, "That's right. We don't like it, but what choice do we have?"

Charles studied the faces around the table and declared, "So you want to give in to blackmail? Give them all big fat raises and a bonus for trashing what was once a great company? Is that upholding our fiduciary responsibilities to the shareholders? Remember gentlemen, Hollister was caught cheating, cooking the books. You're going to hand command back to that thief?"

No one had anything else to add and they all looked like they'd been through a war, a war they'd lost. Charles felt numb, too. "Look, why don't we adjourn? I'll contact each of you within the next day or so. We'll come to some kind of agreement by conference call. Any objections?" There were none, everyone just wanted to go home. "Okay, do I have a motion to adjourn?"

"So moved."

"Is there support?"

"Yes."

"All in favor? Good. Merry Christmas, Happy New Year, let's get out of here." Charles stood up and caught Adam by the arm. "My office."

After seeing the other board members off, Charles and Adam poured themselves a stiff drink from the private bar in the chairman's office. They sat down on the leather couch and said nothing, each lost in thought. After several minutes, Adam broke the silence. "We have been out maneuvered."

Charles grunted, "Seems so. Can't replace twelve senior managers over night can we?"

"Twelve bodies? Sure. Competent bodies? No way. To tell you the truth we would not miss those twelve. But the public's perception of a mass desertion would be devastating."

"Yeah."

"It will take six months, nine months to re-staff this place correctly. We don't have that much time."

"No, I suppose not."

"Word will get out. This whole place will know there is a palace coup going on. Chester and the others will see to that. Our effectiveness will be nada."

"You're right and I'm out of ideas. Just can't believe the lengths that man will go to reclaim his throne. I doubt he even cares his kingdom is crumbling, or that his faithful vassals are worthless. He just doesn't give a damn."

Rocking his drink around in his hand, Adam said, "Kind of sad in a way. I have met a lot of CEO's like that. Guess they figure they got to the top on their own. Probably enough people told them so that they actually believe they can walk on water. They become inflexible, stubborn, egotistical and self-righteous."

"Well, be sure to give me a swift kick if that ever happens to me."

Adam grinned sadly at Charles and said, "Oh, I do not think you have to worry about that, for you will never have a business career. Not after Hollister gets his way. Unfortunately, the same fate awaits me and I cannot teach."

That hurt. "I'm sorry I got you into this, Adam. Looks like I pretty much screwed up your life."

Adam drained the last of his drink and said, "I am a big boy. I took the job with eyes opened. I only wish it could have been different, that's all. Look, I have some things to do. You should call up the two new board members. Fill them in on what has happened."

"Yeah. What a welcome, huh?" Charles held Adam's eyes and said, "We need a miracle. Hollister's going to win if we don't come up with a miracle."

Without hesitation Adam offered, "Fortunately, I do believe in miracles. I shall talk to my guardian angel about arranging one."

Charles finished his drink, sighed heavily and replied, "Use any pull you've got."

* * *

Joyce knocked softly on Ashley's door. "Ashley? A Dr. Hilborn is calling. Is, is everything all right?"

Ashley waved her off, "Yes, Joyce, everything's fine. Dr. Hilborn is the president of LoneStar. I'll take the call." Ashley shook her head. Joyce was acting more and more like a mother hen lately. Hopefully, it was just a lunar phase or something.

"Dr. Hilborn? Ashley Taylor-Bishop, here."

"Ms. Bishop? I'm happy to get this chance to talk to you. Do you prefer Ms. Taylor-Bishop?"

"I prefer Ashley."

"Yes, of course. Please call me Charles. Ashley, I'm calling to fill you in on a few events that have recently developed at LoneStar. Events that have a direct bearing on the company's future."

"Really?"

Charles paused. "I apologize. Sounded rather dramatic didn't it?"

Ashley laughed and answered, "Well, yes."

"I'll start all over again. Ashley, on behalf of the directors of LoneStar International Corporation, and as provided for in our By-Laws, I welcome you to our board of directors on an interim basis. Please pass my warmest regards to Ms. Lauren Washington as well. The board approved both of you at today's meeting. Your term of service will be starting now and run until the next annual meeting. Congratulations, I'm looking forward to working with you."

"Thank you very much, Charles. I must admit, this is the first directorship I've ever held."

There was a discernible surprise in his voice. "Oh?"

Hearing the implied 'disappointment' Ashley asked, "Is there something I'm missing? Or are you just having a bad day?"

Now he sounded confused. "I thought my wife was the only one who could read me so well, at least over a telephone."

"I'm pretty perceptive on the telephone. What's up?"

"I owe you an explanation Ashley. Since you're now an insider . . . ah, out of curiosity, how much LoneStar stock do you own?"

Ashley made a mental tally. "I believe we're over six million shares. Obviously, some of the stock has been purchased on behalf of our clients, and I also have a personal position, though not nearly so grand."

"Well, since you're an insider now, you'll have to conform with strict trading practices in regards to buying or selling LoneStar stock. But I expect you already knew that."

"Yes, I've read about that somewhere. We'll file all the required papers, don't worry. So you were saying about your day?"

"Oh, sure. We had a special guest at today's board meeting. Our former Chairman, Brett Hollister. He handed out copies of a letter signed by twelve of our senior executives demanding numerous actions be taken or they'd quit. Chief among these actions is my removal. So I'm afraid this may be our first and only conversation."

Making a fist with her hand, Ashley smacked the top of her desk. She was too late to warn him. Hollister had moved faster than expected, faster than her information source, Gary Nash expected. This was unbelievable. "The board isn't going to give into blackmail are they?"

"I don't think we have any choice. With that many key executives leaving all at once the banks will trigger 'Material Adverse Change' covenants, causing our lines of credit to go into default. Once in default all bank lending stops, and all our debt becomes due and payable. Without liquidity . . . well, LoneStar simply dies."

This had to be someone's idea of a sick joke. "Charles, I'd like you to tell me everything that occurred today, and I'd like you to have someone fax me the letter Hollister handed out."

"Done. You may want to make yourself comfortable, this story could take awhile."

Ashley did as suggested and said, "Fire away."

Twenty-five minutes later Charles finished the day's events. He was drained. Even Ashley was drained and she'd mostly listened. Closing her eyes, she sorted out the jumble of facts floating throughout her head. Foremost was the responsibility she felt for placing such a big bet on LoneStar . . . and using other people's money! What if she lost? Don't even think it.

After what seemed a very short time, but in reality wasn't, Charles spoke again, "Ashley? Are you there?"

"Yes, yes, Charles. Just thinking, that's all."

"Oh, for a moment I thought I was alone."

"No, you're not alone. We're in this together. Listen, your immediate concern is the bank group that's lending you money. Email me a list of who they are and how much they're lending you. Include a directory of your loan officers, I want their titles and phone numbers. Also, email me a short biography on the twelve LoneStar managers who're holding us hostage. Include their current responsibilities. What's the temperature of the board members? Do they want to roll over or would they just as soon tell Hollister to fuc . . . kiss off?"

"They're frightened. They know a coup like this will cripple us. They have to look at what's best for LoneStar."

"Fair enough. Call them up and tell them you're working on some alternatives and you'll keep them posted, but under no circumstances are they to talk to Hollister or any of the dissident managers, or anyone else for that matter. Also, call up Arthur King, he's not a Hollister fan either. I'm pretty sure you can get his bank to throw in with us."

"How do you know about Arthur King?"

"Ah," Ashley thought for a moment before answering, "Oh, I've been following LoneStar for a few months. After a while you learn a little here, a little there."

That sounded reasonable. Anyway, a noticeable air of enthusiasm was building within Charles. "Okay. Say, I don't mean to sound overly anxious, but do you have a plan?"

"Let me be frank with you, we have very little time and Hollister is holding all the aces. But I've been in similar circumstances before."

"So what'd you do?"

"I kicked over the card table. Listen, once I look at the information you're sending to me, and you meet with King, we'll talk again. I suspect it'll be necessary for Lauren and me to fly down to Dallas, have a counsel of war. I'm afraid none of us will have much of a Christmas."

"Ashley, I'll set up whatever you want whenever you want. I have to confess I've never been in this kind of situation before, neither has Adam Sanchez. We'd be very grateful for any help you can provide. If you're up for it, I'll even give you total command of our defense forces."

"My first battlefield promotion? Thanks Charles. Here's my email address . . ." Upon hanging up the phone Ashley yelled out, "Joyce. Get everyone into my office. Now!"

CHAPTER 30

Monday, December 23, 3:05 P.M.
LoneStar Offices, Dallas

Chester Bennett had not been fired, since there were eleven other senior managers backing him up. Nor was he summoned to speak to Hilborn or Sanchez, which was also fine with him. It gave the general counsel more freedom to walk through the other departments, talking to managers and rallying support for Brett's imminent return. He'd never forgive Hilborn for kicking him out of the board meeting. Who'd that arrogant professor think he was? Picking up the phone he dialed Brett at home. "Jackson? This is Mr. Bennett. Is Mr. Hollister available?"

"One moment, sir. I'll go fetch him. He said you might be calling." Chester grinned to himself. Old Brett was still in top form, still in command of the situation, still pulling all the strings.

"Chester, how goes the war?"

"Brett, it's unbelievable here. Hilborn and the Mexican are holed up in their offices, burning up the phone lines but not talking to any employees. The newspapers picked up what's happening and are running gossip stories. I guess all those anonymous calls worked." Both men were pleased with the well conceived, covert operations being executed so flawlessly. Chester continued, "I'm gonna make sure a copy of your letter gets leaked to the media. That'll really light a fire under the board."

"Good. Have Nash call every bank in our lending group, make sure they know what's at stake. I don't want any of them throwing in with Hilborn, understood? I want all funding stopped until I return. Have Nash let them know I won't be happy if they screw with me."

"I'll see to it. Anything else?"

"Yes, go check on Nash personally. He's got some heavy financial problems and I'm not sure how he's coping. Just make sure he doesn't go off the deep end, at least not until this's over."

Financial problems? Gary Nash? Chester couldn't believe it. That man only invested in money markets. What possible problems could he have other than LoneStar's stock falling a few dollars? Chester felt compelled to ask, "Did you help him?"

"I helped him as much as I'm going to, and more than I should've. Look, Chester, we have more important things to worry about. Just make sure he makes those phone calls."

"All right. Anything else?"

In an exuberant voice, Brett said, "Nope, not now. Remember to keep me posted." Brett was sounding more and more confident; things were going just the way he'd expected. "We're going to win, Chester, we're going nail'em good. You'll see."

"Never doubted it, Brett. Bye."

Same day, 3:35 P.M.
Smith-Palmer & Co., Detroit

This was the best and worst Christmas he'd ever had. Rick wanted nothing to do with Stephanie, which certainly strained the holiday spirit at home. On the bright side was Ashley. All he could think of was her face glowing when she opened her present tonight. He'd been counting the hours and couldn't wait to see her. "Rick. Call for you on line one. Ashley Bishop."

Rick fumbled with the phone, knocking a stack of files off his desk. "Oh, damn. Hello? Ashley? I wasn't expecting to hear from you so soon. I'll leave now and . . ."

"I'm sorry, dear. I know I promised but something's come up. I won't be coming."

He was crushed. Unable to speak he simply stared at the phone. It took a long time for him to finally say, "Oh, oh I see. Ah, well, that's okay, can you make it next week?"

"I don't think so, Rick. I might be out of pocket for a while. I'll call you when I know a little more of what's happening."

Was she in trouble? "Are you okay? Is everything all right?"

"Sure, I'm fine. This is just a business deal going sour, but thanks for asking. I'm truly sorry for doing this. I'll make it up to you."

That sounded promising. "Oh, sure, don't give it a thought." Wanting to prolong the conversation for as long as possible, he asked, "Ah, say did you see those newspaper reports about LoneStar? Looks like there's a palace coup going on down there. Sure am glad you warned me about that place. The price's down to thirty-three after Cypress dumped the stock."

"Well, don't believe everything you read. I've got to run, call you soon. Merry Christmas. Love you."

"Merry Christmas. Love you, too." God, he felt miserable. Only a few minutes ago he was ready to conquer the world. Now he didn't want anything to do with the world. Hanging up the phone Rick wondered why she said, "Don't believe everything you read." Hitting a few keys on his computer he began studying some financial charts to pass the time. One thing was clear, he sure as hell wasn't in the mood to go home.

Same day, 4:25 P.M.
LoneStar Offices, Dallas

The sun was out, the sky was clear and the steady stream of aircraft ferrying holiday travelers to and from Love Field was a sight to behold. Gary was standing with hands clasped behind his back, squinting out his office window, but beholding nothing. A rather hurried Chester entered the hushed room and said, "Gary, I just got off the phone with Brett. He wants you to do something for him." Gary kept his back to the door and didn't move. "Gary, did you hear me? I said I just talked to Brett." Chester took a few steps closer. "Gary?"

Gary finally turned around. Chester's mouth dropped open. Never had he expected this. Gary looked like hell, with bright red lines floating in watery eyes surrounded by black circles and an unnatural gray colored skin. There was also thinning hair matted against the scalp, a foul odor emanating from somewhere, a ragged beard stubble casting a dark shadow on his jaw, and a suit appearing to have been slept in. "Gary, what's happened to you?"

The pending financial crisis had seared Gary's brain, burned it to a crisp. Day and night, all he could think about was the shambles he'd made of his life and Pamela's. All his plans for early retirement, all that time wasted paging though Colorado real estate magazines, the bank account that carried so many dreams, the tickets to the South of France . . . and Pamela, dear Pamela who thought the world of him. He couldn't go home to her, not now.

He'd begged Brett to lend him more money, but Brett said no. A hundred and fifty thousand was tops, and don't ask for more. The inference was clear . . . Gary Nash wasn't worth any more. Then Bob Bell called him Friday with worse news yet. The final tally was in: Gary owed two million three hundred thousand dollars and some change.

He didn't have it. Not with the new mortgage, the one hundred and fifty thousand dollars from Brett and liquidating all his company stock, money markets, watches, rings and cuff links. He was well short.

But Bob Bell didn't care. He said he was out on a limb too, since he'd allowed Gary to trade without sufficient collateral. No one had expected the market to turn so quickly, so dramatically, but that's what markets do. "Just lucky LoneStar pulled the SWAP's in time," Bell said, "or you wouldn't even have a job." But reality really struck when Bell said, "The guys in credit are all over me for being so irresponsible with your account, and they're sending some lawyers after everything you own. I can't help you. I can't even help me."

It was there for all to see. Within days Gary would be publicly humiliated. All that he'd worked for was about to be taken from him, and his wife Pamela knew nothing. She simply thought he was immersed in several important business meetings. She was busy at home wrapping presents and baking cookies, getting ready for their grown children who'd be visiting tomorrow. What could he say to her? Gee, hope you're not upset I lost every cent we own. Oh, and I'm not sure I have a job, either.

Wrinkling his nose, Chester tugged on Gary's arm. "Gary, are you all right? Hey, my friend, talk to me. What's wrong?"

Gary's secretary came into the office looking very worried. "Mr. Bennett? Mr. Nash has been like this all day. He won't talk to me or take any phone calls. He hasn't left this office and I think he spent the entire weekend here. He just stands by the window and I don't know what to do."

"Call his wife. Find out if—"

As if jolted by an electric shock, Gary shouted "*No. Keep her out of this. You hear me?*"

Chester jumped back, startled at the unexpected outburst. "Okay, Gary, okay. Just take it easy. Everything's gonna be fine. Look, how about you and me going to the Club for a drink? I know I sure could use one. What'd ya say? Come on, it'll do us both good."

Gary hesitated, wobbled a little and stared at nothing in particular. He finally nodded his head and said, "Yeah, yeah. I'd like that."

"Great, c'mon. I'll drive." Chester held onto Gary's arm and steered him out of the office as the secretary looked at them, biting her lower lip.

Same day, 7:15 P.M.
Trump Towers, Atlantic City

Early evening neon lights flashed outside the big bay window spraying bright colors throughout the plush room, and Paul Victor took pleasure basking in them. No, actually, he was wallowing in them. He'd done it. He'd pulled it off. Seven million shares of LoneStar stock had been sold short. Even the lower than anticipated blended selling price of thirty-five fifty a share couldn't dim this celebration. The stock was now trading at thirty-three, giving Paul and his partners a cool seventeen point five million dollar profit. *Seventeen million dollars.* In less than two weeks, he'd made seventeen million dollars. Finally, he was *the man*.

Sure, it was also true that Cypress booked a loss of over fifteen million from the original shares they owned, but that was history. Everything was just as that bitch Bishop predicted, the stock was falling like a rock. With each dollar drop another seven million profit was added to their wallets. He'd have to thank Ashley sometime.

But the glory didn't stop there. A couple of high rollers from Atlantic City who'd jumped into the deal were rewarding Paul with an all expenses paid trip to their fair city, complete with penthouse suite, a sack full of casino chips, free flowing liquor and food, two beautiful ladies for his amusement, and all the white powder they could sniff. Was this the life or what?

Padding naked across the thick pile carpeting into the bathroom, he appraised himself in the mirror. Sucking in his gut, he admitted he didn't look too bad, not bad at all. Still could lose a few pounds though. He'd join a gym, start getting back into shape. Patting his stomach, Paul went back into the master bedroom complete with mirrored ceiling. The two girls were still unconscious, still intertwined under satin sheets of the massive round bed. Now those two were worth the price of admission, he admitted to himself. Damn shame they were both asleep, guess they're not used to the good stuff.

Since it was still early, Paul went over to the coffee table and made himself a two-inch long line of cocaine. He carefully placed a stirring straw into his left nostril and inhaled. With sinus exploding, he pulled a bottle of vodka out of an ice bucket and took long, slow swallows. Almost emptying the bottle, he stared back at the two young nymphs. Why not just go wake them up and help himself to an early Christmas present?

All of a sudden he stopped, put his hands on his head to keep it from spinning, lost his vision and crumpled hard to the floor. One of the girls stirred, but didn't get up to see what the noise was.

Same day, 7:20 P.M.
Country Club, Dallas

The aged waiter, Raymond, brought the two gentlemen another round of drinks, placed them on a small coffee table, cleared the empty glasses and left. No one knew why Mr. Nash looked so horrid and no one asked. Grabbing the fresh round, Gary belted back another Jack Daniels . . . his sixth drink in the last two hours.

A little woozy from downing three drinks himself, Chester said, "Hey, Gary. Don't ya think it's time we go home?"

The alcohol was comforting to Gary, building up his courage. "Yeah, sure. Let's go home."

Chester brightened. It was about time. He'd been practically begging for the last hour. "That's great, Gary. I'll have my car brought around and I'll drive you home."

Gary nodded and answered, "Home." Home to Pamela. Sweet dear Pamela. She was probably dressed in something red, waiting for him with a new batch of cookies and a glass of wine. She'd been calling his private line at work all day long, but he'd refused to answer . . . he couldn't.

Pulling his friend to his feet, Chester said, "C'mon, let's get you out of here." As the two members wove their way through the clubhouse, Raymond approached with the bill. Chester didn't even look at it, merely scribbled his name on the bottom and said 'Happy Holidays.' Raymond watched the two leave and remembered an old adage about the blind leading the blind, and that nothing good would come of it.

The parking attendant eased Chester's midlife crises soothing bright red 1967 Jaguar XKE convertible to a stop in front of the club then helped Gary into the passenger seat, all the while thinking what a waste it was to watch two old dudes wedge themselves into this babe-magnet.

Taking in a lung full of air, Chester steadied himself and climbed behind the steering wheel.

"Okay, Gary. Home we go. Hey, don't forget to buckle up. Never can tell what'll happen with me driving." Chester giggled as he started the car, shifted into first gear and pulled away.

Gary's head was spinning, so he let his head roll back against the headrest and closed his eyes. In his mind he went over his situation once more. Somehow the more he thought about it, the better it got.

Time had no meaning to Gary; it was as if everything was happening in slow motion. Chester pointed the car towards the nearest entrance to the Dallas Toll way and pressed the accelerator, luckily there wasn't much traffic. "Everyone must already be home for the holiday," Chester said with slightly slurred speech.

Rolling his head to the right and looking at the onrushing landscape, Gary could tell they were heading north. They'd just passed the Mockingbird Lane exit and in a few more miles they'd be passing the LBJ Freeway intersection, which was real close to the restaurant he and Bob Bell had dined at so very long ago. A lifetime ago.

Chester pushed the Jaguar up to sixty and with so little traffic he started to nudge the speedometer up to sixty-five, then seventy. Gary looked at the clock on the dashboard, did a little rough calculating and determined he'd be home in less than twenty minutes. Fighting to hold back tears,

Gary told himself to make it right. Couldn't very well have Pamela out on the street just because he screwed up. Gary sniffed and rolled his head over to the left. He looked at Chester, Brett's good buddy. While they were drinking back at the club, Chester practically gagged when Gary asked for a half million-dollar loan. Brett had probably already warned him, told him to keep his distance from "Nash's" problem.

Chester noticed Gary staring and said, "You're almost home. Won't be long. I'll call you in a day or two."

Slowly enunciating his words, Gary said, "Sorry, Chester. Didn't mean to involve you in my troubles."

Chester looked at Gary, obviously relieved he wasn't going to be asked for money again. "Hey, don't worry about it. What're friends for? Anyway, you just reminded me, Brett wants you to call our banks and tell them not to work with Hilborn. Ah, Gary? You listening? Brett wants you to tell them that—"

In a blur, Gary reached over grabbing the top of the steering wheel and jerked it down, turning the speeding car hard right, aiming it straight into an abutment. Chester screamed, Gary closed his eyes.

The bright red XKE smashed into the solid structure at seventy-seven miles an hour. The unbuckled passenger was thrown through the windshield and into a cement wall, dying within seconds. The driver's side seatbelt saved Chester's life.

* * *

It wasn't until thirty hours later that Chester awoke in a hospital room. Someone informed him he had broken bones and lacerations all over his body, and then they asked him some questions. Chester couldn't remember what happened. The police knew he'd been drinking and attributed the accident to driver error. Too bad about Gary Nash they said outside Chester's room. Mr. Nash was a solid citizen . . . a real shame.

CHAPTER 31

Tuesday, December 24, 8:05 A.M.
Parkland Memorial Hospital, Dallas

The Nash's family lawyer and friend found Pamela sitting alone in the hospital waiting room; she'd refused to go home. A senseless accident . . . nothing more would appear on the official police report. The attorney sat down beside her and held her hand. Pamela couldn't control the tears, she buried her head into her hands and between sobs said, "If I'd paid more attention . . . maybe he'd still be alive."

The attorney put his arm around her shoulders, consoling her. "Pam? I know this isn't on your mind right now, but it will be in a little while. Listen, you don't have to worry about anything financially. Gary had several million dollars of personal life insurance not to mention those special policies with LoneStar. Like I said, you probably don't want to hear about this now but I wanted you to know, he left you well provided for. You'll never have to worry about money . . . ever."

The attorney leaned his head back against the stark smooth wall and closed his eyes. No sense telling her about Gary's investment problems, not now. He'd just make sure the mortgage was paid off and Bob Bell's company was pacified . . . that Wall Street weasel sure was rude on the phone. Anyway,

Pam would have enough cash to keep her comfortable the rest of her life.

Looking at him with tears streaming down her cheeks, she remarked, "Thank you. I'm not surprised you know. Gary's always been a good provider." Standing on shaky legs, she smoothed her festive red dress and said, "He always liked me in red during the holidays." No longer wishing to remain in the hospital, Pamela Nash weakly stated, "Please take me home. I have so much to do."

Same day, 11:15 A.M.
LoneStar Offices, Dallas

A limousine deposited Ashley and Lauren at the front of LoneStar's ten-story building. Lauren gazed skyward at the glass and marble edifice, took a deep breath and followed Ashley inside. As they entered the lobby, Lauren was overwhelmed . . . overpowered. "Uh, Ashley. We ain't in Kansas anymore."

Ashley grinned, "No, Dorothy, we're not. Click your heels three times and come on, they're waiting for us." Grabbing Lauren by the elbow, Ashley steered her toward the round reception desk. "Steady yourself, Ms. Washington. Remember, you're a director."

Within moments of announcing themselves, they were ushered into Charles Hilborn's private office, which was twice as big as the paint peeling, drafty apartment Lauren and her three brothers, two sisters, mother and aunt called "home."

Standing to meet them, Charles and Adam exchanged second glances. Neither man had anticipated a knockout like Ashley. This was indeed an unexpected surprise . . . pleasure. Introductions were made, small talk was quickly dispensed with, and seats were taken in Charles' conference room, now dubbed: The War Room.

Charles couldn't take his eyes off Ashley, but managed to speak without slurring his words. "Well, thank you both for coming. What I'd like to do first, is ah, fill you in on the latest developments then turn it over to you for any questions, suggestions or ideas you might have."

Ashley and Lauren nodded approval so Charles said, "Fine, to begin with, there's been an accident. It happened yesterday. Chester Bennett our general counsel and Gary Nash our treasurer were involved in an auto accident. Somehow, Chester lost control of his car and hit a cement wall. Sadly, Gary Nash was killed. Chester is pretty banged up, but not seriously . . ."

The shock rocked Ashley's body and she froze. Time stood still. "He's dead?"

All three participants looked at Ashley who had an unfocused, blank stare on her face. Adam spoke first, "Ashley? Are you all right? Can we get you anything?"

Next, Charles injected, "Did you know him?"

Snapping out of her trance, she replied, "I, I did know Gary . . . Mr. Nash." She breathed deeply a few times, "I sat next to him at your last annual shareholders meeting. We talked some. Just can't believe he's dead."

Now Charles remembered. "That's where I saw you. Sure, that's it. At the annual meeting. You were the one who asked a question about some takeover rumor. Right, you wanted to know why Brett hadn't disclosed anything about other firms wanting to buy LoneStar."

Ashley smiled, "Good memory, Doctor. Yep, that was me. Guess I was wrong about that rumor. Sorry for the interruption. Please continue."

Accepting her remarks at face value, Charles added, "I took your advice and met with Arthur King. He'll be more than happy to offer whatever assistance he can. I'm afraid his bank isn't big enough to make much of a difference; their legal lending limit is forty million. Unfortunately, the smallest line of credit we have with any bank is fifty million, but it's a start."

It was a start indeed. "Good. Sometimes perception goes a long way with big shot bankers. Merely having Arthur and his bank eager to join LoneStar's banking group will send those other bankers a strong message. By the way, Lauren here is intimately familiar with capital markets and bankers." She turned to Lauren, "You have any comments?"

Pulling out a sheet of paper, Lauren directed her remarks to the two men. "Well, I've looked at the list of banks and bank officers you sent us. Fortunately, I know most of them. They're the same ones who get involved with financing mergers and acquisitions, so we've all worked together before. The good news is they've all had a banner year. M & A activity is way up and their profits are awesome.

"Add to that, the holidays are upon us when almost every decision maker is gone. I've already talked to them and they'll cut us some slack. The bad news is they ain't stupid. Losing your entire senior management team won't sit well with them for very long."

Charles thought for a moment. "King did offer to talk to Emmet Griswald. Presuming Emmet would be willing to return, that would fill up one of our open slots. I suppose bringing back a controller with knowledge would be well received by your banker friends."

Ashley sat up a bit straighter and offered, "Sure. I also think Lauren could be your treasurer. She knows cash management backwards and forwards, and she's thoroughly familiar with securities and investments. The bankers you're dealing with know her too." Ashley looked at Lauren and continued, "Of course a suitable employment contract would have to be worked out, but I think it would be fantastic. A major plus for LoneStar."

Delighted with the suggestion, Charles said, "Lauren, I've seen your résumé and I hope you'll say 'yes.' Nothing against Gary, but it sounds like you can step in today."

Lauren was flattered, but hesitant. "Dr. Hilborn, how do you suppose the board of directors and your southern middle managers will respond to having a black female treasurer?"

"You know," Adam offered, "probably a lot better than they did me." Everyone chuckled at the all too true joke.

"Okay," Lauren said with appreciation, "you've got yourselves a new treasurer." She turned to Ashley and said, "Thanks, thanks for giving me this shot." Lauren hesitated, then said to Charles, "You may not know this but Ashley's put together a team of very special women. Each of us had baggage of one kind or another that kept us outta the game, couldn't get a decent job. But this lady here gave us a break, a chance to make it. No one else was willing to do that."

Brushing away the compliment, Ashley declared, "Actually, all I did was hire some very talented people at bargain basement prices. We helped each other."

Adam was looking at the list of departed senior managers and observed, "So now we have two of the twelve slots filled."

"That's right." Ashley moved over next to him, scanning the same list. "I know some very competent corporate lawyers, any one of them would make an excellent interim general counsel. I'll have them email their credentials to you Charles, now that Mr. Bennett is incapacitated."

Adam followed Ashley's thought process and said, "We can also hire consultants, fill each critical position with someone who's experienced and nationally known. The bankers couldn't object at that. Some we'd eventually make an offer to, others we'd replace with candidates supplied to us by executive search firms. I'll call some people I know."

"Love it," Ashley said. "This is getting better and better." Next she spoke to Charles, "Okay, let's say we can fill those ten slots with qualified people, how soon before this place can make real money? What can we tell the bankers?"

Charles motioned for Adam to respond. The consultant answered, "Ladies, this place was a mass of confusion and disjointed operations. It was totally out of control. Assets were being sold to make debt payments; there was no focus, no strategic plan. On top of that, management was self-indulgent and no one was accountable. As you may be aware, we have been cutting expenses and reorganizing. To date, we have stopped the cash drain from the systems group and did some re-engineering. Thankfully, our debt burden is two hundred million dollars lighter than before . . . you may remember Cypress converted their interest bearing bonds into stock. That alone saves us twenty million annually in interest payments.

"We're planning on cutting some more people, but mostly from the bloated upper management ranks. We also have to take a long hard look at the common stock dividend and more than likely adjust it downward. All in all, we can spin a pretty good story to the investing public, but a strategic alliance with a larger, better capitalized firm wouldn't hurt either. Is that something you can help us with?"

Ashley considered for a moment. "Sure, once we clean this mess up, get our balance sheet in order, make sure our cash flows are positive, then we can approach a couple of firms. It would be useless to talk to them now. They'd only pay pennies."

"I'm beginning to understand how corporate America works," Charles said. "I'd also like to accept those outstanding senior officer resignations. Can anybody give me a reason for not doing so?"

All four participants were silent. "All right, I'll take that as support of my decision. Adam, will you contact our Human Resources department and have they initiate the necessary paperwork."

There was a tapping on the door followed by Charles' secretary entering the conference room. Suzanne was noticeably anxious. "Excuse me, Dr. Hilborn. Mr. Hollister just called, I told him you were in conference, but he said for me to tell you he's waiting for your answer. He wants to know if you're going to accept his conditions."

Leaning back in his chair, the history professor addressed the small group of defenders as if they were students. "I'm reminded of an event that happened toward the end of World War Two. The Germans launched a major offensive in the winter of 1944, into the Ardennes region of Belgium. It became known as *The Battle of the Bulge.* Happened during Christmas as a matter of fact. Anyway, soldiers of the 101st Airborne along with elements of the 10th Armored Division, were trapped in a town called Bastogne and surrounded by the German Army. With no apparent hope for escape, the Germans sent surrender terms to the besieged defenders. A certain general, General A.C. McAuliffe, gave a most eloquent reply, which I feel is suitable in our situation. Suzanne, send Mr. Hollister our reply. Tell him . . . *NUTS!*"

CHAPTER 32

Friday, December 27, 9:01A.M.
Cypress Offices, Manhattan

Mrs. Paul Victor and her younger sister, Terri Rothman, were cooling their heels in the same conference room where her husband recently had his "most important" meeting. She'd been escorted there by the receptionist who wanted to get this raving lunatic out of the lobby. It didn't make a very good impression with office visitors to be confronted by a woman screaming to see a senior partner.

Pacing back and forth Cindi Victor kept punching her hands together, as if warming up for a twelve-round heavyweight bout. Over in the corner, Terri was sitting and quivering, not enjoying the situation she'd been dragged into. A man with a neatly trimmed beard suddenly appeared in the doorway and said, "Excuse me, ladies. My name is Theodore French, how can I be of service?"

"I'm Mrs. Paul Victor, and this is my sister, Terri Rothman." Cindi stepped right in front of him and asked, "Are you a senior partner here?"

"Yes, yes I am. May I say I'm very sorry about Paul? I understand he had some sort of relapse."

"Relapse? I don't know what bullshit's flying around here, Mr. French, but dear Paul overdosed with drugs, booze and cheap whores." She almost spat the words out.

Moving away from the vindictive bleached blond, Theodore 'Teddy' French took out his handkerchief and dabbed his forehead. No one had prepared him for this. "I'm . . . ah, sorry, truly sorry."

Showing indifference to the man, Cindi continued, "Save me your sympathy. That greedy little bastard got what he deserved. I just hope you're not going to give us any trouble."

Teddy was taken aback. "Trouble? I don't understand."

She moved in front of him again. "Look, I'm not going to put up with any horseshit, you got me? We know our rights, and neither you or anyone here is gonna screw us out of 'em."

"Madam, I assure you, I . . . we have no intention of doing anything of the kind. Please, Mrs. Victor, please sit down."

She reluctantly found a chair and sat down, eyeing him suspiciously. "All right, fine. I want to close out Terri's investment in something with The Excel Group."

"Your investment? But that's your husband's. Paul set it up. He formed a new company so he could invest in a new . . . business venture. You can't just come in here and demand that we cash him out."

Pounding the table and frightening her sister, Cindi hollered, "Don't give me that crap, French. Terri is the legal, one hundred percent owner of that company. Paul Victor is not mentioned on any documents, none what-so-ever. She's the only legal representative and what she says goes."

Teddy was horrified, "But you can't—"

"*The hell I can't!*" She slid a couple papers over to him. "Look at those. I had a lawyer friend make sure everything was in order, totally legal. Those papers say she can do exactly what I'm telling you. Now, *cash us out.*"

"But, Mrs. Victor. I happen to know Paul only made your sister the owner of the company because he couldn't personally be involved. He's cashed in all his investments, everything, and put the money into his . . . I mean Ms. Rothman's company. It's everything he owns; it's not really her money."

Cindi glared at him and spat back, "*You got that wrong. That little prick's been hiding money from me for years. Giving me nothing.* He was gonna keep it all for himself. Sure, let Cindi run away if she wants, but she gets nothing . . . and after putting up with him for years. Oh, it's mine all right. These papers give Terri Rothman a legal right to it.

"This is my divorce settlement French, without having to go through all the muss of a courtroom battle. Instead of getting screwed by Paul's fancy lawyers, I'm walking away with everything, just like god intended. Now, do I have to get nasty? Do I call my lawyers? How about the Securities and Exchange Commission?"

Teddy was stunned. He slowly got up and addressed the sister, "Ms. Rothman. You don't really want to do this, do you?"

Moving quickly and placing herself in front of the shaking sister, Cindi declared, "She knows exactly what she's doing. Now, do I make those phone calls?"

Stroking his beard, Teddy said, "If you'll excuse me for a few moments I'll see what I can do."

"Just don't be too long. I've got people waiting for a phone call, you know?"

Teddy hurried into the office of their legal counsel and explained the situation. Several phone calls later a small meeting of available partners was convened. Each partner was shocked at what was transpiring but legally helpless to stop her. Cindi and Terri had every right to do what they wanted. Legally, it *was* Terri's money.

A couple more calls confirmed their worst fears. They could all be sued if they tried to block the demand. A quick review of the trading ledgers showed that Paul . . . well, Terri Rothman, had five million one hundred and fifty-five thousand dollars of investments and profits in the account. That was Paul's life savings but what could they do? They couldn't even call him up at the hospital . . . he was still unconscious.

A handful of partners returned to the conference room with Teddy, tried to convince the women the errors in their thinking. No such luck. Every time they tossed a new line of reasoning, Cindi grabbed the papers, waved them around and threatened to sue each one of them personally. After a few rounds of getting nowhere they quit.

Finally, Teddy spoke to Mrs. Victor. "All right, madam, we'll do as you wish."

She smiled victoriously at Teddy and said, "Please call me Cynthia. I want you to cash in all of Terri's investments, everything. Then I want you to wire the proceeds, every penny, to this account. Here are the wiring instructions." She slid another slip of paper over. Teddy looked at it and his jaw dropped. "*The Cayman Islands? You're wiring Paul's life savings to a bank in the Cayman Islands?*"

Cynthia smiled all the more. "Yeah. Once you wire it, don't try to trace it 'cause it'll be moved again. Now when do I get my money?"

Teddy shook his head, "I don't know. These things take time what with the holidays."

"*Bullshit. That's pure bullshit.* The documents say cash on demand. I want my money this afternoon or I'll start suing." With that, Cynthia stood up and stomped her way out of the conference room and back to the lobby, obviously willing to wait until the transaction was completed. A petrified Terri Rothman scurried after her sister.

One of the other partners stuck his head into the conference room and said, "Teddy. I don't care what you have to do but get that money wired today. I never want to see that bitch again." All the other partners concurred. Too bad for Paul they all thought, but he had brought it upon himself. Besides, they couldn't waste any more time with her, they had to ensure the same wouldn't happen to them!

Same day, 10:10 A.M.
Parkland Memorial Hospital, Dallas

A telephone was ringing somewhere off in the distance and it was waking Chester Bennett from his sleep. He wished it would stop, but it kept ringing. After the seventh time he swore at the nameless fool for not picking up the damned phone and answering it. It rang again. Finally, opening his eyes, Chester was greeted by semi-familiar surroundings. There was a television mounted on the wall in front of him, some pretty flowers in vases adorning aseptic furnishings, tubes running in and out of his left arm . . . there went that phone again.

During the next ring Chester realized the phone next to him was shrieking. He cautiously maneuvered his unrestricted right arm towards the sound. After a few clumsy attempts he was able to retrieve and place the receiver next to his ear. Trying to speak he found his mouth so dry that no sound came out.

"Hello? Hello, is that you, Chester? It's me . . . Brett. Is this Chester Bennett?"

Chester groaned, grabbed a glass with clear liquid and a straw from a serving tray, swallowed a couple mouthfuls and said, "Brett?"

"Damn, Chester, how are you? How do you feel?"

"I'm not sure. I keep drifting in and out of sleep."

"Yeah, I know. I was over yesterday; you were out like a light. But the docs' say you're gonna be just fine. Damned lucky they said."

"Yeah, lucky."

"Do you remember what happened?"

"No, nothing. Can't remember anything."

"That's what the doctors said would happen. They said you suffered a concussion and that some memory loss is pretty common in cases like that. Anyway, I'm glad you're doing okay."

"Thanks. Ah, do you know what happened?"

"Only what the doctors said. Seems like you lost control of your car driving home from the club. You hit a cement wall on the Toll way. You don't remember any of that?"

"No, not a thing. Was anyone else hurt?"

"Uh, well, kind of."

Had he hurt someone? Did he kill someone? "Did I hit another car?"

"No, no. Nothing like that. Ah, but there was someone else in the car. Um, Gary Nash was with you."

Chester's heart was beating rapidly. "Gary was there? He's okay isn't he?"

"Well, no. No, I'm afraid he's dead Chester. They say he was killed instantly."

"Oh, no." A pain gripped Chester's chest. "No, no it can't be. I couldn't have killed . . ." Tears started welling up in his eyes. "No, please no."

"I'm real sorry to have to be the one to tell you, Chester. Nobody's blaming you for anything, but just so you know, there were traces of alcohol in your bloodstream. Seems that you and Gary were at the club having a few holiday cocktails."

Chester's head was spinning and he was finding it hard to breathe. "I don't remember any of this. What have I done?"

"Sorry, Chester, real sorry. Ah, listen, I was wondering if you remembered to talk to Gary about contacting the bankers."

Tears streamed down his cheeks . . . Gary was dead? "What are you talking about? What bankers?"

An anxious Brett replied, "Gary was going to call up our banks and tell them not to help Hilborn, remember?"

Chester was still sobbing. "Gary? Dead?"

"*Yes, he's dead.*" Brett took a couple of deep breaths and said, "Look, I'm sorry I raised my voice but you've got to think. You've got to remember, Chester. I've been trying to contact our bankers but none of them are returning my calls. I've got to know if they're siding with me, if I can count on them."

"I don't know, can't remember."

"Damn. Call you again, bye."

Chester didn't have the desire or the strength to replace the receiver. Within a few moments a continuous buzzing emanated from the phone.

Same day, 1:20 P.M.
Smith-Palmer & Co., Detroit

The small Christmas present for Ashley was still tucked in his bottom desk drawer. Picking it up, Rick cursed himself for not giving it to his wife instead of the perfume. How the hell was he supposed to know she hadn't worn that fragrance in years? Well, that started another argument focusing on his lack of interest regarding her and the kids. He told her she was imagining things, and decided to return to work early. Why didn't he just run away to New York and stay with Ashley forever? "Rick. There's a call for you, line two. Someone named Ashley something."

A surge of adrenalin coursed through his body, speeding his arm towards the receiver and knocking over a half full cup of coffee on its way. He picked up the phone and tried to clean up the widening coffee spill, "Shit, oh, I mean hello." Damn, why am I such a klutz?

"Hello to you. Not exactly the kind of reception I was expecting."

Rick sighed, "I'm sorry. I just spilled coffee all over my desk. Ah, Merry Christmas. Will I see you soon?"

"Real soon. I wasn't sure you'd be at work today."

"Yeah, well I'm just a dedicated kind of guy. Ah, so how's that business problem going?"

"Rick, it's an adventure down here, believe me."

"Down where?"

"Oh, didn't I tell you what I'm doing?"

"No. You only mentioned some business you had to take care of."

"Oh, I apologize, forgive me. Guess my mind's been elsewhere. Things were, well, things are still pretty hectic, but the light's at the end of the tunnel."

Rick's spirits brightened, "So you'll be finished soon? You'll be going back to New York by way of Detroit? When?"

His eagerness was contagious. "Soon, that's all I can say. I miss you."

"I think about you all the time. I want to be with you all the time. Nothing else seems to matter to me anymore."

Her voice bubbled, "You keep this up and I'll quit my job and just sponge off you for the rest of my life."

"Deal."

"Not so fast. First, I've got to complete a job here."

"So where's here?"

"Dallas. I'm with LoneStar now, well, not exactly with them. I'm on their board of directors."

"You're a director for LoneStar? You're kidding."

"Nope. I was just appointed a few days ago."

"But why? That place is going right down the tubes, you said so yourself. You told me to issue a 'sell' recommendation, which by the way was the best advice I ever got. The stock has dropped from forty-six to thirty-three and Cypress just dumped their entire holdings onto some poor fool."

"Ouch. I'll have you know I'm probably that poor fool."

"What?"

"I'm the poor fool who bought all that LoneStar stock recently. My holdings are around seven million shares."

"*Seven million shares? Are you insane?*"

"Whoa, control yourself. I know what I'm doing. Listen, whatever I tell you from now on can only be a matter of public record, understand?"

"Sure, you're an insider now, I understand."

"That's right. So pay attention. Hilborn and Sanchez are kicking asses and taking names. Adam Sanchez is really good at turning around bloated organizations. Hilborn's just all around sharp.

They've got a contract to sell the systems division, which was bleeding the company dry, changed auditors, implemented cost cutting measures, refocused the credit card solicitations, and the list goes on. Right now a whole new management team is being formed. They keep this up and someone who wants to diversify into the financial services industry is going to come courting."

"Wait a minute. You're down there now, helping them?"

"Exactly. We've got a plan, well, most of it anyhow. Now all we have to do is implement it. Mostly we need the right people, simple as that. I was impressed enough with the potential down here to recommend this stock to my clients, and I still feel that way."

"I see. Ah, okay, thanks. I appreciate it. Do you have any idea when you'll be coming back?"

"Well, could be in a couple of weeks. I'm standing up in a wedding in the Detroit area. An old college friend of mine is getting married."

A couple weeks? "Really? That'll sure give me something to look forward to. I do love you, you know that don't you?"

"Yes. Yes, I believe you do. Take care of yourself, lover. Bye."

Rick replaced the receiver and went to get himself another cup of coffee, along with a stack of paper napkins for the next time she called. Returning to his desk he made himself comfortable, hit a couple keys on his computer and pulled up the latest market data on LoneStar. The stock was trading in the thirty-three range but there wasn't much volume due to the holidays.

There were also some major 'short' positions on LoneStar, meaning someone was betting big money that the stock was going down further. But if Ashley was right and they fixed that place and some suitor took a run at them, the stock price would soar. If that happened those poor bastards with the 'shorts' would be scrambling to cover their position. They'd be buying stock and pushing the price up even further, making their losses astronomical. That was the problem with holding shorts, rising prices will kill you.

Anyway, if he assumed Ashley still had her golden touch and knew what she was talking about, then right now would be the best possible time to accumulate the stock. Hours from now, or tomorrow or next week or next month, the opportunity might be lost. LoneStar's price could shoot back into the forties burning all the analysts with "sell" recommendations.

Rick hit a few different keys and reviewed his last report on LoneStar. Had Ashley ever been wrong? The answer was 'no.' Without giving it another thought he immediately started changing the text, switching from 'sell' to 'buy.'

Same day, 1:35 P.M.
LoneStar Offices, Dallas

After talking to Rick, Ashley tried but failed to throw herself back into work. This was the first time the man stating he loved her wasn't drunk, trying to cop a feel, or had ulterior motives. She'd almost given up hope. Sure, some had come close, like with the film star Antonio Veron. But then one evening he confessed he wanted children . . . his own children. "I can't have children," she sadly admitted. That ended their budding romance in a heartbeat.

It was better if she didn't get herself all worked up. Rick still didn't know a thing about her. Why not get back to work and let fate sort things out? Speaking of work, Ashley needed to check in with her own company. Dialing the office number she waited for Joyce to answer.

"Taylor-Bishop Company."

"Hi, Joyce. It's me."

"Hi. Everything going okay?"

"Yes, fine. Make sure you keep sending me my mail and messages by overnight delivery. How're you doing?"

"We're cold. Wind chill must be minus ten. Other than that, all the girls are pitching in and taking up the slack for you and Lauren. Any idea when you'll be back?"

"Nope, not yet. Say, do me a favor. Get hold of Jackie Wells, tell her to take the next flight back to

New York. When she comes into the office hand her all of her personal belongings packed neatly in a box along with a severance check for two weeks. Tell her we're sorry but things just didn't work out. Tell her to try The Cypress Group."

The giggling secretary replied, "You got it. Anything else?"

"Mention to the girls I appreciate their chipping in. I'll call later. Bye." Overlooking the pile of papers and files strewn about her, Ashley wondered what it would be like spending New Years Eve with Rick. Spending a lot of New Years Eve's with Rick.

Same day, 2:50 P.M.
Blaine Residence, Birmingham

The two boys were keeping to themselves, playing with their new video games. Stephanie was sitting at the kitchen table, finger massaging her throbbing temples. The brash ringing of the telephone made her wince and she picked it up immediately. "Yes?"

"Hi, Steph."

Stephanie Blaine brightened at the sound of her sister's voice. "Court. I'm glad you called. You getting nervous?"

"Yeah, a couple butterflies have taken up permanent residence in my stomach."

"Well, it'll all be over soon. Sounds like everything's coming together. The Ritz Carlton in Dearborn confirmed a room for the wedding reception. The Abby is set. So I think we're good to go."

"Thanks for all your help, Steph. I could never have pulled this off without you. You're one in a million."

Stephanie paused and said, "I appreciate that, Court. Glad I mean something to someone."

The message was plain and Courtney could sense her sister's grief. "I take it things aren't any better between you and Rick?"

"No, no better. We either don't talk or we argue. Now we're arguing about the stupidest things . . . like who's turn is it to take out the trash, or why can't you call if you're going to be ten minutes late? Honestly, Courtney, the list is endless. It's just not fun being together anymore."

"I'm so sorry. Is there anything I can do?"

"No, and pardon me for ruining your day."

"Do you want Mike to choose another usher for the wedding?"

"No, but thanks for asking. Is your friend still planning on getting out of New York, you know, to stand up at your wedding?"

"You mean Ashley? Yes, she said she would. She's traveling a bit, somewhere in the south I think. But I'm sure she'll make it. She mentioned to me something about having a boyfriend in Detroit, so that's two good reasons for her to be here."

A tiny smile broke across Stephanie's face and she remarked, "So love is all around us, huh? Well, who knows?"

"That reminds me, I've gotta start telling everyone the official date. Okay, see you in a few weeks. You take care of yourself; you're my favorite sister you know."

That brought out a worn chuckle. Stephanie replied, "Yeah. Just so happens I'm your only sister too. Goodbye."

Monday, December 30, 10:40 A.M.
Parkland Memorial Hospital, Dallas

The sound of the phone wasn't nearly so distant this time. Chester Bennett knew what it was and managed to pick it up on the third ring. "Hello?"

"Chester! *You fucked up!*"

Why did people have to keep reminding him? Every time the accident was mentioned, Chester felt his heart burst. "I know, Brett, I know. I feel so bad about Gary that—"

"I'm not talking about Nash. You fucked up with the damned banks. You and Gary never called them, did you?"

Chester was totally confused, "Call the banks? For what?"

"Damn you, Chester. I told you and Gary to call the fucking banks and make sure they screwed Hilborn. You didn't do that!"

"Please stop shouting, and I don't know what you're talking about. I don't remember you saying anything to me."

"You dumb, stupid bastard. Because of your incompetence, Hilborn and that wetback got the banks to back off. Shit, even that spineless jackass Arthur King threw in with them. I'll fix that bow tie wearing back stabber someday, just like I fixed his daddy. But if the other banks hold firm, I'm screwed."

"Don't swear, I don't like it. What's all it mean anyway?"

"It means that I got a message from that bastard Hilborn. That son of a bitch mails me a letter with one word on it . . . *NUTS*. They're not going to give in. It means all of you dumb asses who signed that resignation letter don't have jobs anymore. Hilborn's accepted your resignations. That prick even hired a black treasurer to replace Nash, for Christ sake. The stock's going to fall through the floor and I'm selling every damn share I own today. I don't care what price it's at either."

"Wait. What do you mean I don't have a job anymore?"

"You're usually not this slow, Chester. You resigned, so now you don't have a job."

"Oh no, we had an agreement. You said you'd hire all of us, that we all had jobs waiting with you."

"Hey, I'm not going to pay you guys to sit around doing nothing. I'm not LoneStar, you know?

You'll have to go out and find real jobs, but I doubt any of you will get half of what I was paying you. None of you are worth a damn."

"You can't do this. We have an agreement. We signed that letter because of what you represented to us."

"Tough." Brett slammed the phone down.

It took a few moments but Chester eventually replaced his receiver too. That son of a bitch can't do this, especially not to Mrs. Nash. Chester picked up the phone once again and punched in a number he'd memorized a long time ago but had never used. It was a very private line to a lawyer in Fort Worth. An old raspy voice answered on the first ring. "Who's this?"

"It's me, Mr. King. Chester Bennett."

"Chester Bennett? Well, well. Sure didn't expect to be hearing from you."

"No sir, I don't suppose you would. I just woke up, that's about all I can say."

There was silence for a moment and then the man said, "All right. Sorry to hear about your accident. You doing okay?"

"Yeah, just great."

"So, do you need me to sue the club for letting you drive home impaired, or the guys who erected the cement abutment?"

Chester smiled. This man was a real character but the best damned litigator in the State of Texas. "Listen, I want you to prepare a suit, breach of a verbal contract. I'll give you the names later but it's going to be twelve against one and the one is Brett Hollister, former chairman of the board of LoneStar. Being sued by prominent Texans won't make him real popular, I'm guessing. I want to sue him for big bucks, everything he has . . . every last dime. I want to sling as much mud as possible. I'm thinking you'll like that part."

"Damned right I will. Can I tell my boy Arthur what I'm gonna be doing?

"Yep. Tell your son, file the papers and then leak it to the press. I want people to know just what kind of liar he is."

"This'll hit him hard. I love it."

"Excellent. Ah, this is kinda special to me."

"What'd ya mean?"

"One of the plaintiffs against Hollister will be the estate of Gary Nash. I want to see his wife is well provided for."

"Sounds like a good thing to do, Chester. Let me get working on this. I'll be in touch. Bye."

Chester put the phone back. How stupid could he have been? All those years working for Hollister didn't mean a damn thing to the guy. He immediately took a long drink of water to clear his throat. There were calls to make.

PART 7
FINAL JUDGEMENT

CHAPTER 33

Tuesday, January 14, 9:15 A.M.
Cypress Offices, Manhattan

A much thinner Paul Victor ambled into the lobby of The Cypress Group, waved at the receptionist and continued walking to his office. Everyone he passed in the complex gave him a weak smile like he was an unwanted relative showing up for an unscheduled visit. Reaching his office he found it to be exceptionally clean as if no one was working out of it. Sitting down he tried to re-acclimate himself, but where were all his files?

There was a knock at his door and Teddy French walked in. "Hello, Paul. We, ah, didn't expect to see you . . . so soon I mean."

"Hi, Teddy. Naw, they wanted me to stay longer but I sort of snuck out. Thought I'd come in for the morning, get caught up a little then go home. I'm still not a hundred percent."

"Well, you're looking fit."

"I look like cow dung, Teddy. Lost over twenty pounds. Found out I have an ulcer too. My body's for shit. Better take good care of yours."

Stroking his neat beard, Teddy said, "Uh, Paul. There's a couple things we need to talk about."

"Yeah, sure. You can bring me up to date. Hell, I haven't even seen a newspaper in weeks. Doctors said no phone calls, papers, magazines . . . no cable news . . . nothing. Guess I was in pretty bad shape. Too much stress . . . and I had that viral infection."

"Right, stress can really mess you up. Listen Paul, we need to talk. A few weeks ago your wife came here—"

"Cindi? She came here? What'd that bitch want? Shit, you know she didn't even come visit me in the hospital? I mean, she's my wife. Nobody else came either but you'd figure at least your wife would, right? Hell, she hasn't even called me for the last couple of weeks."

Teddy's eyes widened. "Do you mean you haven't talked to your wife for more than two weeks?"

"Nope, so what? We're not all that close anyway."

"Look Paul, she came here demanding—"

"The bitch probably wanted to go through my office, looking for checkbooks or savings accounts or something, right? She's one stupid woman, thinking that I'd leave something like that just laying around for her to grab. But now that you've brought her up, it's kind of funny she hasn't been home. Guess she's staying with a friend or something." Paul's feeble smile wound up being a clenched jaw as he pictured her screwing some migrant gas station attendant.

"Paul, I don't think you fully understand the situation."

"Hey, don't worry about her, she's just your classic dumb blond."

"I don't think your wife is as brain dead as you believe."

"She doesn't know shit. Hell, know what? For years I've been putting the bulk of my assets into different foreign accounts and she has no clue where to look for them." Paul winked at Teddy and added, "That way if she ever tried to divorce me, she'd end up with practically nothing." Paul chuckled, shaking his head at his dim-witted wife.

"Paul, why on earth would you cash in all those investments and put them into a company controlled by your wife's sister? You obviously don't want her to know about the money, so why?"

Paul shrugged, "I didn't want to miss out with LoneStar, and Terri's the closest thing I have to a . . . a friend. Besides, she wouldn't know what to do with that company I set up anyway. I made sure to make it as complex as possible. Hell, she'd need a battery of lawyers to figure it out."

"Paul, they found a lawyer and figured it out."

An icy cold chill wrapped itself around his gut. "What lawyer?"

"The lawyer that pierced your complex set up, the lawyer who produced the necessary documents for your wife to come in here with Ms. Rothman and demand a full settlement."

Blood drained from Paul's face, his head started spinning and he had to clutch at the desk to keep from falling over. "You didn't let her . . ."

The dapper dresser Teddy French opened his hands and said, "Paul, Ms. Rothman is the owner, the president, the chairman, the sole member. Christ, what were you thinking? Of course we complied with her wishes; it's her damn money in the eyes of the law."

A hysterical man shouted, "Noooooo!" and leapt across the desk knocking Teddy back through the office door, sending them both crashing into the hallway. Paul grabbed Teddy's throat and started to squeeze, all the while yelling, "*You son of a bitch. You gave her my money. You gave her all my money. You son of a bitch.*"

Associates and clerks were screaming, Paul was screaming . . . Teddy was screaming. Three portfolio managers managed to pull Paul off Teddy, but Paul was still kicking and shrieking as they pushed him back into his office. General chaos reigned for another ten minutes while a security guard was summoned. Teddy took another ten minutes to straighten his suit and tie, regain his composure, and reenter Paul's office.

Still a little breathless, Teddy said, "I'll forget what just happened, Paul. I'm sure the combination of hearing about your wife, your prescription drugs and your weakened state all contributed to this regrettable incident. Let's just get on and be done with this, okay?"

Paul was slumped in his chair, depressed, dejected and defeated. "What more is there? You just told me my wife has all my money." A glimmer of hope surfaced and Paul asked, "Teddy, what bank did you put the money into? Maybe I can still get it back."

"I'm afraid not. The wire went into the Caymans and is long gone."

Slouching back into his chair, Paul said, "Sorry for grabbing you, didn't know what I was doing."

"Well, let's just move on shall we?" Teddy made sure the now present security guard was paying attention. "Paul, it is my sad duty to inform you that your employment with The Cypress Group is terminated. I was hoping that we could have transacted this under different circumstances, but we simply had no idea you were going to show up today."

Another cold arctic blast hit Paul square in the face, inhibiting his breathing. Fired? No way. "What the fuck?"

"You're out of here, Paul. We'll accept your resignation or you can be let go . . . your choice."

"You can't fire me. I've got clients, investors who'll follow me wherever I go. I'll take everyone away with me."

Stroking his beard, Teddy said, "Don't think so, Paul. You're not too popular with your clients or investors. Actually, you're not too popular with anybody."

"Bullshit!"

Teddy shrugged, "Call them. See for yourself. Most of your clients have already left."

The world was collapsing around him and he didn't know the reason. "Why would they leave? I've made them a ton of money."

"No, not really. I guess you've missed it but LoneStar's now back up to thirty-eight and a half, three bucks *above* our short. Some hot shot research analyst in Michigan came out with a 'buy' recommendation a week ago and turned the fucking stock around. Christ, it happened fast. We couldn't react quick enough . . . still have millions of shares left to cover. We've got a book loss of over nineteen million, and that's *not* including the fifteen million you already cost us with that damned convertible bond fuck-up, remember? Plus, you managed to accomplish all this during a fucking bull market. Not a good performance, you agree?"

"But you can't just drop me . . . we're friends."

"Yeah, right. Tell me, you always fuck your friends? The partners and our best clients are short millions of shares and we're in a classic squeeze. The fucking market's running the price up and we're looking at a potential disaster here Paul, a fucking *personal* disaster. If that damn stock climbs much higher we'll all lose everything because of you. So your friendship means nothing to us."

"But what'll I do?"

Glowering at him, Teddy answered, "I don't give a rat's ass what you do. Just make sure you're out of here within the hour. The security guard will assist you in carrying out your personal property. We packed them all into a box; it's out in the lobby. Goodbye, have a nice life." Nodding to the security guard, Teddy left.

Paul didn't move, couldn't move. Every dime he owned was gone, his job was gone, his health was gone, his wife was gone. What the hell else could happen? As if to answer him, the lone phone on an otherwise empty desk rang. He looked at it . . . it rang again. Picking it up he said, "Yeah?"

"Paul, it's Jackie! Where the hell have you been? I've been calling for weeks."

He closed his eyes, no way was he in the mood for Jackie Wells.

"Paul, you owe me fifty thousand dollars and I want it. That bitch Ashley just fired me, all because of you."

"What do you mean, because of me?"

"*She knew about me and you. I just got fired.*"

Paul's voice cracked, "Wh . . . wh . . . when did she know?"

"When did she know what?"

"*About you working for me, you dumb slut.*"

"Hey, watch your mouth. How should I know when she figured it out? Anyway, I need a job. So how about you hiring me?" Paul started to laugh uncontrollably. The security guard nervously placed his hand on the revolver at his hip.

Tears were rolling down Paul's cheeks, "Oh, this is priceless. Don't you see what she did? That bitch fed me a bunch of shit through you. She knew I was going to do exactly what she wanted me to do. Oh, this is fucking beautiful. Here I was going to screw her to a wall, take down the great Fallen Angel and I wind up getting fucked. All my clients are gone, I don't have a job and she's making millions with each uptick of that damned stock. What a chump I turned out to be." Rolling his head back, Paul continued laughing.

Not so Jackie. Filled with fury she screamed, *"You owe me fifty thousand dollars for getting you that disk. And I need a job. New York is expensive and I need money."*

Jackie's latest outburst caused Paul to laugh all the more, "You stupid whore. I haven't got a dime and I got fired today too. So what are you going to do?"

There was fear, terror and desperation in her voice. Jackie spat back, "I'll kill you."

Holding his sore ribs, Paul managed to say, "Fine, you just do that. Save me the trouble." He hung up the phone, exited his office, followed the guard to retrieve his box and was escorted out of the building. Once outside in the cold, Paul wasn't laughing anymore. Reality began settling in. Paul looked up and down the slush filled bustling streets. He had nowhere to go.

Thursday, January 16, 2:55
Detroit Metropolitan Airport

It was bitterly cold. The winds blew and snow was flying, stinging the unprotected faces of baggage handlers working along curbside. Oh, it was cold all right, although not exactly an unexpected occurrence during the month of January, especially in Michigan. In spite of the inclement weather, Detroit Metropolitan Airport was hustling planes in and out without incident, unlike certain southern cities that clog up at the sight of one fluffy snowflake.

Several airlines utilized Detroit as one of their main hubs, which usually meant congestion . . . today was no exception. Sisters Courtney Keller and Stephanie Blaine were waiting in the baggage claim area. Courtney had brought along a small white cardboard sign that read 'Bishop,' and was holding it like they do at La Guardia.

As Ashley flew first class she was one of the first passengers to reach baggage claim. The college friends immediately saw each other, ran together and embraced. Laughter, giggles, smiles, hugs and kisses were all lavished upon one another. It had been such a long time. Introductions were quickly made and the three girls talked until the flashing light signaling that the New York flights baggage was ready for pick up.

While Ashley was at the slowly moving carousel trying to locate her luggage, Stephanie gently pulled her sister to the side and whispered, "My God, she's gorgeous. What is she, a model or something? Check out every male in this place, they're falling all over each other to get a better look." Indeed, one young man actually tripped over some luggage as he attempted to get closer, much to the annoyance of his girlfriend.

In an equally quiet voice, Courtney replied, "She's a knockout, always has been. Never had trouble finding a date, that's for sure. Actually, one of her dates helped me get into medical school but that's another story."

Two men offered to carry Ashley's bags wherever she wanted. Declining politely the three girls each grabbed one suitcase and trudged out into the open air parking lot. For the first twenty minutes in Stephanie's car, Courtney and Ashley yakked and yakked, just like old friends are supposed to do. The roads had been recently plowed and salted, so driving wasn't too tasking. Stephanie finally managed to get in a sentence, "Ashley, you know you're more than welcomed to stay with us. Court's in the guest room and Mike's bunking with the boys, but I know we can find you room. No need to stay in a hotel."

From the back seat Ashley leaned forward and said, "I really appreciate the offer but I've already made other arrangements. Could you just drop me off? Oh, I almost forgot to ask about the rehearsal."

Riding in the passenger seat, Courtney turned around and recited, "The rehearsal is tomorrow at seven, at The Abbey. Steph was able to arrange it for me. We'll have dinner right after. Do you prefer steaks, French, Italian or Greek?"

"Anything's fine with me. You two choose."

Stephanie looked into the rearview mirror at Ashley and commented, "I understand you have a boyfriend in these parts."

Unable to hold back the smile, Ashley beamed and replied, "Courtney never could keep a secret. Yes, I do. Unfortunately he's away on business. But I expect him back in time for the wedding."

Courtney perked up as she thought of a wonderful idea. "Hey, Stephanie's husband's traveling too, so why don't we girls go out on the town? You know, one last fling for the blushing bride?" All three laughed. Turning to Stephanie, Courtney asked, "Know any good places where we can get into trouble?"

A grin from ear to ear almost split the elder sister's face, "Yep, know just the place. It's across the river in Windsor. You two will love it. Beautiful hunks of male flesh prancing and dancing and taking their clothes off right in front of you. Totally nude!" By unanimous consent they agreed to visit Canada.

Courtney looked at Ashley and said, "We'll drop you off and come back around seven. Where're you staying?"

"The Townsend, it's in Birmingham."

The car suddenly swerved. Stephanie quickly regained control but was noticeably disturbed about something. "Hey," Court said, "something wrong with the Townsend?"

Shaking her head Stephanie replied, "No, nothing at all. I'm sorry, I just . . . no nothing. It's a very nice hotel, I'm sure you'll like it." Gripping the steering wheel, she pushed out the image of Rick having an intimate dinner with another woman. Sure he had denied it, but she could tell he was lying.

Exchanging curious looks, Courtney and Ashley let the incident pass.

Friday, January 17, 7:05 A.M.
Blaine Residence, Birmingham

Morning came far too early for the party girls. Sleepy eyes found it very difficult to wrest themselves open, and a number of pillows were pulled over throbbing heads vainly trying to keep any light from attacking raw senses. Stephanie and Courtney rolled out of their respective beds, neither capable of speech. After brisk showers, mouthwash, aspirin and a half pot of black coffee, a degree of normalcy returned. The sisters spent the rest of the morning snickering at each other and making crude remarks regarding what the other had done the night before.

Stephanie's two boys flew in and out on their way to school without uttering a word. Bemused by their quick entrance and rapid departure, Courtney asked, "Did they get something to eat?"

Stephanie shrugged and answered, "Naw, they'll fill up on something wholesome like pizza and fries once they get to school. You hungry?"

"After last night, I may never eat again." Both girls laughed, blushed and popped more aspirins.

Wiping tears out of her eyes after Courtney finished recanting the story of getting her engagement ring stuck in the well endowed cowboy's scanty briefs while stuffing down a ten dollar bill, Stephanie leaned on the kitchen table and said, "Ashley's really a lot of fun. I thought I'd hate her for being so attractive, but I can't."

"Yeah, I know what you mean. Many is the time I thought of cutting off all her hair, but she's so sweet. Although at times she can be pretty bitter. Comes from her childhood. I've never mentioned it to anyone before, but I know she won't mind me telling you . . ."

Shocked . . . appalled . . . sickened. That's how Stephanie felt after hearing about Ashley's past, one that she'd never-ever imagined possible . . . her heart ached. What a vile, loathsome way for anybody to grow up. "Imagine the scars she must be carrying."

Court nodded, "Yeah, I just hope she can find somebody soon. I'm worried about her, she's becoming callous. I hope this latest boyfriend works out."

"Makes you just want to hold on to what you've got even more, huh? Could be I've been out of line with Rick. I suppose I should try harder."

Court brightened, "Say, speaking of Rick, did he call?"

"Yes, one of the boys' took the call last night. He'll be flying in tonight. He should make the rehearsal in plenty of time."

"Great. I know my Mike wants to fawn all over him. I guess he just made another killing with one of Rick's recommendations. Your husband sure knows how to pick winners."

Hearing the subtle hint, Stephanie admitted feeling pretty proud of her husband. What other husbands could do what he's doing? Glancing at her watch, Stephanie said, "Let's get dressed and go pick up Ashley. We can walk around the streets of Birmingham, it's a great place to shop. You can bring Mike if you'd like."

A bewildered look overcame Courtney and she replied, "Are you crazy? I don't think I want my future husband ogling Ashley all day long. Oh, no, he can stay right here, thank you very much." The women nodded to each other knowingly and went to fetch Ashley.

Same day, 7:55 P.M.
The Abbey, Birmingham

The Reverend Ryan Sladden had obviously done this sort of thing before. He was able to instill a sense of well-being and control even with the absence of one of the ushers. Ryan patiently explained what each person in the wedding party was supposed to do, making sure that Courtney's dad knew enough to brief his son-in-law about the duties of being an usher, as Rick's returning flight was delayed at Chicago's O'Hare Airport.

After a couple of false starts, the dry runs went off without a hitch so everyone congratulated the bride and groom, piled into several cars and drove to a local tavern. The men wanted to eat somewhere with large flat-screen TV. "No use missing a good basketball game, is there?" The girls begrudgingly decided to go along. It was mostly guilt from last night's acts of depravity that induced them to be such good sports.

While the men whooped and hollered the women sipped Diet Cokes as far away from the noise as possible. Being the first chance for the women to sit back and get to know each other, Ashley volunteered to Stephanie, "Sorry your husband didn't make it, I'm looking forward to meeting him."

Checking her watch again, Stephanie shrugged and said, "Yeah, I'm sure Rick is looking forward to meeting you too."

A glass of coke froze in mid air as a terrible thought occurred to Ashley. Then a cold sweat seized her. Ashley's mind whirled back to the introductions at the airport. They'd been so quick. Courtney said, "Ashley, I'd like you to meet my sister, Stephanie . . . Blake, Black, or . . . no, couldn't be." Ashley hadn't really heard a last name; she was too busy hugging Courtney. Speaking as calmly as possible, Ashley asked Stephanie, "I ah, don't think you ever told me what, ah, Rick does. Something auto related?"

"No, he's a stock analyst. That's someone who tells investors whether-or-not they should invest in a specific company. I really don't fully understand . . . Ashley? Ashley? Are you all right?"

Ashley's complexion paled and her hands began shaking. Standing up she had to catch herself as her head spun out of control. What had she done? Sleeping with Stephanie's husband? Bile rose into her throat, her knees buckled and she stumbled against a chair.

Quickly jumping to assist her new friend, Stephanie asked, "*What's wrong?* Courtney! Help me get her outside." The two sisters hurriedly supported Ashley and took her outside into the cold, crisp night air. "What's the matter?" All three faces were in varying states of shock.

Gulping in oxygen Ashley held her head and said, "Nothing, I'm fine." The acidic taste in her mouth caused her to gag but she gathered herself together enough to say, "Listen, do you mind if I go back to the hotel? I think all this night life is getting to me." Within the hour Ashley was back in her room at the Townsend, alone, throwing up in a very posh bathroom.

CHAPTER 34

Saturday, January 18, 7:35 A.M.
Blaine Residence, Birmingham

The condemned man sat in the master bathroom resting his head in his hands. The gallows awaited him and he could do nothing to prevent the execution. He'd cheated on his wife, and by a vicious twist of fate was about to confront both wife and lover at the same event. What were the chances?

Rick had barely walked in the door last night when both Stephanie and Courtney were found running around, trying to decide what to do about Ashley. "Ashley? Ashley who?"

With a quick kiss hello, Courtney said, "My friend, Ashley. She's standing up in my wedding and she's sicker than a dog. I've got to call her . . . see if she's any better." A quick call ensued and Rick overheard his sister-in-law asking for Ashley Bishop's room.

Rick was speechless, dumbstruck, terrified. All the while the groom-to-be, Mike Kilpatrick was shaking his hand, slapping his back, telling him how much money he'd made off Rick's advice. Mike vainly tried to hold one sided conversations, but to no avail. Claiming jetlag, Rick said goodnight and hustled himself off to bed, although he didn't sleep much. In point of fact he was awake most of the night.

All sorts of different scenarios flashed before his mind's eye. None of them ended well. What a nightmare. At morning's first light, Stephanie turned towards Rick and was visibly concerned, he looked terrible. She told him to stay in bed and brought him tomato juice and toast. Coddling him like a sick child made him feel all the worse. One thing was amazingly clear to him though, if he could wipe the slate clean, if he could start all over again, he never would have jumped into that limo with Ashley . . . but he had.

Same day, 10:05 A.M.
Townsend Hotel, Birmingham

Ashley was settling her bill at the cashiers' window when Courtney Keller stomped up next to her. "What on earth are you doing?"

Jumping at the sound of the familiar voice, Ashley gasped and turned around. There in front of her was her best friend, the only girl who treated her like an equal, never looked down on her, never threw her past into her face, never used her, and even quit a sorority for 'deactivating' her. Now her best friend was getting married and expecting Ashley to stand up with her, which she couldn't do.

Staring at her with hands on hips, Courtney repeated, "I said what are you doing?"

"I . . . I thought, it would be better . . . I don't feel so well . . . need to go home."

Courtney's eyes widened, "You can't leave me. Not now. Not today!"

Ashley tried to smile but nothing happened, "Just not a good idea, having me—"

With stone-faced determination, Courtney said, "You stop that kind of talk. What's the matter with you? Get a grip on yourself. This is supposed to be the happiest day of my life and you're ruining it. Now march right back into your room and lay down and rest until I pick you up for my wedding. You've got five hours. March!"

It was useless to resist. Ashley couldn't say 'no' to Courtney, not now, not ever.

Same day, 5:50 P.M.
The Abbey, Birmingham

The strain between Ashley and Rick was evident. They each had on false smiles, said little to anyone and noticeably avoided each other. No one could figure out what the deal was, but with a wedding to finish there were more important matters at hand. Amazingly, the wedding went off like clockwork. Everyone did their jobs exactly as Reverend Sladden had drilled into them the night before. After the vows were exchanged and the good reverend declared them husband and wife, the bridal party walked out of the sanctuary, and hid themselves away from the guests until the church emptied.

The agenda allowed the wedding party a brief fifteen minutes before a few hundred pictures of them would be snapped by the photographer. The girls all went to their designated area to freshen up, while the guy's found a radio and tuned to a basketball game.

* * *

Miserable didn't even come close to expressing the way Rick felt. Every time he looked at Ashley he knew he was in love. When he looked at Stephanie guilt and shame flooded his entire being, incapacitating him from any lucid thinking. All he knew was that he never wanted to tell Ashley goodbye.

Barely listening to the radio broadcast he struggled over deep moral issues tearing at the seams of his soul. Could he simply leave without facing Steph? Doubtful. Could he make her understand the compassion he had for Ashley? No. Is any of this what he wanted? Nope. Should he continue feeling sorry for himself, since none of this was his fault to begin with? Totally!

* * *

Strolling off to be by herself, Ashley found a long stone corridor with stained glass images of past religious notables along a wall. Regrettably, the beauty displayed was shrouded by thoughts ripping *her* apart. She knew it wasn't right but she'd fallen in love with Rick. She wanted him. Wanted to run away with him. Passing an office with a familiar face who was pecking on a computer keyboard, she poked her head through the open door and said, "Hello. Catching up on some work?"

Ryan Sladden looked up from the computer screen, and replied, "Why, hello." He stood up and gestured for her to come in and sit down. "What a lovely surprise. The men are listening to a basketball game, something that never interested me. So I thought I'd just review my sermon for tomorrow." He smiled at her and added, "You're invited by the way."

Ashley settled into an old wing chair. "You certainly make me feel welcome but I'm not much of a church goer."

"Well, if you ever change your mind." He closed some books and gave her his full attention. "It was a lovely wedding don't you think, they seem so much in love. I understand you and Courtney went to college together."

"Yes, yes we did. You have a beautiful church."

"Well, thank you, although I can't take too much credit. It was already here when I arrived."

Ashley traced her fingers along the worn upholstered arm of the chair. After a few moments reflection, she said, "You gave Court and Mike a wonderful wedding. Thank you, for both of them."

Walking over to his fireplace, he lit one match and expertly started a roaring fire. Seeming overly pleased with himself, he returned to his desk chair. "I really love doing weddings. As a matter of fact, I'd be honored to perform your wedding someday."

Flames licked up from the kindling. Ashley watched the burning embers for a moment, then said, "No, not likely. Say, can I ask you a question?"

"Please."

Lowering her head and focusing on clenched hands resting on her lap, she said, "Well, I'm about to do something that will make me very, very happy. Happier than I've ever been in my life. But at the same time it's a very selfish thing to do, and someone else, well, a lot of someone else's will be awfully hurt by my actions." She looked up at him. The eyes that could mesmerize now only showed sorrow.

"Are you asking me if the others will ever forgive you?"

Ashley looked surprised, "Oh, no. I'm wondering if this will shut the door on me with God. I don't think I'd ever expect them to forgive me; I'll probably just have to accept that. But I'm not familiar with how God thinks."

"Well. If that's your concern, then you shouldn't have a concern."

"How's that?"

"Ashley, God doesn't hold grudges. His whole purpose is to get us to accept Him, His Word. He wants as many of us as He can get, not as few. So He's made it very easy for us. No long lectures, no multiple choice tests, no required manual labor, no sacrifice. You want to be accepted? You want forgiveness for anything that you've done? You want salvation? You want to make sure you spend eternity with Him? All you have to do is read and follow Romans ten, nine . . . If you confess with your lips that Jesus is Lord, and believe in your heart that God raised him from the dead, you will be saved."

"That's it?"

Ryan chuckled, "Yes, it's not very complicated, although once you've accepted the Word, I'm hopeful you'd want to continue to grow in it, to reap the benefits it offers. But for forgiveness or salvation," he paused and shrugged, "it's simply a matter of accepting grace."

"Sounds awfully easy." Ashley glanced at her watch and added, "We'd better be getting back for the picture taking."

"All right, shall we?" Leading her back along the corridor to the waiting wedding party and photographer, Ryan pointed out numerous objects of historic significance. An hour and a half later a caravan of eight cars exited the Southfield Freeway at Ford Road and turned into the Ritz Carlton. There they were guided into a magnificent ballroom, formed a greeting line and spent the next half hour either shaking hands or kissing cheeks with about a hundred and fifty guests. Shortly thereafter, the band began playing and the traditional wedding reception commenced. A good time was had by all . . . all but two.

* * *

About an hour into the festivities, the Best man, who had a delicious sense of humor, gave a totally unrehearsed ribald wedding toast at the expense of the groom, which thoroughly embarrassed Mike while delighting Courtney and the other listeners. The audience laughed and applauded and everyone toasted the happy couple. Ryan Sladden was then pushed to the microphone by Courtney's mother and pressed into giving an impromptu speech of his own.

The party then kicked into high gear, all the while Rick managed to avoid Ashley. Then fate stepped in. As Ashley was talking to Courtney, the bride suddenly began waving her hand at him, motioning for Rick to come over. He froze. Courtney waved again. Caught, he managed to travel the twenty feet to the girls without fleeing, tripping or collapsing.

Grabbing him by the arm, Courtney said, "There you are. I don't think you two have said ten words to each other all night. I want you both to loosen up." As she finished, another wedding guest tugged at her, pulling Courtney into another conversation leaving Rick and Ashley alone to stare at each other.

After a brief moment, Rick said, "You look lovely. I'm sorry I haven't spent much time with you, but, well, I guess I feel kind of awkward."

"You look very dashing in that Tux. You're a very handsome man, Rick Blaine."

He blushed a little and scanned around them for eavesdroppers. Speaking in a low voice, he said, "I'd like to leave with you right now. Just run out of here, never come back."

Ashley grinned and replied, "That would be a bit tacky, don't you think?"

He took her hand and said, "I suppose so." Realizing what he'd just done, he dropped her hand and lowered his voice another notch, "Can we go soon?"

"Yes, soon."

"Okay, whenever you say."

She studied him carefully. "Rick, how did you feel towards Stephanie before you and I met?"

He thought for a moment, "I suppose I . . . well . . . um."

She nudged him, "Go on, I really want to know."

He gave a half smile, "I guess I thought I loved her. Not like us. I mean it's different with you. I don't know, is it important?"

Shaking her head, she said, "No, just curious, that's all."

"Why don't I go get us a drink, we'll toast each other. I'll be right back."

Ashley watched the crowd laughing and dancing around her and thought about Stephanie, about all the Stephanie's dancing with their husbands or boyfriends and having a wonderful time. Suddenly, Courtney reappeared and grabbed Ashley's arm, "What's wrong with you? This isn't a funeral you know."

Snapping out of her trance, Ashley said, "I'm sorry, I really am." She reached out and took Courtney's hands, "I'm so happy for you."

Giving Ashley a hug, Court beamed and said, "Then act like it. Go dance with any of the dozen or so men watching you with their tongues hanging out."

Ashley nodded, "Okay, I'll go flirt."

Courtney grinned and laughed. "That's the old Ashley. Now you're talking." They hugged again as Stephanie joined them.

"Court, mom and dad want you over by the cake. I think they have a couple pictures left in their camera, so smile pretty." All three women smirked, and Courtney left to weave her way through the crowd and into the bright lights of flashing bulbs.

Before Ashley had a chance to move off, Stephanie turned and said, "You look so lovely tonight. Is your boyfriend going to make it?"

Wrong topic. "*No.* I mean, I'm not sure."

"I hope he does, I'd like to meet the man who can sweep you off your feet. He must be really something."

The conversation was making Ashley really uncomfortable, "Yes. He's something special all right."

"What do you think about Rick?"

A shiver bolted from her head to toe. "Excuse me?"

"I mean . . . oh, I don't know what I mean. Ashley, I'm sure you've noticed Rick and I aren't doing so well. He's off in another world, we're drifting apart. I still love him, more than ever but he's so distant from me. I was just wondering if you could give me some advice." Stephanie's shoulders sagged and her eyes were downcast. With effort she added, "I don't think I'm attractive to him anymore. That's not an easy thing for a woman to admit."

Ashley saw Rick over by the bar area with Mike. He hadn't noticed that the two women in his life were standing next to each other, talking. Mike did and waved, and when Rick reflectively turned his eyes widened. He slowly maneuvered his way to the edge of the dance floor where he stood watching them helplessly.

"It's important to me, Ashley," Stephanie continued talking. Ashley refocused her attention onto the lamenting wife, whose pale blue eyes were watering, practically begging Ashley to tell her what to do. It was obvious how hurt she was but instead of being compassionate, Ashley thought about what she'd had to contend with growing up, the abuse and humiliation, the total lack of love or caring in her life. She'd been alone, scared, cold, hungry, abused and no one came to *her* rescue. No one gave a damn . . . not until Rick. He was the only one who made her feel . . . respectable.

A tear rolled down Stephanie's cheek. "I'm sorry, you don't deserve this. It's my problem, not yours. I'm just more desperate than embarrassed. I thought a woman like you, well, you could help me." Stephanie chewed her lower lip; she was a very frightened woman. "I'm afraid to lose Rick. I think he's seeing someone else and I don't know how to get him back."

Staring at Rick again, Ashley noted he was still standing in the same spot almost as if his feet were lead and couldn't move. Well, he'd be exiting soon. They'd be off together, hand in hand, leaving everyone and everything behind.

Screwing up her courage, Ashley dismissed Stephanie's grief and thought again about her own happiness. Her face hardened, and she said, "Stephanie . . ." Ashley thought of all the years she'd be with Rick. Together, they could do anything, go anywhere. A contented smile grew on her face, thinking of making love in the little cabin of her dreams, in front of a roaring fire, finally enjoying life.

Wiping away a tear, an anxious Stephanie said, "I thought . . . you could tell me how to, ah, make him happy. I'll do whatever you say."

"Steph . . . ," this was hard but someone had to tell her. Inhaling deeply, Ashley said, "I'm sorry, I'm very sorry. But if he's causing you this much pain then I'd get a divorce. It's the best thing for both of you."

Terror seized Stephanie. "No, you don't understand. I love him . . . I know he loves me."

Ashley had done her duty. Abruptly turning she walked away, gesturing with her head for Rick to follow.

Pushing her way through the ballroom she found double doors leading outside onto a circular driveway. It was freezing, she didn't notice. Ashley leaned against the brick wall and waited for Rick to find her. There was a clear night; thousands of stars dotted the heavens. Within seconds Rick was beside her, taking her in his arms.

"Are you all right? You're shivering, you're cold. Here, take my jacket."

His breath was warm against her skin as he slipped his dinner jacket around her shoulders. Could she ever love anyone as much? "Rick—"

"Shhh. You don't have to say anything."

"Yes, I do."

Forcing his arms off her, Ashley's voice took on a distinctive edge, "I think I owe you an apology. I've

apparently mislead you." Every other thought
screamed: STOP!

"Don't talk." He reached for her again. "I want
to—"
Before she melted into his arms never to reappear,
she stated flatly, "You want to what? You want to
leave your wife? Okay, do it!"

"No need to take that tone. I love you, we're
going to live together—"

"*What*? Whoever said that? I don't want a mate
for life."

Rick went pale, "I mean, you and me . . . we're
going to—"

Grabbing his face between her hands, she
said, "Look, you're a nice guy but I know lots of nice
guys. I *don't* know a lot of men who can issue 'buy'
recommendations on particular stocks whenever I
want them to, or 'sells' for that matter . . . so I paid
you special attention. You were great by the way."
She smiled rather cruelly at him and said, "Admit it.
We were good for each other's career, weren't we?"

Stammering, he said, "No, no. You can't—"

Patting his cheeks, Ashley said, "Listen, no
hard feelings, it was just business. I've got to head
back now." She then pointed to the parking lot and
said, "That's the way out." Ashley started walking
towards the double doors, turned her head and
smiled a most sensual smile. "If you're ever in New
York, give me a call. You're a good lover and I

wouldn't mind seeing you again. Bye." She let his jacket fall to the ground, leaving Rick standing by himself out in the icy night air.

Quickly making her way to the nearest Ladies Room, she found an empty stall, fell to the ground and used the bowl as her stomach twisted and recoiled. With body still shaking, she wrapped her arms around her knees and sobbed as silently as possible. Tears streamed down her cheeks and the hurt inside was unimaginable.

* * *

Moving hesitantly back to the wedding reception, Rick was dazed but nobody seemed to notice. He found his way to the wedding party's empty table, sat down heavily, observed his own shaking hands and set them on his lap. Looking at the partially eaten dinner before him and the half filled glass of wine, he thought of the time Ashley had undressed in front of him at the Townsend. There was half eaten food and drinks there too. Why would she treat him like this? It couldn't have been "just business" like she said.

He sat by himself for what seemed hours but in reality was only a few minutes. A smooth, cool hand suddenly caressed the back of his neck. He looked up at Stephanie who was standing there with a tight smile on her face. Rick could tell she'd been crying.

Sitting down next to him, she confided, "I think I upset Ashley."

He didn't understand. "What?"

"I said I think I upset Ashley. Just a few minutes ago someone told Court one of her bride's maids was in a bathroom crying. So she grabbed me and we went there. It was Ashley. Oh, I feel like such a . . . such a . . ." Stephanie started to sob again. Rick instinctively put his arm around her shoulder.

She looked at him with puffy eyes, and confessed, "I must have really upset her but I didn't mean to. I was asking her for some personal advice. I know it was stupid of me but I just wasn't thinking. I kept pushing and pushing. I must have touched a raw nerve from her past, I don't know, but I feel so terrible. I was only thinking about me, I didn't care about her."

"Her past?"

Grabbing a table napkin, Stephanie sniffed, wiped her nose and nodded, "Yes, Courtney told me. Ashley's had a really rough life, alcoholic mother, foster homes, raped repeatedly by legal guardians, physically abused in prison . . . I guess prison was really hard on her, particularly since she'd confessed to cover up for a self-serving boyfriend's crime. Lying bastard then dumps her. The way she had to live to survive, no one should have to live like that. It's so . . . inhuman."

Twisting the cloth napkin in her hand, Stephanie said, "I figured because she's so attractive and the way men look at her and everything she'd know how I could get you to notice me. Lord, what was I thinking?"

Rick felt numb. What an ass he'd been. A total ass. "Steph, about Ashley's boyfriend here in Detroit."

"You know, I think she made that up . . . about having a boyfriend, 'cause he never showed."

Leaning over he said, "You didn't do anything wrong, Steph. My guess is she did meet her boyfriend tonight and he just turned out to be another . . . another huge mistake." Rick's eyes were glistening as he whispered into her ear, "I'm so sorry how I've treated you lately, can we start over again?"

Turning around, she faced him and wiped a tear from her eye. "I'd like that very much." He reached over, pulled a fresh bottle of champagne out of a bucket and poured them each a glass. They held hands . . . the drinks forgotten.

Sunday, January 18, 9:40 A.M.
The Abbey, Birmingham

The choir was just finishing up the hymn. Ryan Sladden sat behind the pulpit out of view from the congregation. In another minute he'd make his way up a few stairs and deliver his sermon. Adjusting his robe, he waited.

* * *

Stephanie and Rick had arrived late, again. Sleep had been in short supply, what with the wedding reception only fizzling out sometime after two in the morning. By the time all the goodbyes had been made plus the drive home, their heads hadn't hit the pillows much before four o'clock. Their resolve was severely put to the test when the alarm went off at seven-thirty this morning, but somehow they managed to pull themselves together to make the nine o'clock service. They were in the front row holding hands, but Rick didn't mind being in the front row this time.

* * *

Stepping up into the pulpit, Ryan noticed Stephanie and Rick directly below, holding hands. He smiled at them both, so glad everything had worked out. Scanning the rest of the congregation he was startled to see another familiar face from the weekend. There towards the back looking far less radiant than at yesterday's wedding, was Ashley Bishop. Ryan nodded to her and she smiled back weakly. Welcome, Ashley.

CHAPTER 35

Monday, January 19, 8:35 A.M.
Taylor-Bishop Offices, Manhattan

"Welcome back." Joyce smiled as Ashley entered the office and passed her. "How was the wedding?"

Opening the door to her office, Ashley turned and said, "The bride was stunning, the church was spectacular and the minister was extremely interesting. But to be truthful, I don't think I ever want to go through another weekend like that again." She shook her head as she entered her office and repeated, "Never again."

Following her in, Joyce said, "Lauren called and asked that you call her back. She sounds like she's enjoying herself."

Ashley nodded, "Yes, she seems to have found her niche. I expect she'll do very well." Walking to her desk she punched eleven digits on her telephone.

"LoneStar International. Ms. Washington's office."

A big grin covered Ashley's face, "Good morning. This is Ms. Bishop returning Ms. Washington's call."

"One moment please." Ashley shook her head and wondered how Lauren's family was going to adjust to Dallas.

"Ashley?"

"So did you make it to a Mavericks game yet?"

"Not yet. But next time you come I'll get us floor seats. I did buy some cowboy boots." Both girls laughed.

"So fill me in."

"The newspapers picked up the story about ex-LoneStar employees suing Brett Hollister for breach of contract. I'll email them to you. Looks like it's going to get real nasty, at least as far as Brett's concerned. Everyone including Chester Bennett is running around making all kinds of accusations. They're suing Brett for two hundred and fifty million. The Dallas papers are eating it up. Sure makes Brett out to be a real louse. I just heard the other companies he's a board member on have asked him to resign."

"Somehow, I'm not surprised."

"Our stock's has a forty handle. We're making a comeback. Emmet Griswald and the other new managers are really clicking together. Adam Sanchez seems well suited to run this place. Charles thinks so too. In fact, Charles is spending more and more time back in Michigan, leaving the daily operations to Adam."

Ashley chuckled and said, "With the stock rising, those jerks at Cypress will be jumping outta the windows pretty soon. I figure they've already lost fifty million or more. We've also picked up a dozen of their clients and I understand Paul Victor has dropped from sight."

"Don't be surprised if those bastards at Cypress come knocking on *your* door looking for a job."

Ashley smiled and said, "Now that would be fun. I'd whistle at them, tell them to turn around and show me their cute butts."

Laughing at the mental image, Lauren added, "Hey, video tape those interviews for me, okay?" The girls laughed again.

"Ashley, thanks again for putting me here. I really appreciate it."

"I didn't do anything. I happen to own a fairly large portion of your stock and I'd like to make a reasonable return. So the better you do, the better I do. I must admit, so far we're both doing pretty well."

"Yeah, sure. You're a real hard ass aren't you? Oh, Adam said to say hello. I think he kinda likes you."

Holding onto the mental picture of the handsome consultant for a moment, Ashley finally said, "Say hello to Charles *and* Adam for me. I'll see you all next month at the board meeting. Call me if I can help. Bye." Ashley sat down in her chair and stared at her blank computer screen.

After yesterday's church service, she returned to the hotel, packed her bags and called a cab. A message was handed to her by the cashier as she was checking out, it was from Rick. The note was simple, and very touching: *"I appreciate what you did. I'll always love you. Rick."*

* * *

Still standing in front of her, Joyce made a throaty sound and then said, "Ashley?"

Realizing that she wasn't alone, Ashley took one last look at Rick's note, crumpled it into a ball and tossed it into the wastebasket. "What's up?"

"I was wondering if you're disappointed about not being able to sell LoneStar short like you'd originally planned."

Ashley paused and reflected for a moment. "Well, we won't make the fortune we thought we would, but I suspect the stock will continue to rise. We're doing okay for our current clients and we're picking up some new ones from The Cypress Group. So on balance, I'd say we did better than average. Why?"

"Well, I was just wondering. Remember when we were all running around here trying to figure out which company to target?"

"Sure, and I picked LoneStar."

"That's right. But do you recall there was another finalist?"

Ashley bolted from her seat. "Joyce. You're a genius! I love you. Where is it, where's the other file?"

Taking a few steps closer, Joyce brought the file out from behind her back.

Ashley punched a single digit on her phone, "Vanessa, grab Allison, Sarah and Alexis. I want you all in my office, *now*. You've got a new assignment." Ashley took the folder from Joyce and skimmed the Executive Summary with a ravenous appetite.

"Joyce, I want you to book me on a plane to Los Angeles on the twenty-eighth, I'll return late the twenty-ninth." The private secretary stood there perplexed. Ashley winked at her and added, "These guys are having their annual meeting next week." Towering over the file, Ashley wore an expression memorialized by that fabled spider who seduced a hapless fly. Was this her Holy Grail?

62006759R00325

Made in the USA
Lexington, KY
26 March 2017